BROKEN ANGELS

∞

Also by Harambee K. Grey-Sun

The EVE OF LIGHT Series

The Novels
BloodLight: The Apocalypse of Robert Goldner (*Prequel*)
Broken Angels (*Book I*)
Divinities, Entangled (*Book II*)

The Short Stories
FoolKillers
The Lark
Heaven's Gun
Knotty & Ice
Rogue Beauty
Deviant-Hunter's Sabbath

By Harambee Grey-Sun

Poetry
Spring's Fall (Autumn Numbers • Book I)
Wine Songs, Vinegar Verses

BROKEN ANGELS

Eve of Light ∞ Book I

Harambee K. Grey-Sun

ISBN: 978-1-64044-003-6

Cover design by The Cover Collection

Published by HyperVerse Books
http://www.hyperversebooks.com/
writing between and beyond the lines

Fourth Edition: March 2017

The mind is its own place, and in itself
Can make a Heav'n of Hell, a Hell of Heav'n.

JOHN MILTON, PARADISE LOST, BOOK I

Chapter 1

Robert Goldner bent the light around his body, making himself invisible.

No alarms went up. Better, no gang signals. The kids stayed put. They appeared to be minding nobody's business, just waiting for the day of reckoning. Eight years after the emergence of the White Fire Virus, though, Robert damn well knew the younger the potential threat, the greater the potential danger.

It was a Friday afternoon in September, and none of the kids seemed to have anything better to do. The nine boys and two girls probably should've been in…junior high school, from the looks of it. But they were hanging out in front of a pizza place and a check-cashing shop. Smoking, joking around, dressed like thugs-in-training. Robert wondered if they were just truants or if they were staking out territory early, waiting for the needy folks who were done with their workweek to come by and cash their paychecks. Big kids, or little criminals?

Hard to tell what anyone was really up to these days. Easier not to trust anyone.

Six, seven, maybe even eight years their senior, Robert could probably take them. But he didn't like fighting kids, even if they thought they were adults, even if such confrontations came with the territory of being a Watcher. Anyway, he needed to conserve his strength for the hunt.

He maneuvered through the cluster, none of the kids suspecting a thing. The parasites inside Robert may've been slowly killing him, but thank fortune they didn't leave him defenseless. He stayed invisible as he ran on toward the target house, five blocks away.

Generations have trod, have trod, have trod…

Funny—lines from Hopkins's poem about the grandeur of God often shot through his thoughts during this part of the hunt. The poet had surely seen his share of wretched scenes from the big picture of a downtrodden human family and its ravished home. Hopkins may not have witnessed as many underpass-and bus-stop-dwelling Jellyheads, the shit-and-piss-stenched fiends of no permanent residence strung out on Jelly Raptures, sprawled out amid the irrepressible scatterings of condom wrappers, broken beer bottles, 7-Eleven chili dog boxes, and all the rest of it, but life wasn't all that wonderful one hundred and fifty years ago either. Still, Robert couldn't bring himself to share the poet's optimism that "nature is never spent."

Oh, well—"Don't Worry, Be Happy."

Funny how he often recalled the lines of that dumb rhyme during these hunts as well.

What was the worry anyway? The odds were against his surviving to witness humankind's last day. He could die within the next few seconds, stopped cold on the way to potentially winning this week's mystery prize. He might even be successful and come out a hero, only to have the billions of parasitic microbes living in his skin and blood cells kill him shortly afterward. *Generations have trod, have trod, have trod…*

This one was a long shot, he'd been told. Probably a Friday afternoon wild goose chase. But he was never one to waste time. On the sidewalk and across lawns, he moved as fast as he could in jeans and a windbreaker. If he'd been wearing less, he could've moved even faster, gliding over the ground, skating on thin air. But, invisible or not, he wasn't about to strip down to his drawers.

It had nothing to do with shyness. He'd never been accused of being infected with modesty. It was his actual infection that was the problem. Baring too much skin to light was equivalent to inviting the parasites within to feast—get drunk then unruly. Hopefully, though, never to the extent of what he saw when he rounded the corner.

Robert had actually heard the sound of it first, the labored breathing like the sound of a large sack of junk being dragged slowly over a gravel road. Even in silence, he would not have missed seeing the man, naked except for his underwear, socks, and one shoe, propped up against the blue postal box in front of a seemingly deserted apartment complex.

The man didn't have much further to go. Even from forty feet away, Robert could see the patches of skin that had fallen off, patches matching the thinness, brittleness, and colors—if not exactly the size—of maple leaves in autumn. It was a clear day, and the sun shined freely. The parasites had overdosed, and the man was being eaten away, rapidly, by the frantic microbes inside him. The Virus was claiming him, overtaking him, exposing more and more of his insides to the outside world, the world empty of anyone who'd see—except invisible Robert.

The man was beyond blind at this point. But Robert remained unseen as he studied him, approaching ever more cautiously lest the leaking radiation resulting from the man's death throes envelope him, causing the parasites within Robert's body to go ballistic.

No more than a dozen skin patches had fallen from the dying man, and what was still hanging on was turning the hue of rice paper, or the color and texture of tree bark, dotted all over with dark silver glitter that sparkled from black to red to orange to yellow to green to blue to indigo to violet and then briefly to silver before going back to black, each piece of glitter sparking through the color-cycle at its own unique pace.

Robert had seen it all before. It wasn't all that shocking. He did briefly wonder what Hopkins might think of this Pied Ugly; certainly not "Glory be to God for dappled things—" But Robert's brief imagining turned back to stark reality as he stepped nearer, looked closer, and saw something unusual.

The man still had skin covering most of his abdominal area. Robert concentrated and pushed his vision down the spectrum into the range of x-rays, trying to figure why the wheezing man's stomach appeared be getting redder than a cranberry as it swelled more and more with each breath.

Robert saw through the layers of skin and muscle. He saw the man's intestines breaking all of their bodily connections to form one long worm.

Part of him wanted to wretch, but Robert couldn't take his eye away.

A chunky vomit, looking like milk four weeks past its expiration date, oozed out of the left side of the man's mouth as the intestine-worm thrashed violently in the limited space provided to it inside the self-destructing body. It didn't take long for the thing to find pathways around rotten, mushy organs and bones that were more flexible than pipe cleaners, the head and tail of it writhing and wriggling in opposite directions as it searched for freedom.

In his time, Robert had seen a lot that was fantastic and horrific, but when one end of the intestine-worm wriggled out of man's anus as the other end simultaneously wriggled out of his mouth, he almost lost it—his consciousness, if not his sanity.

Robert backpedaled and turned, almost tripping over his own feet, then trotted a few steps more to regain his balance. Covering his mouth and nose with the inside of his right elbow, he put three fingers on the face of his right-wristwatch. The man was dead, but it would be nice to have the authorities swing by and pick up the body before some roving hooligans found it and did who knows what with it.

After transmitting the message to his superior, Robert glanced back once more at the corpse. There but for the grace of medication goes he.

Robert shook his head to stop his full-body shudder then continued on his way.

He ran just under a sprint until he came to the quiet, middle-class neighborhood. He slowed, paying extra-special attention to his surroundings as he jogged toward the target house. It had a manicured lawn, an empty driveway, a wreathed front door, and plenty of windows—with closed blinds. Blinds Robert couldn't see through, with or without his x-raying vision. This wasn't another Friday-afternoon wild goose chase.

He used his right-wristwatch to contact his superior again. Robert had a hunch, a good one, and he needed backup—a few cops, some FBI agents, or something even better. The superior's response: all official authorities were occupied elsewhere. Something about gunfire and explosions in the area of Pentagon City. Robert and his partner would have to handle this hunt, together and alone.

Sure. His partner. The partner who should've been by his side since daybreak. The partner Robert hadn't seen since the day before. Just a little more than a year older than Robert, he wasn't acting much better than the truants on the street corner, minding nobody's business.

Robert used his left-wristwatch to send his partner a message he knew would go unanswered. He then continued his reconnaissance.

As the minutes passed, his sense of dread increased. Whatever story was hidden inside that house, it was one full of terror, and one eager to be told. Robert would have to make a decision, soon, about whether he was willing to hear it alone.

Chapter 2

Blessed are the stingy, for they know how to preserve time and money as well as energy—all precious resources in these damnable times.

Darryl Ridley still remembered the first time he'd heard the bad joke: on late-night television, nine years ago. It was harder to figure when the dumb joke morphed into an actual creed. Hell, for all he knew, it had been around for millennia. Maybe it was humankind's first Big Belief.

Big or small, the woman in front of him had somehow managed to live by it for the greater part of her thirty-four years. It was just one of many terrible beliefs she held. Darryl was sure he could change her mind about all of them, here and now.

It was just the two of them, standing in the middle of the three-bedroom house she used to share with roommates. Just Darryl and the woman he affectionately called "T," the first initial of her first name. The reason she'd called in to work sick and invited him over on a Friday afternoon was clear, but he'd accepted the invitation for a very different one.

She was wearing a pale pink chemise and nothing else. She could've been wearing a burqa for all he cared. What he wanted from her, he could only find by looking deep into her naked eyes.

He took off his shirt.

T. started to say something but stopped to stare. She was evidently taken by the sight of his bare stomach, chest, and arms. Darryl knew the faint lavenderish skin-tint she'd seen during all their previous intimate moments was deepening, darkening, and becoming more conspicuous. She was speechless, watching his skin modify its tone.

It was all a matter of skillful concentration. Whatever else they were doing inside of him, Darryl had long ago figured out how to make the parasites work for him. He didn't give a damn about whatever the government's propagandists said. At a certain point in a relationship, Darryl wanted the woman, or man—whatever the case—to know there was something different about him, something beyond rational explanations, something that could change lives.

"I'm not your lover," Darryl said as the woman's eyes slowly rose from his chest to meet his. His irises faded from their usual shade of violet and gradually brightened, approaching the color of wisteria. "I'm more like an angel."

His corneas twinkled, and the air around his body filled with suspended particles, looking like not-quite-clear raindrops, each of them smaller than a thumbtack.

The drops multiplied. After an uncertain number of them had appeared, they moved, scurrying until gathered into two crescent shapes that hovered just above and behind his shoulders. Before T. could say anything, the crescents unfolded, cascading down and down in waves of intangible watery light. When it was all over, two large, radiant wings featuring various shades of violet extended from Darryl's back.

The wings burned with a chilled glow. The skin on Darryl's bare arms, chest, and stomach sparkled with pinpricks of silver.

His would-be lover looked at everything and everywhere except at Darryl's smiling face. In order to finish the process he started, though, he had to get her to focus on the right target.

"Like all angels," he said, "I am essentially a messenger." He extended his hand to her. "I can give you something better than sex, something that can erase all false notions of love from your pretty-pretty head."

Perhaps entranced more by the sight than the words, the woman stepped forward and placed her hand in his. Darryl drew her closer. With his other hand, he raised her chin until their eyes met; he then twinkled his eyes twice more to establish a psychic link that would make their two minds temporarily one. With confidence, he could now shut his eyelids and finish sharing his message with her through a kiss.

There was a faint buzzing sound when they touched lips. When they separated moments later, viscid strings of saliva kept them connected until Darryl stuck out his tongue, wound the nectarous strings around it, and swallowed them all with a smile.

T. opened her eyes. Darryl knew if everything had gone as intended, she wouldn't see his smiling face for several seconds. She'd see nothing but a mélange of beautifully strange colors, beyond violet, all of them dancing with, around, and into one another, maybe communicating an otherworldly message to her with their movements.

"Next time you see a clear blue sky," he said, "don't think of displaced seas. See it as a symbol of the haven for those escaping Love for Peace."

Darryl kept his smile as he backed away from her and turned toward the front door; it wasn't until after he'd turned the knob that he traded it for a different expression.

He bent the light around his body.

It was the last time he'd see the woman. He had nothing more to say to her. There was nothing more he could do for her. It was time for her to move on, live the rest of her celibate life spreading the word, and the word only—pay the act of charity forward. If the loving acts of his teenage years resulted in him contracting the White Fire Virus, the least he could do was use his parasite-given talents to keep others from falling into love's careless traps.

He was just one man, but it was clear as day he was doing a much better job at curtailing the spread than those who got paid for it.

The consensus among US government officials and other interested parties was that there was no need for the general public to know the skin of Virus-carriers was not only hypersensitive to the properties of light but many of the infected could also, within a very limited range of their bodies, manipulate the properties of light, bending it and other forms of electromagnetic radiation to their will. They weren't gods; they were humans. Very sick humans. Most chose seclusion over attention-grabbing antics. Regardless, government researchers and doctors and the officials they advised all figured general ignorance was the best policy until they themselves could figure out just how all these electromagnetic tricks were being performed. So what if the more vocal and flamboyant carriers of the Virus made no secret of their true condition and what they could do? They were sick, in body and in mind. Incurable. Not to be believed or trusted. And most often, such types ended up being shot, or "disappeared."

Even more amazing than some of the beyond-belief abilities many of the carriers displayed was the fact most people seemed to buy into the Heartland Security Agency's propaganda campaign: what credulous witnesses saw was nothing more than random acts of generic magic. The success of the campaign had the related-but-inverse effect of people not heeding the warnings about contracting and spreading the Virus. After all, it affected less than .002% of the people on the planet, so it was really nothing to worry about. But those who worried least were those most at risk. As a clever Heartland Security official once described them, the biggest risk-takers were "those young men and women unwise enough to make promises of undying love to one another, and dumb enough to make haste to seal those promises with quick moments of nude stupidity."

Some carriers spread it before realizing they even had it, before experiencing the seizures that could send their broken minds to a place worse than Hell. The White Fire Virus wasn't the deadliest sexually transmitted disease, but it was the most worrisome. Those who knew all about it knew to be concerned. And some turned their concerns into creativity.

Darryl didn't believe himself to be a literal angel, but thanks to the Virus, he could pretend well enough and long enough in order to drive his special message home.

He and T. had dated for about five weeks. When he first saw her in the nightclub, she was chatting happily with girlfriends about her engagement to someone Darryl knew to be an unrepentant philanderer. Darryl had a low opinion of the man, and he had an even lower opinion of the wonderful idea T. had conjured to make sure her husband-to-be stayed loyal and settled: she'd have him get her pregnant, before the wedding. The husband would just have to stay loyal with a baby on the way. It was an idea Darryl had overheard T. express to friends over the third round of appletinis. Sitting halfway across the room, he hadn't been able to tell if she was serious. It was such an atrocious idea, but it had been spoken by someone Darryl had figured to be a desperate thirty-something; there was a fifty-fifty chance she'd make a serious attempt to carry out the plan. So Darryl had introduced himself, right then, using every talent available to him to charm her. Soon the engagement was broken.

Since that first night in a crowded watering hole, the two of them had dined at some of the area's most intimate restaurants. They'd been on several private boat rides. They'd gone horseback riding. They'd been to the aquarium and even the zoo. They had done everything but what most American lovers say is the highest expression of love. Darryl knew T. had wanted to since day one. Today she thought she'd finally have her way.

Darryl hated having to do it. Even though he did it to prevent the world from dipping deeper into an abyss filled with tainted relationships, deranged parents, and unwanted, unhappy children, he hated it. Making the very thought of lovemaking repulsive in the minds of those who otherwise wouldn't act responsibly, knowing he was stealing from their lives all future moments of joy that were experienced during sex, none of it was easy for Darryl. Adhering to the second half of the Diamond Rule—"Spare None"—was the nastiest part of the business. But he accepted it. After all, he deserved to live the life that a former life of recklessness had created for him. Golden Rules were for a golden age. This time and place demanded a new philosophy.

Darryl wouldn't put his shirt back on until he'd gotten a few more blocks away, closer to where he'd parked his Miata. He did, however, refasten his watches to his wrists. He'd almost forgotten about them, stuffed in his pants pockets. It was against IAI regulations for Watcher agents to remove them for any extended period of time. "Only when showering" was the actual instruction. But in Darryl's mind, charity work trumped these regulations. The work was delicate, requiring his complete attention. He couldn't let an incoming message snap his concentration and ruin the process. And it seemed the messages were more and more frequent these days.

Sure enough, he felt a sensation on the pulse of his right wrist before he could even open the driver's side door. Someone at the Isaac-Abraham Institution was signaling him. Darryl touched his index and middle fingers to the watch's face. After a few seconds, he intuited the message: He was to meet his partner in Arlington; Robert might have found a missing girl, and he needed help with the recovery.

Darryl made himself visible, slid into his car, and sped off. It would take him fifteen to twenty-five minutes to get there, depending on traffic—and the message was a Level 4, second highest priority—so he figured he didn't have time to make a detour to his apartment to arm himself. He hoped his usual accessories wouldn't be necessary.

When he got within a good walking distance of the target site, he parked his car on an adjoining street and strolled toward the general spot where he was to meet his partner. Since he wasn't exactly sure where Robert was, he wanted Robert to see him, but to all others he wanted to appear nonchalant, as if he was just out for some exercise or fresh air.

"Up here."

Darryl didn't look up. He instead looked all around him to ensure no one was watching before he made himself invisible. He then looked and saw Robert a few dozen feet above him, sitting on the stout branch of a tree.

Him and trees…With his brown skin, the nappy black hair flecked with rusty-red hairs, and his penchant for dressing in dark jeans and never-bright T-shirts, Robert barely had to put much effort into twisting the light around his body to blend in. Darryl could tell that his T-shirt today was actually a red-wine color even though Robert was making it appear more like a black coffee. His ever-present black windbreaker hung on a branch, patches of it invisible, the rest appearing as leaves. Nice trick, for a show-off.

Darryl concentrated, twisting the electromagnetic radiation around his own body, and climbed up to the branch liked a winged cat.

"Glad you could make it," Robert said as Darryl crouched down beside him. "Thought I'd have to go treasure-hunting alone."

"I had an appointment." Darryl exchanged his invisibility for tree-leaf camouflage.

"Not with a therapist, I'm guessing," Robert said. "Unless maybe it was a massage therapist?"

Darryl narrowed his eyes.

"Sorry," Robert said. "I know how much your oh-so-great charity work means to you, and how much you think it means to the world, but—"

"Just shut up, Goldner. Tell me what we've got."

"That blue house over there. See it?"

"I can see fine."

"Adam thinks there's a strong possibility the girl we're looking for is somewhere inside."

"Which girl?" Darryl asked. "There're about twenty on our list now."

Robert crooked an eyebrow. "Marie-Lydia McGillis."

Darryl gave him a blank look.

"From Spencer, Virginia," Robert said. "The redhead on all those videos."

It took a few seconds for it to come together for him—but only a few. "The high school."

"Yeah."

Darryl thought about the lost opportunity of making that detour on the way over. "Shit."

"Adam says not to hurt her," Robert said.

"Uh-huh."

"But it looks like maybe you got the message ahead of time, showing up without your bow. And your *corresq*, too, I assume."

Darryl thought about the accessories he usually carried on special recoveries, those situations where there was a strong possibility the lost child might be held captive by a few dangerous types who didn't want the child to be found.

"I came here straight from where I was," he said. "I didn't have time to pick them up."

Robert laughed. "You wear two watches and still can't manage your time."

"I can manage just fine with my bare hands."

"Sure hope so."

"Did you case the place?"

"I got into the yard, tried to peek inside. I couldn't x-ray the walls. Looks like the window blinds are turned just a bit, letting in a small amount of light, but I couldn't see through them either."

"Losing your touch?" Darryl asked.

"I almost lost my patience and went in without you."

"But Adam told you to wait."

"Adam didn't have to tell me a damn thing," Robert said. "There's something strange about this. It looks suburban-normal on the outside, but I can't see through the façade, at any range. The place seems designed like a clubhouse for The Infinite Definite. I'm not stupid enough to go into something like that alone, not if I don't have to. One foot inside and I could be lost in a box of melted crayons."

"Nice metaphor." Darryl squinted at the house, trying hard as he could to see through the walls and windows. He was within range to use his ability, but it just wasn't working for him. Most interesting thing he saw was a scrawl on the front door, in the center of the wreath: a clumsy-looking "W" and two dots, written in blood with a finger. Some kind of gang tag, probably. Unfamiliar. He assumed very dangerous.

"Yeah, you're right," Darryl said. "It's best we do this together."

If it were a clubhouse for the Virus-infected terrorists known as The Infinite Definite, Darryl knew if either he or Robert went in alone, there'd be no chance of making it back out alive. He again regretted coming unarmed.

"No assistance from the badges or feds, huh?"

"Nah," Robert said. "Better things to do at the moment. Besides, you know the boys in blue-n-black wouldn't do anything but bust in with voices blarin' and guns blazin', putting the girl in even more danger. That's why we're getting first crack, to get in unseen and unheard. See what we can see, do what we can do."

"Search warrant?"

"Don't worry about that. Peter's got us covered." Robert flexed the muscles in his arms. "Ready?"

"To get lost in a box of melted wax and colors?" Darryl said with a grin. "Yeah. Let's go."

The two turned themselves invisible and left the tree. Darryl adjusted his vision so he could still see Robert as they approached the house. They walked slowly, trying to detect any signs of life or movement inside. Darryl also kept a lookout for passersby, but only as an afterthought. The streets and yards had been empty of cars and people since his arrival.

As they walked up the driveway, Darryl used his hands to signal he was going to circle around to the backyard and Robert should stay up front; they'd communicate via their left-wristwatches until they were ready to make their presence known to others. Most important, once they made themselves visible, they were to keep their facial features blurred, for misidentification purposes.

Robert waved at Darryl and positioned himself at the edge of the front yard so he'd have a full view of the front of the house. Darryl went to find a similar position in the back.

Rounding the side corner and scaling the fence, Darryl took in the small backyard's beautiful landscaping. He'd seen a fraction of it from his vantage point in the tree, but now, standing in the freshly cut grass and steps away from the well-tended flower garden, he was even more impressed. One would think that it was late June rather than the eve of autumn. All of the flowers were in full bloom. Darryl wondered at all of the work put into it, and at all the work put into erecting the eight-foot-high vertical fence, a custom-designed structure marking the boundaries between neighbors' properties, a wooden obstruction preventing anyone from entering or seeing the pretty, well-kept yard without an invitation. Pity. He agreed the careless shouldn't be allowed to trample upon a beautiful scene, but he also believed everyone had a fundamental right to bear witness to pure beauty.

He looked at the house. He still wasn't able to see past the walls, or even through the vertical blinds on the other side of the patio's glass door, but he could now hear sounds. Nothing distinct, but he at least knew the house wasn't empty. He touched the screen on his left-wristwatch, communicating the information to his partner. Robert signaled back that something was about to come out of the garage.

Darryl itched to circle back around and meet the threat with him head-on, but he couldn't risk leaving the back unguarded. He didn't want to risk having something escape with the treasure.

He touched his watch and sent Robert a message that he should neutralize whatever threat emerged from the garage then use it as an entry point into the house; as long as the garage remained closed, however, he should maintain his position. Darryl would find a quiet way in from the back.

He wasn't sure if Robert had gotten the entire message. Before he finished sending it, Darryl heard voices from the front of the house: Robert's and the voices of two others. It wasn't friendly conversation or innocuous banter. They were fighting.

Darryl muttered a curse as he dropped his invisibility and picked up two of the larger bricks edging the flower garden. One after the other, he threw them at the patio's door. The glass shattered, and he rushed on through, parting the door's blinds with his eyes wide open, looking for the girl, and ready to attack anything that made a move against her or him.

He'd burst into the kitchen. Empty. Darryl didn't move three steps, though, before someone came in from the next room.

The man began to yell something in a foreign language; Darryl didn't want to wait for the translation. He squinted, concentrating a large amount of infrared radiation in the area of the man's face. The man screamed and ducked down. Darryl hopped onto the kitchen table, stepped, and jumped again, kicking the burned man in the head on his way down to the floor. He punched and kicked him again before moving into the next room.

Darryl paused and surveyed the room's furniture. He spotted all the closed and open entrances, saw a bright wide-screen television displaying hardcore pornography, and counted up to three agitated men before the one closest to him took a swing. Darryl grabbed the fist, caught the elbow, and swung the man into the wall. He then swung the man back the other way and released his hold, hoping he'd collide with the other two.

One of the men stopped to shove his oncoming pal out of his way. Darryl pointed two fingers at the other one and flicked his wrist, snapping his fingers. A bright flash of light appeared, momentarily blinding and stopping the man. Darryl rushed forward and punched him on both sides of his jaw before repositioning his body to kick the next man closest to him in the stomach.

A door slammed in another part of the house. Darryl figured there'd been at least one other person in the room who'd escaped through the open entranceway before he had a chance to spot him, and now that person had escaped…Outside, through the front door? Inside, holed up in the room with the lost girl Darryl and Robert had come for? Wherever, Darryl had to get to him quickly.

He ignored the man coming from the kitchen behind him, the man he first attacked. He pushed aside the others who were still standing in front of him and rushed for the open entrance. He couldn't get out.

Darryl felt an intense burning sensation on the back of his neck and stumbled. He realized what had hit him—a taste of his own infrared medicine—before a fist hit him in the back of the head. He went down to a knee and translated himself into invisibility. No luck. His attackers could still see him. They surrounded him, burning, punching, scratching, and kicking him. After delivering a few swift kicks, one of them ran into the kitchen.

An Infinite-Definite clubhouse, Darryl thought as he withstood it all. Spot on. He hated it when Robert's instincts were correct. He hated it even more when his junior partner saved him.

Darryl didn't see it, but he heard the hollers and screams of his attackers. He opened his eyes to find Robert standing in front of him, reaching down with an open hand.

"Bet you wish you'd brought your corresq now," Robert said.

Darryl thought of the flat, six-inch circle composed of hard metal and designed so that a talented Virus-carrier could use it like a short-range boomerang. He knew the corresq would've been helpful but only said, "I would've gotten them. Just another second." He got back to his feet without assistance.

"Can't afford to waste any seconds," Robert said. "We've got a whole house to search."

Darryl looked at the other men in the room. All were lying prostrate on the floor or leaning against furniture, holding their eyes.

"What about the guys you met outside?"

"Dealt with," Robert said. "Come on." He rushed out of the room.

Darryl began to follow, but the man who'd run into the kitchen ran back out, shouting in an incomprehensible language, brandishing a knife and a brick. Darryl couldn't get out of the way fast enough.

He grunted when the jagged, heavy object hit him in the shoulder. Darryl winced and instinctually brought his free hand up to cover the area of impact. He'd no time to think to defend himself before the man lunged at him—but there was time for Robert to direct a beam of light from the television into the knife wielder's eyes. In mid-lunge, the man tripped and stabbed himself in the arm.

"C'mon!" Robert said as he rushed out of the room again. "There're more in here—find 'em, blind 'em!"

Darryl hated it when Robert shouted instructions at him. That wasn't the junior partner's role. But Darryl knew telling him that would do no good; he'd have to reassert his authority by bold actions alone.

Darryl hurried out of the room and stopped behind his partner. They stood in front of the next big obstacle.

A pool table sat in the middle of the room, overlaid with a strange-textured cloth. Scattered billiards resembling giant marbles were on top of it. On the right-hand side of the room was a large mirror, covering more than half of the wall. On the left-hand side were the front door, another door that presumably led to a coat closet, and a halfway open door that led to the laundry room and the garage. On the other side of the pool table, directly opposite them, was a darkened hallway containing the doors to the rest of the house's rooms.

Darryl knew Robert had hesitated not because of the pool table, but to adjust his sight so he could peer down the blackened corridor with utmost clarity after counting all corners, intuitionally measuring all angles. Robert, the mathematically gifted genius; it was his habit. Darryl didn't know how Robert did it, but he knew now wasn't the time to ask. He instead put his vision to use finding the answer to a minor puzzle.

He soon solved it. The walls were lined with a foil-like material, which was what had prevented him and Robert from seeing through from outside. The window blinds were lined with it, too. Yes, it was definitely an Infinite-Definite clubhouse. The foil-like material probably also explained how, despite the low level of light in the house, he, Robert, and the Virus-infected kidnappers were able to manipulate light almost as skillfully as they would've been able to if they were outside in the sun.

"I count four doors," Robert said. "Can't see beyond them."

"Of course," Darryl responded. "Foiled."

The two began to make their way around either side of the pool table.

"Careful," Darryl said. "Assume each room has at least three hostiles. You know how they like to pack up a house with too many."

Robert grimaced. "You smell that?"

Darryl started to reply, but the room suddenly lit up.

He looked toward the ceiling above the table and, before flinching and averting his sight, saw that what at first glance appeared to be an out-of-place disco ball was now a bright, checkered globe. Half of the sphere's squares were mirrors, while the other half were multicolored windows allowing light from the high intensity bulbs inside to shine through. The pool table's surface material and the mirror on the wall helped create the thin-air appearance of amorphous, undulating blobs of light, widespread throughout the room.

Darryl and Robert both cursed at the onslaught of heat and lights—the fulfillment of the half-serious prophecy spoken back up in the tree. It wasn't quite melted wax, but there were plenty of colors, and the experience was hellish.

Both agents screamed when the intangible blobs touched their bare arms, necks, and faces. On impact, Darryl felt and saw patches of his skin burning, bubbling, peeling off, detaching from his body to float off into the air and evaporate. It was no less painful for being an illusion.

Notwithstanding all the confusion, they were too well trained to stay still and succumb to it.

Robert ducked under the pool table.

Darryl clenched his teeth and withstood the searing radiation as he made his way through the colorful storm, searching for a switch that would shut off the globe. He made it to the opening of the dark hallway, only to fall back again when one of the doors opened and—almost in a blur—a teenage girl spun out and into the hall, bounced off the walls, and kicked him in the face and stomach.

Darryl was forced back against the edge of the pool table. He was preparing to push himself forward when the girl smacked him, twirled, kicked him in the knee, and whirled away, out of his reach, while he grunted and snatched at her.

The girl grabbed a pool cue from the rack in the corner of the room as Darryl saw someone else coming out of the same hallway door. No time to determine the age, gender, or danger before he saw the more immediate threat—the girl swinging her cue down at his head.

Darryl couldn't duck. He could only try to catch the cue with his hand. He grunted when the wood smacked his palm. He made a much louder sound when the boy who'd emerged from the hallway's door planted the tip of his steel-toed boot into Darryl's chest with a swift kick.

The boy and the girl shouted as if they were at a sporting event. Darryl suppressed a mild urge to shout for Robert's help. Not today. And definitely not for two little brats.

The boy drew his foot back for another kick. Darryl released the pool cue and lunged at him. Caught off-balance on one leg, the boy did little as Darryl pushed him, forcing his back against the corner where the room met the hallway. The boy screeched in pain. Darryl wanted to make him screech again, but he spent the next moment spinning to the left, out of the way of the stick-swinging girl.

He stopped in the darkened, narrow hallway and stood facing the grimacing, sloe-eyed teenager who guarded its entrance. Over the girl's shoulder, he saw the four punks from the TV room entering the poolroom. Apparently they'd all recovered at the same time, or maybe they'd waited until they were all rested and ready to jump their quarry at once. Whichever, he had to get back out there to help his partner. And he had to do something about this girl in front of him. As usual, time was not an ally.

Darryl neither blinked nor saw the starting action, but he did see the reaction of the girl shouting in surprise and stumbling forward. She came one step into the hallway but was blocked from entering thanks to the size of the pool cue. It seemed Robert had come out from under the near side of the pool table and shoved the girl from behind before she could turn around to see him. Darryl didn't hesitate to take advantage of her temporary disorientation.

He drew some of the abundant light from the pool room into the hall, gathered it in his palm, and then forced it forward, straight at the girl's face. She screamed at the impact and dropped her cue. She was infected all right; an attack like that would've inflicted temporary blindness on an uninfected person, but no pain. When the girl brought both hands up to her face, Darryl grabbed one of her arms and pulled her back into the hall with him. Before turning his back to the poolroom, he saw Robert had hopped on top of the table and was fending off the four punks surrounding it. Darryl would join him soon. First things first.

He twisted the girl's arms behind her and pushed her chest-first up against the wall, making sure her face was turned away from the bright playroom.

"You want to be the one who cooperates and walks away relatively unharmed?" Darryl asked.

Before she could say anything, the boy in battle boots got back to his feet and rushed at them. Darryl squinted and concentrated, hitting the boy in multiple spots on his face, neck, and arms with bundles of infrared radiation. The boy fell to the floor, burned and unconscious.

"It won't be him," Darryl said. "Or the vermin who're trying to hurt my friend out there. We're going to take them down. Hard. Find out what secrets you-all've been hiding. You're the only one who's being given a choice."

"Get out of our fuckin' house…" The girl managed one complete sentence between grunting and struggling.

"You lose your right to being left alone when you go after others—"

"Didn't go after nothin'…You 'tacked us!"

"Take precious property that doesn't belong to you," Darryl continued, "keeping children from their proper guardians—"

"Our parents live here!"

Her words surprised him, but before asking any questions about her story, Darryl needed to know the ending to another.

"I'm not talking about you," he said. "I want to know where the redhead is. Marie-Lydia. I also want to know what you people—"

"Darryl!"

"What fuckin' redhead?" the girl said.

He'd heard the shout. Robert needed him. Now. But he couldn't let the girl go free. She'd attack him again, no question. He had no choice. She was at least sixteen, seventeen years old. Practically an adult. She could take it.

"You had your chance."

Darryl put his hand on just the right spot of the girl's neck and twisted his wrist. She collapsed, unconscious.

Darryl rushed into the poolroom and assessed the situation. The four thugs still had the table surrounded. Three of them were armed with pool cues. The fourth—the self-stuck pig—was wielding the same large knife. Robert was holding his own, jumping from one spot on the table to the next, trying to avoid the rolling billiards and, with less success, trying to avoid the swinging sticks. He was clearly having trouble keeping his senses and balance under control while in the thick of all the colorful globs.

An average person might regard the disco ball's lightshow as a welcome or even necessary aid for dancing and partying, but to almost any victim of the Virus, the radiation-shower could be nothing less than plain torture. Robert wouldn't last much longer. Darryl saw the tear in his pants and the gash underneath. He knew what had triggered Robert's call for help. With no bow and no corresq, Darryl also needed help.

He took a deep breath, pulled off his T-shirt, and entered the lightshow.

As expected, Darryl's hypersensitive bare skin reacted to the exposure. The parasites inhabiting the upper layers of his skin were thrown into frenzy. For them, it was feeding time. Darryl concentrated and did what he could to keep them under control, trying his best to stay conscious as he used every inch of bare skin to manipulate the radiation that was violating him. Indigo pools of liquid-light gathered in his pores as most of the hairs on his skin seemed to stiffen and self-ignite. It felt as if the hairs were burning themselves out and laying down the remains in the indigo pools, and from the mixture, from the pores emerged a glistening substance, a viscous perspiration that tingled and burned his skin as it changed the skin's appearance, its texture, seeming to convert Darryl's epidermis into a thin shell, even as that shell—he felt—began to crack.

Despite the excruciating pain, Darryl was in control.

He extended his hands and redirected a good portion of the light beaming down from the sphere above. As the spinning ball used the bits and pieces of the environment to produce confounding blobs of color, Darryl used the light to combine all of the amorphous blobs and then divide them, creating intangible puppets, allies that looked more-or-less like him and were alive enough to move at his direction and engage two of Robert's attackers.

Darryl manipulated his zombified beings of light toward the knife-wielder and the closest stick-swinger. The former was too obsessed with trying to draw blood to notice anything, but the man with the cue turned and swung twice at the projected hologram, without effect. Not being as stupid as he first appeared, the stick-swinger soon gave up on the puppet and went after the string-puller himself. The man color-shifted his appearance to blend into his surroundings and make himself harder to see. He too was a Virus-carrier, and before he got close enough to swing at Darryl, the man sent forth a burst of infrared radiation to burn and disorient him—successfully—seconds before tagging Darryl on the arm with the stiff wooden stick. Darryl hollered and lost the concentration to control his marionettes. He tried to counterattack, but his sloppy punches only swept the air as the pool cue tagged him twice more.

Darryl was facing an enemy he couldn't quite see, but he did see Robert reach down, scoop up the nine-ball, and fastball it in his direction. The ball pegged the stick-swinger in the back of the head; he lost his camouflage as he fell face-forward. Darryl hit the man with an uppercut and didn't wait to see him hit the floor; he rushed forward to take out the man with the knife.

Darryl grabbed the wrist of the hand holding the blade and twisted it as violently as he could to make the man drop his weapon. He then grabbed the forearm that was inches away from the stabbed shoulder, brought it behind the man's back, and jerked it up as he rammed the man's forehead against the pool table's edge.

The odds were evened. Two against two.

Darryl punched his chosen opponent into unconscious submission while Robert found his way off the table by hitting his attacker with a few billiard balls. On level ground with his enemy, Robert wrestled the man down to the floor and put him to sleep with an expertly applied hold. Darryl found the light switch to shut off the mirror ball.

The two stood for a moment and surveyed their work, attempting to catch their breath before moving on.

"Why didn't the ones who attacked you in the garage come back?" Darryl asked. "You didn't—"

"Tied them up with a rubber hose," Robert replied. "Just a man and a woman. Got them by surprise. Went down easy."

Darryl stepped back into the hallway; Robert was two steps behind him. He surveyed the room with the open door while Robert surveyed the room across from it.

Darryl saw nothing but a bedroom oversupplied with electronic equipment, most of it still in boxes. Robert had found nothing but an empty bathroom.

They moved on to the next door and found another bedroom, also messy with electronic equipment.

Darryl twisted the knob on the door to the final room. It was locked.

"Break it down?" Robert asked.

"I've got it." Darryl started fidgeting with his belt buckle. He pulled out what appeared to be a short metal pin and inserted it into the keyhole.

"A key?" Robert asked.

"A tool," Darryl said. "Special metal. Ask Zel about it."

He jiggled the tool and the knob and, within seconds, the knob turned.

Both agents tensed and readied themselves, prepared to face head-on whatever had holed itself up in the room.

They weren't prepared.

There would've been no way to prepare themselves for the sight of the girl—in torn, burned, and blood-stained clothing—strapped to a bed surrounded by video equipment.

She didn't see them enter. She hadn't seen anything for some time.

Darryl saw she was asleep, in a deep sleep, but not dead. He recognized the girl as the same one from the videos, those all-too-popular videos recorded at a Spencer, Virginia high school and illegally available to those willing to visit, pay, look, and play in the pits of the blackest holes in cyberspace.

Yes, the tip had been right, but something was all wrong. She didn't have red hair. She wasn't chubby. She was a few years older than the fifteen-year-old girl they thought they'd find.

"She's alive," Darryl said.

"But it's the other girl," Robert said. "Right movies, wrong star."

"Yeah. Contact The Burrow. Tell Adam what happened, and what we found. Get the proper authorities out here. Quick."

Robert touched the face of the watch on his right wrist as Darryl turned to walk back down the hall.

The defeated remained motionless on the billiard room floor, but no telling when some of them could come to. Before tying them up, Darryl decided it would be a good idea to first check on the two Robert had secured. It was possible they could've gotten free or, worse, called for backup. Darryl wanted to make sure they were still down and out.

Near the entranceway to the TV room, he noticed for the first time an odd smell. Probably the smell Robert had mentioned earlier, before the disco ball of pain had been switched on. Darryl looked around until his eyes stopped on the coat closet near the front door. He tried to see through the closet's door, but couldn't. He had to open it in order to find the decapitated woman, and the bound and gagged child in whose lap her head rested.

Chapter 3

Robert listened to these lyrics, sung in the most perfect way, as he studied the singer's eyes, and lips, and throat. As much as he wanted to believe it, as much as he felt it, he wasn't naïve enough to believe that unique voice was singing songs only for him. Without thinking about it, he picked up the knife.

He weighed it in his hand for a while, and then dipped it into the glass.

It was the same glass of grapefruit juice he'd ordered when he first came into the club, two hours ago. What was left had become too warm to drink, but he wasn't even considering it. Only the movement, the motion…Stirring was his way of dancing to the performance piece of slow poetry and cool melodies.

An admired artist was onstage, performing and testing snippets of a larger dramatic work she and her troupe had been developing. The crowd was small, but it didn't matter. Many artists' past experiences had shown, no matter how seemingly empty, this particular dawnclub always managed to have the right mix of people, a good cross-section comprising a fair and honest audience open to hearing new experimental music.

Robert sometimes lacked the courage to be completely honest about what he saw and heard, even to himself. He usually preferred music without words, or in a foreign language, giving him the chance to provide his own lyrics in his mind. But Sin Limite, the multilingual singer on the stage, had been a favorite since junior high school. He'd discovered her during a pretty rough time. She was such a different type of vocalist, he put her in a special category. No matter what she said or how she said it, Robert valued every word. And he felt no shame in smiling and applauding at anything she did, even if it was simply making a brief appearance on stage to do nothing but raise her finger.

At the moment, Robert saw someone else make an appearance. He didn't wave or signal. He just shifted his eye and stared, waiting for his partner's eyes to meet his. Darryl saw him. Robert turned his attention back to the attraction on the stage.

Sin Limite had turned the song over to a chorus of five preteens. They and the jazz ensemble accompanying them were just one small part of the performance artist collective known as "Phantasie's rEVEnge," or "The Phantasie" to loyal fans. Even though he didn't care for most of The Phantasie's work, Robert followed Sin Limite. Keeping tabs on her latest projects, he knew The Phantasie as a whole was working on developing a multimedia production of *The Blackbook of Autumn Numbers,* a two-volume book of narrative dramatic poetry Robert considered to be little more than unburned trash. He still found it interesting the troupe was making an attempt to translate the book into a complete work of art. The singers, musicians, poets, dancers, and others who were members of The Phantasie were determined to dramatize the poems in the book, telling the book's story using a connected series of performance pieces involving music, dramatic readings, dancing, interactive videos, and other types of experimental art, all of which would be presented as a coherent whole on the Internet some day.

"Hey—" Darryl started to speak, but Robert held up his hand.

"Wait till this piece is over," he whispered.

Sin Limite finished her song:

> "It goes against all sense—
> > why do children love to play
> in the rain, begging for a later illness
> > to take from their days of joy?
> I had an umbrella in hand,
> > but it's useless against what the wind carries.
> So I returned home
> > to save it for a lighter day."

The crowd applauded as the singer waved and the group left the stage. A saxophonist was coming up next. Robert signaled to the bartender he was ready for another drink, and then he turned his full attention to Darryl. Darryl's attention was on a blonde sitting at the bar.

"Okay." Robert touched his partner's arm. "What's up?"

Darryl passed another smile to the striking beauty then frowned at his partner.

"It was a band of identity thieves," Darryl said. "A good one. Even the kids were involved. And the headless woman."

"You kidding me?"

"No. They'd been making their living through financial fraud, using aliases. They're wanted in five states. The good citizens of the Heartland Security Agency were pretty happy to finally get their hands on them, after we got our hands on them. They weren't too happy about that part."

"So we got a little rough," Robert said, "so what? We had no choice, and no backup. No Peacemaker agents to help us out—"

"There was an incident at one of the hotels near Pentagon City," Darryl said. "Three jihadists tried to take the whole building down. There weren't any Peacemaker agents readily available."

"Yeah, I know, I know," Robert said, then with a grin, "Funny. Most Americans think Muslims are the biggest threat to civilized, God-fearing society."

Darryl nodded. "No surprise you would find that funny."

"What about our identity thieves?" Robert asked. "Were they affiliated with The ID?"

"The teenage girl and three of the guys are carriers. The rest were just regular punks and scum. No one's sure yet of any affiliation with The Infinite Definite."

That would've been interesting. Identity thieves associated with The ID. Even though the abbreviation was an intentional nod to Freud and pronounced the same way as "id," Robert always considered the concept of personal identities—shifting and lacking—when pondering how the terrorists operated. They were hard to identify, until they attacked. And once they'd left a bloody scene, despite the near ubiquity of HSA surveillance cameras, they were near impossible to track.

Well, hell—affiliated or not, these identity thieves seemed just as vicious as any Infinite-Definite terrorist to Robert. "Who killed that woman?"

"There's little love and even less loyalty among thieves, Goldner. It didn't take long after the HSA boys started grilling them for each of them, one by one, to start painting by the numbers. They killed the woman several days ago then locked her and her little brother in the closet. That girl who came at me with the pool stick, she was their sister, the middle child."

"What?" Robert said. "You told me she said her parents lived there."

"They did. They were the two you tied up in the garage. One of the older men was the stick-dancer's boyfriend, and boot-boy's father. The rest were just buddies and friends of the family, and the primary buyers of the drugs most of them used. Apparently they turned against the dead woman when she refused the advances of one of the older men, and also refused to go along with a job they'd planned."

"Didn't her parents—"

"They were the first to start beating her," Darryl said. "Her parents cared more about the potential money than the kids. Only the girl's little brother tried to stick up for her. That's why they ended up sticking him in the closet with her corpse. They'd been beating and torturing both of them for several weeks—starving them, whipping them, burning them with matches and hot water, violating them with pliers and screwdrivers. They moved them both to the closet when they had to make room for an unexpected guest."

"The girl we found on the bed," Robert said. "She's not with them?"

"They all say they don't know her, just that she—like we—attacked them."

"And what does she say?"

"Nothing. She still hasn't woken up yet. They planted her deep under. Sam took a look at her before they took her to a secure hospital."

"Deep under, huh?" Robert said. "I wonder if she'll grow into something old or new when she finally opens her eyes."

"Will she be herself or something else? Sam wondered the same thing. She's at the hospital now."

"Good," Robert said. "Sam's smart enough to judge the true condition of an awakened deep-sleeper based on their first two words. Let's just hope the girl doesn't cry like a baby, but instead says—"

"Hello."

Both of them turned to look, but only Darryl looked happy to see the speaker. Well-toned legs, intriguing smile, and a hairstyle from a different time…It was the same blonde with whom Darryl had just exchanged glances and smiles.

Robert wasn't surprised. The connection began within the usual timeframe. Within ten minutes of walking into most places, Darryl caught the eye of at least one interested observer. Very affectionate verbal greetings were never far behind.

Robert was never surprised. With Darryl's smooth skin and its lavender hints, the unusual eyes that literally twinkled, his seductive smile, and the enigmatic and sometimes poetic manner of speaking, Darryl was an attractor. It was a status Darryl manipulated—he believed—for the greater good.

In the past, Robert himself had often been entranced by his partner's velvet mannerisms, as were most others who came into close contact with Darryl. But unlike most of those others, Robert had grown tired of it. He was tired of women and men interrupting him and Darryl as they tried to talk in private; tired of Darryl's excuses for engaging them in conversation and leading them on, down to an unsatisfying conclusion, doing more harm than good; and tired of Darryl acting as an illusionist, working his charms and magic, all in the name of "peace." Robert had lost his patience with the entire charade.

"We're a little busy here, miss," Robert said.

"Miss Blake," the blonde said, extending her hand to Darryl.

Darryl extended his and made a motion as if he would kiss hers, but he stopped short. "Mister Ridley, Miss Blake. And my rude friend here is—"

"Going to check on my drink. Excuse me."

Robert stood up. Halfway to the bar, he glanced back and saw Miss Blake hadn't hesitated to take his seat. He snorted and went on his way.

"Sorry, baby," one of the bartenders said as he sat on the stool. "I was just about to bring it over."

"S'okay, Sonya."

"We're a little understaffed this morning." She placed the glass of juice in front of him. "Plus I had to deal with the *artistes*."

"I didn't come up here to rush you," Robert said. "I just needed some breathing space."

"You and me both." Sonya signaled for another bartender to take drinks to a table. "The crowd isn't big this morning, but they sure are needy."

Robert took a little plastic bottle from his pocket. "Saturday morning customers always seem to be tough, no matter how many there are."

"Yep. It's only the Saturday night boozing that softens 'em up for Sunday morn."

Robert laughed. "So what about tomorrow? Anyone interesting showing up?"

"Not this week," Sonya said. "Couple of recurring acts, same flavor as usual for a Sunday. Light and mellow. Nothing you haven't seen before."

Robert grunted as he swallowed his medication with a sip of juice. "I may be in the mood for something like that before this week is over."

"Just one more day."

"And plenty of ways for it to turn nasty," Robert said.

"Well, if you're willing to stay up past your bedtime tonight, there's an absolutely *insane* act performing at DC9, on U Street. Starting around ten, I think."

"In the city?"

"Don't sound so disgusted," Sonya said. "I live in it you know."

"Sorry," Robert said. "That's not how I meant for it to come out. It's just that, being on city streets after nightfall, something about it makes my hair itch."

"You won't be on the streets. You'll be inside a building. Unless your pleasant attitude gets you thrown out on your ass."

"Yeah, well, you know me." Robert smiled, and then he felt a sensation on the pulse of his right wrist. A communication was coming in. He muttered an obscenity and said, "Excuse me," to Sonya as he walked toward a window and touched the face of the right-wristwatch. While staring out at the sunrise, Robert intuited the message. He had to go to the hospital. Now.

He rushed by the bar and tossed a few bills near his unfinished drink.

"Later, Sonya."

She nodded at him as he turned and looked for Darryl. They'd both received the same communication, so Robert expected to see his partner making his way toward the exit, or at least rising from his seat. Instead, he only saw Darryl and Miss Blake, seated, hand-in-hand, almost nose-to-nose.

Unbelievable, he thought as made his way back to the table.

"C'mon," he said when he was within earshot.

"Just a second," Darryl said.

"We don't have a second. Didn't you get the message? She's up. The doctors are only giving us a small window to speak to her."

"I got it," Darryl said. "You go on ahead. I'll meet you there."

Damn it. Robert turned away and hurried toward the door. Charity work—work that does all harm and no good. Was Darryl so blind that he couldn't see that?

Robert ran to his car and sped off for the hospital to meet Sam. The found girl needed to be questioned about the still-missing one. Since Darryl and Robert were the two who found her, it made sense for them to be part of the process.

In an absence of common sense, I left my shelter, went out under a sweltered ice-sky.

The line from Sin Limite's song "Rainfall" went through his head as he tried to maneuver through Saturday-morning traffic.

Like some kind of spell, lines and verses from the whole damn song invaded his thoughts, and stayed. He couldn't shake them, probably because it all rang so true to life. His life.

He'd once succumbed to passion. A few times, actually. *In an absence of common sense…*He'd made a lot of mature decisions at a young age. He decided to stop being a momma's boy and go out for the wrestling team in junior high, the first move in a seven-step personal remodeling project designed to capture himself a girlfriend. His first true girlfriend. He wanted a steady girl to have and to hold through the remainder of his school days and on into marriage.

He never made it all the way up the steps. Robert was diverted, his life pushed and dragged through episodes of cruel comedies and darker tragedies: withstanding the unspoken and whispered suspicions in the wake of the mysterious (at the time) death of his best friend Davin; becoming a pariah to all but a couple of his remaining friends; and getting kicked off the high school wrestling team and expelled from school. Hell, by the time his ex-girlfriend's dad had tried to put buckshot through his skull, Robert was about ready to end it all; he'd fall in a bloody, delirious fit of laughter. But something compelled him to save himself that day—for the even worse episodes that were to come.

It had all seemed so unrelenting until that clear, sunny day when he saw Darryl…

His right hand was trembling. Robert looked at it. His nails were turning blue. The hairs on the back of his hand were stiffening, sticking straight out. His finger joints popped—painfully—when he bent them. On the periphery of his vision, he saw the phantom gnats, the indigo and crimson dots that couldn't be seen straight on but only existed to taunt, to act as a signal. *Shit.* Speaking of fits…This wasn't going to stop on its own. It was actually about a minute away from getting worse. He kept only his left hand on the steering wheel, but it would soon follow suit. He wouldn't be able to steer at all. And he couldn't count on a crash to put him out of his misery.

Robert stepped on the gas. He'd been driving through a residential neighborhood, a linked set of one-way streets that, in times of heavy traffic on the primary route, Robert knew as a shortcut to the hospital. There was nowhere to pull over, and he couldn't just stop. All of the driveways were full, except the one he'd spotted a bit farther down.

He slowed at the first stop sign, didn't bother for the second. Robert swung into the open driveway and put his foot down hard on the brake. His left hand couldn't reach the stick to shift the car into park; his right hand was useless; so his foot stayed pressed on the brake pedal while his left hand fumbled with his inside jacket pocket for his pill bottle.

He twisted the cap off with his teeth and poured two pills into his mouth. He let them sit on the middle of his tongue while the back of it worked to get enough saliva in his mouth in order to smooth the pills' passage down his throat.

Robert had to swallow twice to get them all the way down. He then closed his eye and waited for the illusion of normality to retake his body.

This shouldn't have happened. He'd just taken his damned medication less than fifteen minutes ago. Looked like from now on he'd have to start taking twice as many pills every few hours, and remember to ask Sam when he saw her if any of the government's medical geniuses have yet come up with anything stronger to keep the parasites tame.

What a charmed life he led. If anything, he should be the one lying in a hospital bed.

Robert had known what alleged "sin" he'd committed, how he'd opened the door for the Virus to enter his body. What he didn't know—what no one knew—is where those translucent flies had come from in the first place. They'd appeared in random areas on the planet one early spring, and then they disappeared on the eve of summer, long before they could be classified or properly studied. Left in the wake of their biting and blood-feeding spree were the millions of parasitic microorganisms they'd injected into the skins of thousands of people. The human immune system defeated many of the parasites almost immediately. But in a few unlucky people, once they hit the bloodstream, the parasites thrived. They multiplied and took up residence in their hosts' red blood, skin, and brain cells, introducing the human species to the White Fire Virus.

Robert hadn't been among those bitten eight years ago. But when the parasites began to use their new hosts to propagate themselves in manners other than biting, well…Robert eventually got caught up in the waves of victims that came after, all of them struck with something that started like malaria and rapidly evolved into something more like HIV. But what had the victims done—what had he *really* done—to deserve such a punishment?

Was it a sin, or a blessing? Or were both equally false words, having no relevance to real life?

Robert's viral condition—at least when controlled through a combination of willpower, smart attire, and frequent medication—allowed him to do some good in the world. But who really gave a shit whether he lived or died? Who'd given a shit about that poor old man he'd seen literally falling to pieces? Known Virus-carriers were treated worse than the homeless. And if one had the misfortune of being homeless and infected, well…

After eight long years, the total number of the infected—both dead and living—remained relatively small, and mostly ignored. It was estimated that, at any given time, there were one hundred thousand to two hundred thousand living Virus-carriers on the planet. The vast majority of those who contracted the Virus died shortly thereafter or were quarantined; treatment of victims varied from country to country, locality to locality. In the United

States, far too many of the country's elected officials and opinion-makers abused the out-of-sight-out-of-mind philosophy. They felt only a few million Virus-carriers dead or on the verge of dying worldwide over the span of eight years was nothing for them or the populace to get too excited about. After all, the ordinary flu killed somewhere between a quarter of a million and half a million people worldwide each year, and very few people got too worked up about that. Besides, overpopulation and a tightening economy were far more dire problems.

Those who ran the Heartland Security Agency agreed with this assessment, but they were also smart enough to give the Virus some attention. Almost from day one, the Agency had been at the forefront of an educational campaign that tried to prevent its spread, while at the same time orchestrating a propaganda campaign to persuade the public that carriers of the Virus couldn't really perform the amazing feats numerous witnesses had seen them perform.

Robert chuckled as he thought about some of the propagandistic acrobatics the HSA had performed over the years to explain away the actions and misdeeds of Virus-carriers. Their supernatural-seeming performances were, without fail, dismissed as mere illusions, sophisticated-but-still-amateurish magic tricks. Nothing to worry about. Professional stage magicians, circus freaks, and any halfway decent clown at a children's party could perform tricks just as amazing. Whatever fantastic tricks anyone thought they saw or heard about could be illuminated by rational, common-sense explanations, courtesy of the HSA's wordsmiths. The government's expert debunkers could also easily disprove any of those fantastical tales told by bloggers and others on the Internet about isolated happenings in other countries.

No wonder no one gave a damn about the Virus and whatever catastrophes to which it might be a party. Lies, ignorance, and illusions—all of them were so blissfully sweet. Reality was much too pungent for the senses.

Robert opened his eye. He'd heard someone shouting at him. He turned his head and saw a frazzled-looking middle-aged woman in a yellow bathrobe, half hidden behind the open front door. His Mustang was idling in her driveway, and she was none too pleased about it. Only some of her words were in English; all that Robert understood were a couple of racial slurs and something about getting a gun if he didn't get out of there.

His drug-assisted rumination was over. The medication had steadied his hand. His nails were the proper color. Time for him to get on with his official duties.

Robert arrived at the hospital in ten minutes.

He passed through the security check on the first floor then went to the fifth floor, where he had to pass through a second check before getting to the right hall. When he saw Sam, he had many questions for her, but she was the first to speak.

"Where's Darryl?"

"On his way, I guess." He hoped. With Robert's unexpected ten-minute detour, Darryl should've arrived already. He surely wasn't all that caught up in that blonde; one really didn't have to spend too much time sweet-talking her type in order to get a first date, or whatever else. "Adam's message said the girl was awake. You speak to her yet?"

"Briefly," Sam said. "I wanted to wait for you two."

"What did she have to say to you?"

"First thing? 'Where's Marie-Lydia?'"

Robert sighed.

"I'm not well-versed in interrogations," Sam said, "but I figure it wouldn't be useful to ask her the same question she asked us."

"I'll make a note of it," Robert said. "What did you say to her?"

"Well, since I don't know where Marie-Lydia is, I just told her where she was—in an Arlington, Virginia, hospital—and why—we found her beaten and unconscious in a house full of addicts and criminals. I told her the people who found her were on their way to talk to her."

"She gave you a name, right?"

"Hers? It's Ava Darden."

"She's not listed on any of our registers," Robert said.

"No, but Adam's running a full search, trying to locate any relatives in the area."

Robert approached the door to Ava's room.

"Aren't you waiting for Darryl?" Sam asked.

"No. But you can." He closed the door behind him.

Ava shifted her head when he entered the room. She was still weak, but she didn't seem the least bit troubled.

Robert smiled. "Hi there."

Her eyes narrowed.

It was impossible for him to know for sure, but from the expression on her face, the slight movement of her irises, and the slight contraction and dilation of her pupils, Robert figured she was studying him, from bottom to top, taking an extra amount of time to focus on the black patch over his right eye, shielding an injury, a loss.

Ava blinked before speaking. "Hello."

"My name is Robert Goldner." He moved a step closer to the bed. "I'm an agent with the IAI, the Isaac-Abraham Institution. It's a nonprofit group that, among many other things, helps find missing kids. Yesterday, we found you."

"Was I missing?" she asked.

"Well, we weren't exactly looking for you," he said. "But we found you."

Her lips approached a smile. "You're an honest one."

"I was raised to be."

"I'm Ava. Ava Darden."

"And you're not from around here," Robert said.

"No. Spencer. Spencer, Virginia."

"What were you doing in that house?"

"House?"

"The one we found you in. The woman who was in here earlier told you—" He hesitated. "Do you know where we found you?"

"Oh. Yeah. The den of drugs and thieves."

"Why were you there?"

"I wish I knew," Ava said.

The room's door opened. Sam entered, followed by Darryl.

"Uh, Ava, you've already met Sam Goins. This is my partner, Darryl Ridley."

The two exchanged greetings and Darryl said, "Sorry I'm late. But you know Saturday morning traffic. Everyone trying to get to the malls."

Robert snorted as Sam said, "We don't mean to crowd you, Ava. But all three of us are very interested in knowing your story."

"I'd be interested to know it myself," Ava said in a murmur.

"We can all leave if you need us to," Sam said. "Should we get the nurse back in here?"

"No," Ava replied, sounding even weaker.

Robert looked at Sam, who just shrugged and shook her head. He then turned to Ava and asked, "What's the last thing you remember?"

"I was in the gym. The school gym. I was trying to stop Marie-Lydia from killing everyone."

"Marie-Lydia McGillis?" Darryl asked.

Ava perked up and, in a foolish attempt to sit up, aggravated the wounds on her abdomen. She grunted and fell back as Darryl and Sam rushed to her side.

"Are you okay?"

"Do we need to call the doctor?"

Ava winced but said, "I'm fine." She took a moment to catch her breath, and then she opened her eyes wide, looking at each of them in turn. "Where is she?"

"We don't know," Darryl said.

"We were looking for her when we found you," Robert said.

"But you said something about a house," Ava said. "Is she involved with—?" She grimaced as her body tensed.

"Okay, that's enough for today," Sam said. "Gentlemen, out in the hall. Ava, dear, I'm calling the nurse for you. We're leaving you alone now, but we'd like to speak with you again later."

The nurse rushed into the room after Robert and Darryl left. Both agents took their time walking toward the nearest lounge area.

"That wasn't much use."

"There'll be another time," Darryl said. "After her wounds heal and she starts to think clearer. Anyway, it's a cold trail again. There're other kids to find. Let's concentrate on the warm ones."

"Don't you want to wait and see what Adam finds first?" Robert asked.

"What do you mean?"

"Didn't Sam tell you that this girl wasn't on any of our lists of missing kids?"

"Yeah, so what?"

"Aren't you curious why?"

"I know why. She wasn't missing."

"If you're right, that should make you even more curious."

"Curious about what? What are you talking about?"

"What's with you?" Robert asked. "Where's your head these days?" They weren't meant as rhetorical questions, but he wasn't about to wait for answers. "Ava said the last thing she remembers is fighting with the redhead—Marie-Lydia McGillis—which is the entire plot of all those videos we've reviewed. It's the last thing Ava remembers, and it's the last time anyone saw the McGillis girl awake and conscious. Ava was the last one to see her. We get a tip that the McGillis girl may be in a house, but Ava is there instead."

"Yes," Darryl said. "And?"

"You're the senior in the partnership," Robert said. "Can't you put all of that together to reach some sort of conclusion?"

"No, I can't. Because it doesn't mean anything."

"At the very least, it means the trail isn't cold."

"It means we're back where we started," Darryl said, "and there's nothing warm or encouraging about that."

Neither, Robert thought, was Darryl's lack of commitment to the Watcher program he'd signed up for.

"Well, I'm heading back to The Burrow to check on the sources of our information," Robert said. "Maybe you'd like to work with me, unless you have another appointment for tongue-wrapping and spit-swapping?"

"Listen, Goldner—"

"She's not in as terrible shape as she seems." Sam entered the lounge area. "I spoke to the doctor again. She said Ava's more fatigued than anything. Another good night's rest will do wonders." Robert and Darryl followed Sam toward the elevator bank. "I left her our contact information for when she's ready to speak to us, if she wants to, but the police and feds get the next crack at her. We only got dibs as a favor from the HSA."

"They owe us more than one," Darryl said.

"Funny," Sam said as they got onto an elevator cab. "They've been claiming it's the other way around. We have another briefing meeting with them on Monday, bright and early."

"Maybe they'll brief you on the status of my application," Darryl said.

Robert felt like laughing himself to tears; Darryl had to be joking. He'd been slacking as a Watcher agent, noticeably and dangerously. Did he really think he could be effective as a federal agent?

"I've been waiting to hear something for three months now," Darryl said.

"Maybe you should clean out your ears and realize silence means they don't want you."

"Don't be so sure," Sam said as Darryl glared at Robert. "The HSA is searching for some new Peacemakers, and I believe Darryl would make a good fit."

"Then what's the holdup?" Darryl asked. "I thought I did well during my first round of interviews. But since then, nothing. No yay or nay."

"I'll be sure to ask for an update on Monday," Sam said.

Darryl sighed as the elevator's door opened. Robert also sighed. Picturing Darryl with a gun was a sad sight. Armed and mentally preoccupied with getting on to the next charity case, he could cause all kinds of collateral damage.

"I'd like to know the Agency's decision one way or another," Darryl said, following Sam toward the building exit. "Soon. Before I turn twenty-two and Adam kicks me out of the IAI for being too old, too much of an adult."

"I assure you," Sam said, "that's not going to happen."

"Yeah," Robert said. "I'm sure Adam's definition of 'adult' includes the phrases 'acts responsibly' and 'exercises mature judgment.'"

"Well, your position's secure," Darryl responded. "Keep making those stupid babyish remarks and your place in the orphanage of Watchers will be assured for the rest of your wise-alecky life."

Robert grinned. As if either of them was destined to reach old age, or even middle age. "This baby is wise enough to know that neither of us is going to get much older before we're through. We're just crawlin' till we fall."

"Cutely phrased," Darryl said. "Every nursery needs a rhymer."

"And every government agency, a self-righteous prick who—"

"Will you two cool it?" Sam unlocked her car. "Who's coming back to The Burrow?"

"I am," Robert said.

"I have some business to take care of." Darryl turned and walked toward his car.

"Yeah," Robert said, "the HSA will just love to hire a Peacemaker who insists on moonlighting."

Darryl just kept walking.

Chapter 4

A workshop of toys. That's how the IAI's chief engineer referred to his special room. Robert had a different opinion of it.

It was intimidating. It was a room that seemed to exist in a separate time and reality from the world outside, even more so than the rest of The Burrow. It was a room where futuristic instruments and devices were created, very few of which were intended for use by the masses.

True, Robert figured most people would be lost in a small world of happy wonder when they entered and spent time in Zel Bernard's workshop of toys. But the objects inside were nothing to play with. And in spite of the casual way Zel referred to the products of his work—insisting on referring to them as if they were just amusements for children—the toymaker was careful to limit access to the room to only a privileged few. This Saturday afternoon, Robert was among the lucky ones.

But he didn't enter the workshop to gawk and gander at the many shelves and display cases. Robert didn't request the time to ask Zel about his latest gadgets. He didn't care to see Zel demonstrate how his latest toy worked or hear how effective his specialized instruments would be in certain situations. Something else was riding his thoughts, and Robert wanted to discuss it with Zel, the IAI board member he trusted most.

Nevertheless, just after entering the toymaker's workshop, while looking around for his host, without intending to, Robert picked up a silver object that resembled a deformed ball, a once-perfect sphere that had melted into the grotesque shape of a lump. He paid it little attention at first. But while continuing to look around the large, cluttered room for Zel, and turning the device around in his palm, Robert became more and more focused on the silver object. He soon realized it more accurately resembled the shape of a human heart. Captivated, Robert examined it, noticed the wire loop, and stuck his finger into it. While doing so, he accidentally dropped it—and he saw the heart extend on its string. He instinctively flicked his wrist to return the object to his palm. As the string extended, tiny points resembling metallic thorns had extended from the heart. When it rested safely in his hand again, the object no longer appeared to be a heart, but a smooth silver apple. He figured the device worked like a shape-shifting yo-yo. He released it again, saw little pointy worms appear on the object's surface, then palmed it and observed its new appearance: a jack-o'-lantern. When he released the object once more, sharp metal flames jutted outward. When they retracted, the device appeared again as a silver heart.

"'Mazing, isn't it?" Grinning, Zel emerged from behind a lead-lined screen. "Made one a couple of years ago, only to have it stolen. Just got around to making another one."

As always, the toymaker was covered from head to toe in white, from the shoes to the gloves to the skullcap. The only uncovered area was his face, a face that had its eyes shielded by special wraparound glasses. The black lenses were so beyond black they seemed just a bit creepy to Robert, but he fully trusted there was no malevolence behind them.

"What is it?" Robert asked as he held up the silver lump.

"A toy, of course."

"It looks really, really dangerous."

"Well, it's obviously not for kids."

Robert didn't want to know for whom it was obviously intended, but having a toy heart in his hand helped remind him of the reason he was there.

"Congratulations, by the way," Zel said as Robert went to put the toy back from where he'd plucked it. "I hear you two had quite the successful treasure hunt yesterday."

"Not quite successful," Robert said. "We found a girl, but not the one we were looking for."

"Well, you made a live recovery, that's what's important."

"I suppose."

"Plus, working with Darryl, I'm sure you'll find all the lost girls and boys you're looking for sooner or later."

"Not through any effort of his." Robert took a seat at one of the least-cluttered tables. "He's not acting like the lead on our team. More like a load."

"Nice way to talk about your partner," Zel said. "If I recall correctly, he was the one who found you not too long ago, wandering around naked in some woods just south of Sterling."

"Yeah. Years ago. These days, Darryl has other priorities than searching for missing kids. That's why I wanted to speak to you. His extracurricular activities are more than a distraction. They're a serious problem."

"What activities?"

"His so-called charity work," Robert said.

Zel shrugged and shook his head.

"For a really perverse belief system that he's adopted."

"A belief system, huh?" Zel sat down at the stool opposite Robert's. "Called what?"

"Bullshit, if you ask me."

"Uhm…"

"Sorry," Robert said. "I really don't want to take up your time with a rant. I just need some advice on how to maybe fix this, help get Darryl back on track."

"Maybe you'd better tell me about the charity work first," Zel said.

"Okay," Robert said, "but I'll warn you up front, it's a really abstract philosophy. I'll do my best to make it as coherent as possible."

Zel nodded.

"Well," Robert said, "after Darryl was forced to face the fact that he had the Virus by, you know, having a seizure and being raptured down into XynKroma against his will, he looked for a way to make up for his past lifestyle, erase the habits that caused him to get the Virus in the first place. While he was still in the hospital, or right after he got out—I'm not sure when—he somehow got hold of a book called *Death's Heart*. A book of poetry by some anonymous writer. I mentioned it to some friends once; they did some research, and they're pretty sure it's by the same person who wrote *The Blackbook of Autumn Numbers*."

"Who's also anonymous."

"Yeah," Robert said, "and for a good reason. But my friends and I still tried to work our way through it. Them, for the challenge. Me, for the sake of the partnership. I wanted to get a bit inside of Darryl's head."

Zel chuckled. "Well, there're better ways of doing that."

"Better for whom?" Robert asked. "I'd just as well avoid that route."

Zel said, "Going to XynKroma, under the supervision of Vince, is quite safe."

Robert wondered how traveling to an extra-dimensional realm that could best be described as an unstable marriage of

Heaven and Hell could ever be considered safe, regardless of whether or not the process was being monitored by an IAI board member. "Reading *Death's Heart* seemed to me the wiser option," he said.

"Maybe I should try my eyes at it."

"You shouldn't. *Death's Heart* is a bad story, an allegory told by way of a connected series of convoluted poems. It's about a character named 'Vastion,' or 'Vast' for short. And he…Listen, I'll spare you all the ridiculous details. I can summarize the whole stupid thing by just telling you that Vastion is some kind of supernatural being, from another dimension, and he's worried about the sick condition of *Love,* which is considered a god, or maybe The God, where he's from. What's more, Love is also Vastion's father."

Zel gave him a pained look.

"Yeah," Robert said. "It's kind of an abstract, metaphysical concept. As I said, Vastion's a being from another dimension. So, just stay with me a sec."

Zel nodded. Robert continued.

"Vastion is angry that human beings have been using the word 'Love' in vain and, worse, the perverse acts they carry out in the name of Love are directly to blame for the sick condition of Vastion's God. Somehow, what humans say and do in their dimension has dire effects in Vastion's. So Vastion somehow leaves his dimension and comes to Earth as a supercharged man in order to get people to change how they think about the concept of Love—not to regard it simply as the product of momentary crushes and one-night stands. But while living among humans, as a human, Vastion becomes convinced that Love is actually a false god; rather than misbehaving humans corrupting Love, Love is actually corrupting humans. So Vastion changes his tactics—and his mission."

"That sounds…interesting," Zel said.

"If so," Robert said, "it's only because I'm summarizing and you haven't heard the worst of it. There are five chapters in the book. Five short chapters of convoluted, mind-numbing poetry. They're not named by numbers, but colors, and in the last chapter, the Blue chapter, Vastion gets to the point where he sets out to destroy this false god Love by, in a sense, overloading it. He sets out on a mission to encourage select humans to engage in all sorts of despicable and perverse 'acts of Love.' You can imagine the details; just consider the idea of *sexual terrorists*. Rapes, violent crimes of passion, and so on. Vastion's theory is that Love and its worshippers—lovers—can only take so much. After *too* much, they'll self-destruct. Once the false god is dead, the real God—*Peace, Love's* estranged wife and Vastion's missing mother—will reclaim its rightful place."

Zel thought for a moment then chuckled. "Sounds like a nice little bedtime storybook."

"Maybe for insomniacs in an asylum," Robert said.

Zel put a thumb and finger on his chin as he cocked his head. Robert pressed his lips together and gazed at Zel's glasses, waiting for the older, wiser man to fully digest what he'd just heard.

After more than a full minute of silence, the toymaker said, "I'm sorry. I still don't get it. What does this have to do with Darryl?"

"Vastion is Darryl's prophet, his inspiration."

"In what way?"

"Darryl doesn't just think about peace, or talk about peace," Robert said. "He *inflicts* peace. On every woman and man he can."

Zel hummed and nodded. "I still don't quite follow you."

Robert sighed. "Think about it. The fundamentalist fanatics in this country preach that 'God is Love.' Every pop song you hear, every movie you see, every other insipid television show is telling us all constantly that love is the supreme feeling. Every other person you bump into on the street just can't wait to tell you how happily in love they are, or how they're looking for love, or how they're so miserable because they're not in love. And in spite of all these thoughts and feelings and sentiments of love everywhere, look at the state of our planet, look at the state of humanity. It's shit going down a toilet."

Zel bristled at the language. Normally Robert would have paused to apologize, but he was on a roll.

"That's Darryl's thinking," Robert said, "and he's not a stupid guy. But he read this dumb book when he was in the hospital recovering from his most severe seizure, recovering from the brand new idea that he had a bizarre new virus, an STD. He read those poetic words, thought about the world around us, saw through the metaphors, and he put two and two together, concluding Vastion was on to something. Love really is a false god, the ruler of this crappy world. Peace is what we all should be striving for. Reading that damn book over and over, Darryl came to the conclusion that, as penance for the acts that caused him to get the Virus in the first place, in order to gain some type of redemption, he'd devote as much time as possible to acts of charity, steering people away from love, convincing them to accept peace."

There was a period of silence before Zel broke it by laughing. "Well, I guess everybody needs a hobby!"

Robert only stared at him, his expression unchanging.

Zel cleared his throat. "Okay, seriously, I see your point. Darryl is allowing his charms and good looks to attract women—"

"And men."

"Okay, fine, both, and he uses his, uh, talents to convince them not to bother with trying to find love. Don't even think about it. The pursuit of love is the wrong way to go."

"Exactly."

"So?"

"*So?*" Robert wanted to hit the table. "Look, ignore the fact this book he swears by has a flat-out ridiculous premise, ignore the fact this book he's basing his entire life on is overwritten and terribly written, ignore the fact the philosophy is just bizarre and stupid, and—for the moment—just ignore the fact it's interfering with the work we do for the Institution. People who are in our condition, who can do the things we can do, have a responsibility to either help humankind or stay out of the way. We do *not* have the right to screw with other people's minds."

"What're you saying?" Zel asked.

"I'm saying that he's not just reading them poetry or whispering sweet-nothings in their ears. Darryl's using his talents, his real talents, to hypnotize these women, these men—anything he can attract—to come around to his way of thinking. From manipulating light—standing eye-to-eye, nose-to-nose—it's not a far cry to manipulate another's thoughts too. Maybe even permanently."

"Aggressive hypnotism?" Zel finally looked concerned. "Is that what he's doing?"

"I'm pretty confident."

Robert had a suspicion the act Darryl was performing was closer to an actual lobotomy than mere hypnotism, but he wanted to be careful with his words until he knew for sure.

Zel clasped his hands on the desk and bent his head. It seemed he also wanted to carefully choose his words before he spoke.

"Listen, Robert, I don't pretend to know all of what Darryl does and doesn't do, what he believes and what he doesn't, but he's been with the IAI for longer than you have. I don't know him as well, but I know his reputation. And whatever philosophy, ideology, or theology he believes in—well, actions count far more than beliefs. And Darryl has helped the Institution recover dozens of lost children and young adults, including you. If he is taking whatever messages he sees in this book to heart, I'm sure he's taking to heart only what he sees as good and useful, and rejecting all the rest that's bad."

"*None* of it's good."

"Maybe he really is just talking about living a careful life of peace," Zel said, "just clean living and meditation, and hypnotism never comes into play. I haven't spent enough time with Darryl to feel as if I could get inside his mind, but I have spent considerable time with someone who has actually been there. You shouldn't worry."

Robert looked downward and shook his head.

"You know that Darryl has spent dozens of hours working closely with Vince," Zel asked, "assisting him with his experiments in Xyn?"

"Yeah," Robert said, "and those experiments have only helped convince Darryl that what he's doing is having some effect, bringing order—piece by piece—to chaos."

"And maybe he is."

"I don't buy it," Robert said. "There's no way to bring order to a plane of existence whose environment is constantly being altered by a countless number of minds. Every sentient being's thoughts, whims, and wishes combined…You go into that realm confused and come out even more confused. I just don't buy into the idea there's any way to bring order to it."

"Okay, well, what would you buy?"

Robert hesitated before responding. "I just want to know why—*why* is it that so many who have this damn Virus have to create these stupid, personal, religified fictions based on bad books of poetry."

"Would you be happier if the books were better?"

Robert frowned in response to the toymaker's smile and said, "All these damn Creation and Reformation myths, all of them variations on each other while being at odds with one another. Just like their Believers. None of them completely sensible—"

"Just like their Believer's actions."

"Right."

Zel reassumed a straight face and said, "Robert, you know as well as I that most victims of the Virus create or adopt mythological narratives because they *have* to. They have to find a way to survive, mentally cope with the rest of their lives after their horrific experiences of a realm like XynKroma."

Robert didn't believe "horrific" was a strong enough description for an extra-dimensional realm composed of polluted light, a realm that didn't adhere to the known laws of physics or even what the wackiest spiritualist would call common sense. He also didn't believe there was only one way to survive after having traveled all the way there and back.

"I didn't," Robert said.

"So you keep telling yourself," Zel said.

"And I'll tell the same to anyone who'll listen. I never came out of the experience wanting to go on a messianic crusade to mess with people's minds under the pretense that I was in some way saving the world."

"No," Zel said, "but not long after your first extended stay there you joined the IAI and our crusading efforts to help save lost children, to help prove to them that they were never forgotten."

Robert took a deep breath.

"Yeah, okay," he said. "After my first experiences of Xyn, I was convinced that the human family needs strengthening. But none of us need any fictions to tell us that, or to help us solve the problem."

Zel hunched his shoulders and leaned forward. Robert couldn't see his eyes, but he could sense they were looking straight at his, maybe even through it.

"Robert," he said, in a tone far more serious than Robert had ever heard him use, "you're much younger than I am, and I know you've been through a lot in your short time on this Earth. But you've never had children. You've never raised them, neglected them by paying too much attention to a woman who wasn't their mother, or lost them before their time. I have. And I've had time to think about the experience—all of it—long after it was over. About the moments of happiness, about what made those moments so happy for us. And about how I could find joy in life after resolving myself to the fact that those moments were gone, irrecoverable and irreplaceable. And I can tell you, from experience, that elements of fiction *are* necessary help heal certain wounds, improve certain conditions; they can save the little personal worlds of most men and women, and maybe even save the bigger one."

Several moments of silence passed after Zel stopped speaking. Robert felt like he'd been punched in the stomach and, in spite of it, wanted to say he was sorry. But, beneath it all, he also felt that Zel was still missing the point. There was a rage within. Within Darryl, definitely. Within Zel, maybe—maybe once upon a time. But in his partner, Robert knew there was still a self-loathing, a hatred for his very existence and everything he'd done before he lost his family, everything he'd done before he was left alone. Just like Vastion felt when he found out he was the seed of a false god, a god who made its worshippers sick, worshippers who in turn made their god sicker. Vastion coped by setting out to push the worshippers to indulge in acts that would consume them all. Zel coped by making complicated and dangerous toys, and would do so until the White Fire Virus consumed him. And Darryl? Whether it was mere hypnotism or more like a lobotomy, Robert knew it was wrong for Darryl to screw with anyone else's mind, with or without their consent. And who knew what else he was doing with them? Hell, what were these women and men going on to do after Darryl had his way with them? Robert believed these so-called acts of charity were far worse than any one-night stand. After all, Vastion, the promoter of sexual terrorism, was Darryl's poetic prophet. But Robert just didn't know what more he could say to Zel at this point.

The toymaker broke the silence.

"Maybe you should meet with Vince, talk all this over with him. He can give you far greater insight than I possibly could."

"Yeah," Robert said. "Maybe. Or maybe I should just—" He felt a sensation on his right wrist and looked at his watch. "Damn it."

"Problem?" Zel asked, rising from his seat.

"Maybe. Adam wants to see me."

"Oh, must be important," Zel said as Robert rushed toward the door. "If he's sending you back out into the field, I'll be here if you need to come back and borrow a yo-yo or something."

"Thanks," Robert replied over his shoulder, "but I hope I won't need to."

He stepped through the sliding door and entered a hall of The Burrow. With the exception of a couple of agents from other Watcher units, it was empty. Normal for a Saturday afternoon, and most other afternoons.

The Burrow served as the central office of the Isaac-Abraham Institution and was comprised of three secure, mazelike floors located deep underground, beneath one of Northern Virginia's many shopping centers. Like the toymaker's workshop, the compound was a world apart from the greater world beyond it. Inside of its reinforced walls were things most people in the outside world would never see and would probably never understand. The IAI did, however, share the organizational structure of many other Washington-area nonprofits: a board, an advisory committee, and "researchers" like Robert.

The Burrow housed offices for advisory committee members, conference rooms, and special training rooms for Watcher agents. In addition to more traditional offices, the Institution's nine board members had their own personal workrooms. Zel, Adam, and some of the other board members even had their primary living quarters—fully furnished apartments—in The Burrow. There were also spare rooms that Watcher agents or "special cases" could use on a temporary basis.

Adam Smith, the chairman of the board, had the initial idea for the IAI, primarily because he had no idea what had happened to his own children, or if he ever even had any. Like Robert, and Darryl, and Zel, and most everyone associated with the Institution, Adam was a victim of the White Fire Virus, one of the earliest. Among other maladies, the Virus caused the infected to have seizures and severe mental breakdowns, once or several times during the course of a victim's abbreviated lifetime. One of Adam's early breakdowns had been so severe he lost all knowledge of his family and background, including his real name. But the man still retained a large amount of technical knowledge in spite of the fractured state of his memory. He took on the name "Adam Smith" and, rather quickly, managed to raise enough money to fund and build his short-term dream project—the Isaac-Abraham Institution, dedicated to the deep study of familial relations and to the recovery of missing children, particularly Adam's own.

Early on, Adam established a relationship with the Heartland Security Agency in order to avoid any unnecessary legal issues. Thanks to the IAI's board members' brilliance and ability to provide important research, information, and other tools to assist the struggling Agency, certain government officials had figured it would be wiser to work with them—both organizations providing the other with mutual favors—instead of treating them as infringers or nuisances. As a result, Adam had been allowed certain liberties; few other nonprofits were permitted to have armed agents (though guns of any kind were a definite no-no).

One liberty Adam would never be allowed, however, was the freedom to venture out into the sunlight unshielded or inappropriately attired. When the skin of Virus-carriers was exposed to too much electromagnetic radiation from a certain section of the spectrum, their bodies became like puppets on invisible strings, out of control, manipulated by a mindless sun or other source. Some of the infected, like Darryl and Robert, were sensitive to the properties of light but also possessed the ability to manipulate those properties to their advantage. Other victims, like Zel and Adam, were simply at light's cruel mercy. If their eyes or sections of bare skin were subjected to too much light, they would experience severe epileptic seizures, seizures so intense they would feel as if each and every fiber of their muscles was unraveling, their bones dissolving, and their skin melting, layer by layer. To prevent that experience, they usually stayed covered from head-to-toe, often dressed in white, and stayed inside, underground, and away from windows as much as possible. Adam rarely left the premises of The Burrow, but his manner of dress was unusual even for one of his condition.

Robert stopped in front of the closed door of Adam's office. He pressed his fingers to the keypad and positioned his face so his eye was level with the scanner. After a few seconds, he heard a recorded voice announce, "Enter, Mister Goldner." The door slid open. Robert hurried on through before it closed again.

He stood in a dark reception room, the part of the office where Adam would sometimes meet and speak with his visitors. It was empty, as expected. Robert looked at but didn't approach the second door, the door to the main office where Adam spent about twenty hours a day—most days—working. No one was supposed to approach it without an invitation. Adam always knew when someone had entered the reception room. He would open the second door and enter the room, or allow his guest into the main office, when he was good and ready.

Robert took a seat and began to wonder why Adam wanted to see him. He'd come up with two good guesses before the door to the main office slid open and Adam called his name. Robert hurried through the portal then stopped just after crossing the threshold.

He was always in awe of the large room. It was a lot to take in. There was the seven-foot long, oval-shaped glass desk, the black-leather swivel chairs, and the monitors—dozens and dozens of various-sized computer and television monitors on the walls all over the room. The pictures on the screens were always scrambled whenever Adam had a visitor, so Robert could only guess what Adam watched when alone. But he knew whatever Adam saw on his screens was important, as was anything Adam had to say to him.

"Please come in. You are not a stranger here."

Robert did as he was told, but he did feel like a stranger, no matter how many times he'd visited and how many times Adam had told him otherwise. Adam's appearance wouldn't help anyone feel at home. From the top of his head to his fingertips to toes, he wore attire that, in Robert's eye, resembled the armor of a post-modern knight.

At first glance the suit of full-body plate armor seemed to be composed of pieces of a silvery white alloy, custom molded and strategically fused together. In reality, it was made up of a different material—a more flexible, porous material that was at least as strong as steel but that also contained innumerable slits, each of them an inch long and not more than a pinhole's size in width. These fissures allowed slivers of air and light to pass through, enter, and presumably touch the man's undergarments or skin. In keeping with the motif, Adam also wore a helmet that covered his entire face and neck. The front of it was a smooth concave mirror that gave a funhouse view-of-self to anyone who spoke with him face-to-"face." Curiously, while the suit had its openings for light and air, the front of the helmet had none Robert could see. Still, even though there was something off about the way the man talked, Adam's voice wasn't distorted or muffled. One could hear only a thin metallic echo when Adam completed a sentence.

The suit may've appeared ridiculous or frightening in the eyes of many, but Adam's mobility would've been severely limited without it. Even with it, he needed the assistance of a sturdy iron cane to walk. Most often, as now, Adam was seen sitting uncomfortably in a high-back swivel chair.

He wasn't offered a seat, so Robert didn't take one. He just stepped forward, stopped in front of the desk, and crossed his hands behind his back.

"You wanted to see me, sir?"

"Yes," Adam said. "I have managed to dig up some information on your latest find. Ava Darden."

"Oh," Robert said. "Shouldn't—? Is Darryl coming?"

"You can fill Mister Ridley in later. There is not much, but since you happened to be at The Burrow, I thought I would just tell you face-to-face. Some of this information was previously gathered—last year, to be exact—when we first began to look into the disappearance of the McGillis girl and the incident that preceded it. All of their classmates were questioned last spring and summer."

"So we knew Ava was missing?"

"No," Adam said. "She was never officially reported missing. So I kept her name off of our lists."

Robert thought it odd that, whether reported missing or not, finding the Virus-infected girl who'd stopped a school massacre wasn't considered to be a task just as important as locating the one who tried to pull it off. But he kept silent and listened.

"Her legal name is Stavan Darden. She would have graduated from high school last May if she had not disappeared shortly after her engagement with Marie-Lydia McGillis at that very same high school in March of that same year. As you have seen from the videos that made the rounds on the Internet, the girls fought each other so intensely, they beat each other into unconsciousness. Both girls ended up comatose. They and many of their classmates were taken to the hospital after that fight. Stavan—or 'Ava'—was visited by one relative. Her mother. She came to see her daughter several times, but she probably never got to see her wake up. We could not find anyone who did. Ava simply disappeared from the hospital one day or, more likely, one night."

"Just disappeared?" Robert asked. "We're sure her mother didn't take her out?"

"If she did," Adam said, "she left no trace of coming or going."

"Didn't the hospital report her missing?"

"Apparently there was some confusion at the time. They thought she had been properly discharged, but now they have no records to confirm that. After you and Mister Ridley found her, we tried alerting her mother, but we had no success."

"What do you mean?"

"She seems to have disappeared as well. The authorities have already started questioning her old neighbors and acquaintances. No one has seen her in over a year, since last April, right before her house burned down. So far, it seems like she slipped off the face of the Earth."

Just like my father, Robert thought. "So Ava's a lot like us, like the other Watcher agents here, I mean."

"Yes," Adam said. "An infected young adult without parents."

"Scary to think that our numbers may be growing."

"You can add it to the list of items to be scared about. I have heard reports of secret clubs forming in the Carolinas, Texas, and other states, organized solely for hunting and killing people who have the Virus. Parlors have been set up, very close to home, for the sole purpose of allowing patrons to bet significant sums on confrontations involving Virus-infected combatants—a lopsided mix of willing and unwilling participants. I have seen reports from Atlanta concerning mutant strains of the Virus. There are talks of quarantines. And, of course, there are the Virus-infected terrorists—The Infinite Definite—an ever-growing, multifaceted problem."

"Yeah." Robert let his eye unfocus as his thoughts drifted. Adam's list was more depressing than scary, but something was beginning to worry him. He refocused on Adam's mirroring mask. "You think this Darden girl's connected somehow to The ID? I mean, I know it seems she's on the right side, attacking those identity thieves and all, but maybe she just came at them for drugs or money or something?"

"It is on the list of possibilities," Adam said. "Unfortunately, we have a long list with this one since there is more than a year missing from her life on record—and from her mind as well. We do not know what she has been up to. One thing we do suspect is that she was never reported missing because her mother disappeared before she did."

"Or at the same time."

"Possibly. For the time being, all we can do is keep a close watch on her now that we have found her. Certain individuals at the Heartland Security Agency are also deeply interested in her, so they will be keeping a close watch as well."

"One more question," Robert said. "Did Ava disappear from the hospital at the same time as the McGillis girl?"

"No. Much later. The McGillis girl was only there for a day or two before vanishing."

"And her parents didn't," Robert said. "They're still around."

"Around and angry enough to sue the hospital and anyone else they could think of."

"Did we—?"

"Yes," Adam said. "They were questioned about Ava's mother. First thing. They did not even know her. Or Ava."

Robert looked down at his feet, thoughtful again. But the thoughts were incomplete, running half-circles in his mind.

"I will keep you updated," Adam said. "But that is all I have for now."

"Thank you." Robert nodded and turned to leave as Adam turned his attention to one of the keyboards on his desk.

The chairman was a busy man, serving as the sole facilitator of communications between IAI members. Robert always felt humbled and a little surprised when Adam took time out of his duties to speak to him in person. He usually feared overstaying his welcome, but not today. As he walked down the hall, considering everything Adam had just told him, Robert became more and more convinced Adam hadn't told him all that he could have.

In the old days, even as recently as six months ago, Robert would've met with Darryl to discuss the situation, going over and over every minute detail. They'd spend the evening discussing probabilities and possibilities. But these days, Darryl's evenings were usually booked. And most others at the Institution had shown increasingly little interest in his hunches. Robert had no choice but to turn to his other resources.

Chapter 5

"And what does it mean, Mister Ridley, that you haven't found a wife yet?"

Miss Blake asked Darryl the question after he'd quoted her a snippet of poetry. He could tell, rather than admitting she wasn't impressed, she was trying to change the subject. Darryl admitted—only to himself—the verse was pretty bad, but he felt there was good meaning behind it. He wanted to make that meaning plain to her. But he wasn't pushy, and he could take a hint. He allowed the subject to be changed.

"It means, Miss Blake, I'm not a sucker, that's what," he said.

"Pardon?"

Darryl laughed, a little embarrassed. So soon after leaving T., he for some reason wasn't feeling at the top of his game. "I just meant I'm a giver, not a taker."

"Oh, I get it," she said. "Not a sucker, but a stinger—is that it?"

They both laughed this time, but Darryl still felt embarrassed. He deserved it. After meeting and talking with her in the dawnclub earlier that day, he was the one who'd asked her out, thinking she'd be a relatively quick fix. When she admitted she was glad to see him walk into the club because she'd been looking for some company for the weekend, Darryl decided right then she'd be his next charity case. He knew her type. He was glad he'd seen her too. And when she told him she was some kind of artist, Darryl knew he had her pegged. He definitely knew her type. But that was no excuse for him to get sloppy in style or technique.

The two of them had agreed to meet for lunch just before noon in downtown Washington, near the National Mall. After coffee, they'd walked by but decided against going into any of the Smithsonian museums. One of them had said and the other had agreed that on a warm, sunny day like today, the best beauty could be found in full display outside, in nature and architecture, in people and other creatures. So they'd chosen to walk around the grounds of the Mall, listening, looking, and talking.

"All the relationships I've had over the past few years," Darryl said, "none of them ever lasted more than two months, tops. But we always part on peaceful terms."

"Always?" Miss Blake said. "That's unusual. You must have some streak going."

"Yes," he said, "it seems like I keep getting mixed up with the self-destructive types. We start out fine, but things sometimes get a little rough after a while."

"I'll bet."

"But still," he said, "I do what I can to make sure we both walk away from each other happier, and wiser. I'm happy enough if she walks away determined to never follow the path of the Beauty Fools."

"Beauty Fools?" Miss Blake looked askance at him. The look almost made Darryl laugh, but he had to keep it together. It was an important subject.

"Yes, Beauty Fools," he said. "From the poem." A different one than the one he'd quoted earlier, but it was worth spelling out to her. "They're the types that fall over and over again into the same traps, following the lure of their own poor definition of beauty, making judgments based only on surface appearances, and ignoring everything else, especially common sense. Like the woman who walks down the street, bemoaning the existence of calendars, thinking: 'All these damn dates, again and again…No good men—wait, that one looks cute…I want him!' She cries for more and more candy and cakes, but she can't figure the cause of her recurring tummy aches."

"*Bemoaning,* huh?" Miss Blake said, shaking her head. "The existence of *calendars?* And it's just gotta be a 'she,' right?"

"Well, no," Darryl said. Yes, it was all strangely phrased, but, "That's just the way the poem goes. The roles could be reversed. Men can certainly act like fools in the face of beauty."

"Uh-huh. You don't sound convinced by what you're saying, Mister Ridley." She smiled as Darryl wondered what made her think so. "Maybe you believe women are the greater fools when it comes to love? Maybe you believe women are naturally self-destructive?"

"I just believe in peace, Miss Blake," he said in a solemn tone.

"Oh puh-lease." She laughed. "Is that your standard line? Is that supposed to entice the ladies?"

"Well it's certainly not a threat."

She laughed again. "Do women, does *anyone* fall for that line?"

"No," he said, "but some trip themselves up while laughing at it."

He smiled and reached for her hand as they stepped off the curb and into the street.

"Ah," she said after they made it to the other curb, barely avoiding the car that wouldn't slow down for them, "so you throw bad jokes and worse poetry at me, then, when I'm off balance, you go for my hand to pull me along. Sly maneuvering." She glanced and grinned at him. "I see how you do."

Darryl grinned back. He was trying his best to stay cool, trying to hide his discomfort. He hoped it was working.

He'd purposely overdressed, even though he'd known the day's temperature would climb to almost eighty degrees and the sky would remain cloudless until nightfall. He was usually adept at controlling his body's involuntary reactions to full-on sunlight—he took his medication religiously—but it was a first date. He wasn't used to this one yet. She could say or do anything to surprise him. It was bad enough being in proximity to her was making him feel goofy. Pills or no pills, a lapse in concentration and too much exposed skin was a loud and clear invitation for the sun to play dirty with him. So he'd put on khakis and a long-sleeved button-down over a T-shirt, just to be safe.

Miss Blake was much more daring. Even though she didn't seem to be infected with the Virus, Darryl still thought she bared more skin than was wise. She wore a pink tank top, and on the left shoulder for all to see was an indigo tattoo of a swastika. Rather than the more familiar right-turning direction, it faced to the left. Even more curious, it was encircled by a bigger, fuchsia-hued tattoo of the Star of David. Darryl hadn't bothered to ask her about the body-art's meaning. It would've been pointless to ask for an answer he wouldn't trust. He instead decided to research the symbol later and ask her about it afterward. If her answer jibed with what he'd found on his own, he'd consider that it just might be the truth.

The two strolled around the Haupt Garden and stopped in the Moongate section, where Darryl explained the symbolism behind the garden's square and circle forms—the former representing the mundane, and the latter, the transcendent. Having been through the garden so many times before, he knew the explanations by heart. His commentary almost always impressed. But when Miss Blake asked him, "What about triangles?" Darryl faked a sneeze and suggested they move on to the sculpture garden.

This time, without comment, Miss Blake held up her hand for Darryl to hold before they crossed the street. When they reached the other side, he loosened his grip, but she only tightened hers.

They remained hand-in-hand as they reviewed each sculpture, taking an extra amount of time in front of Auguste Rodin's *Crouching Woman*, Aristide Maillol's *Nymph,* and Emile-Antoine Bourdelle's *The Great Warrior of Montauban*, a bronze sculpture of an excessively muscular man whose left leg was cut off at the knee and whose right was cut off in the middle of the thigh. After Darryl commented it appeared to be only six- or seven-eighths of a complete man, Miss Blake said, "It's still frightening, even more so." Maybe to her. To Darryl, it appeared vulnerable; after a series of conquests, it was ready to be finished off in a final battle.

The last sculpture they viewed for longer than a DC-minute was Darryl's personal favorite, Gaston Lachaise's *Standing Woman,* majestically standing to show off her wide hips, pouchy stomach, thick thighs, muscular calves and biceps, large breasts, and pinched hourglass waist.

"Her head seems to be the smallest part of her."

"She looks proportional to me," Darryl said.

"Is that so?" Miss Blake asked.

"Sure."

"Yeah, figures—I guess all those cakes and pieces of candy got packed into just the right places."

"Maybe she was born that way," Darryl said as they headed for the garden's exit. "Appearing grotesque and bizarre—even ugly—to some, but having hidden depths, depths containing shards and flints of true beauty. Someone, in the right frame of mind, who can see beneath the skin, may see one of these shards or flints, and based off of that one tiny fragment, judge the whole, the entire woman, as being truly beautiful."

There. *That* was a standard line of his. But Miss Blake said nothing in response. She only squeezed Darryl's hand harder. He turned to look at her; she returned the look with a quick and awkward smile before turning away. It was then a thought that had been fluttering about his mind all day finally settled down on its object: her hair. Miss Blake had cascading blonde hair that fell just past her shoulders, and long wavy tresses of it fell over her face, obscuring her right eye. Occasional awkward smiles aside, the woman walked and carried herself in such a graceful manner that the shrouded eye remained hidden, the hair in front of it only swaying slightly. Darryl wondered if the effect was due to the fluidal way in which she moved her body or if she'd somehow styled her hair to obtain that effect. He then wondered about her overall style—the blonde hair, the unhidden blue eye, and the star-and-swastika tattoo—putting them all together. It all had to mean something. Probably nothing profound, though.

"You talk about appearances, and the surface of skin," Miss Blake said, "but what about the surface of your language? Switching between bad poetry and poor philosophy—it may've charmed some of the sillier women you've been with, but is it really authentic? Can't help but wonder what's really underneath those sugary words of yours."

"Well, you won't have to wonder for long. Just keep your eyes open."

"*Cute,*" he thought he heard her mutter.

"Not more words," Darryl said, "but a person's actions make his words into lies or truths. I agree with what you might be thinking, that the words are just a lot of gossamer. But that's not how I mean them. To be honest, I prefer action to speeches. As they say, talk is cheap, and usually worthless."

"So I shouldn't spend my time listening to what you say?" Her tone was playful. Darryl matched it, but kept his meaning serious.

"Ignore it, or absorb it," he said. "At my age, I've had plenty of time to learn, over and over, that a man can hardly talk to a woman without her expecting him to expect something deep to develop from it."

"A tangled sentence for a tangled idea," she said with a sigh. "Something deep like what? A good, honest friendship?"

"No, like—" Darryl didn't want to say it. "You know what I mean."

"I don't," she said. "And just how old do you think you are anyway?"

Darryl laughed. "You know, Miss Blake, I've also learned that if I were to ask any adult woman that question, I can expect a five finger reply, if I'm lucky enough not to get just one."

"Grown men and women can be civil and friendly with each other, Mister Ridley," Miss Blake said, "*close* without being *closed* to each other, without expecting anything sexual to come out of it."

"Are you talking about the man's expectations, or the woman's?"

"I'm talking about self-assured, secure, reasonable adults."

"Oh," Darryl said. "So neither then."

"Ha ha, comedian." She bumped him sportively with her elbow. "You know, you didn't hesitate to engage me in conversation this morning, or to ask me out to lunch. What outcome were you expecting?"

"An engaging conversation," Darryl said, "and a nice meal."

"That's it, huh?"

"A rest on a bench would be nice. But I'm not greedy."

The two settled themselves on the first clean and shaded bench they could find. They sat in silence for a few moments, watching the passersby on the grass and the gravel walkway in front of them. Darryl was about to remark how, despite the fact most of the people who passed by were tourists, there was far more variety in their languages, dialects, and accents (totem poles of babel) than in their styles of clothing. But she spoke first.

"Wow. I just realized. You and I are on the exact same bench as you and she were."

Darryl looked at her. "Me and who?"

"That short, kinda plump, really dark-skinned girl." Darryl drew a blank, until she added, "The one with the Jamaican accent."

Now he had it. He remembered that girl's name, but then he thought of the name of the woman currently sitting next to him. Forget the cute, flirty "Miss Blake" stuff…Veronica. *Veronica Blake.* Was that a familiar name? How did she know about him and Joyce?

"Joyce, right?" Veronica asked. "Wasn't that her name?"

"How do you know that?" Darryl asked. "Do you know her?"

"No. But I remember seeing you two sitting here."

Darryl thought for another moment. He hadn't seen Joyce in two years. "You remember that?"

"Well, yes, of course," Veronica said. "I remember seeing you. You have a very memorable look, with that out-of-this-world tan and all."

"Okay," he said, "but Joyce's name, how did you know that?"

"Picked it up during one of the times I passed by. Picked up her accent too."

"One of the times?"

"I was jogging," Veronica said. "I was in better shape back then. Running 10Ks every other week."

She'd passed by multiple times, and he hadn't noticed? Not enough to remember?

"What are you mumbling?" Veronica asked.

Had he been mumbling? He must've been so deep in thought he failed to mind his mouth. If so, undoubtedly he'd been mumbling what he'd been thinking. "I, uh, just said you've got a scary memory."

Veronica laughed. "You find it scary that I can remember something I saw more than a year ago? I think it's a sign of good mental health."

"Some might find it intimidating."

"Aw, poor baby, intimidated by a li'l ole woman's memory, bullied by the idea of settling down into marriage."

"Yes, ma'am." Darryl matched her mocking tone. "And don't forget my paralyzing fright at the mere sight of a baby carriage."

They both laughed. Only Veronica's sounded as if it came from genuine amusement. The undertone in Darryl's voice no doubt gave him away. As she looked at him with a coy, playful smile, he could see something he didn't like in that bold blue eye of hers. He was happy it didn't linger on him. Veronica turned to gaze at the people on the grass; Darryl turned his attention inward.

This one was different. Unlike any of his previous charity cases, this one was able to keep up. She wasn't the annoying silent type, and she wasn't the type who'd get too confused at his philosophical-poetic musings. And she wasn't shy about disagreeing when any of those musings expressed something she didn't like, but she wasn't the angry, argumentative type either. A far throw from the type he'd grown used to. In conversation, she could keep up, even trip him up. It was all so different than the vapid conversations of most first dates. And unlike with the others, he figured he could push on, wrap up this particular case quicker than usual. No need to wait for their third or fourth date to begin it. He'd start the process now so it'd be done in a week or so. Veronica Blake was different, but she wasn't on the bright path. Not yet.

She was an artist, or so she claimed. True or not, he knew her type. Whether talented or not, she had to be *sensitive*, unsure of herself, insecure about her place in the naked world. The scarred, blemished, *sick* world. Whether they'd admit it or not, Darryl knew all self-proclaimed artists sought in some small or big way to create their own perfect world, a world perfect in their own eyes. If their vision wasn't strong enough to overcome the entire real world, it was just as well. Their little world could remain in a tiny bump on the greater world, noticed or unnoticed. A mole on the face of reality. Maybe regarded as a beauty mark to some onlookers, but to others—

"What?" Veronica asked.

His thoughts interrupted, Darryl reentered the reality before his eyes and at his fingertips. "Huh?"

"I heard you mumbling again. You said something about an ugly spot. And something about 'the heart of death.' Sounded really weird."

Darryl was sure, almost positive this time, he'd said nothing while he was ruminating. But even if he hadn't said a word, she'd mentioned the words "heart" and "death," words from the title of the book that gave his life meaning and directed him toward redemption. Still, whatever she thought she'd heard him say, he'd have to spin it some other way. In the process of peace, words were to be elusive, actions direct.

"I was just thinking about the concept of *peace*," he said, "which I guess some poets might refer to as the *heart* of death."

Veronica rolled her visible eye. "Here we go with the poetry again."

"You're right," Darryl said with a smirk. "To hell with poetry. Actions trump words."

He exerted just the right amount of pressure with his arm. She turned toward him, matching his smile as he tightened his muscles, pulling her closer, looking into her eye, preparing to look much deeper after the spirit-weakening first kiss. Step one in the treatment. She looked ready; she seemed willing, so easy—then she turned her head to the right, letting Darryl kiss the hair that fell over her left ear.

"Hey," she asked, "where's the sock hop?"

Darryl blew off the hair sticking to his lips. "What?"

"Check out those two," she said.

Darryl looked toward where Veronica nodded. "What the…?"

Michael and Christine were walking on the gravelly path on the other side of the grass.

Michael and Christine, one of the terrorist duos associated with The Infinite Definite.

So conspicuous…How had Veronica's untrained eye spotted them before he did?

Darryl slid his arm from her shoulder.

The terrorists were dressed in their usual outfits, just like cartoon characters—though there wasn't a damn thing funny about them. Michael wore his black jeans, white T-shirt, and black leather jacket, copied from the generic greasers seen in most modern movies about the rebellious youth of the 1950s. His look never varied. His companion was different. According to the photographs Darryl had seen and the descriptions he'd heard from fellow agents, her outfit stayed the same while the colors changed. This time she was wearing the red skirt with white poodle, white blouse with white poodle, red chiffon scarf, and red cats-eye glasses. All that red, so vibrant and eye catching. It made an angry Darryl again wonder why he hadn't spotted the two on his own. What kind of a Watcher agent was he?

The duo was on their way to a dance, all right. Darryl knew he had to cut in before they forced anyone else to spin with them.

"Whoa," he said as he fingered the watch on his right wrist. "Time almost got away from me." Darryl stood up from the bench. "I really have to run."

"Another date?" Veronica asked as she stood. "Are you blessing calendars instead of damning them?"

Hah—a reference to the woman in the poem. Darryl chuckled feebly as he again thought of the power of Veronica's memory. "No, I *bemoan* them. Just like *she* did. But I can't manipulate time."

Veronica smiled and shook her head. "Well, I can only say 'till tomorrow' to you then. Let's meet for brunch, if you're not too busy. Call me."

She moved closer, stood on her toes, and leaned in. Darryl pulled her even closer and kissed her, straining to keep as much of his own saliva in his mouth as possible. The use of his signature honey-trick (a strange-but-happy side effect of his Virus medication) would have to wait for another time.

They disengaged, and Veronica turned to walk toward the Metro station entrance. Darryl stood still and waited for—*There*—the moment she turned back to smile and wave at him. He returned the gesture, and, when she turned away, he turned himself invisible. He didn't care about any others who may've witnessed the sudden disappearance, just so long as she didn't. Not yet.

Darryl scrambled off the path and up into the nearest tree. He stripped down to his T-shirt and boxer shorts. On other days he would've been thankful if a strong wind were rustling the leaves, masking the sound of his presence in the tree. Today, it didn't matter. He'd make his presence known soon enough.

Leaving his clothes hanging on the branches, Darryl took his corresq out of his hidden shirt pocket. He kept himself invisible as he drifted back down toward the ground, stopping to levitate just one inch above it. He then glided toward his targets, who, for the moment, were strolling along the pathway like two young people casually in love with each other. He knew they were really scoping out the territory as they decided on the best spot to tag the most victims. He knew their kind.

The Infinite Definite was a loose association of Virus-carriers who had dipped themselves once too often into the dirty-light pools of XynKroma. The result for each was a scrambled mind, conscious thoughts stained with uncommon sense, an inclination toward wild artistic expression, and an uncanny ability to manipulate the twisted laws of physics that ruled the extra-dimensional realm of Xyn wherever they went. They were the mentally undead. Magickally talented zombies. Like most Virus-carriers, they could manipulate light, but they took it to whatever extremes they could by performing what had become known as Dirty-Light Magick tricks—fantastical feats that were too, too real and always used in the service of mayhem and chaos. If they believed in anything, associates of The ID believed the nonsensical rules of XynKroma, the Ultimate realm of Reality, should rule over all realms of Reality, all planes of existence. They may never say so outright, but Michael and Christine subscribed to this messy philosophy; one could tell by their actions, their special brand of violence.

Both the greaser and his chick were in their mid- to late-teens. Darryl had never faced these two before, but he'd had two or three discussions with Watcher agents who'd encountered them. Their modus operandi was to draw attention to themselves by putting on a dance display in a public setting. After a sufficient number of individuals had gathered around to watch them, snap pictures, and applaud, the duo would snap and begin to hurt as many of the onlookers as they could before the authorities arrived. Today, they were taunting their luck; an authority was already here.

Darryl continued to follow them, studying them as he kept a distance of fifty feet and remained invisible to everyone around him. From what he'd heard, Michael and Christine wore the same basic outfits whenever they were in public, and they never manipulated light-and-shadow to hide, blur, or alter their facial features. They were among the most audacious couples associated with The Infinite Definite. Still, it was rare for them to cause alarm when they went for a stroll. People usually either took them as eccentrics and ignored them, or smiled at them with broad amusement.

Damned tourists. They were a big part of the problem. Though bold, Michael and Christine were also smart enough to frequent only the touristy spots in Washington and Northern Virginia, the places area residents saw often enough but rarely stopped to visit unless they were entertaining guests from out of town. A few residents of the area knew of Michael and Christine's antics—how they looked and what they did—from brief mentions on the nightly news and small items published in the local papers. On the occasions sharp-witted residents spotted the duo, or even thought they did, they would either flee or call the police; unfortunately for local law enforcement officers, there existed a large number of social clubs devoted to the culture of "1950s America," clubs whose membership included law-abiding adults and teenagers fond of dressing in 1950s fashion and speaking in 1950s slang. The police often found themselves answering to false alarms. These two in Darryl's sight weren't false; he'd been looking at them close enough and long enough to see they were exactly who he thought they were. But he couldn't do anything. Yet.

In spite of all the complicated deals and arrangements the IAI had with some law enforcement agencies, the Watcher agents were in no way considered true officers of the law. Darryl couldn't touch either one of them until they'd proven themselves to be a threat; then his status would change. He'd be allowed just enough legal authority to put an end to the threat, like someone making a citizen's arrest. Watcher agents had unofficially been given a bit more leeway to act over the past two years, but there still were limits by which to abide. A tightening economy had led to increased crime, underfunded and overworked security forces, slower response times, and formerly borderline lawbreakers crossing the line more and more often as there was a greater chance they'd get away with it. That was just another reason Darryl wanted to join the HSA as one of their armed agents—fewer limits, more authority to act. He'd never again have to bide his time, waiting for someone who was clearly guilty, clearly the enemy, to make the first move. He'd already sent a message to Adam asking him to contact the proper authorities, but it could take up to thirty minutes for them to arrive. Something would surely happen before then. Darryl considered himself patient, but young terrorists lacked that virtue.

After walking the Mall's gravelly path all the way to Fourth Street, Michael and Christine turned around and started walking in the other direction, on the grass. The show was about to start. Unseen and undetected, Darryl followed them until the pair stopped in the grassy area of the Mall right between the Natural History Museum and the Smithsonian Castle. It was no random spot. It was an area almost equidistant from the Metro entrance and the entrance to the sculpture garden, and very near the children's merry-go-round. It was the area with the highest concentration of people. And at two o'clock in the afternoon, the sun seemed to shine down on the spot from directly above. It was perfect.

Although the merry-go-round's tune was loud and distracting, the greaser and his girl most likely blocked it out and, in their own minds, substituted the music of Bill Haley or one of his contemporaries as they began their dance routine. Darryl was the first member of their audience; little by little, however, more and more curious onlookers stopped and stepped closer, wondering at the spectacle, talking about it, laughing at it, and taking pictures.

Michael and Christine moved deftly on the grass. Darryl was sure he was the only one to notice they had raised their bodies to stand a quarter of an inch above the ground's surface. They were literally dancing on air.

Many Virus-carriers could perform some amazing feats. They couldn't fly, but they could defy gravity within very severe limitations. Vince Ceniza once told Darryl it had something to do with the Earth's magnetic fields and the "magnetic" part of carriers' electromagnetic talents. Michael and Christine's talents included some phenomenal dancing skills.

The two weren't dancing as if they were in a 1950s dancehall. They were performing physical riffs on 1950s dances, mimicking while adding modern touches to them so that, while the movements made their nostalgic nods toward the fads of a simpler and more conservative time, they also seemed to be smart, forward-looking, and more than a bit threatening, dangerous, like all truly experimental artworks. Michael and Christine moved and threw each other around as if they were trying to kill themselves, and knowing the mind-state of the terrorists associated with The ID, Darryl believed that maybe they actually were, themselves and whoever else got close enough.

In spite of the frenetic display of some amazing stunts, Michael and Christine didn't draw a large crowd. Those who did approach stayed only a few minutes before moving on to go about their sightseeing. After they'd been at it for a little more than ten minutes, Darryl knew the two wouldn't wait much longer to strike.

And they didn't.

When about fifteen people were within a good enough range, Michael released Christine to twirl, spin, and dance by herself as he pulled an object from his pocket and made a motion as if he would run it through his hair. A comb? Darryl wondered as he squinted at it. No—a switchblade, he realized too late as Michael threw it, hitting a man several feet away in the back of the neck. It happened so fast and far away from where most eyes were focused that no one in the crowd moved or screamed until Christine reached for the woman standing closest to her, put her hands on the woman's cheeks, dug her false nails into the skin and jerked her hands down, ripping deep gashes in the woman's face.

The woman's scream was infectious as members of the crowd caught on and tried to run. Most who had gathered in close to watch the duo were older, middle-aged individuals and couples, some with young kids, none of them in the best shape for sprinting. Their attempts to get away were slow and clumsy.

Michael ran, leaped, and glided a couple of inches above the grass for several feet toward three of the most vulnerable runners—a beer-bellied man, his hysterical and paunchy wife, and their obese eight-year-old. They scrambled to run away, but the handholding family only succeeded in running into one another. Michael had drawn another switchblade and was just moments away from reaching them, getting his hands on one of them.

"Gonna carve some of them steaks outta ya, big daddy!" the greaser said. "Then gonna milk yer cow! Hear her squeal while I make veal!"

Darryl flung his corresq. The metal circle sailed out from invisibility and hit its target, breaking the skin on Michael's wrist. He yelled and dropped his knife. Darryl then stepped out from behind his unseen screen, appearing as a thing enshrouded in bluish shadows and purplish light, intangible violet and orange wings spreading out behind him as he rushed toward the costumed hoodlum.

The sudden appearance of a seemingly alien being failed to intimidate Michael. As swift as Darryl was, Michael was even swifter in removing his leather jacket and tossing it at his attacker.

In an ordinary circumstance, such a maneuver would slow Darryl down by only half a moment; he'd step aside instead of stepping forward, moving out of the way of the tossed object. But this maneuver wasn't made by an ordinary opponent. After the jacket left his hand, Michael used a Dirty-Light Magick trick to withdraw all light surrounding the jacket, making it appear as a large and growing black blanket. Darryl couldn't see beyond it or anything around it, and within a sliver of a second, a thick wall of blackness had appeared in front of him. He was forced to stop.

He was then forced backward when Michael emerged from the wall a few feet in front of him, swinging his fists at Darryl's head.

Darryl fought back, swinging and connecting, hitting Michael in his throat and his right temple. Michael stumbled to the left, and Darryl made sure he went all the way to the ground by clasping his hands together and bringing them down hard on the back of Michael's neck.

He turned around to locate the other one; he spotted her farther down field, finishing up a dangerous dance move with her unwilling elderly partner. The dancing partners parted for good when the tip of one of Christine's saddle shoes made violent contact with the underside of the old man's chin.

Darryl couldn't make it down there in time before she hurt any others, so he stayed put, squinted, and concentrated. Christine began shrieking almost immediately, feeling the infrared radiation burning her face. Apparently confused about the cause, she didn't run; the girl only collapsed to the ground, hiding her head under her arms. Darryl let up and turned away, just in time to see Michael lunging at him with another knife.

Darryl raised his left arm in defense and grunted when the blade slashed his forearm. He used his right arm to grab for the wrist of the hand holding the knife, leaving himself open to a punch in the right side of his gut. Darryl brought his right arm back, backhand-slapped Michael across the face, and followed it up with a quick punch under the jaw.

As the greaser stumbled backward, Darryl considered himself lucky that Michael lacked the strength to make the punch in the gut mean much, but he was also frustrated he was fighting like an amateur. The Watcher agent was too skilled for that, or felt he should've been, especially against someone who was proving to be nothing more than a punk kid.

Michael recovered in no time and rushed at him. Darryl back-pedaled with three quick steps before launching himself to skate on the air, gliding several inches off the ground for several feet backward. When he landed, he spread his arms and drew a greater amount of light around his body. The light already enshrouding him flared, making him seem like a taller, wider being of light and shadows—a fearsome angel. His intention was to make it nearly impossible for the enemy to locate the real being of flesh and blood at the center. One who had Michael's abilities could have found him, given time—but Darryl wasn't about to waste any.

He rushed forward, sending eagle-shaped flares of light ahead of him in order to misdirect Michael's attention. The greaser backed up, almost tripping over his own feet, before turning around to retrieve his jacket. Once in hand, he swung it at every shape of light that came near him.

Perhaps Michael thought the black leather flag would kill the lights, or maybe he was just panicking. Whichever, it did nothing to help him as Darryl got within ten feet, stopped the lightshow, and dived, tackling him to the ground.

He delivered three rapid punches to the punk's face before realizing he'd forgotten something. Darryl remembered that something when the saddle-shoed foot kicked him the back of the head. He fell forward, and Michael pushed him off as he scrambled up to his feet.

Darryl's head throbbed. The wound on his bleeding arm stung like a fresh grease-burn. He felt winded. And he had trouble thinking of what to do next as he lay on his back, looking up at Michael and Christine standing on either side, looking back down at him.

And this is how it ends. This couldn't be right…

"It's been a big tickle, daddy," Michael said.

"Yeah," Christine said, "but you shoulda split after you got your first lucky shots."

"Ain't no one around left to pound."

"'Cept you."

Darryl laughed. "You two goofs are the ones who shoulda cut out," he said with a smirk. "The heat'll be here any second."

"Fine," Michael said. "But we got plenty of time before they make the scene to end you."

The greaser held his switchblade up near his face and smiled. Christine followed her partner's lead and held up her hands, curling her fingers, giving them the appearance of a panther's claws.

"Good lord," Darryl said. "You two look and sound like a couple of fuckin' idiots…I'm sorry, but I can't be seen like this."

He turned invisible and maneuvered his body, grabbing Michael's foot as he kicked at Christine's legs. He managed to keep both of them off-balance as he got to his knees.

Darryl had planned to duck and roll away from them, but he wasn't quick enough. Michael swung his blade, cutting through Darryl's T-shirt, breaking the skin.

Darryl winced.

The knife had cut a line at least four inches long. Not a deep cut, but a stinging one (the blood-cell parasites in both of his open wounds were getting excited). Darryl didn't make a sound, but he did make up his mind about what had to happen next. He had to go all out. He couldn't continue to stall. He couldn't continue to engage these two as if he was self-evidently their superior. He had to put them down, now, or die.

He became visible again, and Michael swung the knife down again, straight at Darryl's neck. Darryl used both of his hands to catch the wrist, then twisted it. Between clenched teeth, he said, "Drop it or—" He broke it, declining to give the kid a choice in the matter.

Michael screamed louder and longer than Darryl had heard anyone scream in a long while, but somehow through that cloud of sound, the Watcher agent heard distant sirens. He looked in their direction and didn't see them but determined by the noise they made that three law enforcement cars were on their way.

He turned his attention back to Michael, who was now crying as well as screaming.

"What's fifties slang for 'I'm gonna break your neck, you dumb li'l shit'?" Darryl asked as he applied more pressure to the broken wrist.

Michael continued to scream and bawl as Christine looked around frantically.

It wasn't until Darryl released the wrist and hit Michael under his jaw that the girl went back on the offensive, raising her arms and opening her palms toward Darryl. When he turned toward her to try to figure what she was doing, he felt the answer. Infrared radiation enveloped his body, the heat steadily increasing its intensity.

Darryl didn't move a step. He again clenched his teeth and fought back, focusing on the girl's nose, giving her a bit of the same offense, concentrating in one small area.

Christine screamed, dropped her arms, and brought her hands to her nose as she turned to run away, away from Darryl and away from the sirens. With both hands on her face, she appeared to be galloping in the general direction of the Metro entrance. Maybe the girl thought she could escape on the subway. No way, Darryl thought.

He hit Michael thrice more in the jaw to ensure he'd stay put. The boy was already on the ground, but Darryl hit him until he was flattened. He then scrambled to retrieve his corresq and looked for Christine. She'd tried to shield herself with bent light. Nice try, honey.

Darryl adjusted his vision, located the invisible girl, and sprinted in her direction. When he was within a good enough range, he stopped and hurled the corresq. The silver circle sailed through the air in a straight line for fifty feet before hitting

Christine in the back of the neck, the metal cutting into the skin as the impact forced her forward. She became visible again as she fell face-first into the grass. Once down, she didn't move. She didn't even make a sound.

Now to shut down the other one.

Darryl turned around, but the police cars were now in view, turning off Seventh Street onto the Mall's grass. They weren't far from Michael. They'd get him.

Darryl waved his arms in the air, pointing at Michael and gesturing toward Christine to make sure they saw both. He then went to get his toy back.

Darryl began to feel a little sorry as he neared Christine. He hadn't meant for the corresq to hit her so hard. He'd only intended to stun her, slow her down. He'd have to talk to Zel about modifications, but for now, what was done was done. Two Infinite-Definite terrorists defeated and captured. Another victory.

Still, they were truly a third-rate pair. Their fighting skills were nowhere near the level of their dancing skills, and Darryl had barely managed to hold his own against them. If they hadn't given him a chance to catch his breath…Darryl didn't want to think about it. He'd more important things to do.

Chapter 6

Robert was seated in a cushioned booth, but he was far from comfortable. He was trying to think, trying to focus, and trying his damnedest to ignore his two best friends. It would only be a matter of time before they tried to pull him into their latest argument. He wished a waiter would hurry up and drop off a basket of rolls or something.

"Research and personal experience have taught me," Kurtis said, "that women don't like to be stared at."

"Of course not," Anika said. "You needed research to teach you that? It's common sense. It's rude to stare at people."

"And yet," Kurtis said, "women put a lot of attention into how they dress, are neurotically concerned about their appearance, spend considerable amounts of time making themselves up—from hair to face to shoes—just so people, men and women, will look at them. But if a guy looks too long, he's a rude dog. If a woman does, she's probably a jealous cat."

"You're such a chuckhead," Anika said.

"Rob, am I not right?" Kurtis asked. "Aren't women confused about what they want?"

Robert again glanced over his left shoulder. "I'm probably not the best person to ask."

"They're of a divided mind," Kurtis said, "wanting every on-looker's two eyes to operate independently—one admiring the view, the other going about its own business, staring into space or whatever."

Robert had the talent to see in two directions at once, with a little concentration and under the right conditions. But these conditions weren't right. He felt a lot of things weren't right. He'd had an odd feeling ever since entering the restaurant. Shortly after taking a seat in the booth with his friends, he began to feel he was being watched by someone—someone behind him, probably seated at the bar. He didn't trust the reflections he saw in his knife and spoon, and he didn't want to make his suspicion obvious. In-stead, for the past five minutes, he'd been using over-the-shoulder glances, trying to spot his spy while pretending as if he were look-ing for his table's waiter. So far, nothing.

"Oh, nice, Kurt, really nice," Anika said. "Take a crack at Rob's vision impairment. Just because he doesn't agree with you and is too polite to say so."

"That's *not* what I said. The only impairment among us three, Nika, is your hearing. I was taking a crack at certain individuals' opinions on social etiquette, not Rob. His one eye is better than your two ears. Anyway, our boy seems to be too busy doing what the divided minds want rather than caring about what I say about it."

"Yeah, Rob, what are you looking at anyway?" Anika leaned to her right, out of the booth, peering past Robert and toward the restaurant's door. The rushing waiter behind her had no time to stop or swerve when Anika's head popped out in front of him. The head made contact with his hip, causing the waiter to lose his balance, his tray of food to topple, and the food and dishes on the tray to tumble to the floor.

"Oh, I'm so, so sorry!" Anika wailed as the stooping waiter bit his lip to hold in his language.

Damn it. More eyes turned in their direction. That wouldn't simplify anything.

Anika continued to make apologies as she stooped down to help the grumbling waiter pick up whatever could be picked up before restaurant's cleaning staff could get there. After Kurtis finished a healthy round of chuckling, he nudged Robert with his elbow, signaling he wanted to slide out of the booth and help. Robert stood up and let him out, but rather than join his friends, he took the fact that two drops of alligator stew had landed on his shirt as a good excuse to remove himself from the center of all eyes and comments.

"I need to go wash this off my shirt," he said, happy that the mess in front of him was blocking the direct route to the bathroom. He had no choice but to turn around, head toward the door, turn left into the primary dining room area, and then head toward the bathroom. The U-shaped route would take him through the entire patron's section of the restaurant, giving him the chance to get a good look at everyone, seen and unseen.

Counting, subtracting, compartmentalizing—using only the instruments of the eye and the mind…Robert felt proud his mathematical skills were one of the few abilities the parasites hadn't given him. He'd been an intuitive math whiz long before he'd gotten infected. Beyond the electromagnetic effects and the physical agility, his adding, subtracting, and measuring skills were often the most useful in dangerous situations. But maybe not tonight.

By the time Robert reached the door of the bathroom, he was still unsure. He'd seen no one who raised his suspicion, no one whose eyes lingered on him too long, absolutely nothing that looked out of the ordinary. Nothing except for the spots of stew on his shirt.

Inside the restroom, he took the plaid handkerchief out of his pocket, wet it, added a dab of liquid soap, and worked on the stains.

Robert stared down at the sink while waiting for the small areas to dry. He didn't want his eye to meet the reflecting glass dead on. Staring into a perfect mirror, he knew what the results would be. He just couldn't afford to have his body break down in a public place, especially not now. Not when he needed his friends' help. Not when everyone at the Institution to whom he'd normally turn had other priorities. Kurtis and Anika had been his best friends for over a decade, and in all that time, they'd remained the best code-breaking cyber-sleuths and quickest researchers he'd ever met. Best of all, they know how to keep secrets on lockdown. They had the skills to perform research discreetly and securely. But he'd yet to tell them what he needed from them now. Anika had asked him to meet them at a spot where they already had dinner reservations; Robert now wondered why he hadn't tried to persuade her to meet in a more private setting.

He glanced at the mirror, just to make sure he looked fairly presentable. A glance was all it took. He looked fine, eye patch and all. He smiled a wry smile.

On some of the rare occasions he had trouble falling asleep, he wondered how other people saw him—when he wasn't con-sciously altering his appearance, that is. He wondered if the eye patch inspired fear, or pity.

"Fear" would be the runaway winner if those who gawked knew what the patch really concealed.

Enough parasites had congregated in his right eyeball to com-pletely remake it. It had ceased being an "eye" long ago. It was now a little black sphere—whose exposure to too much free-flowing air would cause it to react and produce a beam of unclassified radiation. Just thinking about those little bastard alien microorganisms made his head ache.

Robert glanced at the mirror again. This time he couldn't look away so quickly.

His "normal" eye had taken on a new appearance. He could see well enough out of it, but looking directly at it, it appeared as a miniature moon lodged in his eye socket—pale, cratered, and lifeless. Those goddamned parasites...

Some Virus-carriers were skilled enough to control the color of their irises, as they could manipulate the light reflecting off their skin and clothes, changing their appearance at will. But Robert had no part in what was happening now. Something had inspired the parasites in his head to make him see what wasn't real. Him thinking of them—resenting them—concentrating too much on what they'd done to his body...

Robert took his pill bottle out of his pocket and swallowed one, to kill the hallucination if nothing else.

As his eye's appearance began to regain normalcy, small sections at a time, he grinned at the thought of those parasitologists and other scientists who insisted the microbes associated with the White Fire Virus were nonliving. Some people could be insistently brilliant but remain consistently clueless.

Call it a sixth or seventh or nth intuitive sense, but Robert just knew the parasites weren't the microscopic equivalent of zombies. The tiny creatures hadn't come from nowhere only to occupy human cells, feed on recipes of blood and light, multiply, and eventually die. They weren't only alive, they were communicating with one another—like a colony of tiny alien ants, or bees. And their method of parasite-to-parasite communication just had to be, at least in part, responsible for most of the hosts' supernatural abilities.

Robert imagined a vibrant community of conspirators, living inside each and every Virus-infected body—a community that sometimes softened the reflexes, seemingly unconcerned with alerting its host to immediate danger.

Something banged into Robert's elbow.

"Oh, sorry dude." The guy who'd pushed the door into him didn't seem sorry. "You done?"

"Yeah," Robert said as he brushed by the jerk.

Time to turn his attention back to business anyway. Just the right time, it appeared.

Robert was surprised to see the mess by his table had been cleaned up so quickly; he was even more surprised to finally catch sight of someone who looked out of place.

A long-legged, raven-haired woman was sitting at the bar, near the door, alone. It wasn't the attractive woman's lack of companionship that set off his suspicion. It was her drink. Coffee. Unusual, he thought. And he thought so again when he saw lipstick on the cup. This was the first Robert was seeing of the woman; neither his round-the-restaurant count nor his over-the-shoulder glances had picked up even a hint of her. Had she entered the restaurant, ordered coffee, and added something to it in order to cool it enough to allow her to take more than one comfortable sip, all while he was in the bathroom? Improbable.

But maybe he was overreacting, trying to justify the suspicion he felt due to one look cast in his direction the moment he came out of the bathroom. At least it seemed like a "look." It was difficult to know for sure. As Robert approached his table, watching the woman the whole time, he saw—in the slim moments when she turned her head—the woman's eyes were in constant shadow, such a deep shadow that he could barely see the whites of her eyes, never mind the irises. There could be no telling what she was looking at. To his eye, though, the woman appeared to be a little nervous about something, trembling in a very warm restaurant.

"Probably afraid of being alone, feeling alone in such a crowd," Kurtis was saying as Robert sat down. "Hey, Rob."

"What are you two talking about?"

"Why Melodie Might feels the need to cry onstage during her performances."

"Every time," Anika said.

"Who?" Robert asked.

"Melodie Might," Anika said. "The ballad-singer. With The MadPoet Experience."

"The what?" Robert asked.

"Man, you don't know about The Experience?" Kurtis regarded his friend with a mild look of disgust. "Where've you been?"

"Oh, relax," Anika said as she backhand-slapped the air toward Kurtis. "Not everyone has heard of them yet." She said to Robert, "They're a collective of artists that stages these humongous concerts at The Poet's Pit every other weekend, when they're not on the road, that is."

"All types of artists," Kurtis said. "Singers and skaters, dancers and martial arts experts, actors and mimes, ice-sculptors and magicians, acrobats and contortionists—"

"It's a real circus," Anika said.

"Sometimes they all perform at once," Kurtis said, "but for some numbers, only one of the artists performs. Melodie Might is a singer, but she never finishes a song because, in the middle, she starts crying."

"Melodie *might* make it to the end, one day," Anika said. "We guess that's the reason behind the name."

"We're catching one of their shows after dinner. Want to come?"

"I'll pass," Robert said.

"Ready to order?" the waiter asked. This was his first official visit to the table, but there was impatience in his voice. Robert saw why. It was the same waiter Anika had sabotaged earlier.

"Death by Gumbo," the girl said. "And again I'm really, really sorry."

"S'okay," the waiter said. "We won't charge you for it. This time."

Smart guy, Robert thought. Only one accident so far, but he'd already correctly figured she was probably going to cause more.

"And you, sir?"

"I'll try a bowl of that alligator stew," Robert said. "Two drops weren't enough."

The waiter didn't get the joke, or found it unfunny; he only looked at Kurtis, who responded, "Death by Gumbo for me, too. And can we get a refill on the ice teas?"

After the waiter left the table, Robert thought of the earlier accident and took another look at Anika. During the confusion, he'd seen a few drops of food touch her clothes too. They were now gone.

"Didn't take you long to clean up," he said to her.

"I don't like to spend a lot of time in the bathroom," she responded.

Robert ignored the wise-aleck response mumbled by Kurtis and asked, "When you were going in, was someone else coming out? Someone tall, with dark hair?"

"A friend of yours?" Anika asked.

"Unlikely," Robert said.

"Then who are you talking about?"

"That short-haired, porcelain-white woman at the bar. Near the door. Don't look, Kurtis. And don't make it obvious, Anika."

Both ignored the request without hesitation then spoke at the same time.

"Who?" "There's no one at the bar who looks like that."

Robert turned and saw they were right. The woman had vanished. Another woman was in her place. A short, stocky, strawberry blonde who was chatting happily on her cell phone and downing the last of what appeared to be a martini.

Robert sighed as he turned back around, taking his bottle of medication out from his jacket pocket. What he'd taken in the bathroom probably hadn't been enough.

"Sure that stuff's helping," Kurtis asked, "and not just messing with your mind?"

"If anything's messing with my mind," Robert said after swallowing, "it's not the pills. These things help me keep control."

Anika shook her head. "So you say. But from what I've read, any medicine offered for…those who have what you have is either dangerous or just a placebo."

"These are neither," Robert said. "They keep their promise."

"You're too trusting," Kurtis said.

"I've heard different."

"Well, I heard that a ring of identity thieves was broken up yesterday," Anika said, "and that maybe a certain nonprofit group profited nicely by finding a lost girl."

"I guess there's nothing wrong with your sense of hearing after all," Robert said as he smirked at Kurtis.

Kurtis only rolled as his eyes and mumbled, "Congrats on the find," before taking a sip of his tea.

Robert didn't know how they found out about the previous day's hush-hush activity—the HSA had taken full credit and released next to no details to the press—but it was a good sign. They were still on their game. He leaned forward and lowered his voice. "I need another favor."

"Research?"

"Yeah. I need you to find out about this girl, Stavan Darden, from Spencer, Virginia. First name is spelled S-T-A-V-A-N and pronounced STUH-von, but she goes by 'Ava.' Approximate age is eighteen or nineteen. Do whatever electronic magic you do to find out every tiny bit you can about her. Especially stuff someone like me might find relevant."

Robert felt a tingling sensation on his right wrist. "Damn it." He put his fingers on the face of his watch, intuiting the message. "*Damn* it."

"What's the matter?" Kurtis asked as Robert stood up.

"Gotta go. Emergency." Robert tossed a twenty on the table to cover his cost of the meal. "Let me know when you find something." He rushed for the door. On his way out, he glanced at the seat where he'd seen the snow-skinned woman. It was empty, but the lipstick-stained coffee cup was again on the bar. Several bills and change were lying next to it. He furrowed his brow but kept moving.

He felt a chill when he stepped out onto the sidewalk. Even though the sun had already set, September's early evening air was still warm enough to get by with just a T-shirt. Robert was wearing a T-shirt and a windbreaker. Regardless, he'd felt a chill. He nonchalantly looked all around him as he crossed the street. He looked around once more as he headed for the parking lot between the paint store and the pharmacy. And he glanced all over one last time before he unlocked his car's door. He swore he was being watched—and followed. But neither his parasite-given abilities nor his mathematical tricks helped him detect a thing.

No time to dwell on it. Adam had contacted him to tell him that their most recent find had disappeared again. Darryl was otherwise occupied, apparently, so it was up to Robert to get to the hospital as quickly as he could.

He was there in thirty minutes. He spent the next thirty minutes questioning everyone he could about what had happened. They had very little to tell him. The nurse who'd checked in on Ava around three o'clock saw she was sleeping soundly. When the nurse checked in on her again a short time later, Ava was gone. No one had seen her leave the room, or the hospital.

Robert wasn't surprised. He'd spent much of the day studying the videos in the IAI's archives of her fight with Marie-Lydia Mc-Gillis. He was familiar with her abilities. Ava was skillful enough to sneak undetected out of a big busy building like a hospital, no matter how secure it allegedly was. The recordings made by the building's surveillance cameras would be worthless, he knew, even though someone affiliated with the IAI would review them anyway. After relaying to Adam what he'd found, there was nothing left for Robert to do but go home…or maybe go looking for Darryl. Pin him down, stage a one-man intervention.

But he felt it again after he passed through the hospital's sliding doors. A chill. This time he felt it and shivered more than once before reaching his car. Again he looked all around him. Again he saw no one.

The enhanced abilities of his eye and ears only went so far; instinct always went further. Robert knew he was being watched and followed even though there was no good evidence, and there was no way he was going to lead a potential threat straight to his doorstep. If his stalker wanted that prize, he or she would have to survive a maze of fast tracks and blind curves.

Robert walked away from his car, out of the parking lot, and kept on walking until he was able to catch a cab.

"East Falls Church Metro station, please."

He planned to start out on one of the outlying Northern Virginia stations of the area's subway system. He would ride it into and under the District before coming up in Maryland for air, checking it for pollutants. If he couldn't lose his spy on the road, he'd lose the looker on the rails. At the very least, he hoped he'd lose his funny feeling.

But the nerve-prickling sensation at the back of his neck branched out to other regions of his body the moment he stepped onto the platform of the Metro station.

Damn parents. There were none in sight, or at least none who were acting in the role. The platform seemed crowded with nothing but a range of children and teenagers—some of the older ones so drunk or drugged up they could hardly walk, and the youngest so young they'd probably only started walking within the past year. The noise-level of their voices was tolerable; the volume-level of their tiny portable media players was bearable; but the words Robert heard were something else. Much of the language coming from the mouths and seeping from the loose earbuds was as foul as the atmosphere. Despite being an outside, above-ground platform, the odors didn't move very far from the many that smoked cigs and joints, drank from bottle-shaped brown bags, and ate from greasy bags of fast food, in blatant violation of the posted signs and occasional loud-speaker announcements about Metro station rules.

It turned out adults were present, just not willing to take up their rightful mantle of supervision. Some appeared oblivious to the goings-on; others were participating. Robert did spot five or six who were trying to keep their heads down and stay out of the way as they waited for the train to arrive and carry them to safety. Some had better luck than others. The giddy young roughhousers rarely stayed within their own play-zones, and unwilling participants were bumped and shoved almost as much as those who were in on the childish games.

Authority figures were also on the grounds—downstairs, on a different level, sitting inside their big-windowed kiosks, probably talking about last night's Nationals game or, more likely, napping. No one would disturb them with questions about ticket purchases at this hour; they could rest in peace. The station's surveillance cameras provided only a wink to security. If something were to happen, something spontaneous and big, Robert wondered how many people would end up beaten and bloody before sufficient help arrived.

He didn't like the situation, but he'd been in it so often, he was almost inured to it. Almost. It took all but superhuman strength of will not to allow himself to lapse and fall in with those resigned to the way things were, with those who didn't give a shit and had just given up on society, themselves, and the future of human civilization.

Kids…There was more than one way for their parents to lose them. They weren't all runaways, abductees, or premature corpses. Some kids stayed close to home, with no direction in life, lost to themselves and anyone else in the world who would be close to them. But it wasn't Robert's job to keep them in line, only to find them when they ended up too far astray. At the moment, he had to perform the tricky task of ignoring them while searching for something else that might be astray.

As he maneuvered through the drunk and the joyous and the careless, Robert kept his ears perked for immediate threats and his eye alert for anyone who might be watching him with too much interest. He detected nothing, but he found a clear spot from where he could keep a lookout over the rotten slice of nightlife around him.

Robert did give the revelers some credit. When the train arrived, they were smart enough to toss their tobacco and weed sticks, declining to bring them onto a cramped car that had limited ventilation. He was happy to see they adhered to some rules of civilization, or at least fell back on the instinct of self-preservation.

He was less happy to hear the noise-level only increased when the train's doors opened. The higher volume and a packed car would only make personal surveillance much more difficult. But he fought for one advantage.

Robert had posted himself near the train's last car and—manner to ladies and children be damned—he made sure he was one of the first to get on. Nudging and pushing, he made his way to the end of the car and leaned his back against an emergency door, putting everything and everyone in front of him and only the door behind him.

There he stayed while the running train slid underground, traveled beneath Washington, and resurfaced for a few stops before reaching the end of the line in Maryland. During the ride, he'd been the subject of many dirty looks, a few bad jokes, and some good nonverbal taunts (eye patches weren't popular, and those who wore them even less so, especially if they didn't have a strapped or muscular crew standing with them), but Robert hadn't seen anything that was a serious threat to him.

After riding through a few stops on the train heading back in the other direction, on a whim he decided to switch lines at the Gallery Place station. He hopped off the orange line train and ran onto the green line train just as its doors were closing. He was attempting to confuse whatever unseen person or persons had been following him; instead he'd only succeeded in jumping into a pit of potential danger.

Robert had entered through the middle door of the car, a car filled with rowdy individuals who by their words, clothes, and actions made clear their intent to wild-out all night long. Shortly after the train made its first jerking motions forward, two of the more menacing riders stepped toward him.

The two teenaged boys were shirtless and sockless, clomping toward Robert in unlaced shoes. Their ratty vests and tattered, ripped jeans were faded and grimy, as if they'd gone through multiple cycles of being machined-washed and hand-dragged through soot.

"Yo ho ho, matey," one of the grinning boys said as they closed in. "Lookin' for some swiggin' swag?"

"Or some shakin' *booty?*"

The oil-stain colors on the boys' tongues and the look in their eyes made it clear they'd had a low dosage of Jelly Raptures; no more than one or two beans apiece. The night was still young for them.

Robert ran his eye over both druggies, then said, "Don't bug me, man."

The word "man" wasn't an accurate description, and it wasn't meant as a sign of respect. Robert had simply meant it as an indirect warning to what looked like a fifteen-year-old and his younger friend: Push me and I'll take you on like an adult. With their body art and piercings, it was clear they were no strangers to pain. The lines on their faces showed they'd already experienced trials beyond their young years. He wouldn't need to go too easy on them.

"Where'd you get that faggoty lookin' eye patch, man?" the younger one asked.

"From your father," Robert said, "back in the alley."

The questioner stopped grinning. He balled one hand into a fist and took two steps forward. Robert left his fingers outstretched and furrowed his brow, letting the iris of his eye fade from a mahogany brown to a shade of maroon before trading its hue for a bright cherry-red.

"Bug me," Robert said, "and get zapped."

Fighting young ones to save young ones—another one of life's beautiful contradictions. When Robert was the only one being threatened, he had a choice, and he almost always chose to remove himself from the situation, if allowed. If not, he tried to encourage the aggressors to remove themselves. Retreat without regrets.

The boy stopped advancing, uncurled his fingers, and looked as if he wanted to say something, something that would erase what he'd just said to Robert. His friend put a hand on his shoulder and pulled him back a step to whisper something in his ear. The older boy's moving lips were hidden from Robert's line of vision, and he only heard the word "back," but when both retreated from his personal space, he figured he could safely ignore them.

Robert avoided looking at the two Jellyheads and, at the next stop, left the car for another one. He saw them leave the car after him, but he didn't realize they'd followed him into the new one until after the doors had closed. He'd entered at one end of the car, they at the other. The throng of people between them made the two difficult to spot at first, but shortly after seeing and recognizing them, Robert again made a conscious decision to ignore them and find a position where he could keep an eye on more serious happenings—like the something happening in the middle of the car.

A little boy was approaching a woman in a wobbly manner, babbling and pointing at her headscarf as he neared. The woman, presumably a Muslim, was with two small children, most likely her daughters. A teenage girl was sitting adjacent to the woman, her cell phone oriented in the direction of the boy. Robert saw the phone's camera function was on, recording. The snickering girl was anticipating something. Something funny. Robert looked at the boy to try to guess the joke.

He initially figured the boy just wanted to know why the woman's head was covered. Today's kids were not only curious but also bold. This one was having trouble expressing himself. The woman said something akin to, "What?" in her original tongue as she leaned nearer, bringing her face closer to the boy. Robert had a second guess about the boy's intent just one second before he smacked the woman across the face. "Bold" wasn't the word for it.

"Happy slap! Happy slap!" The girl with the cell phone yelled with glee as her companions howled with laughter.

The boy smacked the woman twice more before turning to her children, the children who were barely old enough to walk and nowhere near old enough to defend themselves.

Robert cursed as he looked for the nearest emergency call box and cursed again when he spotted it next to the emergency exit door. An embracing couple stood between him and the red button, a couple so lost in each other's affections they could have no idea of the emergency taking place. Robert nudged them over with his shoulder and elbow, into the seats and onto the laps of another amorous couple.

He didn't wait to talk to the questioning voice that came through the box's speaker in response. Someone who heard it might have responded with "Fight!" or something similar, but all Robert heard was the laughter, crying, and screaming from the commotion.

A small area of space had cleared so the victims and victimizers were clearly defined. Most of the bystanders—whether appalled or amused—had moved themselves as far out of the way as possible, clogging Robert's route to the scene.

He unfastened his belt with one hand while he pushed and shoved with the other, maneuvering his way through what felt like a suffocating crowd while focusing on the rampaging boy who had cornered the family in their seats. Robert felt he was losing breath as well as time as the boy continued to screech and swing his arms, yelling and scratching at the woman and her children. The targets buried themselves deeper and deeper into their seats as they tried to fend off the child and shield themselves.

It took Robert almost thirty seconds to make his way through the mass of people—much too long. Once through he didn't waste any time taking a breath before going straight for the wild boy.

He pulled the child over and away from the tormented family with one arm while, with the other, he bound the boy's wrists together with his belt. He then pulled the belt close to his own body so all the boy could do was scream and kick against Robert's legs.

"Let go my son!" An older girl sitting next to the one with the cell phone cursed and yelled the command as she lunged for Robert.

He preferred not to lay his hands on a woman, of any age, but Robert hesitated only a moment before hitting her across the face with the back of his free hand. She didn't go down, but she stumbled before rushing at him again. Robert used the same hand in reverse motion, balled into a fist, to knock the girl down and out.

The train had stopped but the conflict only escalated.

The child screamed louder and kicked harder when his mother fell; the two friends of the bad-boy's mother expressed foul-mouthed shock that someone had dared to hit her while laying his hands on her son; and Robert suppressed a desire to deal with them in the same manner—but they were coming for him. He had to do something.

Never mind the bruises that would appear on his legs tomorrow, he wasn't about to let the child go, not until some responsible adults showed up and took charge. There was only one option.

Robert focused his eye on the face of the attacking girl closest to him. Her cry of anger became an even louder cry of confusion after he ensured that, no matter how often she blinked, she'd see nothing but an opaque blanket of blackness for the next several minutes. As he'd hoped, she collapsed down to her knees in order to stabilize herself.

He had no time to shift his eye and try the same trick on the other one. He used his free hand instead, pointing a fist toward her face and unfolding his fingers, showing his palm. Before the young woman could stop and think what he might be doing, he'd redirected a good portion of the subway car's lights toward her eyes. She wouldn't see anything but a stew of colors as she fell to the floor.

Robert began to wonder about his next move, and then a hard object hit him in the back of the head. He grunted and stumbled forward as he heard, "Let the kid go, booty pirate!"

He recognized the voice. Rather than turn around to see and confirm, Robert turned himself and the kid invisible.

He wanted to wait until his head stopped spinning before making his move against the two punks, but Robert had little time, and no real choices. One of the punks held a knife. The other, a cheap handgun. Nice to see the repeal of the Second Amendment was still having its desired effect eleven years after the fact.

The confusion caused by Robert's disappearing act would last only a few seconds before that piece went off. The crying boy would give away their exact position soon enough, and Robert wasn't about to let him go. Again, he had only one option.

Robert focused and concentrated a thin, sharp beam of infrared radiation at just the right spot on the gunholder's wrist, stinging him, causing him to relax his hand and drop the weapon. Before he or his friend could make another move, Robert reappeared with the gun in his hand, pointed at the two punks.

He didn't say a word. He didn't need to.

Robert's back was against one of the car's side doors. No one could get behind him. He was in a safe position, but an unhappy one.

He couldn't be seen like this, holding someone's bawling kid hostage with a belt while pointing a black-market .38 Special at two teenagers. Some stupid riders might try to rush him. Inspired by false courage or misplaced bravery, some idiot might force him to make the situation five times worse. So much could go wrong from here, and Robert was far from sure of the right way out.

He began to silently count up to the inevitable—*one, two, three, four*—until the emergency exit door at the right end of the car opened and three Metro transit police officers rushed in.

One of the officers stayed by the door as the other two advanced.

"Nobody move!" one of the approaching officers shouted.

"You!" the other officer shouted at Robert. "Drop the weapon! And let that kid go!"

Robert shouted back. "Not until you get over here!"

"I said drop the gun!" the officer repeated as he and the other officers quickly drew their weapons.

"I drop it," Robert said, "one of these assholes snatches it up and shoots me and the kid! And maybe you! Get over here and I'll give you the boy and the gun!"

The officer stopped shouting orders at Robert and started ordering others to back away from him. When they were close enough for him to feel comfortable, Robert loosened the belt and let the crying child go running. He then laid the gun and belt on the ground.

"Get your hands up! Now!"

Robert did as he was told and said nothing. The officer flattened him against the side of the car and cuffed him. Another officer radioed the train's operator, telling her to restart the train, pull it into the next station, and keep the doors closed.

The officer who'd cuffed him ordered Robert to sit crossed-legged on the floor then read him his few rights as the other two checked on the boy, his recovering mother, and her visually impaired friends. Using a lot of fast and high-pitched words, the Muslim woman talked at the two officers as she pointed at the women, the kid, and Robert. Neither of the officers had any idea what she was saying. One of them tried to calm her down. Robert remained silent. He only glared at the two smirking punks as they did what they could to blend in with the car's more innocent riders. Bastards. He should've burned new tattoos into their foreheads.

When the train reached the next stop, one of the officers received a call on his radio. Robert could only hear one side of the conversation, but it was enough. He knew it was good news.

The officer took out his earpiece and looked at Robert. He then helped him to his feet and turned him around. Robert felt the officer's hand reach into his back pocket and pull out his wallet.

"Can you verify your full name, sir?"

"Robert Omari Goldner."

"Okay," the officer said as he unlocked the handcuffs. "When these doors open, you're free to go. We'll contact you for a statement later."

The officer returned his wallet and Robert went to stand by the nearest door while the officer whispered something to his colleagues. He didn't even attempt to eavesdrop. He could figure the scenario. Someone from the Heartland Security Agency had seen what was happening on the train, thanks to at least one of the three surveillance cameras on every car. They made a positive identification on those involved in the commotion—or, at least, a positive identification on Robert—and did a quick background check. They realized he was affiliated with the IAI, contacted them, and someone at The Burrow used their influence to keep one of their birds uncaged. It was a good thing he hadn't bothered to use light and shadows to blur or alter the appearance of his face, which is exactly the method of disguise Adam had instructed all Watcher agents to use in such situations.

The system works, Robert thought as he shook his head.

"Okay, ladies," one of the officers said, "you three are not free to go. You either, ma'am," he said to the Muslim woman. "We're going to need a statement from you all right now."

"And a translator," one of the officers said.

"When these doors open," the first officer said, "all of you are going to need to come with us. Stay close together. Don't even think about doing anything else."

One of the English-speaking women asked in slurred slanguage if they were being arrested.

"You will be if you don't do what we say," one of the officers said.

"We might need a translator for that one too," another officer said to his colleague.

Robert left the car the moment the doors opened. He remembered too late that, as soon as he was uncuffed and nothing he said would be used against him, he should've told the officers about the two druggies and the fact one of them still had a knife. But the punks had fled, and Robert hadn't the time or the desire to look for them. That wasn't his role anyway. If he pursued them, he could end up arrested, and rightly so this time. Last place he wanted to be on a Saturday night was a DC jail.

He brushed himself off and took deep, satisfying breaths of relatively fresh air as he left the Metro station. It took him fifteen minutes to hail a cab and almost twice that amount of time to get back to the hospital's parking lot. During the drive, Robert thought about why he'd decided to travel such a convoluted route home in the first place. At least his funny feeling had disappeared. Whoever or whatever had been following him, even if just a specter of his imagination, was long gone. Thankfully. He wasn't sure he could find the energy to handle another confrontation.

After parking his car in its usual spot, Robert punched in the numerical code on the pad at his apartment building's entrance to unlock the doors. The lobby was dead quiet. Not so unusual, even for a Saturday night. As he passed by the laundry room on his way to the stairs, he glanced through its glass door and saw it too was empty. Common, especially for a Saturday night. Who would want to do laundry when they could go to a club, house party, or restaurant instead? All Robert wanted now was a good night's rest. He had a big day ahead of him.

He pushed the security-shutoff button on his keychain and unlocked his apartment's door. He opened it, took one step, and stopped short. There was a big surprise in front of him. He was sure he didn't have the energy to deal with it.

Chapter 7

Robert slammed the door behind him. Scowling, he balled his hands into fists. His eye glowed as its iris color-shifted to a rusty-red hue.

Ava Darden stood in front of him. Her uncombed auburn hair framed a plainly pretty face with unblinking sapphire-blue eyes trained on Robert's.

"Miss Goins gave me your information."

Ava hadn't flinched when he'd opened the door, nor had she flinched when he'd slammed it. She may have appeared calm, but Robert stayed ready to attack and defend himself.

"She gave you my address?"

"Your phone number," Ava said. "I found the address on my own."

Damn landlines. He almost regretted not trading off for a cell phone like Darryl and pretty much everyone else in the country. "Why'd she give you my number?"

"She left me a couple of contacts. I chose yours."

"Seems your memory loss is getting worse," Robert said as he unclenched his fists. "You've forgotten there're laws about breaking and entering."

"I'm sorry," she said, "but I had nowhere else to go."

"You could've stayed at the hospital."

"No, I couldn't. I—" She almost looked away from him. Robert could tell she was choosing her words carefully. "I didn't feel comfortable there. I kept feeling like, at any moment, something would come and swallow me up."

"Right," Robert said.

"I couldn't let that happen."

"Of course not."

"Especially since"—she did look away from him now—"I'm just starting to remember…bits and pieces…"

Robert tensed, ready to hear something good or useful. "About what?"

"About me," she said.

"Yes?"

"You're an honest one, Robert Goldner. I trust the impression I got at the hospital this morning. And even though I'm not back to full strength yet, I think I can go ahead and trust you with the one bit of information I do know about myself. An important bit."

"Okay, let's hear it."

"I'm—I am—" She stuttered a couple more times before saying it outright. "I'm an angel. The Arkangel Ava."

Oh good, he thought, another one of these.

It seemed to him a small but steadily increasing number of Virus-carriers considered themselves to be "angels." Some literally, some metaphorically. Darryl fell in the metaphorical camp; Robert stayed out of both. He thought it was all foolishness, just another symptom of the silly fictions people adopt to help them get by. Problem was, most carriers had the abilities to convince others of the truth of their personal fictions. Robert wondered what Ava's angle could be.

"I was hoping you'd help me with something."

"What," Robert said, "you want me to help you break into someone else's place?"

"I think I know a way to help me remember more, help me rearrange the messy bits and pieces in my head, get them in some kind of order."

"Oh?" Robert approached the girl. "What did you have in mind?"

"Well," Ava said, casting glances around the studio apartment, "we could use your bed, after you change the sheets. Or the couch. It looks comfortable enough, but we'd have to position ourselves like—"

"Whoa, whoa, whoa." Robert held up his hands and took a step backward. He realized what she was getting at, and he wouldn't go there. Not tonight. Not in his apartment. And definitely not unsupervised. "We just met. Let's just sit and relax first. You, over there."

Ava looked at the black leather chair with some reluctance. When she finally sat, Robert began to look around the apartment to see just what had been tampered with. He thanked fortune his laptop was still at The Burrow, broken and slowly being repaired. He'd gotten a little frustrated a few weeks back during a research project and took his anger out on his computer, but he'd downloaded so much he didn't want to just chuck it and buy a new one. For the first time, he was happy the IAI's technician was taking her sweet time fixing it. He didn't need Ava snooping around on it.

"Can I get you something to drink?" he asked.

"I'll take a glass of your orange juice," Ava said. "Your tomato juice has expired. And the grape juice is flat."

Charming, he thought. "Did you check to make sure the ice trays were filled?"

"Yes."

Perfectly charming. Robert sighed and shook his head as he started toward the kitchen. Ava stood up again and approached one of his bookshelves. She certainly wasn't the type to stay put.

Robert did a quick survey in the kitchen, making sure everything was as it should be. As he opened the fridge, he heard Ava say, "Very interesting looking…dolls you have."

"They're more like action figures," Robert said about the six-inch-tall toys on his bookshelves.

"Oh."

"For adults." He wanted to clarify without giving away too much. "Specially made by a friend of mine. An engineer."

"He made them especially for you?"

"For my apartment. There's much more to each of them than meets the eye. Or, tonight, maybe much less." Robert didn't hide his disappointment at the failure of his apartment's unique security system. He doubted Ava could know the real purpose of the strategically positioned toy robots, and he doubted Zel's devices had all malfunctioned at once, but somehow she'd gotten into his apartment without any of them either sounding the loud alarm or emitting the mosquito-like whine that was supposed to render unconscious anyone who was within a twelve-foot range of them. The robots just seemed dead.

Ava was still examining the toys when Robert came out of the kitchen, bringing her a glass and a coaster for the coffee table. She only turned her attention to him after he sat on the couch and cleared his throat.

He waited for her to take her seat and her first drink, and then he asked, "Suppose you tell me every single important bit and piece that you remember about yourself? I'm sure you've had plenty of sleep over the past day or so. And I'm willing to stay up all night."

After her fourth sip, Ava began. "I've checked a calendar. My last clear memories are from over a year ago. It was around that time, last March, when I thought I was about to die. I kept seeing these, all these, visions and strange things, like bugs, teeny tiny spiders, living under my skin. And Death. A living, walking, talking *Death,* watching me, following me, following me everywhere…" She took another drink, no doubt hoping the words would begin to flow more easily. "Then one day, finally, this Death confronted me and revealed itself—herself—as an Archangel. She gave me the good news, telling me I wasn't sick, and I wasn't dying. I was being helped. Not cursed, but blessed. Blessed with the chance to become an angel, a true-to-life angel on Earth, just like her."

Robert did all he could to maintain a straight face. For once he felt thankful for the eye patch; there'd be less chance of her seeing him roll one eye than two.

Still, better to roll an eye in annoyance than have a good belly laugh at the black joke of people calling themselves "Arkangels" and "Archangels." The terms sounded similar when pronounced by some, but when spoken by true believers, there was an added emphasis on the first syllable of "Arkangel," causing one's throat to catch a little when saying the word. Robert got tripped up pretty much any time he had to say anything about "angels." "Sick humans" rolled off the tongue much more naturally.

"This Archangel showed me different realms of Reality," Ava said. "She took me down to the lowest levels of Reality, the Ultimate realm—"

"XynKroma."

Ava seemed a little too happy to hear the word. She composed herself before continuing. "Yes. Of course you've been there."

"I've had my unfair share of visits," Robert said.

"Well, like you, I had more than a few, each one with the purpose of *inverting* me, rebirthing me into my destined rank, that of an Arkangel." She paused and studied Robert's face for a moment before asking, "What rank are you?"

He showed her a puzzled expression before erasing it with a smile. "I just prefer to think of myself as nothing more than a Watcher."

"Huh." It was Ava's turn to look puzzled. "The Archangel didn't mention Watchers. But I know the scriptures do."

Robert made a mental note to do some research on what book or books of scripture she could be talking about, first chance he got on Sunday. He figured the meaning of "inverting" was probably very similar to that of "converting," but he'd look into that too.

"I'd almost completed my training in Xyn," Ava said, "but before taking the final step, I was forced to undertake an inholy mission on Reality's surface."

He'd have to look into the meaning of "inholy" as well.

"I learned that right in Spencer, right in my own hometown, one of my closest friends had become corrupted. She was also an angel, but one of the worst kind."

"Marie-Lydia?" Robert said.

"Yes. It was the Tuesday after spring break. I was at home when I received the revelation. She was at school, trying to kill everyone. I got there and did everything I could to stop her. Last thing I remember, I pinned her down in the gym, and took her down to XynKroma."

"And next thing you knew—"

"I was in a hospital," Ava said. "In Arlington, Virginia. On a September day, far away from home." She finished her drink.

"Yeah, well, I guess you already found out about your mother," Robert said as he stood and reached for her glass.

"My mother?" Ava asked. "What about her?"

He stood awkwardly in front of her. "Didn't you try to call home today?"

Ava opened her mouth and closed it just as quickly. For the first time, she appeared nervous.

"I didn't call anyone today," she said. "When I was ready, and able, I just left the hospital. And I made my way here."

Robert took a deep breath. He sat back down and leaned forward, ready to take her hand and try to comfort her if necessary.

"Ava, after you told us your name, we tried to find your parents. And, we…Well, we found no record of a father. And your mother, she's gone."

"What do you mean?"

"We couldn't find any trace of her," he said. "We're still searching, but…"

Robert broke off, feeling his throat catch, remembering how he felt when he was told the same news about his father more than three years ago. A fine comforter he was.

He managed to control his emotions well enough to notice Ava didn't seem all that upset about the news. In fact, she no longer seemed anything—not uncomfortable, angry, depressed, or even perplexed. Her facial expression showed nothing but a blank. She was suppressing it, Robert decided. She was repressing something.

"I'm sure if she's to be found," Ava said, "someone will find her."

She stood and stretched her arms, then looked all around the room in a nonchalant manner. Robert stared at her. She was communicating exactly what she intended not to. Uneasiness. Was there some issue with her mother? Did Ava have no use for her after her *inversion* experience with this so-called Archangel? Just how did that house burn down?

Robert shifted his focus from Ava's body language to her clothes: a wheat-colored jacket over a cream-colored tank top, black capri pants, and matching black ballet flats. They weren't the clothes he and Darryl had found her in. And that diamond pendant in her cleavage…She'd made at least one other stop before coming to his place.

Apparently tired of averting her eyes and not knowing what else to say, Ava asked if she could use his bathroom. Robert said yes and asked if she wanted another drink. She said yes and closed the bathroom door.

Robert hurried to pour the juice, then, after checking that she was still in the bathroom, he put two fingers on the face of his right-wristwatch. He contacted Adam and gave him an update on all that had happened since they'd last communicated. The responding message asked that he bring Ava to The Burrow, immediately. They'd set her up in one of the spare apartments for the night. Adam had plans for her.

He was about to send a message to Darryl using the watch on his left wrist when he heard the bathroom door open. He picked up the glass of juice and turned around. Ava was standing three feet in front of him. Startled, Robert released the glass.

Ava grabbed it. "Thank you."

"Sure." It was too hard to tell whether she'd grabbed the glass from his hand or from the air after he released it.

"You know," she said after taking a drink, "you don't have a mirror in your bathroom."

"I realize that."

"Any particular reason?"

"Yes," Robert said. "I have reasons."

Neither spoke as they stared at each other. She'd lose the contest. There was no way he was going to deal out personal information to a stranger. Especially not this stranger.

Ava didn't blink, but she eventually turned her back on him to return to the sitting area. "You know," she said, "I was thinking."

"Oh?" Robert followed her.

"If you're prioritizing, it would be best to concentrate on finding Marie-Lydia, rather than my mom."

"Any particular reason why?"

"Yes," Ava said as they sat down. "I have reasons. One's an adult and can take care of herself. The other…is young. And a danger to herself."

"And to others. We know."

"I want to go to XynKroma, Robert. It's where I took her, last time I saw her. It's the only way I can pick up her trail. And I can't go alone. I want to go with someone I trust."

Robert sighed as his eye unfocused.

His former pastor used to preach that Heaven and Hell weren't actual places, just metaphors for certain states of mind. They were conditions of existence to be experienced in *this* life; one experienced Heaven or Hell based on one's attitude and actions. There were no other planes of existence. But Robert's former pastor didn't have the White Fire Virus. He knew nothing about XynKroma, even though he'd come close to a good enough description in some of his sermons.

Robert was neither a preacher nor a poet, but even his best description of Xyn sounded like something delivered from a pulpit to a congregation of born-again beatniks. It was another dimension, a realm comprising the deepest, lowest levels of accessible Reality. Xyn was what university professors of philosophy and religion would call "Ultimate Reality." Not a dreamscape or a fantasyland or an imaginative figment, but an actual plane of existence made up of dirty light and sentient beings' polluted thoughts, the fundamental energies of life.

Heaven and Hell may've been fictional realms for the afterlife, but XynKroma was an experienced fact, particularly for those infected with the White Fire Virus. A seemingly infinite realm, Xyn was like Heaven and Hell after they'd been combined, folded up into a pea-sized nugget, and relocated to exist simultaneously—and unstably—at the core of every sentient creature's mind. In theory, anyone could visit the extra-dimensional realm, but thanks to their hypersensitivity and electromagnetic abilities, it was much easier and much more common for Virus-carriers. As far as Robert knew, the realm could only be accessed by practicing a form of intense meditation and staring deep into one's own or someone else's eyes, tunneling to the center of the subconscious mind. Ava clearly wanted to go the latter route, his eye and hers locked, strangers embraced, their bodies entwined like lovers, if only for one night…

It was too dangerous. For the body and the mind.

Energy from every living being's mind—their hopes, fears, desires, hates, wishes, *everything*—fed into Xyn, like rivers and rainfalls feeding an ocean. Hence the realm's chaos. The flowing energies from the minds of every living being competed with one another in Xyn, resulting in the creation of archetypes and other symbols that manifested as dangerous settings populated by even more dangerous creatures: unclassifiable monsters, innumerable giants, fire-and-ice fairies, and so on, ad infinitum. Hell's demons and Heaven's mistakes on ever-shifting terrains. More than once, Robert had referred to Xyn's low levels of Reality as the *Scalp of God*. He didn't remember where he'd first heard that phrase, but he didn't mind using it. To enter this realm was like treading on the balding scalp of the Creator, a Creator in the throes of senility. The exact experience was unique for everyone, but almost always horrific, and definitely life-changing.

Robert had experienced more Hell than Heaven during one of his earliest visits, which began with him floating weightlessly while suffocating in bluish beige smog. It wasn't his flesh-and-blood body that was floating and choking, but it was *him*. The essence of his consciousness had translated itself into a taffy-like body that could exist in Xyn with only a minor measure of comfort.

The smog eventually cleared to reveal a monstrous free-floating tree. No ground or sky—just Robert and an enormous tree, whose roots immediately snatched him up. They stretched and strangled his neck, arms, and legs while teeth-bearing fruit appeared (possibly shaken loose from the malicious tree's branches) to nibble at his exposed sections. Peaches, plums, nectarines, and cherries of various hues nipped and pinched, taking bits and pieces out of Robert while, between screams, he heard the harsh music of the tree's leaves. It seemed to his strangely enhanced sense of sight that each leaf was vibrating and shaking in its own unique way, despite the complete lack of wind.

He was bitten at least a hundred times before something snapped—and Robert found himself in a new experience. His "body" had become wood. He'd become the tree. And he'd been planted atop a high mountain made up of the slowest quicksand, a quicksand containing a colony of ravenous, alien termites. The mites went to work on his roots while his trunk, limbs, and branches were subjected to the most extreme elements of all four earthly seasons, and maybe even a fifth or sixth one. It had been hard to tell what was what in the middle of all the rain, snow, heat, and incessant shedding of leaves, whipped up by tornado-like gusts. It all came to a stop only when a gorilla-like creature straight out of a drunken Dante's infernal dreams grabbed him by his trunk and pulled him out of the quicksand. Robert had apparently been seasoned to the point where he could be happily devoured by the giant demon. In the pit of its stomach, Robert felt a bliss he'd never felt before or since as what passed as the stomach's acids dissolved him. He regained consciousness in his familiar body on Reality's surface, imperceptibly but definitely a changed man.

To those who'd been to XynKroma, the real world in which most humans lived and played—the Earth and its comprehensible universe—was regarded merely as the *surface* of Reality. The dimension of Xyn was Reality at its limits. It was fairly easy to get lost when visiting such a place, and there was a low chance one would even find an exit back to a relatively coherent and familiar realm of Reality rather than becoming lost in the mind, in *everyone's* mind, having one's senses and sanity permanently scrambled, as had happened to the numerous associates of The Infinite Definite.

Just three years ago, after one of his longest visits, seventeen-year-old Robert had been lucky enough to leave XynKroma and reenter his familiar realm of Reality, but what he'd learned during his visit wouldn't allow him to ever consider *any* part of Reality as coherent or sensible again. It had been during this visit Robert that learned the fate of his mother, the final fate of the woman who'd carried him for nine months.

That goddamned day.

His parents had left him at home alone, sleeping through dawn on his eleventh birthday. His father had set off for work while his eight-month's pregnant mother had set off for a cousin's house. Out of the town of Wallace, Virginia, into the heart of its bordering city, his mother had gone to gather the gifts she'd stashed far away from where her too-curious son would be able to look, far away from where he would even think to look. She'd been determined to surprise him, and Robert had been. Later that day, he was surprised to hear how his mother had been ambushed.

The cousin wasn't a close relative. Barely an acquaintance, in fact. Just a bloodliner who'd relocated from Louisiana only six months prior. No one in Robert's house had any clue of the thirty-year-old's addictions, or her associations. Robert's mother had arrived at her house just as the Ecstasy- and heroin-fueled gathering of shady characters was breaking up. Most of the drug-fiends scattered back toward the dark corners from which they'd come. Three remained behind. Two eyed the stomach of Robert's mother. And one had an idea.

The cousin. She ran to the kitchen, retrieved the second largest knife she could find and, as her drug-addled associates restrained Robert's mother, she cut the unborn baby from her womb.

Minus some of the details, this was the story Robert had been told on the afternoon of his eleventh birthday by a less-than-sensitive cop who'd interviewed the missing cousin's accomplices. The officer thought he was just doing his duty by talking to the victim's son. Six years later, in XynKroma, Robert learned every minute detail of the story, and its epilogue. A denizen of Xyn, a fantastical creature that had spent every moment of its possibly immortal life in the realm, had told him all about it.

Unlike Robert's mother, the creature said, her baby hadn't died on the day it was snatched from her womb. The cousin had stolen it, stolen away with Robert's baby brother to parts unknown. And the baby had the White Fire Virus. Robert's mother had had the Virus. She'd been infected right around the time she got pregnant, a couple years before the new-and-out-of-nowhere Virus infected the first "official" victim, according to the "official" history. During the gestation period, the unborn baby had been subjected to the raw experience of XynKroma; its mind-and-soul had practically lived there. The final bombshell: Robert's father was not the true father of Robert's little brother.

Robert never had a chance to ask or confront either of his parents about any of the many questions raised during his extra-dimensional sojourn. After leaving Xyn with this new and improbable information, after awaking from his deepest of deep sleeps, his father was nowhere to be found. Disappeared without a trace.

How trustworthy was the story Robert had heard while he'd been in Xyn? How trustworthy was Xyn's denizen, the three-mile-long albino serpent who told Robert the story while it devoured itself? How trustworthy were any absurd words heard on any level of Reality?

There was a line beyond which he wouldn't humor the ridiculous. There was a line beyond which he even refused to entertain the preposterous. But there were other lines he was obligated to cross in order to do his duty.

Ava stared at Robert. She may have been holding the gaze during all the minutes of silence that had passed while he was remembering the tragedy of tragedies. He must've been staring at her the whole time without fully seeing her.

He blinked twice, shook his head, and asked, "Would you like to go for a ride?"

Chapter 8

Robert had been told there was no need for a blindfold. Adam was sure someone of Ava's abilities would be able to see right through it anyway. Robert was sure that none of this was a good idea.

It was a lot to decipher from such a short message—Robert's pulse and watch and intuition working in mysterious harmony to break the encryption—but it seemed Adam believed Ava deserved a proper introduction to the Isaac-Abraham Institution. After all, she was a young Virus-carrier with no parents and nowhere to go. Not only did Adam want her to trust the IAI to keep her safe, he also wanted to see if he could trust his instincts about her. She might make a good Watcher agent.

Robert didn't have time to protest, but he was wary of the whole set-up. They still knew so little about her. What if she was affiliated with The Infinite Definite? What if, once inside The Burrow, she revealed her true colors and went berserk like her friend did inside the high school? Yes, they could take her down, but how many would she take down with her? Robert had studied the videos in the archive. She was tough. And if she did escape and meet back up with her terrorist associates with information about The Burrow's secret location…

"Why so quiet?" Ava asked.

"Just thinking," Robert said.

Ava went silent for a few moments before asking, "How long have you been looking for Marie-Lydia?"

"Since her parents reported her missing."

"Any good leads?"

Robert took a long breath. "Just you."

Silence seemed to disturb her. The thought of this made Robert want to prolong it even further. Spurred by nervousness, Ava might blurt out something interesting. But her only words during the rest of ride were questions about some of the buildings they passed. Robert said next to nothing until they drove into the parking garage.

"The Isaac-Abraham Institution is a publicly known organization," he said, "but its main office, which we call The Burrow, has always been a well-guarded secret. It's located underground, for various reasons, the most important one being that almost everyone in there has the same condition you and I do. Even though we're not officially affiliated with the government, we have connections, and the location of the facility and the nature of much of the work is top secret. Adam Smith is the chairman of the Institution. He insisted I bring you here, without blindfolds or any other of the simplest security measures. He didn't tell me to request it, but I'm asking that you please keep anything you see or hear strictly to yourself."

"You have my word, Robert. This angel doesn't lie."

"Yeah," he said as he pulled into a parking space.

They walked to one of the garage's elevator banks, and Robert pushed the "up" button.

"I thought we were going underground?"

"We are," he said after looking around them for busybodies. "Just wait."

The first elevator cab had four people inside. Robert waved them off, saying they'd catch the next one. The people gave them funny looks. Robert ignored them. Ava smiled and shrugged.

They waited for three silent minutes until an empty cab arrived. After entering, Robert pushed the button for the door to close, selected a key on his keychain and stuck it into a slot near the buttons. He then pushed the button for the highest level.

At the top level, the door didn't open. Instead, the cab began to vibrate.

"What's happening?" Ava asked.

"It's turning around."

When it stopped, the door opened onto complete blackness. Robert adjusted his vision until he saw through the opaque wall of nothing. There was another elevator ten feet away. He moved forward with Ava close behind. He pressed some of his fingers against a pad next to the second elevator and stooped down so his eye was level with the iris scanner. The door opened, but Ava hesitated. The inside of the cab was as pitch black as the space outside it. Robert waved her inside.

"The door will shut in less than seven seconds."

She just made it.

After the door closed, Robert again touched some of his fingers to a pad and looked into a scanner. The cab began to move. After a long, silent descent, the door opened. They stepped out into a darkened corridor.

"Follow me," Robert said.

He led Ava through halls and around corners, down stairways and through several doors. They didn't pass anyone. The place seemed deserted. But Robert knew better.

When they reached Adam's office door, Robert pressed his fingers to the keypad and lowered his head until his eye was level with the scanner. For the second time that day, he heard the recorded voice announce, "Enter, Mister Goldner."

The two stepped into a room lit by three low-wattage lamps. Robert was surprised to find Adam already waiting behind the reception area's desk. He was even more shocked to find Darryl sitting in one of the three metal chairs in front of it.

"Come in, both of you," Adam said as he gestured toward the two empty chairs. "I ask you to please excuse the dimness, Miss Darden, but I am sure you can see just fine."

"Yes, thank you." Ava sat in the seat next to Darryl. Robert sat on the other side of her and then scooted his chair back a few inches so he could get a clearer view of Darryl. The sleeves of Darryl's shirt were rolled up to his elbows, and a bandage was on his left forearm. Must've been a tough charity case.

"I am Adam Smith, chairman of the Isaac-Abraham Institution."

"Pleased to meet you," Ava said with a respectful nod.

"First, I would like to know if you are feeling okay," Adam said, "considering everything you have been through over the past few days."

"Yes," Ava said. "I guess I'm feeling as well as I can be, considering."

Yes—what was she feeling? As far as Robert could detect, she didn't seem the least bit put off by Adam's exoskeletal suit or his atypical manner of speaking. Then again, Robert didn't have a full view of her face, and the funhouse reflection on the front of Adam's helmet was of little help. Ava's actual facial expression may've revealed something her tone of voice didn't.

"Good," Adam said. "For now, I just want you to relax. I did not ask Mister Goldner to bring you here for an interrogation. I wanted him to bring you to a place where you could be sure, and we could be sure, that you would be safe."

"Thank you," Ava said.

"I have also called Miss Goins, our medical specialist. She is on her way here to have a quick look at you. Then you will be shown to one of our secure apartments so that you may get some rest. But before all of that, I thought it would be wise to tell you what we are all about."

Ava nodded as she crossed her right leg over her left.

"The Isaac-Abraham Institution," Adam said, "is a nonprofit research center that is devoted to the advanced study of familial relations—how and why families disintegrate, how we can put them back together, and how we can keep them that way. That is a very basic summation. We advise and disseminate the results of our research to federal, state, and local government entities, social workers, and many others who share our goals.

"The Institution began as a three-person operation. Me, two associates, a few computers, and a rapidly growing electronic and paper library of information. It was my associates who came up with the name for the Institution, names not being a very strong area for me…"

Ava cocked her head a little.

"You see," Adam continued, "eight years ago, I was severely crippled, and my subsequent recovery only brought me so far to a state of normalcy. In the wake of my accident, I lost quite a bit of my memory, the most valuable parts, almost everything having to do with my personal history. My name, knowledge of my family… But during my recovery process, I came to believe the answers to my past would lie in the work I could do for the future. I retained important pieces and bits of other types of knowledge I had acquired during my travels through life, and I put that knowledge to use while trying to find the most significant parts of both my past and my future—my children."

When Adam paused, Robert saw Ava lower her head and whisper something. He couldn't quite make it out.

"Yes, Miss Darden?" Adam asked. "Do you have a question?"

Ava's head jerked up. "Oh, I'm sorry, sir. I was just, uh…"

Robert figured something Adam had said triggered something within her, something causing her to fall into a momentary trance and whisper something to herself. Instructions, maybe. The sight of it just added to Robert's unpleasant feeling about all of this.

Ava cleared her throat. "You're saying you lost most knowledge of your background, but you remembered you had children?"

"That is one of the few bits of which I am certain, yes. I just do not remember how many, or any definite names. It must sound strange, I know, but I believe that however many there are, at least one of them has a name that rhymes or comes close to rhyming with the letter 'R,' or the word 'air.' Possibly Claire, Carey, Blaire, Aaron…The possibilities are many, but not endless.

"However, as our research on my past seemed to lead us only in circles, and as our resources began dwindle, we thought it would be a wise idea to expand our mission and our search. Six years ago, we offered to assist the Heartland Security Agency with part of its mission—a mission for which it did not have the manpower at the time—in exchange for government grant money. As we began to acquire other types of researchers and specialists, and a substantial amount of private donations from various sources, we offered to assist the Agency in other ways as well. Now we have come to the point where the Agency and the Institution assist each other as we both stretch and reach for the goals of strong, unbreakable families—the fundamental units of a truly secure society."

"Noble idea," Ava said.

"We all think so," Darryl said.

Robert shot a glance at him, barely managing to suppress the rude noise that came close to leaving his lips.

"The scores of individuals who are now part of the Institution," Adam said, "each of us is here to help benefit society, to give it a peace it has never truly had, but most of us are also here to recover missing pieces from our own lives. I do not know how much Mister Goldner has told you of his own story, but both he and Mister Ridley are without parents. We have several other young adults and teenagers who are with us. They too have lost their parents."

"They—" Ava turned to look at both of them. "You two are orphans?"

"Yes," Adam answered on their behalf, "Mister Goldner, Mister Ridley, and all of the other specially gifted orphans here were recovered either by us or, almost by accident, by certain law enforcement agencies while their agents and officers were carrying out their other duties. All of the orphans had parents who either died or disappeared or, in some of the rare two-parent households, both. Because of their status, and because each of them happened to be endowed with abilities the world does not fully understand or appreciate, they were each given a choice to be temporarily adopted by the Institution for the duration of that crucial stage: the passage through adolescence into full maturity. We offered food, shelter, loaner cars, a generous allowance, and all sorts of real-world training in exchange for their assistance with some of our research projects. And they accepted.

"Mister Ridley and Mister Goldner here make up one of our many Watcher units. They are responsible for assisting the Institution by doing field research. Primarily, they assist us, and the government, with locating and recovering missing children. We also have an advisory committee of adults. These individuals take time out from their full-time jobs to assist the Institution with their expertise, in areas ranging from medicine to law to physical therapy to engineering to psychology and many others. And then there is the board. It controls the Institution. We board members came to be referred to as 'MatchMakers'; I believe Mister Levy, one of our government liaisons, came up with that term, I suppose for our stated goal and occasional success in matching children to their rightful guardians. All together, we like to think of ourselves as one tight-knit community."

"Robert told me that everyone, everyone in this community, is like me."

"Not exactly like you, Miss Darden," Adam said, "but yes, almost everyone affiliated with the Institution has been *blessed* in such a way as to set them apart from most of humanity. And there are others who have been similarly blessed, at least in their own eyes. They are not a part of this community, or any other true community."

Robert saw an odd reflection in Adam's mask. Was Ava smiling? He repositioned himself in his chair to get a better view of her face. He'd a feeling her expressions were about to tell on her.

"There are young adults in this and other areas," Adam said, "most falling within the range of thirteen to thirty years of age, who also seem to lack parents and responsible guidance. They wander the streets and haunt certain locales. They are specially *touched,* like us, but unlike us, they use their gifts and abilities to assist them as they maim and torture and murder others, and escape detection and capture by those who would stop them."

"Fallen angels," Ava said, almost whispering again.

"That is one way of putting it," Adam said. "But we and the authorities have classified them as 'The Infinite Definite,' or 'The ID' for short. We have only managed to gather a relatively small amount of information on them, but then there is only so much information we could gather on a rootless, faceless gang that operates under the principle of Leaderless Insistence."

"Leaderless Insistence?" Ava said.

"Go to your core, submit to your basest urges, and do what comes naturally," Darryl said as he rubbed his bandage. "That's what it means, and that's what they do."

"They are a terrorist gang without any known leader," Adam said. "And as they can manipulate light like you do, they are quite adept at hiding their faces, their identities, escaping detection for long periods."

Adam went silent. It was only for a few seconds, but it was long enough for Ava's thick, cold surface to begin to crack. She uncrossed her legs as her shoulders tensed. She was becoming defensive before she even said anything, before anyone could even say it to her outright. She looked from Adam's smooth, featureless mask to the detailed, staring faces of Darryl and Robert.

"What?" she said. "Are you accusing me of being a part of that? Of being one of *them?*"

"I am not," Adam said. "But I thought by making you aware of them, it might help you to remember if you have ever encountered their like. Say, recently."

"I don't think—" Ava began to respond but stopped. Robert guessed why. As she'd said, this angel doesn't lie. She probably couldn't even tell an outright lie about herself to save herself.

"They travel in pairs," Robert said. His eye stared at her, but in his mind he was replaying what he'd seen on the videos he'd studied earlier in the day. "Tribes of two. That's the closest they come to being organized. We happen to know you can handle yourself pretty well physically. And, based on your last known association—"

"Robert, what—?" Ava turned as much of her body toward him as her chair would allow. "*What* association?"

"Marie-Lydia McGillis." He answered her with just a twist of frost in his tone. She appeared ready to lunge at him; if she did, it would help prove his point. "She's a definite fallen angel, as you yourself have admitted. And, as we've found, a very, *very* close friend of yours back when you two were classmates."

Ava stared wide-eyed at him; she had no words. He responded with a cold glare. He also saw that Darryl was now looking at him instead of Ava. He wanted to tell Darryl he could've reached the same conclusion if only he'd joined in the research after they left the hospital that morning, but he kept his neck rigid, kept facing toward Ava, kept waiting for her to—admit, deny—say something.

"Robert, I told you I was trying to stop her! I *did* stop her!"

"And after that, what?" Robert said. "You two went to Xyn-Kroma together. When you came out, maybe you were more like her? A fractioned memory, and more than a year missing from any public record. With a profile like that, we are smack-dab in Infinite-Definite territory. A territory of young mentally mangled terrorists."

Earlier, she'd accused him of being honest. He could only hold back his honest suspicions of her for so long.

"That's enough, Goldner," Darryl said.

"Yes," Adam said. "Miss Darden, please understand we are not accusing you of anything."

"I understand fine," she said.

"But Mister Goldner is correct in asserting your friend is most likely, in some way, connected with The Infinite Definite. We are well aware of the damage she caused in your hometown. And we have many strong reasons to believe she is now in the Washington metropolitan area. We desperately need your assistance in finding her so she may be rehabilitated and reunited with her family."

Ava stared down at the glass desk, her lips scrunched together.

"As I said," Adam continued, "I did not call you here for an interrogation, and I will not force you to help us. It is your decision. But please, sleep on it. And know that, whatever you decide, you may stay with us for as long as you need to."

Ava raised her head. Her lips began to slowly part, as if she had something to say. They quickly closed again when a recorded voice spoke from behind her.

"Enter, Miss Goins."

Sam entered and nodded greetings at everyone before saying to Adam, "My apologies, but I got here as fast as I could."

"It is okay, Miss Goins," Adam said. "We were just having a nice little chat."

"Quite a scare you gave us," Sam said to the back of Ava's head. "We feared we'd lost you again."

"No." Ava didn't look at any of them as she spoke. "Not yet."

"Miss Darden, if you prefer to go straight to bed, Miss Goins will be happy to show you to the apartment we have prepared for you, but I strongly suggest you let her look you over and give you a quick physical examination before you turn in. We do not want to find out about any injuries later than we need to."

"No," Ava said as she rose from her chair. "That is the last thing we need." She didn't look once at Robert or Darryl as she turned and only glanced at Sam's smiling face before lowering her eyes toward the floor. Sam prepared to reopen the door.

"Oh, Miss Darden?" Adam said. "I did have one question for you."

She turned toward him. "Yes?"

"Where did you get that necklace?"

Robert focused his eye on the pendant as Ava pressed the dime-sized diamond between her fingers, holding it up and away from her skin as she gazed at it. It looked to him as if she were appraising it, deciding on what it was worth to her, what she would get out of telling this interested audience about it. Or maybe she was slipping into another short trance.

"It was a gift," Ava said. "From an old instructor."

"I see," Adam said. "Very lovely."

"Very generous teacher," Darryl said.

Sam and Ava stepped into the hall after Adam bid them good night. Robert heard Ava ask for directions to the nearest bathroom. After the door slid shut, there was a period of silence.

Robert wanted to stand up and stretch but thought it would be rude to be the only one. It could be taxing having an extended meeting with the chairman, a man who barely moved his head or even his hands while he spoke.

"She knows more than she has said," Adam said.

"And what she *has* said," Robert said, "is enough to for us to know she's trouble."

Darryl sighed as he lowered his head, shut his eyes, and pinched a thumb and forefinger on the bridge of his nose. "All right, Goldner," he said with a strained voice. "Why the attitude?"

"You mean the attitude of wanting to find the redheaded girl?" Robert asked. "Marie-Lydia McGillis? Remember her? Don't you share that attitude? Or maybe you're too preoccupied trying to find your next—"

"Mister Goldner, please," Adam said. "I believe Mister Ridley simply wants to know why you accused Miss Darden of being in league with The Infinite Definite."

"I didn't. I—" Robert took a deep breath. "Well, not directly. But she's in league with someone. And, with all due respect, sir, I think it's a bad idea, a very bad idea, to bring her into The Burrow. She escaped from a room in a secure wing of the hospital, tracked down where I lived, broke into my apartment without setting off any of Zel's security devices, and took almost a complete inventory of my place. All that has shown me she's resourceful. And sly. And everything she's said, put together with what I've gathered from my review of the Institution's materials on her, tells me she's definitely been trained and prepared by someone, for some purpose."

"Fine," Darryl said. "But you know those affiliated with The ID aren't like that. They're more erratic, like wild animals."

"I know, which is why I wasn't necessarily accusing her of being affiliated with them, but maybe with something else. Another gang or breakaway sect, a more organized version of The ID, with a more sinister purpose."

"Oh, really?" Darryl chuckled. "And what can be more sinister than raping and murdering for no reason?"

"I don't know. But maybe we can get her to tell us."

"Dangerous thinking," Adam said. "If you let your thoughts travel down a straight enough route for a long enough time, you could reach the conclusion our Watcher units are nothing more than a more organized version of The Infinite Definite. But we have no sinister purpose here. What you have seen so far places her more on our side than theirs."

"Yeah, come on, Goldner, really, what is it about her that's setting you on edge?"

"Well, unlike you," Robert said, "who just wants suckers to believe he's an angel, this Darden girl really does believe she's an angel. A true-to-life angel. Not like in the Bible or Qur'an, but in a modern-day scripture. Not an Old Testament or a New Testament but a *Now* Testament that she and her allies are composing by their actions, by the lives they live."

Darryl cocked his head. "She said that?"

"Not exactly that, but she didn't just call herself an angel. She used a key term: Arkangel. I've run across their kind before."

"When?" Darryl asked.

Robert squinted at him. "When you were busy elsewhere, partner. These so-called Arkangels, they're on a mission from Xyn. They think they're some kind of artists, like a lot of Infinite-Definite associates think of themselves, but these Arkangels are artists in the process of remaking themselves into something else, beyond artists, beyond angels. The lives they live are supposed to be like the poetic scripture or allegorical legends that'll be the basis of the next Creation. They're not using words for their compositions. They're using actions."

Darryl shrugged. "Okay. And?"

"So the idea of a *next* Creation implies that something will destroy *this* one," Robert said. "Something like The ID's Flood. These Arkangels just have to be allies of The ID, somehow."

While carrying out their duties for the IAI, Robert and many other Watcher agents had heard rumors of the Flood, a deluge that could consume the entire Earth, and even extend beyond it. Through dimensional leaks, XynKroma could seep into, rain on, and flood all levels of Reality. Heaven&Hell could relocate to exist far beyond subconscious minds—invading dreams, invading the conscious, invading what is known as "real life," the four-dimensional world and universe—forcing everyone and everything to live in XynKroma's anarchic muddle. It wouldn't be anything so banal as governments collapsing and roving citizens behaving like jungle creatures (as if that hadn't already been happening for the past decade). No—it would be a flash flood of unrestrained consciousness, giving reign to Xyn's senseless, incomprehensible laws of physics. All of space and time could be totally reconfigured. It would be as if a Meth-addicted Ovid were given a heavenly pen and hellish license to rewrite all of Creation into a hyperverse. The events described in the Roman poet's *Metamorphoses* would seem commonplace by comparison.

Robert once read a theory on the Internet explaining how the present universe came into existence fourteen billion years ago. The original universe had ten dimensions rather than four, but it was unstable. Thus, it broke down, resulting in a six-dimensional universe and a four-dimensional universe, the latter's rapid expansion causing the Big Bang, an explosion of matter that eventually resulted in the cosmos more or less known today. The six-dimensional universe shrunk down to a size smaller than an atom, and it may in some way account for teleportation, time travel, and the other fantastical weirdness experienced by particles at the quantum level.

Robert's math skills only took him so far. Not being a physicist, he didn't fully understand what he'd read (he later read there were maybe more than ten dimensions involved). He also didn't completely comprehend how the Flood would occur, but he was able to see the parallels between the scientific theory and actual happenings. Dimensional leaks from Xyn were a fact, and something was causing them. Over the past year, there'd been sightings of some leaks, most dubious, a few credible, but all of them reports of fantastical creatures, constructs, or settings that didn't belong on this planet, or even in this solar system. Maybe they were aberrations, maybe not. But if anyone could turn all of Reality into a horror-show, it was the practitioners of Dirty-Light Magick—The Infinite Definite.

One of the more talkative and articulate Infinite-Definite associates Robert had subdued four months ago volunteered to tell a bit about a goal he and his like-minded fellows all ultimately shared. "It's DNA strands taking on lives of their own," the terrorist had said, "literally becoming and acting just like satanic serpents. It's a magickal Eve plucking atoms and biting them, splitting them, trillions at a time." Robert knew these were just poor metaphors for universal chaos. That's what many and maybe all in The ID were fighting, playing, living, and killing for. It was only within the past hour Robert had begun to contemplate what an Arkangel's role in all of this might be.

"Did Ava say anything about a flood?" Darryl asked.

"No," Robert said, "but—"

"Mister Goldner," Adam said with slight note of impatience, "I am not following your logic."

Robert clenched his teeth. He wasn't exactly following it himself. He was trying to make an intuitive leap and hoped Adam would at least humor him, saying he'd at least consider what Robert had said. He tried again.

"These Arkangels could be using The ID as shock troops of some kind. Unwitting dupes. Useful idiots. And in the meantime, the so-called artistic actions taken by Arkangels on Reality's surface are somehow being translated in Xyn. What they're doing on the surface, in *this* plane of existence, is having a direct effect *there*, so that after the realm overwhelms us…" Robert lowered his head as his eyebrows knit together. He was stuck. He wasn't a learned art critic, or even a casual student of art; he didn't have the tools necessary to even guess the Arkangel-ID connection. "I...I don't know." He'd talked himself into a wall, but he just knew he'd been on right track.

"That doesn't make much sense," Darryl said.

"Of course it doesn't make sense, damn it, I'm talking about XynKroma!" He may've been up against a wall, but it was no obstacle to his frustration.

"Please calm down," Adam said. "You are overreacting."

He knew he was, and he felt he had a good reason. But out of respect, Robert took a deep breath and began again, this time getting at the root of his suspicion and interrupting Darryl, who'd begun to say something meaningless about artists.

"Let's look at this mathematically," Robert said, irritation still evident in his voice. "This Ava girl shows up in a place, out of nowhere, where we thought we'd find her friend, the sociopathic Virus-infected Marie-Lydia McGillis, who used every electromagnetic trick she could to try to kill everyone at her high school. Okay? Clearly something an ID terrorist would attempt, right? Ava stops her by taking her to XynKroma. They go there together. Now Ava shows up with a chunk of her memory missing, believing she and Marie-Lydia are real angels, truly supernatural beings, and she's anxious to be hooked up with Marie-Lydia again, her long-lost partner."

Neither Adam nor Darryl said a word or shifted his gaze from Robert as he paused for another deep breath.

"Add it up," he said. "This memory-loss stuff is not an accident. Her mind's been purposely screwed with. She's been electromagnetically hypnotized." Robert shot a glance at Darryl as he said it, but Darryl's face seemed to show he didn't get the reference—probably because Robert hadn't used the word "charity." "Ava's just waiting for a trigger," Robert continued, "something visual or verbal. The student interview notes say her friend Marie-Lydia was set off at the school by seeing a picture of Ava engaged in some sort of kinky sexual act with an older black woman."

"Really?" Darryl leaned closer. Yeah, Robert thought, now his interest was piqued. As usual, he focused on exactly the wrong things. If he focused on what was important, he would've had the student interview notes memorized by now.

"Once Ava's trigger is pulled," Robert said, "it'll set her off. She'll be complete. She'll become, I believe, a threat, a dangerous threat to everyone. Which is why I believe it's a bad idea to have her here. She's been trained to do something, and it's not going to be cute."

"Fine," Adam said.

Both Watchers stared at him. Only Robert, after shaking off the initial shock, managed to say anything. But he stuttered and made little sense as he tried to ask Adam a series of follow-up questions.

"My grand hope," Adam said, "is that whatever she is hiding, whatever she may think she is, we can rehabilitate her here and make her one of us. She has the potential to be a great Watcher agent, or a dangerous enemy. Either way, I want her close so we may keep an eye on her, and perhaps discover the hidden purpose of this…*artist,* as you put it."

Robert plunged into deeper thought, continuing to calculate all the relevant information he'd gathered, while Darryl spoke up.

"Sir, Goldner may be right to be worried. Really worried." The tone of his voice had changed. Robert and he were finally on the same wavelength. "It can take a while to rehabilitate someone. And unless we plan to lock her up—"

"That is not how we operate, Mister Ridley."

"But, sir, I—"

"I know the trigger," Robert said. "At least, I think I do. She believes she's a real angel, right? She emphasized that to me, and she never said one word about the White Fire Virus. If she knew about it before she got it, somehow those memories must've been blocked or erased. What happens when she finds out that there aren't any angels—fallen or otherwise—just a bunch of sick, parasite-ridden humans?"

"You may be on to something," Darryl said.

"Yeah, so our next step is obvious."

"We let her believe she is truly an angel," Adam said.

Robert was about to say they should lock Ava in The Burrow's physical training room, surrounded by seven or so Watcher agents, one of them telling her all the gruesome details about the Virus and another one showing her even more gruesome pictures of carriers in the final days of their lives; then let what happens happen. Robert couldn't believe what he was hearing from the chairman. This time, he didn't even attempt to speak. It was Darryl who asked the questions.

"But sir, why? I mean, how could we even pull that off? She's bound to find out about the Virus. It still pops up in the news, in spite of the propaganda campaign. It's only a matter of time before she picks up a newspaper, turns on a television, or starts surfing the net only to come across a story about it. She'll recognize the symptoms and effects of the Virus, and then…What if Goldner's right?"

Adam didn't answer immediately. He instead shifted in his chair to reach for the iron cane propped against the wall behind him.

"We will deal with it," Adam said as he stood. Robert and Darryl glanced at each other before rising to stand in front of their chairs. Both crossed their arms behind their backs as Adam continued. "That scenario, however, will not take place. Something you did not see in the files on her, Mister Goldner, is something that I neglected to record because I was not sure about it. At least, not until I got to view her up close.

"Miss Darden is a rare type of Virus-carrier. Most of those who get the Virus, and live, can manipulate the properties of light with their bodies and, beyond their control, may have their bodies manipulated by light's properties; a smaller number, like myself, are simply affected, manipulated by light when it makes contact with our skin; however, a tiny minority occupy the opposite category. They can manipulate light according to their will, but they are no more affected by it than a person who does not have the Virus. Miss Darden is in this category."

Robert wondered how he could figure all that just by looking at Ava. Had to be something about that helmet of his. What else could he see?

"The news reports fail to discuss this sort of Virus-carrier," Adam said, "because this type is known only to a miniscule number of specialist researchers. And these carriers are unlikely to call attention to themselves for two primary reasons: their numbers are small, and they do not experience the epileptic attacks, the periods of mental disorder and bouts of sickness the rest of us do. At least, not to the same extent. Hence, they may not need medication or the frequent medical attention. That is why I called Miss Goins in, to confirm or deny if that is the case with this one. If it is, then if and when Miss Darden learns about the Virus, I am sure we can persuade her to believe it is something carried only by those angels who hold a certain rank, a status lower than hers, lower than 'Arkangel.'"

Adam walked with difficulty toward the door of his main office. Both Robert and Darryl flinched with the urge to help the man, but neither took a step. They would hinder more than help. The iron cane alone was the best aid.

"So while I am asking you two to be kind to our guest, I am also asking you—as I will ask all of the Watchers, MatchMakers, and committee members first thing in the morning—to take more kindly to the term 'angel.' After all, as we continue to do our duty, and with more and more success, maybe that is how the world will begin to see us."

The door to the main office slid shut behind the chairman. There was nothing more he needed to say.

Robert walked The Burrow's dark corridors with a bad taste in his mouth. Beside him, Darryl spoke, but Robert didn't hear anything. He was caught up in a dilemma. For the first time, he didn't know whether he should fully trust Adam or follow his own instincts. Choosing either prospect scared him more than he was willing to admit.

Chapter 9

Darryl had heard the whispered words clearly: "Save the Children." He figured Adam and Robert had probably missed them; neither of them had said a word about it during the discussion last night. Ava had whispered the words when Adam mentioned his children, and Darryl had recognized the popular phrase at once. It was certainly popular in some sections of Northern Virginia, where Darryl had seen it spray-painted on walls, scrawled on sidewalks, and—he distinctly remembered—finger-written in the dust of a long unwashed van. It had stood out because it was so different from the slogans and statements one usually read in the area's graffiti, which were primarily the signatures of the region's ever-multiplying street gangs.

Darryl had gotten up at dawn and spent most of his Sunday morning taking note of each location where he remembered seeing the three-word commandment. He hadn't bothered to alert Robert to what he was doing. Or Adam. He wasn't sure he had anything significant, and he didn't want to waste their time with hunches, or waste his own good reputation on a lump of nonsense. Nor did he care to waste his entire morning fishing in an empty pond. He had a very important date, and didn't wish to be late.

After triple-checking his list, making sure he'd noted every location he could remember, Darryl returned to The Burrow. Board member Vince Ceniza greeted him ecstatically after inviting him into his office.

"I've completed a summary of my research based on your most recent trip to XynKroma," Vince said. "Would you like to review and discuss?"

"Maybe later." Darryl waved away the offer to take a seat. "Right now, I was hoping you could review and summarize something I'm researching."

"Oh?" Vince sat on the chair he'd offered to Darryl. "What's the subject?"

"Maybe nothing. Maybe a few things."

"Have anything to do with the girl you and Robert brought in yesterday?" Vince asked.

"Maybe. Last night, when we met with Adam, she gave us a clue about where she might've been before we found her."

Darryl explained his hunch. Vince only shrugged after hearing it.

"It's not unusual for someone to inadvertently repeat a phrase they've seen written in a few places," he said.

"Yeah, it's a psychological thing," Darryl said. "That's why I came to you. I want to know why *she* repeated it. Because she saw it once, and only once, and it held special meaning to her? Because she's seen it a few times and couldn't get it out of her head? Because she had something to do with writing it? The phrase is only written in a few places, that I could find. If she visited those places frequently, even one of them, maybe we can trace and figure out her previous place of residence and her previous activities."

Vince nodded. "You want me to compile and translate this information."

"Yes," Darryl said. "I need a map connecting all the locations and giving as much info about each one as possible, including previous ID terrorist sightings."

Vince Ceniza's official title was "psychologist," but insiders knew him as the Institution's "psychological mapmaker." He spent much of his time sending willing travelers into XynKroma and recording their experiences in detail after they emerged. It was probably impossible to make a coherent map of such a chaotic realm, but Vince firmly believed that patterns could be discovered, that some sense *could* be made of the realm. And he thought a truly skilled traveler just might be able to effect some permanent change, some stability among all the chaos. But he didn't focus all his talents on mapping Xyn. On Reality's surface, he was able to take bits and pieces of dissimilar ideas and hard facts, and then, like a seventeenth-century metaphysical poet, he could combine things that no normal mind would ever connect in order to reach a brilliant conclusion. He was Darryl's favorite board member. The two of them could talk for hours when Darryl wasn't busy.

"I'll see what I can do," Vince said. "In the meantime, I'd really like to discuss my report of your last trip to Xyn with you. Understanding it could have serious consequences. During your next trip there, you're *very* likely to become susceptible to—"

"I'm sorry," Darryl said as he started toward the door, "but we'll have to talk about it later. I've got to hurry and catch Zel."

Darryl thanked Vince again as he left his office. He greeted Zel just as rapidly after being invited into the toymaker's workshop.

"Coming from Vince?" Zel asked.

"Yeah."

"Had a nice long chat?"

"Long enough," Darryl said. "I'm short on time."

"What's up?"

"I need to speak to you about my corresq." Darryl handed him the silver toy.

"Something wrong with it?"

"Not necessarily," Darryl said, "but any chance you've made an improved version?"

"Haven't," Zel said, "but could. Any suggestions?"

"It's a little too rigid. Is there any way you could make one that I could, say, adapt to any situation at hand?"

"You mean create one made of a pliable metallic substance? Something that can be changed into different shapes?"

"Yeah, a softer metal," Darryl said, "like the key-tool you made for me. I get a little tired of having to work with a circle all of the time."

Zel laughed. "That's interesting. Most people tend to think of Robert as a real square."

Darryl didn't get the joke. "I have other thoughts about him," he said as his attention turned toward the laser instruments hanging on a nearby wall. "But they're not worth discussing now."

"You know, before I get started on this," Zel said, "have you considered maybe there's nothing wrong with the corresq? You can already make it suit any and every need that might arise—but maybe whatever faults you see in it are, possibly, attributable directly to you?"

"I'm sorry?" Darryl turned his gaze back to the engineer.

"'I'm sorry,'" Zel repeated. "A common phrase spoken by those who lack confidence."

"I don't lack anything but reliable assistance."

"And I've heard your assistant say the same thing."

"The corresq talks?"

"I'm talking about Robert."

Darryl wanted to shout, but he looked at the floor and took a long breath before responding. "Mister Bernard, he's not something I want to talk about right now."

"Diverting your attention, lack of concentration," Zel said. "Another telltale sign of what your real problem may be."

"I'm not diverting anything. You're the one who keeps bringing my partner up. I just want to know if I can get a new and improved corresq, and how soon."

"I'll work on it, but it won't be a total solution. Among others, at the very least, will you please make an appointment to see the Institution's physical trainers? Go through a thorough workout and assessment?"

"I'll think about it," Darryl said. "Right now, I'm running late for another appointment."

∞   ∞   ∞

Darryl had stopped running an hour ago, just making it. Now seated, he nevertheless felt as if he were on an inclined treadmill, one that sped up with each step.

He was enraptured in her voice, her words. Sin Limite seemed to be literally moving him—until the final tug and shove of the song's last few words.

Darryl had only one comment after the music ended and she took her bow.

"That was pretty creepy."

Vanessa Blake smiled at him from across the table. "Well, their lyrics aren't for the faint of heart. Or the feeble of mind."

"And you've written how many songs for them?" he asked.

"Only a few," she said. "And only when they've asked. Usually I just try to point The Phantasie in the right direction for their inspiration."

"Like *The Blackbook of Autumn Numbers*?"

"It's as good a source for quality lyrics as any."

Darryl took another sip of his orange juice and turned back toward the stage where the same group was performing from the same playbook as when he and the blonde had first met. He noted the coincidence shortly after he entered the dawnclub and joined Veronica at the table she'd reserved. She told him it wasn't a co-incidence. She'd asked him to meet her at this particular lounge because Phantasie's rEVEnge—a group she happened to manage and promote—would be performing. She had to be here. And they were in luck because the lounge's food happened to have an excellent reputation. Darryl nevertheless had opted only for fresh fruit, unbuttered toast, and pulp-free juice. He wasn't in the mood for anything that would weigh heavily on his stomach. Too much was already weighing heavily on his mind.

It seemed nothing could weigh Veronica down. She was al-ready on her second stack of mixed-fruit-topped pancakes and her third cup of green tea. Darryl had initially insisted on paying for the entire meal, but he was half-glad she demurred, insisting they split the check instead. He'd pay for his food, and she'd pay for her own. It was just as well. Coherent fractions seemed to make more sense to Darryl now than deceptive wholes.

For most of the morning, his thoughts had been running through a multitude of subjects, concerning the past, present, and future, all at once: maybe he really was shirking his responsibili-ties with the IAI; Veronica would have to be fixed, set on the bright path, and soon; the performers on stage were really unique and in-teresting, like nothing he'd ever seen before. His head had begun to hurt. Darryl was thankful at least the music had been pleasant.

Then two new singers began a new song.

Their convoluted lyrics had not been adapted from *The Black-book*. When the music started, and before the singers began, Veronica leaned over to whisper it was a new song she'd just writ-ten for them. The duo on stage would be portraying an angry husband accusing his wife of being too energetic and loving with others, and an unhappy wife accusing her husband of being every-thing he shouldn't be with her. The two threw pointed lines at each other, singing them in such a way that their voices and the lyrics flowed seamlessly while the two gestured and moved around the stage, seeming to fight and dance simultaneously without even touching each other. They sang on for six minutes, their lyrics increasing in complexity until the end.

"I loved that," Darryl said, applauding as the singers bowed. He didn't necessarily understand it all, but he'd been entertained. "They're good."

"Harold and Harmony," Veronica said. "They were performing as a duo called 'Red Redemption' before I recruited them for The Phantasie."

"The woman—Harmony, I presume—is particularly good."

"Good woman, and great women," Veronica said. "The first noted for what she does for man in the present, the second remembered for what they didn't do to men back then."

Darryl almost choked on his toast as he turned to look at her. He recognized the words immediately. It was a quote, lifted and recited, almost intact, from the Yellow section of his favorite book, the book of his life.

As he continued to hack, trying to get the crumbs out of his windpipe, Veronica took a casual sip of her tea, looking at him over her teacup with a bright and rheumy blue eye. She picked up a raspberry from her plate, smiled, and said, "Yes—I've read it," before sticking out her tongue and placing the raspberry on the tip of it.

"You've read *Death's Heart?*" Darryl finally managed to say after swallowing some orange juice.

She nodded. "All of it. In fact, I acquired a very good copy some time ago, but it's been a while since I've leafed through it. After I left you yesterday afternoon, I dusted it off, just to refresh my scary memory on a few bits and pieces."

Darryl conceded her memory was "scary." The word could also be used to describe her intellect, its ability to make leaps. On Saturday, he'd only quoted from *Death's Heart* three times, and he'd only made an indirect reference to the book's title. One day later, she was quoting from it. As he'd suspected, Veronica was different. She was different from all those who'd come before.

"I only wanted to begin solving the mystery of Mister Ridley," she said.

Darryl had been staring at her with questioning eyes, and an open mouth, while the aches in his head seemed to increase their pressure. He was discomforted, but he couldn't continue to show it—displays of uncertainty were signs of moral weakness—so his lips gradually drew together until they'd formed a smile.

"A mystery solver, huh?" he said. "Sure you're not following a red herring?"

She smiled back. "I'm no amateur, honey. And men aren't that complex. Honestly, I think I'm getting close to the end of you."

"Is that so?" he asked after swallowing another mouthful of juice.

"Or perhaps," she said, "to the end of what you think you're trying to become."

Darryl gave her a quizzical look. Veronica smiled again. With only one eye exposed to view, in a dimly lit lounge, Darryl thought her smiles were looking more unsettling than they probably should've been. Was it her, or was it him?

"And what's at the end?" Darryl asked.

"A beautiful creation, of course."

"Oh, why, thank you."

"I didn't mean you," Veronica said. "You, Mister Ridley, seem determined to remain incomplete, unfinished, unresolved."

"Excuse me?"

"You're incomplete," she repeated. "Basing your life off of half-formed ideas and pieces of philosophies, each of which may appear beautiful individually—but when taken together as a whole?" Veronica shook her head. "We've got to fix that." She took another sip of her tea.

What was that? He got the reference to his comments in the sculpture garden on Saturday, but what was she really saying? Was she insulting him, or was that supposed to be playful banter? The throbbing in Darryl's temples made it hard for him to tell which. He decided it'd be best to just brush it off, keep cool. Starting an argument wouldn't stop his headache.

"Are you suggesting I re-create myself?" Darryl asked. "Take on a new personality maybe, or a different lifestyle?"

"I'm suggesting the one you have now isn't working," she said. "You're only jerking yourself in circles."

Darryl laughed, but not out of amusement.

"You can continue to just make yourself feel better," she said, "or you can make an effort to help heal the world."

When they met, Darryl didn't tell her exactly what he did; he only said he was a social worker for the homeless. She hadn't asked for details, and Darryl had thought it odd. In the DC-area, the first thing folks almost always wanted to know after meeting was what the other did for a living, and the second thing was where, and there were usually several related follow-up questions. Veronica hadn't pursued it, so Darryl thought it doubly strange she suddenly pretended to know all about him, even if she was speaking vaguely. He'd met pretentious artists before, but she was breaking the mold.

"You may not believe it," he said, "but that's just what I've been trying to do."

"I believe you believe you've been doing some good," she said. "But I also believe you're half-blind."

Darryl looked at the blonde tresses covering her right eye. She had to be kidding him.

"You're blind to your own potential," Veronica said. "I've seen it. And it's huge."

Darryl smiled at a thought that popped into his head. "Is 'palm reader' also on your list of talents?"

She smiled back at him, another one of her discomforting smiles, but said nothing.

"And have you realized your potential, Miss Blake?" Darryl asked.

"Yes," she said, "I'm an artist. Ever curious, but sure of The End: a peaceful beautiful world, a perfect existence. As an artist, I'm living and working for a time and a place that has no time and no place for artists."

The mold of pretention, broken.

"Artists don't live to entertain," she said. "They only exist to remind the world of imperfection. At The End, there's no need for art, there's no urge to imagine something different, there's no desire to change or alter anything. In spite of what all these neo-nihilists and the faux-anarchists and the pseudo-rebellious say they believe in, they and we all want the same end: the place-time after the Greatest Artist has sung-spoken-painted-written The Word, producing the Greatest Work of Art."

That was a mouthful. Darryl didn't quite get what she was saying, but he thought he found it a little interesting. Maybe. His thoughts had become more and more agitated as she was speaking; he assumed that effect had to mean something. He wanted to ask for clarification, but the pangs in his head…He tried to ignore them, play it off.

Darryl pushed his plate aside, clasped his hands on the table, and leaned toward her. "You artists love to use those pretty words," he said with a smile. "Talking in tangles, but strangling all meaning."

"Look who's talking," she said as she copied his actions and leaned closer to him. "I can tell, quite clearly, that you, Mister Ridley, have been living a pretty-pretty perverse life in the name of an artful little book you really don't understand."

Darryl stopped smiling. "Excuse me, Miss Blake, but I've read that colorful little book, from cover to cover, well over a dozen times. I understand its message more than anyone. Maybe you just don't know what you're talking about."

He tried to hide any signs of the anger that seemed to be contributing to the fizzing sensation in his brain's frontal lobe, but he couldn't help but coat his words with venom.

Veronica furrowed her brow and inverted her smile as she opened her mouth, no doubt ready to spit a response dipped in acid. She was on the verge of losing her playful cool. But she swallowed it all back when their waiter passed and placed the check on the table.

Neither Veronica nor Darryl spoke as they retrieved their debit cards and, at the same time, threw them on the table. After the waiter made another pass-by, Veronica broke the silence.

"You know, you're right. Words are meaningless in this day and age. Misunderstandings stand over words, buried."

Darryl thought he recognized her last sentence as a quote from something. A misquote maybe. But he couldn't remember. All he could do was rub his temples with his fingers.

"You know," he said, "you're really making my head hurt, V."

"Am I now? I'm really, really sorry." She seemed genuine. "I didn't mean to talk so much about nothing, but I thought you were the philosophical type. I just wanted to engage you on your level. Talk mind-to-mind, heart-to-heart. How about we go for a walk to try to clear things up?"

"I—" The *fizzing* sensation had become stronger; it seemed to be expanding to other regions of Darryl's brain. Where the hell had it come from? "I don't know. I've really got a lot to do today."

"Now, D., can any of it be more important than taking a stroll down what you may one day remember as lover's lane?"

Lover. The tragic word. Attempting to ignore his headache, Darryl removed his hands from his head and smiled at her. "Is that your way of coming on to me? I'd expect that type of language from a sad, cheesy-rat male, not a smart and savvy female."

"Oh," Veronica said as she signed her receipt, "I promise you're not going to be expecting what comes next."

"I'm not a kid," Darryl said. "I'm sure I can guess."

She responded with a wink then said, "Excuse me for one moment. I want to let the band know I'm going out for a stroll." Veronica rose from her seat and glided her body around the other chairs and tables as she made her way to a door leading backstage. Darryl remained at the table, staring at the flickering flame of the candle at its center. He massaged his temples with one hand and picked up the candle's lighter with the other while all his conscious thoughts tried to focus on the reasons behind one clawing headache.

*Misunderstandings stand over words, buried...*Where had he heard that before? *Had* he heard it before? Regardless, what did it mean? And why did his brain feel like it was shrinking while sprouting multiple birds' talons, talons that picked and scratched at the inside of his skull? Why—?

"Ready?"

Darryl started and almost fell out of his seat. He hadn't seen or heard Veronica approach; she seemed to have appeared from the other side of nowhere, materializing by his side the moment she asked her question.

"Yeah." He tried to keep his equilibrium in check as he got up from his chair. He massaged his temples once more as they approached the exit.

A construction sight dominated their first view outside. Most of the area was still in development, at a stage where the HSA hadn't even set up surveillance cameras yet. Just outside of Old Town Alexandria, it was an area slowly moving toward completion; the economy was its primary obstacle. Like all such works-in-progress, the display of creation showed much more evidence of destruction. The area's construction projects had led to an increased production of garbage, which in turn had led to overflowing dumpsters and overstuffed sidewalk garbage cans. The excess spilled onto the ground only to be kicked or blown farther away by the winds. Adjacent to the littered sidewalks were some brand-new stores and some empty shops with "Opening Soon!" signs in the windows; some had "Retail Space for Lease" signs, while others were just black, providing no reflections, no views, and no hint of their future use. Among the open and operating places in the area were a movie theater, a federal courthouse, some other nondescript buildings housing various government offices, and a yellow line Metro station. There were also assorted restaurants and other eating spots, most nearly empty at any given time. There was really no reason to be in the area on the weekend, unless one was coming to catch a movie or grab a bite. There was nothing else to do but walk, peacefully.

Their brunch date had been an early one. Darryl and Veronica had met at the lounge at nine o'clock. When they left, it was more than half past ten, and much more humid than it had been earlier. Darryl had dressed smartly and had taken the proper dosage of his medication on schedule; he was nevertheless even more uncomfortable outside than in.

In another state of mind, he might've had something to say about the near total lack of cars as he and Veronica walked halfway around the construction project's circular fence, its posted sign proclaiming it the future site of John Carlyle Square. He might've had more detailed and interesting responses to Veronica's remarks about the sign's descriptions of the walkways, the lawn area, the trees, the plants, and the decorative fountain that would all be a part of the completed Square. If he had been himself, Darryl might've suggested a different route for their stroll, maybe the one that would take them toward the Metro station.

But he allowed Veronica to lead him by the hand, down the avenue across Holland Lane, and into the African American Heritage Park. They walked down the long, wide steps onto a gravelly path. Darryl's body was there, but he was looking inward, not fully noticing that, as they followed the pathway, to his left, just across the narrow waterway of Hooff's Run, there were more than a hundred carefully arranged tombstones. Veronica breathed something about "sassy symbolism" and whistled a dreadfully familiar tune, but Darryl paid it little mind.

His scattered thoughts—of conflicted faith and neglected duties, of championed philosophies and limp poetics—only began to draw back together as a tightening cluster of trees darkened the path they walked. At the middle of the wooden footbridge, an area almost completely shielded from sunlight, Darryl saw carvings that had been made by a knife and traced with ink for greater visual effect: "Save the Children." His headache went nowhere, but the sight of the Arkangel's whispered words made Darryl refocus on the here-and-now. He stopped walking, forcing Veronica to do the same. She didn't stop whistling however. She didn't even turn to look at him. Her nose, eyes, and chin were pointed upward. Veronica seemed preoccupied with something nesting in or resting on the branches above them—but Darryl was in no mood to birdwatch. He tried to draw her attention to him.

"Okay, V. Let's talk straight. You were saying something about art, and The End."

"Hmm?" Veronica lazily turned her head.

"At the club. What were you saying?"

The quiet time during the walk had done Darryl some good, despite the headache. Veronica's words, her very strange words about art and The End, couldn't help but remind Darryl of the most recent discussion with Adam and Robert. Veronica was so different from everyone he'd ever met. What insights did she have? What did she really know?

"Oh, yes," she said with an exhalation that sounded like the beginning of a giggle, "all of that. Sorry. But sometimes I play things checkered, just to hear how they'll sound."

Maybe she was too different. While staying the same in appearance, Veronica's language, throughout their date, made it seem as if she were phase-shifting though different personalities. Was she high on something?

"What are you talking about?" Darryl asked.

"That phrase, my love, is a direct quote from the nymphomaniacal Kaprice. The female character, the primary character, of the Indigo section of *Death's Heart*."

"Indigo section?" Darryl dropped her hand. "There's *no* such part. The book has five sections. Red, Orange, Yellow, Green, and *Blue*."

"Your copy does," she said. "Mine has Indigo. An apocryphal chapter. It's where I lifted the lyrics for Harold and Harmony's song."

Darryl had no words. His mouth and throat were dry. His headache sprawled, scratching-clawing-*pinching* on all sides of his skull.

"But," Veronica said, "to misquote a once-popular, now-forgotten singer, 'How can you tell what words are for if no one anymore listens?'" She smiled and turned her back to him.

Darryl hesitated before following her off the footbridge.

As they began up a long, curving set of steps, his thoughts were a scribble. He was having a hard time reconciling the idea that the very book on which he'd based his beliefs and actions for the last couple of years was incomplete. It just couldn't be true. He had many questions beyond the most obvious one, but he kept silent.

The couple stepped onto a sidewalk bordering a section of Holland Lane a block away from where they'd entered the park. Veronica maintained a pace of three steps in front of him. The trees to the left of them provided a good strip of shade, but as far as Darryl was concerned, they could've been walking on lava. He couldn't stay silent any longer.

"Veronica. I have to see this book. I need to read it, study it."

Veronica laughed. "I have a more creative idea." She stopped and turned to look in his eyes. "My girlfriend and I have decided you should rewrite it—with your life."

Before Darryl realized someone had been following them, that someone grabbed both of his wrists and pulled, binding his hands behind his back. Veronica raised her hand and pulled back her tresses, revealing a nonblue eye.

"We *will* solve you, Darryl Ridley."

Darryl heard Veronica's mellifluous voice speaking, almost singing these words as a scratchier voice behind him said, "Don't blink." A cracked second later, his sight and thoughts were taken by a bright rush of raspberry-blonde light.

Chapter 10

Robert thought the discussion had been fascinating and instructive. Once again, the reverend had come through for him.

Whenever Robert called his former pastor with a question on a religious topic, the reverend was always able to give a detailed response right off the top of his head. Ava's comment last night about Watchers and scriptures prompted him to make the call first thing in the morning. Robert felt lucky to have the opportunity to speak with the reverend just before Sunday services, and he was happy to receive such a generous amount of information. Robert now knew what he needed to about the Watchers and the Book of Enoch, the Sons of God, the Daughters of Men, giants, fallen angels, and fair games—all the details of the little-known and seldom-read scriptural story detailing the events before the biblical flood in the days of Noah.

Robert had learned that even though the Book of Enoch was referenced in the Bible's New Testament, it was not a part of the canonical Bible. It was an apocryphal text, considered authoritative only by a small segment of Christians. The reverend told him the book portrays the biblical flood as being a result of mischievous angels who left Heaven and came to Earth primarily to mate with human women, the *fair* Daughters of Men. The beginning of a new sin, these rogue unions produced unnatural offspring that overran the Earth, devouring all the food of humankind, before starting on the flesh of humankind. So God sent a flood. The Supreme Being pushed a reset button on its own Creation.

Robert knew another flood could very well be coming. A deluge of cold fire and hot ice, unrestrained light and untrained thoughts, it too would be the result of tainted "angels." If the terrorists of The Infinite Definite had their way, a Flood of Xyn would warp all of Reality beyond anything Robert could imagine. Alienated young adults, pushing for universal chaos—it almost made sense.

The Arkangels Robert had encountered—including Ava—weren't like The ID. There was the "Arkangel Katrisha" who almost a year ago, on an overcast morning in November, had appeared out of nowhere to help save his butt. Robert was jogging in the woods and had somehow managed to trot right through an area where members of the MS-13 street gang were having a powwow. He'd been running for an hour and was by that time exhausted enough to allow himself to get surrounded by a dozen gangbangers. Robert held his own for a few minutes, but just as his luck was about to run out, the Arkangel jumped in to help even the odds. He'd learned a few days later that her real name was Kate Gyllenhoff, but when she was kicking ass on his behalf, he was more than happy to acknowledge her as any type of angel she wished.

Even when he'd treated her to a "thank-you" cup of coffee, he'd taken her at her word as she told him plenty about the Arkangels. And he'd confirmed it all a few months later, earlier this year, when he'd met the "Arkangel Jessica" and the "Arkangel David-Jo."

They'd surprised him while he was on a treasure hunt in the Eastern Market section of DC. Once they realized they'd no cause to fight each other (and Robert had found the hunt to be a dead end), they had a nice chat. He never figured out their real names, but he did get an idea of what the Arkangels were all about, all of which he'd tried to tell Adam and Darryl last night. No, they weren't *like* The Infinite Definite, but there just had to be some kind of connection. Robert had been dwelling on what it could be from the moment he ended his phone conversation with the reverend to the moment he arrived at The Burrow.

"You owe me an apology, Robert Goldner."

Ava was the first thing he saw when the elevator's door slid open. The angry angel had been waiting for him, possibly for some time. Robert noticed the clenched hands and the diamond pendant right away; then he saw that the whites of her eyes weren't all white. He wondered if she'd been crying, or if she'd been fighting hard not to. The intrusion of tiny off-red vessels to the surface of her eyes gave the once-white areas a fuchsia appearance, vividly contrasting with the irises that had switched from the gem-blue of last night to a grass-stained muddy brown. Robert looked at the color-clashing oddities, blinked twice, and looked away.

"I don't owe anybody anything," he said with a sniff as he stepped around her.

"You owe me an apology," Ava said as she followed. "And an explanation."

"Funny," Robert said, "I was thinking of maybe tossing that statement at you."

"Listen, whatever you suspect me of being, or doing, why not have the guts to say it to my face? One-on-one, like an adult. Like an honest person. You don't like me? Then let's have it out right now."

Robert stopped and ran his eye over her.

"I neither like nor dislike you," he said. "I don't know you. But judging from what I've seen and what I've heard, balancing it with my experience—"

"You don't trust me," she said. "Okay, then, what better way to tell if I'm lying, about anything, to find what I'm holding back, than to come into my mind? Let's go to XynKroma."

"That's just it, Arkangel. I don't trust your mind. I don't know where it's been."

The more he spoke, the weirder her eyes appeared. She was undoubtedly seconds away from taking a swing at him.

"I'll be honest with you, Ava, but you better be honest with yourself. If you're telling the full truth about not having any memory of the past year and a half, then you should be worried. Worried about all the road trips and pit stops you've made during that time."

"I see," she said. "You don't trust my motives, what may be living and lurking inside the nooks and crannies of my cranium, and you're too scared to look."

Crannies, cranium, nooks, look, living, and lurking—Robert immediately recognized the strange phrasing of the statement. With the almost excessive rhyming and alliteration, it certainly would've been strange to hear coming out of the mouths of most people. But Robert knew that many of those associated with The ID were involuntary poets, and pretty bad ones at that. Did Ava intend to say what she'd said the way she'd said it? He wouldn't ask, but he'd keep the question in mind.

"If you were honest with yourself," he said, "and with the rest of us, you'd come out and admit that you're scared and that you don't trust your state of mind, either."

"Do you trust yourself?" she asked. "Your mind?"

"I—"

"I didn't think so."

"I didn't finish speaking."

"You didn't need to. 'Yes' should've been your only response. Anything less is just as good as a negative answer."

Robert had an answer all right. More than one. The honest one wasn't the one he was ready to share.

"Prove to yourself you're as trustworthy as your surname implies," Ava said. "Prove to yourself, and me, that you're serious about finding Marie-Lydia. Let's go to XynKroma. Now."

No. He'd never go back. Not voluntarily. Anything he needed or wanted to learn about his family or anything else he would learn by his own research on Reality's surface. He turned his back on the huffing girl.

"I don't think so," Robert said as he walked away.

"It was the last place I saw her," Ava said as she followed him. "You think I'm the key to finding her? Then come with me. Unless you don't care and just want to get on with the next thing."

Robert slowed but didn't stop. The analogy was there, and very clear, even if it was unintentional on her part. In spite of his true feelings for his partner, Robert would be damned if he let anyone compare him to Darryl.

"Please, Robert."

The tone of her voice had moved away from indignation by just a hair. Robert noticed the shift and looked at her again.

"I have nowhere else to go," she said, "no other idea of what to do. Please help me."

He detected a note of fear, if not just desperation, in her voice and demeanor. Whether it was an act or not, whether she was a sleeper agent of The ID or not, Robert figured maybe the best way to find out the truth on her, and maybe even the best hope of finding Marie-Lydia, was to keep Ava close at hand. Maybe Adam had a point.

"Okay, Arkangel." Robert gestured for her to follow him. "Let's you and I go see the doctor."

∞   ∞   ∞

"We won't talk any more about trust," Robert said. "From now on, you can read it in my actions."

"That's what I've been doing," Ava said. "The story's been a sad and stupid one so far."

Charming, Robert thought.

"That was only a first draft," he said. "We'll start over right now."

After opening the door, in an overexaggerated imitation of a stereotypical gentleman, Robert bowed and waved his arm, signaling without saying "Ladies first." Ava sneered at the gesture but passed by him into the office.

"Hello, Ava," Sam said. "Robert. What can I do for you two?"

"You can tell us, openly and honestly, what your reading is on Ava."

"What do you mean?" Sam asked. Ava looked at Robert with an expression that asked the same question.

"You gave her a thorough examination, right?"

"Yes."

"Well, Ava is going to be working with us—me especially—to find Marie-Lydia McGillis. If I'm going to be working closely with her, I'd like you to tell us both what you've discovered about her. Don't hold anything back. I don't want her to think I came to you behind her back to get the dirt on her."

Sam gave Ava a look, an unspoken request for permission. After some hesitation, Ava gave it to her with a nod.

"Well, first off," Sam said, "as Ava and I discussed last night, there's a problem with how she sees things."

"No kidding."

"Robert, please," Sam said.

"Sorry," he said. "Please go on."

"She views the world, everything she sees, in a pale red tint."

"What do you mean?" he asked.

"To her, it's as if the world has been rinsed with red and white." Sam stopped talking, but Robert gave her a funny look, prompting her to go on. "In other words, it's as if every light bulb inside every building she enters is pink, and the sun's light is scattered on the planet in a very different way than it is for the rest of us."

"Really?" He turned toward Ava with new interest.

"Think of the sky," Sam said. "It only appears blue, most of the time, because the longer wavelengths of the sun's light in the red, orange, yellow, and green sections of the spectrum are far less likely to be scattered by air molecules than blue light. But to her eyes, wherever she looks, light in the red range is scattered. What she's seeing is not a deep, pure red, but more like a diluted or bleached version of the color."

"So diluted that I really didn't notice it until last night," Ava said, "when you gave me that exam. But I suppose it's been like this since I woke up in the hospital. I know for sure it wasn't like this before, even when I was inverted, reborn as an Arkangel."

"So your eyesight's been like this either since we found you," Robert said, "or since you and Marie-Lydia went to XynKroma together?"

"Yes."

"No matter how it happened," Sam said, "we can correct it. Or, more precisely, Zel can. I've already spoken with him, and he's in the process of making some lenses that should do the trick. When he's finished, he'll let you know, and you can get fitted for some glasses."

"What else did you find?" Robert asked.

"Well, she's in exceptionally good shape. And the speed at which she's recovered from most of her injuries has been incredible."

"How bad were they?"

"No broken or bruised bones," Sam said. "Only scratches and cuts, and some strange bite marks. But none of the wounds are open any longer. No need for any bandages, or even Band-Aids."

"That's it?"

"Isn't that enough, Robert?"

"But I mean, no damage to her head? No concussion? Nothing's wrong with her heart or other organs?"

"Not as far as I can tell," Sam said. "I ran every test I could last night with the equipment I have. Of course, I did some blood work and took a urine sample, and I'll need to review the results of those. But for now, as far as I'm concerned, aside from her memory-loss, her eyesight issues, and some bruises and probably a few tender spots, she's fine."

"Really?"

"As fine as an *angel* can be, Robert."

"Oh. Yeah. Got it."

"I'm just as surprised as you are," Ava said to him.

"Doubt it." Robert cleared his throat and raised his voice to thank Sam.

"Yes, thank you Miss Goins," Ava said as she followed Robert back out into hall.

He'd wanted to show her he was willing to trust her, but he didn't want to show her he was naïve. Even though it was unavoidable she'd see more of The Burrow than he thought it smart to allow, Robert wouldn't be the one to give her a guided tour of the place. And he didn't want to leave her to wander around and discover things on her own. Not yet. He wanted to try to discover something about her first.

"Let's go get some fresh air." He smiled at her. She didn't return the expression of mock friendliness, but Ava walked next to him as he headed toward the elevator.

"What was that crack about doubting?" she asked as they waited for the cab to descend. "Doubting my surprise that I'm not worse off than Sam says I am?"

"Nothing."

Ava looked at him. Robert knew she was trying to draw his eye to hers. He wasn't going for it. She couldn't make him nervous. Not someone of his mettle. But the effect of her stare, the effect of just knowing she was staring at him, made the side of his face feel tingly, and increasingly cold.

Finally he said, "It's just that most angels tend to be in pretty bad shape."

"Why?" Ava asked.

He sighed. "Seems like we're all in a never-ending battle with ourselves."

Ava turned away from him. Maybe not a satisfactory answer, but his face felt warm again. Had it just been his imagination, or was something going on with those freaky eyes of hers, something Sam hadn't told him about?

Neither of them spoke until the elevator's door opened. Robert nodded and waved, again the gentleman, allowing her to enter the cab first.

"If I didn't know better," Ava said, "I'd think you didn't want to turn your back on me."

"I'm sure you know better," he said.

As the elevator cab began its ascent, Robert thought it a good idea to clue Ava in on something before they entered the company of others.

"By the way," he said, "most of the general public doesn't know that *angels* are among them. The things we can do, the facts of our condition. A lot of time, effort, and energy have been put into a massive propaganda campaign by the HSA to convince people that when they see us performing spontaneous light-shows or something, they're really just witnessing the performance of some kind of amateurish magic tricks."

"Magic tricks?" Ava looked disgusted. "And people actually believe that?"

"Yeah. It's shocking what people will buy into. Must be something in the water."

"Why?" she asked. "Why is the government doing this?"

Robert chuckled. "Do you really think the country, the world could handle knowing that angels are living and breathing next to them?"

"They're going to have to face up to it sooner or later."

"Yeah," he said. "A lot of us are going to have to face up to all sorts of surprises sooner or later. But for right now, we have to be careful about how we conduct ourselves in public. There are other stories floating around out there about our kind, in the news and elsewhere. Scary and dangerous stories. The HSA's propaganda has been trying to counter some of them and keep the populace relatively calm."

"Calm? In the world we're living in?"

"Sometimes it's wiser not to let too many see too clearly," Robert said. "True magicians never reveal their secrets, and—"

"Neither do angels."

"That's the spirit." And that settled it in Robert's mind. It wasn't simple amnesia. Since she was such a rare type of Virus-carrier, he could almost buy that she never considered herself as having the White Fire Virus, even if she'd heard about it before she'd contracted it. But the propaganda campaign was another matter. Even if she didn't know the HSA was behind it, had she not heard the stories of *magic?* The propaganda campaign had been in effect for several years, far outside the block missing from Ava's memory. No, the stories weren't rampant; they never dominated the news. And, yes, her hometown was a rural one; maybe she never paid much attention to the mainstream media down there. But it didn't add up for Robert. He was convinced she'd been programmed. The next step was to find out for what purpose.

The elevator's door opened onto darkness. Ava nodded and waved, allowing Robert to go first this time. He smiled, and went. The elevator to the parking garage would only come when its sensors detected the cab was empty. The wait could be anywhere from two to twenty minutes. Today, they were lucky.

"Okay, so you know about my eyes," Ava said as they entered the cab. "Since turnabout is fair play, why don't you tell me about yours?"

"Are you referring to my eye patch?" he asked.

"I'm referring to the lack of mirrors in your apartment," she said.

"Let's just say I'm allergic to them."

"Let's say more, shall we?"

Robert took a deep breath and shook his head, deciding it wouldn't hurt to give out just a little. "If I look into a mirror dead on," he said, "it's like staring directly into the sun and being lifted, transported, to travel straight to its center. Angel or not, I'd rather just sit out that whole experience."

"You're able to watch everything but yourself, huh?" Ava said.

"I guess."

"Then I guess, as your partner, half of my duty will be for me to watch you."

"Excuse me?" Robert was not shy about looking into her eyes now, at their crazy colors and all. "Who said anything about partners?"

"That's what you said to Sam."

"I did *not* say that."

"You implied it," Ava said. "Whether the words are explicit or implicit, good angels don't lie when they speak."

The elevator door opened, and three people from the parking garage entered. While they were in the cab, Robert could only grimace and grind his teeth. He certainly couldn't say what he wanted to in front of strangers. But he shifted his position so he could look at Ava, furrowing his brow, hoping she'd hear his unspoken words. She only met his glare with a blank stare, as if she was oblivious to his expression and had no knowledge of what they'd just been talking about. It was almost like holding his breath. Only when the door opened and everyone left the cab, three turning to head toward the shopping center and two walking straight toward the parked cars, only then did Robert feel like he could exhale.

"Listen," he said as he led her toward his car, "I said that you'd be working with us as a witness, not a partner. Darryl is my partner."

"Then where is he?" Ava asked. Robert didn't look at her, but he could picture her smirking as she said it.

"I don't know," he said. "What I do know is that we Watchers have two-person partnerships. That's how we operate. We don't partner up in threes."

"Hmmm. Sounds like something an ID operative might say."

Robert inhaled a large quantity of air through his nose; he could think of no other way to control his temper. After exhaling, he said, "That's not even remotely funny."

"I didn't think so either, back oh-so-long-ago when you inferred it about me. Guess it just goes to show we share the same things in common."

Robert grumbled as he unlocked his Mustang's doors. He didn't bother to hold open the passenger-side door for her.

"So, where are we going?" Ava asked as she fastened her seatbelt.

"Some place where we can walk."

Neither said a word as Robert drove for fifteen minutes through what seemed like a labyrinth of streets—purposely, in order to disorient his passenger—before getting onto Columbia Pike. He then turned onto Carlin Springs Road, drove for a few minutes, and, after passing the elementary school, made a sharp right turn onto an almost hidden path. Signs next to the shaded, narrow route cautioned drivers to go slow. It was a two-way road, but it hardly seemed wide enough for one vehicle. Robert was relieved that after navigating the car around several curves, and having to make way for two casual strollers, he didn't have to negotiate road space with any cars heading the other direction before he reached the tiny, secluded parking lot.

"Where are we?" Ava asked.

"The Long Branch Nature Center is right up the hill there. The rest of this is Glencarlyn Park."

After they got out of the car, Ava stood next to the vehicle, looking at the trees surrounding her.

"Park?" she said. "We're in the middle of the woods."

"Yeah." Robert headed toward the nearest paved trail. "I love gettin' back to nature. C'mon."

Ava took another around-her look before following him on the foot-and-bike trail.

A wide and relatively shallow stream was on their right, beyond a short craggy decline. A man standing on a rock in the middle of the water was talking with a woman sitting on a rock on the bank.

Robert nodded in their direction. "It'd be a nasty spill if that guy slipped and hit his head."

Ava was looking at the scene with some uneasiness; Robert suspected it wasn't for the reason he'd suggested. Did her trigger have something to do with water?

"What is this?" she said. "Why are we here?"

"Turning philosophical on me?" Robert said. "I can't answer all the big questions, professor."

"I'm not joking," Ava said. "I meant why did you bring me here?"

"To relax."

He said it with a smile, but it was a serious response. The park, with its many paths and recesses, was a favorite of joggers, hikers, cyclists, birders, and other nature lovers. It was also a favorite hangout spot for associates of The ID, not to mention a gathering place for some of Northern Virginia's ethnic gangs. This was obvious before they'd even gotten out of the car. At the beginning of the narrow route leading to the park was a sign that used to display the location's name before it was marred by layers of graffiti spelling out gang names and portraying gang symbols. Beyond the sign, graffiti could be seen on trees, on logs lying by the roadside, and even on the pavement, written in chalk.

Robert had wanted to bring his new self-proclaimed partner to just such an environment, a place that was fully out in nature but that also had a lot of people activity—perhaps her type of people—hoping she'd relax, let down her guard, and let something slip or fall out. This was all a test to see if she'd revert back to her nature. Better here than inside The Burrow, where everyone seemed all-too-quick to give Ava the benefit of the doubt.

"We shouldn't be relaxing," she said. "We should be searching for Marie-Lydia."

"And we just might find some clues out here." Robert tried his best to sound convincing. "This is a hot spot for ID activity. Based on what we know of her behavior, I'm positive Marie-Lydia's associated with them, in some way, and they're not the type to stay cooped up indoors. Who knows? She could be hiding out in the plain sight of mother nature."

Robert knew "plain sight" was an ironic phrase to use in an area like this. With so many tall trees, and so many curves in the trails, visibility was severely limited for those with normal sight. He figured that was the point of a recreational park. If people can't see too far ahead of themselves, they'll pay more attention to and maybe appreciate their immediate surroundings. But he was divided on whether the environment would help or hinder someone searching for something besides birds. In more wide-open spaces, it would be easy to miss the objects underfoot, anthills as well as ants; in a claustrophobic setting like Glencarlyn Park, it might be even easier to miss a hiding space made for something someone doesn't want found.

Robert believed that when the sense of sight was hampered, the sense of hearing was sometimes enhanced. But aside from the snippets of unimportant speech picked up from unseen sources, all he heard while walking were the sounds of water, leaves, tree frogs, birds, and annoyingly close insects. After several minutes of this, Ava said, "The ID."

"What about them?"

"Why are they called that?" she said. "I mean, in that way? I know it's short for The Infinite Definite, but why is it pronounced as one word instead of its initials, I.D.?"

"I don't know who first came up with it," Robert said, "probably some word-wizard at the HSA. But the name refers to Freud's concept of the id, the section of the psyche that's totally unconscious, the source of an individual's instinctual drives and impulses. It's appropriate for these terrorists, these fallen angels, as you might say, because they seem to be driven to satisfy some of the most primitive needs, all of them centered on sex and violence, and whatever those two acts have in common."

"Marie-Lydia isn't like that," Ava said.

"How do you know?" Robert said. "You say you can't even remember the past seventeen months. People can change overnight."

"More than a year may be missing from my memory," Ava said, "but I know her. I've known her for years. As you said, we were *close*. She's just not capable of falling in line with some mentally diseased savages."

Robert stopped walking. He closed his eye and took a deep breath.

Diseased.

She said it, and she didn't even know what she was saying. Or maybe, deep down, she did.

Ava stopped in front of a tree that forked into two at its trunk. A few paces in front of her, the trail led to a low concrete narrow walkway that crossed over the stream. It was clear she was hesitant to cross it. She turned away and looked at Robert.

He stared back at her for a few uncomfortable seconds. He swallowed what he wanted to say and instead said, "The ID is a leaderless gang of young viral victims. They live for their own pleasure, and they take the highest pleasure in playing with bodies and minds, using swordplay or wordplay or any other allegedly fun or artistic means available. The only lines are those of Leaderless Insistence. And that's no lines at all."

"Victims?" Ava repeated the less important of the two "v" words he'd used. "Victims of what exactly?"

Robert took another breath as he deepened his stare, hardened his resolve.

"Of nature," he answered. "And God."

Ava's brow wrinkled, and the muscles in her forearms tensed. Robert could tell she was unhappy with his words, probably the last one in particular. Was this it? Was the time bomb down to its last seconds? The muscles in Robert's forearms tightened.

But whatever Ava had felt, it passed.

"This is a waste of time," she said, turning back toward the stream. "In Xyn—"

"Damn it"—Robert started forward—"what is it about you and that place?" He no longer felt like standing still. If she were on the verge of coming out of her cover, he wanted to get it over and done with. "Why do you want to go there so badly? And, worse, take me with you?"

"Why are you so resistant?" she shot back.

"Are you crazy?"

Robert believed only the insane willingly went to XynK-roma—associates of The ID went happily, and frequently, like an addiction—and when the sane unwillingly went, it was probable they'd come out insane. In a calmer moment, he'd admit his accusation probably could've been put into better words, but he wanted to push her. He wanted her to push back. His ambitions didn't allow for language-censors.

"No, Robert," she said, "I'm not crazy. I know what Xyn is. I also know what it could be, what it *must* be before it overwhelms us."

Wish granted. He was almost speechless.

"Overwhelm? So you're admitting—? The Flood—?"

"The Flood is coming," she said. "Nothing can stop it."

He was right. All along he was right. He knew it. She *wanted* the world to be plunged into chaos. She wanted the Earth to pop like a bubble and spill its contents in a stew of pure anarchy. She was definitely an ally of The Infinite Definite. In some way. Somehow. Damn what Adam had said; Robert had all the evidence he wanted, and he had a duty to take her down. Now.

He took a step backward as he squared off, readied himself, and folded his fingers to make fists. Ava cocked her head in response.

"What are you—?"

She'd begun to speak but stopped and jerked her head to the right. Robert flinched. Before he could recover from his withdrawal and counterattack, Ava was already running. She was on the other side of the stream before he could even consider what had just happened. Confused and already several steps behind, he sprinted after her.

As he ran, Robert realized Ava had somehow managed to see just around the shaded trail's bend. She had somehow seen or heard the commotion before he did. In a far-from-neat picnic area, four teenagers were attacking a family of six.

Two boys and a girl were taking turns punching, kicking, and spitting on the short, paunchy father as he staggered, fell, and regained his footing only to fall again in the small space between a tree and a grilling station. The three hoodlums got their knocks in while the mother only had to deal with one: a scantily clad girl who laughed hysterically and shouted anti-Latino slurs as she threw uncooked food, paper plates, and plastic utensils at the cowering woman. All the while, the couple's four preadolescent children ran around aimlessly, crying and screaming amid all the senselessness.

Robert considered how Ava had detected something out of the ordinary happening behind her back while he, facing in the right direction, didn't pick up a thing. She seemed to possess more abilities than the average angel.

However she'd become alerted to it, Ava had been quick to take off across the low concrete bridge, following the pathway's curves. She didn't slow her pace for even half a second as she neared the scene and, as if running up invisible stairs, took three steps on the air and a fourth atop the family's minivan. While leaping off of the maroon vehicle, she reared back with her left arm, gathered a ball of sky-and-tree-filtered sunlight in her hand and fashioned it, shaped it into something longer, slimmer, and more pointed before throwing it to her right, directly at the back of the neck of one of the young thugs. The hit boy screamed in agony, slapping the palm of his left hand on his neck as he fell down to his knees. Although he'd received the first blow of Ava's assault, he may not have been her first intended target; it was most likely the racist black girl, she who got tackled a second after she saw Ava diving for her from the top of the van.

Robert had only been three steps behind Ava in her race toward the violent scene, but he'd stopped running the moment he saw Ava take her first step onto the unsolid air. It was unexpected. All of it. He'd seen her in action on videos, but in-person was something else. He was too amazed at what he was seeing to think of assisting, and Ava's actions made it clear she really didn't need any help.

The slur-spewing girl had been knocked down but not out when Ava forced her to the ground. As the girl cursed and struggled to get back to her feet, Ava struggled to keep her own body straddled on top of the girl. Ava used her hands to hold the girl's head, squeezing it, making the girl's nose point toward hers as Ava looked into her eyes. When they were in the right position, Ava did something with her own eyes and somehow rendered the girl still.

The two delinquents still on their feet left the father alone and ran toward Ava. She spotted them, rolled to her left, and grabbed a fallen tree branch as she came up to her knees. Ava threw the branch at the boy's knees as she looked with squinting eyes at the running girl's throat. Robert could see she was being shot with twin narrow beams of infrared radiation. The girl would feel a sudden sensation, as if a match had been struck on her throat and then left there to burn through the skin.

She felt it. Both of her hands went to the burned area as the girl dropped her head, stumbled over her own feet, and fell, landing on her side.

The boy who'd dodged the tossed branch had been hindered, but he was still coming at Ava. He was less than ten running paces away.

Ava hopped up to her feet and ran three steps to her left, toward the nearest picnic table. She jumped, placing her foot on the edge of the tabletop and pushed off, twisting in mid-air, putting her body in just the right position to kick the boy in his ear.

The boy went down, and Ava was soon on top of him. She rendered him motionless in the same manner she had the girl—by forcing him to look into her eyes.

Robert had stepped off of the paved path and onto the picnic area's grass, nearer the chaos. The panicked mother was trying to calm her four screaming children and rush them into the minivan while the bruised and bloody father stumbled around in a daze. Robert saw but didn't know what he could do to help them.

His full attention shifted back to Ava when she leaped from a picnic tabletop, took two steps on the air, and landed on another tabletop, moving closer and closer toward the boy who'd received an arrow of light in the back of his neck. He was on his feet now, but he was still pressing his palm against the burned area and sucking in small streams of air through clenched teeth. He wasn't exactly in a daze, but it was obvious he was following no particular direction as he took tentative, baby steps forward.

In her second-to-last leap off of a picnic table, Ava tossed another bright arrow at one of the boy's elbows. He screamed when stung. He screamed again when Ava kicked him in the chest. The hoodlum fell back against a tree, and Ava hit him in the jaw—left hook, right hook—before placing her hands on his cheeks and giving him the same treatment as the other two. The boy collapsed on his butt.

Robert got a fleeting-but-close look at the formation of the electromagnetic arrow during Ava's last throw. The arrow itself was a shaft of yellow and orange light that had been sharpened at one end with light in the infrared range. As it took shape in her hand, strange webs of orange and yellow light were visible on her forearm, strangling them, appearing almost like strings, or vines. While he wondered how a Virus-carrier would react to being struck by such an arrow, Ava made quick work of the last delinquent still conscious, the girl with the burned throat.

Ava wrapped her hands around the girl's neck, pressed her thumbs against the burned area, squeezed harder and said, "Look at me." The girl opened her eyes for only a sliver of a second, but it was long enough for Ava to do whatever she'd done to the others.

Four down. But what about the family of six?

Robert turned and saw they'd finally gathered themselves into their minivan. He called out to them, asking them to wait. They were safe now, and the authorities would have questions for them. The father shouted back at him in Spanish while the mother shouted in the same language at her kids, probably in another paradoxical attempt to calm them down.

His pleas ignored, the vehicle sped away, and Robert was left to survey the area, observing how the grass and dirt were littered with food, napkins, spilled condiments, and other assorted rubbish, not all of it a result of the melee. Did anyone respect the environment anymore?

He picked up the trash in his path as he made his way to the picnic table Ava was leaning against. She seemed to be in two modes at once—resting from her activity, and ready to take a swing at someone else. The way she looked at him as he approached put Robert on guard.

"Why didn't you help?" she said, trying to catch her breath.

He did feel a little embarrassed by his inaction, but not regretful. She'd gotten the job done, in short order, and maybe even better than he could have. He wasn't ready to start giving her compliments just yet, though.

"I didn't have time."

"Yeah?" she said. "You're wearing two watches. What happened? They canceled each other out?"

Cute. Rhetorical questions and a terrible joke all wrapped into one by a wise-aleck. Robert felt it was probably deserved, but, more important, the remark reminded him of his watches' primary use. He touched the tips of his index and middle fingers to the face of his right wristwatch to give Adam a brief summary of what had happened and ask him to contact the authorities to round up the fallen. Ava pointed at two of them with her thumb.

"These are the type of terrorists you accuse me of being in line with?"

"No," Robert said as he deciphered Adam's immediate response. "These aren't terrorists. They're just brats. What did you do to them anyway?"

"I froze them," she said. "Put them in an altered state. They'll be fine in an hour."

Robert took another look at the four victimizers-turned-victims. They almost looked as if they were dead. He could see they were still breathing, just very slowly. *Frozen.*

"So, what's that you were saying before," he said as he sat on one of the table's benches, "about the Flood coming?"

Ava smirked at him. "So now you just want to talk, huh?"

Although he still wasn't convinced she was truly on the side of the righteous, he was a bit more willing to consider her close enough, close enough to be trusted as—at the very least—a potential ally. Maybe Adam had seen something in her Robert couldn't. He left her question unanswered as she sat down on the opposite bench, facing him.

"I was saying that I know that the fundamental realm of Reality—XynKroma—is the collective *sunconscious* of all living things, and as a result, the place is a mess. A chaotic collage of nonsense. The apparent indiscriminate result of an unsupervised collaboration of an enormous number of the most abstract artists, poets, and musicians. But it's also a realm of polluted light. And while all angels can manipulate light at will, those of us with higher aspirations have applied our talents to the realm of XynKroma. We're not content with just beating the stuffing out of other angels here on the surface of Reality."

Or freezing the stuffing that's inside the noninfected, Robert thought. The term "sunconscious" wasn't just a cute term combining the words "subconscious" and "unconscious;" it was an apt one-word description of the extra-dimensional realm of low light, dirtied up by the thoughts of an uncountable number of sentient beings. Robert was more used to seeing Virus-carriers use their eyes to burn skin than freeze something deep within.

"I and other angels," Ava said, "like the Archangel who oversaw my inversion, we've sectioned off parts of Xyn and protected them, cultivated them, remade them into Pieces of Paradise. We've created temple-palaces. One grand palace and one surrounding garden per one fit-and-deserving angel. And each temple-palace is inhabited by the caretakers of these pieces. They're attempting to bring and maintain order in Xyn, but they're also watching for the day when the realm spills out to the surface of Reality. We want XynKroma to be as ordered as possible when that happens."

"And you believe this Flood can't be stopped?"

"I know it," Ava said. "The Flood *has* to happen. Creation isn't finished yet, Robert. It's only a work in progress. The Flood is part of the process."

Hence her metaphor about artists and poets, Robert thought. Ava was a clever one. Smart and clever.

"I was once an evangelical Christian," she said, "believing in a superhuman God who created the universe in six days and then guided everything within it, using divine intervention. Answering prayers, teaching people harsh but deserved lessons, and all the rest. But the Archangel taught me the truth about Reality. The Creator did create the prototypical universe, by lighting the spark of consciousness. But as this fire of consciousness burns, as the level of consciousness in living beings is raised, the universe develops, and the Creator is consumed. Creation didn't happen; it's *happening*."

Robert was on the edge of his bench. It seemed that either Ava or this mysterious mentor to whom she kept referring had developed a postmodern take on modern theology, a kind of in-process Deism. Original Deism had its roots in seventeenth-century Europe, during the period of the Enlightenment; its adherents believed a Creator-God designed the universe during a set period of time then, once the work had been done, retreated to observe life and history and everything play themselves out while the Creator declined to interfere in anything in any way—an old-fashioned Watchmaker, watching the finished timepiece tick-tock on its own. In Ava's mind, the Watchmaker was still creating the watch. Once finished, the Watchmaker will have a well-timed heart attack…unless The ID interferes, smashing the unfinished watch and murdering its Maker prematurely.

"One thing I remember," she said, "is what you seem to have forgotten, if you ever even knew: we angels have a duty to ensure Creation's finished state is as perfect as possible."

"No doubt there's a whole boatload of things I should know," Robert said as he looked at the frozen kids to ensure they were still breathing, "but there's only so much I can wrap my skinny head around."

"There's a lot I want to teach and show you," Ava said, "but in order for you to understand it all, to see the entire picture clearly, we have to go to XynKroma. That's where we *have* to begin. My sight and yours are limited here, and I mean that in more ways than one."

Robert considered her words, and his thoughts drifted to Darryl. Darryl was of the firm belief that, with each individual mind he changed on the subject of "love," he was progressively healing XynKroma, the collective *sunconscious*. Each lover he charitably left in "peace" was one step closer toward an improved state of Creation. His philosophy and Ava's were remarkably similar, at least on the surface.

Robert hadn't been to XynKroma in a long while, but this Flood had to be taken seriously. For the first time, he began to seriously consider allowing Ava to usher him to the fundamental realm of Reality so he could soak up as much as possible, learn everything, and, fortune willing, emerge sane and prepared to do whatever he could to stop it. But he still had questions.

"How can going to XynKroma together help us find Marie-Lydia?"

"I told you," Ava said. "That's where I took her. That's where I last remember seeing her."

"But not *her*." Now that she was talking, and now that he was willing to hear her out, Robert wanted to be sure he was clear on everything she had to say. One couldn't travel to the extra-dimensional realm as if simply driving to Canada or flying to Japan or rocketing to the moon. One had to leave all material possessions behind, including the body.

"Yes, I took *her*. Her essential essence. Her *soul,* if you want to get technical."

"Yeah," Robert said, "technically, I suppose that's the best way to get there."

Even though the realm was accessed by traveling to the core of the human mind, its sights and sounds weren't immediately comprehensible to humans, not at humankind's current stage in the evolutionary process. Everything seen in Xyn was metaphorical; everything heard was symbolic. The only hope a human being had of existing and traveling within any degree of comfort in the realm was by concentrating and reshaping the essence of his consciousness into a symbolic or figurative representation of what religious folks would call the "soul." This allowed Xyn to make some sense to a human being. The soul translated the sights and sounds into stuff that was more or less familiar, but there was a price. Whatever happened to a person's soul while in Xyn had permanent effects on the person's body and mind, sometimes minor, sometimes major. These "Pieces of Paradise" and "temple-palaces" Ava had mentioned were also metaphorical, but could also be consequential.

"Marie-Lydia's soul and mine traveled there together," Ava said. "You know she was a corrupted angel"—Robert nodded—"but she wasn't a thoroughly corrupted one; I didn't believe so. I took her to Xyn to reform her. Just like the Archangel inverted me, I intended to reconfigure Marie-Lydia's soul, clean up her way of thinking, remake her into an angelic being that could benefit humanity and help usher in a perfect, finished Creation."

"Noble intentions."

"I just need to get to my temple-palace, Robert. Its caretakers can tell me everything I need to know, maybe even restore my memory."

It was all very interesting to him, but something about her story just didn't seem right. He wondered whether or not he should introduce Ava to Vince Ceniza. The psychological mapmaker might be able to supervise a solo journey through Xyn for her like he'd done so many times for Darryl. Robert hadn't yet convinced himself this was a good idea when three police cars pulled up to the curb.

"Which one of you is named 'Goldner'?" one officer said as she and her partner approached.

Robert raised his hand, got up from his seat, and—when prompted—gave the officers his version of what had just taken place. When they questioned Ava, and she gave them a word-for-word recap of what Robert had just told them, he again looked at the bodies on the ground. Ava's handiwork.

Frozen.

Just what did it really mean?

Chapter 11

"Okay," Robert said, "what've you got for me?"

"Something hot," Kurtis said.

"Burning." Anika glanced at Robert with an odd smile.

It was noon on Monday. The three of them were huddled in a private study-room of a campus library.

After taking a tired Ava back to The Burrow on Sunday evening and privately asking some other agents to keep a close eye on her, Robert had called his friends and asked for an update on their project. They hadn't yet completed their research, but they had some material they wanted him to review. Robert was eager to see it. His excitement just barely compensated for his exhaustion. He'd spent much of the night tossing and turning as he turned over in his mind the concepts of "God" and "Satan" in light of everything Ava had told him in the park.

In Christian belief, angels were beings of light; Satan—a fallen angel—and his demons were creatures of the "fire." Robert couldn't help but think that "fire" and "polluted light" were synonyms. He knew from his long-ago Sunday school lessons that Satan had once been a servant of God, as illustrated in the Book of Job—synonymous perhaps with how The ID were somehow servants of the Arkangels who, according to Ava, were serving the Creator and its work of Creation, a Creation that got its start via a metaphorical *spark*. Before falling asleep, considering it all mathematically, the best he could come up with was that, whatever Supreme Being or Higher Power the Arkangels truly served, it was neither an indifferent Watchmaker nor a Benevolent Deity. Robert was sure in his bones that the space-and-time warping Flood was not inevitable, but these Arkangels were organized to make it so.

He'd agreed to meet his friends during their lunch hour, the only break between classes Kurtis and Anika shared. Robert had arrived not knowing what to expect but hoping it would illuminate what he'd seen the day before.

"What is it?" he asked.

"Hell," Kurtis said, "over the past year, that girl has been busier than a bee trying to get into Georgetown Law."

"Check this out." Anika made a few fast keystrokes on her laptop. Within seconds, the three of them were watching a surveillance camera recording of a confrontation in a strip mall's parking lot. The unusually clear and detailed footage showed Ava fighting with two adults, a man and a woman. It was obvious by their methods of fighting the adults weren't Virus-carriers. It was also obvious the two were trying to do Ava some serious harm. Among a scattering of onlookers, two young children were prominent in the picture. The video had no sound, but Robert could tell by their movements the kids were panicked, crying and screaming. Ava appeared to be trying to maneuver herself around the man and woman, attempting to get at the children, while ducking and dodging the adults and the objects they threw at her.

"What's she doing?" Robert asked.

"Not sure," Anika said, "but based on all we've reviewed over the past twenty-four hours, I'd say she's fighting for those kids you see."

"Why do you say that?"

"I can add," she said, "even when no numbers are involved."

"Some of the other footage we've seen," Kurtis said, "shows her fighting in areas where graffiti is a natural part of the environment."

"Out of all the drawings, symbols, gang-tags and so on," Anika said, "one little decorative message stands out: 'Save the children.'"

"Yeah," Robert said, "I've seen it before."

"We've seen it in two of the videos we reviewed," Kurtis said, "and heard her say it more than once in those that have sound. Look at those kids. They're scared, but they're not running away. They're hoping one of those parties will protect them from the other. We haven't had time to do the digging on those two, but I strongly doubt I'd lose my scholarship funds by betting they're abusive guardians."

"Yeah," Robert said. "Maybe."

"It's not on the video," Anika said, "but I'd wager one of *my* scholarships that one of those kids was smacked or spanked right there in public. I've seen it happen before, in grocery stores, on the bus. The girl probably saw and decided to do something about it."

"Your scholarships are not inheritably more valuable than mine, Nika," Kurtis said.

"I didn't say that they were."

"But you implied—"

Robert shushed them. They could engage in one of their pointless arguments on their own time; he had to focus.

Although bigger and older, the man and woman on the video were clearly outmatched by the spry girl. Using light as her only weapon, Ava knocked them out, grabbed the kids by their arms, and hurried away, beyond the view of the camera. The video lasted less than three minutes.

"I'd like to know what happened to those two kids," Robert said. "And the adults. Maybe she's part of some kind of kidnapping outfit."

"Why don't you just ask her?"

Robert gave Anika a look. She gave him a blank stare. When he realized she wouldn't get the meaning behind the lines on his forehead, he said, "I'm sure amnesia will factor into her answer."

"Well, whatever happened to them," Kurtis said, "I can assure you she didn't take the kids home with her. Before you and your partner found her, she'd been living in HOT houses, moving from one to another."

"The House of Thomas shelters?" There were ten such shelters in the DC-Northern Virginia area that Robert knew of. They were set up for homeless people infected with incurable diseases, homeless people who *knew* they had a disease. "*Really*?"

"Yep," Kurtis said. "Spending her nights there anyway. She seemed to have spent much of her daylight hours adventuring."

Anika grinned. "Kicking ass."

"Sometimes alone, sometime with partners."

"Partners?" Robert asked. "Who?"

Anika tapped a few more keys and pulled up another short video. It showed Ava and two others fighting together at what appeared to be a miniature golf course. It was obvious the footage had been recorded by several surveillance cameras and that, before being launched into cyberspace, the footage had been spliced together and edited to portray a coherent and uninterrupted stream of action; Robert wondered by whom. He didn't recognize any of the individuals he saw on the screen as associates of The ID, but that meant nothing. Only a tiny fraction of the terrorists had been documented by authorities. The video ended shortly after Ava's partners grabbed three kids and turned them and themselves invisible. The last few seconds of the film showed Ava knocking down two tall, rotund men—kicking them in their groins, then their faces—and running away, out of range of the cameras.

"She doesn't play around," Kurtis said.

"She's playing at something," Robert said.

"We saved the best for last." Anika punched a few more buttons on the keyboard. "Look familiar?"

It did. At once.

The setting was a front yard. The yard in front of a house he and his partner had recently visited. The haven of identity thieves, where they found a battered, bruised, and unconscious Arkangel. On the computer screen, Ava was wide-awake. Robert, Anika, and Kurtis watched in silence as she maneuvered from one position to another, using all manners of light tricks and electromagnetic effects, fighting for her life.

Robert was unsure of the total number of fighters Ava faced, but the odds were clearly against her. It was also clear her opponents were all women, and all Virus-carriers. When Ava seemed to almost score a hit against one, the target disappeared and, two seconds later, another target appeared and struck at Ava from another angle, undoubtedly in her blind spot.

Ava's opponents were dressed in short-jackets, short skirts, and high heels. The jackets stopped just above the navel, putting the ladies' bare midriffs on full display. The sleeves had been pushed up to their elbows, and, underneath the jackets, the women only wore bras. Plenty of skin was showing, and what wasn't showing was hidden by parts of an impractical outfit. Robert knew only two types of Virus-carriers would dress in such a way, go out in the sunlight, and engage someone in a fight: those who were suicidal, and those who were highly skilled warriors.

Robert briefly considered that Ava was facing off against only one, one woman winking out of sight to change her appearance and her position, using multiple ways of instilling confusion in her opponent; skilled fighters knew confusion turned into fear, and instilled fear usually led to a self-defeated opponent. Robert's theory was bolstered by the facts that only one other woman besides Ava appeared on the screen at a time and, while the colors of the woman's outfit changed back and forth between a combination of red-and-white-and-black and blue-and-white-and-purple, the outfit remained the same.

But he was wrong. Robert soon realized Ava was fighting not one, but two. A pair of true warriors.

The women came at Ava with sharp nails, sun-charged hand-smacks, sparkling finger-snaps, and well-aimed pointy-heeled kicks. And one in particular was inclined to use her teeth. Robert paid especial attention when this one was on the screen. It was such a bold, unusual method of fighting, especially when used by one Virus-carrier against another. But the method isn't what captured Robert's attention. It was the woman herself, the one who favored the blue and purple attire: a long-legged female of porcelain-white skin and chin-length raven-black hair. It was the same woman he'd spotted briefly in RT's Restaurant on Saturday night. She did exist. She was indeed real. And she appeared to be very dangerous.

He was so focused and attuned when this woman was on the screen that Robert paid much less attention to the other, the one to which he apparently should have paid much more attention the first time he saw her—she who preferred to sport the red-and-white jacket and skirt; she who maneuvered her body so well in the black bra and high heels; she who no matter how she moved, and where, whether she was delivering a blow or dodging one, had only one bold blue eye exposed to the camera's view…Miss Blake.

The two women fought together as a team, but in Robert's judgment, either one of them alone could have outmatched Ava. And that's how they played it, with just one of them appearing at a time. Assault with pepper and disappear. They were toying with her, wearing her out, trying to cut and break skin, inflict as much pain as possible before she would feel no more. The Arkangel put up a good fight, but she did next to no damage to her opponents.

A ten-minute fight scene, an eleven-minute film. One mystery solved: how Ava came to be so battered and bruised. But why had she gone to the house in the first place? The film had been recorded by a high quality device, not a surveillance camera—so who was behind it? And how'd the film end up in a place where Anika and Kurtis could find it?

"MC³ Productions," Anika said after the screen went black. "They have a growing library of films like this. All of them involving Virus-carriers fighting each other or attacking others."

"Almost like fetish porn," Kurtis said. "That's what they specialize in."

"Are you telling me there's a company making money off of filming and selling videos like this?" Robert asked. "A legit business?"

"I don't know if they're making money," Kurtis said, "legitimately or otherwise. But they sure are making a lot of flicks. Their name's out there, and they want it out there."

"But we have no idea who's behind it."

"Then keep looking," Robert said. "Please." He grabbed his windbreaker and headed for the door. "I think two of their stars are scouting the leading men for their next film."

∞   ∞   ∞

Darryl. Where in the name of fortune was he? Robert hadn't heard from him in more than twenty-four hours. He put three fingers on the face of his left-wristwatch and tried to contact him. No response. Still no response, after trying him at every stoplight between the campus and The Burrow. Robert remembered Friday. It was probable Darryl was on another charity case and was just ignoring him. As was his habit, Darryl would get back to him when he was good and ready. But Robert wouldn't let it go, especially if that case happened to be Miss Blake. Robert had to speak to his partner, face-to-face, before it was too late.

He rushed out of the elevator, and found himself face-to-face with Ava.

"We need to talk," she said.

He hadn't seen or spoken to her since Sunday afternoon, nor had he spoken to the Watcher agents he'd asked to keep an eye on her. He did want to talk to them and her—in that order—but he knew he had to prioritize.

"Not right now," he said as he tried to get around her. "I need to figure out where Darryl is."

"So do I."

Robert stopped. "Why?"

"After we got back yesterday, I spoke to Sam about what happened in the park. About everything. I need to go to Xyn, Robert. And if you won't go with me, Darryl might. Sam told me about his experiments with Vince Ceniza. But after taking everything into account, I'm not willing to go alone, supervised or not. You were right; I don't fully trust myself. But, maybe, with Darryl…"

It was there again. The fear in her voice. Robert detected it as she trailed off. She was being honest with him. She was also astonished by her actions yesterday, though maybe for different reasons.

Robert wanted to discuss with her the Internet films he'd seen, one of them in particular. During a serious, detailed discussion, he'd find out what she really remembered. But at the moment, she was the safe one; Darryl might not be. Robert and Ava both shared a more immediate goal than sitting and talking. He'd only come to The Burrow to ask Zel about the key-tool he'd seen Darryl use a couple days earlier.

"Okay," he said. "I need to speak to Zel, then I want to try Darryl's apartment."

"Shouldn't we check with Mister Smith," Ava asked, "to see if he knows where Darryl might be?"

"No. I've already sent a message asking him to contact Darryl for me." And telling him Darryl might be in danger. But whether it was the way the message had been relayed or because Adam was wise to Darryl's habits, Robert had sensed Adam hadn't taken his hunch seriously. "I'm not going to bother the chairman just so I can tell him the same thing face-to-face. It's a waste of time. I know Darryl. I can find him. You coming?"

"Yes," she said, "but Sam warned me not to leave The Burrow again without the glasses Mister Bernard is making for me. I don't know if they're ready yet."

"They damn well better be." They were losing more and more time. "C'mon. Let's go check."

∞   ∞   ∞

"How do I look?" Ava asked.

"The more important question is: how do you see?" Zel said as he looked through the lenses, into her eyes. "Everything clear? No pale rosy tints?"

"No. Everything's fine."

"Excellent!"

"Another work of perfection," Robert said as he paced near the door.

"Maybe," Zel said, "but that determination should be made by the clear eyes of the wearer. Come." The engineer took Ava by the hand and led her toward a full-length mirror. "Take a long peek and give me your honest opinion."

Zel stood close behind Ava as she examined herself. After a moment, rather than saying anything about her own, she asked about the nature of Zel's glasses.

"Without them," he said, "I can see the world a little too clearly."

Ava turned away from the mirror. "What do you think, Robert?"

"They're beautiful. Let's go."

"The frames need to be adjusted," she said to Zel. "They're a little too loose on the nose."

"Behind the left ear too, it seems," he said. "Here, let me tighten them a bit."

Robert sighed and made a big show of looking at his left-wristwatch.

Ava gave him a look, as if to say she was just as anxious as him to leave. Deep down, Robert knew that if Ava was going out in the field with him, it was important she be able to see well enough. Still, time wasn't their ally.

"Okay," Zel said as he handed the readjusted glasses to Ava, "let's try this."

She put the glasses on and, instead of looking at the mirror, looked all around the workshop. Her eyes stopped on an instrument on the wall. Robert followed her eyes and saw the glimmering, multihued, stringless bow that seemed to be made of clear crystal. The colors of white light were broken up and kept bottled up, on full display inside the crystal. Robert had seen it before. Many times. And he'd noticed its lateral position on the wall and its multicolored appearance made it look like a crystal rainbow.

"Like it?" Zel asked.

"What is it?" Ava asked.

"One of my favorite toys," Zel said. "A bow that can only be used by angels. While holding it, a skilled angel can 'string' it and direct light through it with his or her free hand. As the light passes through the crystal, the angel—with some strong psychological assistance—can use the grasping hand to control how the light is broken up within and how it's released, shooting it through the air for a good distance."

Ava couldn't take her eyes off of it.

"A plaything I made for Darryl," Zel said, "but he rarely uses it."

"It really speaks to me," Ava said.

Zel laughed. "Maybe you and ol' Darryl share some kind of connection. He said the same thing when he first saw it."

"Just looking at it," Ava said, "it reminds me of the story of Noah. The rainbow that God put in the sky after the flood. A symbol of the new covenant with humankind."

"Yeah," Robert said, "after all but eight people on the planet were drowned by that god. Funny story. Are we ready yet?"

If Ava heard him, she ignored him. She gazed without blinking until her lips parted and she whispered, "Save the children."

Robert perked up.

"What did you say?" he asked as he approached her.

She turned toward him. "Huh?"

"What did you just say?"

Ava looked at Robert as if he were speaking Greek. Before he could repeat the question a third time, Zel broke in.

"'Save the children.' That's what I heard."

"I said that?" Ava asked.

"Yeah," Robert said, "I heard it too. I've even seen it in a couple of places. What does it mean?"

"Seen it where?" Ava asked.

"Answer my question first, please."

"I—" Ava hesitated. "It's just something I've been saying for years. Kind of like a motto, a life-purpose. It's the reason I first became an evangelical Christian, long before I became an angel."

"Uh-huh." Robert knew there was much she wasn't saying.

"Now, where have you seen it?" she asked.

"In graffiti art," Robert said. "And sometimes without the accompanying art. It's really dirtying up the area. I always figured it was more verbal litter from the associates of The ID, but maybe there's something more to it."

"You'll have to show me," Ava said.

"Later. After we meet up with Darryl."

"When you do," Zel said, "tell him I'm going to be a while with his corresq." The engineer walked over toward the table on which the silver circle lay. "I've figured out how to make the modifications he wants, but it'll take me at least a week to do them."

Robert hurried over to the table. "Did he drop that off this morning?"

"No. Sunday morning. Before he went out for one of his, uh…" Zel glanced at Ava. "One of his appointments."

Robert cursed. He had a hope, just a faint hope, Darryl hadn't met with Miss Blake, that he was somewhere else, caught up in someone else's business. "You heard from him since then?"

"No," Zel said.

Robert cursed twice more. His hope was evaporating.

"What's the matter?" Ava asked.

"C'mon." He waved to her as he rushed for the door. "We've got to go. *Now*."

Chapter 12

Darryl woke up in a circle.

A red circle inside a larger orange circle inside even bigger colored circles.

He was lying on his side, in a fetal position.

He blinked, moving his eyes to every corner, before stirring his body.

Impelled in part by grogginess and in part by an uncertain fear, he came up to his knees, counting his surroundings: five circles, five different colors. It was hard not to see them. Even with his enhanced visual abilities, the circles were the only things he could see. The circles had been painted on the floor with a kind of fluorescent paint in colors that glowed in the otherwise complete darkness.

Darryl knew the source of the circles' glow was black light. He wasn't in any condition to think straight about much else. The remnants of a headache buzzed in his skull. He massaged his temples with the thumb and pinky of his right hand until an idea came to him.

He touched his right hand to his left wrist, and his left hand to his right wrist. They were bare. His watches had been stripped from him. And with the exception of his boxer shorts, so had his clothes.

Darryl's next idea was to test himself, to see if he was capable of standing. He then heard something that made him think it wiser to stay still.

A melancholy voice sang a song without words…a dirge-like song that inspired a vision of his skull breaking into thousands of sand particles, each of them nestling in to irritate his brain.

The voice seemed to come from all around, surrounding him like the painted circles, engulfing him like the darkness. He didn't want to move. Then he heard another voice, a mystery voice, giving the song its appropriate lyrics:

> "Blind, meeting life with a contract,
> a common promise,
> a compromise between false love,
> imperfect peace."

The singing continued after the lyrics stopped, but there was no need for more words. Darryl knew them. They were a perversion of the lines that began *Death's Heart*. He opened his mouth to speak, but someone else spoke first.

"There's something very primal about poetry, don't you think?"

This too was familiar. The voice, not the words. It was the same chalky voice of the woman he'd heard but not seen a moment before he blacked out…when? How long ago had that happened?

Questions, questions—Darryl had a bagful. He chose one closest to the top.

"Where am I?" he asked.

"At the heart of what really matters," someone answered.

Riddles. Darryl was in no mood or condition to deal with them.

"Who are you?" he asked.

"What am I not?" the voice responded. "A knot of your peaceful deeds—blessings kissing sins—made flesh."

Damn it. Darryl's headache flared. He decided to try one last time before switching tactics.

"What happened to me?" he asked. "What are you doing?"

"You should be more careful about what you drink." These words were spoken by a far more familiar voice. "And about what you think."

"Veronica," Darryl said.

"What happened to 'V.,' honey? Or 'Miss Blake'?"

She or someone else at the club had put something in his orange juice. He'd been drugged. That had to be it. That was the source of his headache. Some kind of drug used to help tenderize his mind before knocking him out with a burst of concentrated light. Drugs, music, poetic words—a magick concoction. Whatever Veronica had done, she was keeping it going.

"What the hell do you think you're doing?" he asked.

"Helping you save your life," she said. "And helping you save our world."

Darryl couldn't figure her position by just listening to her. He got to his feet and looked around, in every direction, turning and readying himself for a confrontation. The glowing circles didn't help.

But he didn't need them.

Veronica emerged from the blackness less than ten feet in front of him, giving Darryl a start. She stopped at the edge of his red circle. It took him a moment to notice that, as she appeared, her partner had done the same directly behind him. The similarities and differences in the two women's appearances were striking, and strange.

Veronica wore a cloud-white halter gown that showed off both shoulders and the fuchsia-and-indigo tattoo that had disturbed Darryl enough to do some quick Internet research on its meaning; he'd only discovered the symbol represented something called "Charma." In the area of her right thigh, Veronica's white gown displayed a tilted tomato-red cross; Darryl couldn't imagine what it might represent. Veronica's partner wore the same outfit, only it was midnight-black instead of white and had a tilted lightning-blue cross on the upper half of the gown, over her left breast. She had no tattoos, but her skin had the color, sheen, and smoothness of a clean, white ceramic vase.

"Welcome to the dark room," she said.

Maybe it was because he was seeing her for the first time, or maybe it was because he wanted to get a good look at the one who'd managed to evade all of his Watcher-agent-honed senses before pinning his arms behind him with unusual strength. For whatever reason, Darryl's eyes were drawn to this woman. He made a quick study of her long cherry-red nails, her chin-length, ink-black hair, and her expressionless face. In her wide-open eyes, eggplant irises were on clear display, as if her top and bottom eyelids were magnetically repelling each other. She seemed incapable of blinking, and Darryl had to make a strong conscious effort to do so when his pupils were in direct line with hers. The link was no easier to break than it had been to establish, as she was at least a full head taller than him. He had to look upward and she downward in order for their eyes to even meet. But he managed to snap the line, and he saw she was barefoot.

Darryl turned to look at Veronica, who was also barefoot and standing nearly seven feet tall, as if she'd undergone a significant growth spurt since he'd last seen her, outside, out in nature's air and light. Despite the dizzy-ill feeling the dark and boundless room gave him, Darryl wasn't confident the women's heights were an optical illusion.

"Don't look so worried, honey," Veronica said. "Soon you're going to see a beautiful day."

"We're going to help make all your fantasies come true," the other woman said.

"Skip the fucking rhetoric, riddles, and other bullshit." Darryl tried to figure a safe position from where he could keep his eyes on both of them at once. "Just tell me plainly what the hell's going on, what you want from me."

"Charity." "Clarity."

Veronica and her partner spoke the rhyming words simultaneously, but they were less of an answer and more of a cue. Once spoken, three more women appeared out of the black. One of them wore a tangerine-colored gown; another, a lemon-yellow gown; the third, a lime-green gown. With the exception of the tilted white cross on each, the gowns were uniform in their color. The three women stood on the painted circles that fit them. None wore heels or any other kind of footwear, but Darryl saw they all appeared to stand nearly seven feet tall, just like Veronica and her partner.

He couldn't find a position where he could keep his eyes on everyone at once. The ladies had him surrounded. Darryl would have to keep turning, keep spinning around, and keep making contributions to his increasing sense of dizziness as he watched them.

"The girls and I had a little book club meeting the other night," Veronica said with a distorted smile. "Lots of wine and giggles. I know you'll just love to hear what we discussed."

"*Death's Heart*," her black-haired partner said. "The book of your despicable little life."

Another cue—the women all rushed to speak at once. Each offered her own commentary on the book, her own unique interpretation, and her own biting criticism. As they talked, Veronica and her partner stood still while the ladies in orange, yellow, and green walked along the paths of their colorful circles—two clockwise, the third counterclockwise—revolving around him. Whatever they were saying meant little to Darryl; he couldn't even understand most of them. But he recognized the tactic. It was taken from *The Blackbook of Autumn Numbers.*

Another book of narrative dramatic poetry, *The Blackbook* detailed the exploits of a lecherous teenager, a young man who at one point was confronted by the phantoms of his conquests. The armed phantoms taunted him about his past crimes of indifferent passion, cutting him with their words and with very sharp swords. The protagonist ended up okay, physically, after he fought back with a bigger sword and very few words of his own; it turned out the confrontation was just a dream, a fantasy with the theme of revenge; but he woke up psychologically damaged.

Darryl knew his present experience was no dream, and he couldn't fathom how he might survive it, psychologically or otherwise. So he retreated by resorting to his first tactic of defense, asking questions, and hoping for coherent answers this time.

"I don't know what any of you are talking about," he said. "I just want to know, why am I here?"

"To fill the holes in your holey book, honey," Veronica said.

Darryl ignored the others and looked at her, in her visible eye, remembering their last time together.

"Veronica," he said, "please. Just tell me what all this is about. Why've you brought me here?"

"You brought yourself here," she said. "This is a place of *peace,* after all. At least, in a very warped sense. Just as *warped* as you've left the minds and senses of too many women. Pretending to do them favors by rearranging their consciousness, washing white their minds while babbling to them about the blues."

"What? Listen, what I did—"

Something caught in Darryl's throat. It was too dry. He was dehydrated. He hacked while the other women in the room took the opportunity to throw more accusations at him, more insults, and more damning criticisms. He ignored them, and, when he could summon the words, he responded only to Veronica, but he spoke loud enough for all to hear.

"I did what I did—to women and men—to *help* them. That's all. If you had any sense, if you could see and think clearly, you'd know and understand this world is nothing but pain and suffering. Falling in love for most is a just a trip into an imperfect peace, an illusion that just makes things worse. I gave security to the insecure."

"The world doesn't need your gifts," Veronica said. "It needs those of a true saint."

"An artist," the woman in the green gown said.

"The Greatest Artist," the woman in orange said. "Clearly not you."

"But you do have a great value," the woman in yellow said, "a real use."

"You just need a little more seasoning," the woman in black said.

"We got to you just in time," the woman in green said. "For you, and for the world."

"If you'd been allowed to go on your merry way," Veronica said, "eventually you would've ventured into apocryphal territory, following in the footsteps of Vastion."

Darryl remembered. Veronica had an expanded version of *Death's Heart*. He again looked at that bold blue eye.

"How did it end?" he asked.

"*Death's Heart*?" she asked. "Not with a beautiful creation. Your supernatural role model, Vastion, was a fool in Love, and a greater fool outside of it. I guess that's what happens when boys lose their fathers."

The other women in the room laughed. Darryl ignored them. Only what Veronica had to say was important to him.

"In chapter Indigo," she continued, "among his other crimes, that son of Love Vastion sires a *child* on a human woman, a child who, while still a fetus, is preternaturally aware of its own nature. Seeing itself as too good for a world ruled by the false god Love, the child kills the mother, Kaprice, a worshipper of the false god, while still in her womb."

"*What*?" Darryl said.

"Oh, it gets worse," the porcelain-skinned woman said.

Darryl turned and found himself again staring into her eggplant-dyed eyes. He felt his headache blossoming and heard a faint humming as he gazed through those irises into the pupils.

"But there's no need for you to know the rest," she said. "You know enough."

Darryl broke the visual link with another herculean effort and turned away, resolving not to make eye contact with any of them again.

"I don't believe you," he said, looking at their gowns. "I don't believe any of this."

"Oh, no?" the woman in the yellow gown said. "The empty gift-giver doesn't believe? No surprise."

"What you have believed," the woman in orange said, "has been dangerous enough."

"There's no room in your proud philosophy for anything meaningful," the woman in green said. "No progress. Nothing."

"Only spaces for the absence of love. No positive creation."

"Couldn't you see that?" Veronica asked. "Were you read-ing that stupid book with your eyes closed?" Her tone carried far more anger than Darryl thought her capable of. "Didn't it occur to you that Vastion was heading down a twisted path when he said, 'She wants to pursue the wrong man? Let her have him. She gets mistreated, that's her dessert, her problem'? Those dumb lines said nothing to you? Those ignorant lines, from the last poem in the version of the book you've *memorized*?"

She walked to her right as the woman in black walked to her left. They were trading places, keeping Darryl between them.

"See, I know you, honey," Veronica said. "You're fundamentally a good person. But you've gotten out of touch with the fundamentals."

Darryl struggled against what they were saying, what they were doing, and what was happening within his own skull. He was done speaking, and tired of listening. He put his hands on his ears and shook his head, but their words continued to come through.

"It's time for you to settle down, honey. Make a different type of commitment. We'll put you on the path that leads beyond Vast, beyond Indigo."

"We'll introduce you to The Beautiful One."

"But you can't meet her in your present condition."

"First, we need to get the Red, Orange, Yellow, Green, and Blue out of you."

The white-skinned woman spoke the colorful sentence, and she punctuated it with a shove. Darryl stumbled toward Veronica, who grabbed his arm and used his momentum to swing him toward the woman in yellow. He managed to stop himself and sidestep out of the way of the woman's swinging fist, but his years of training with the IAI failed him. He couldn't think to counterattack. In fact, Darryl had no reaction at all when he looked up at the yellow-clad woman's face and saw she had assumed the appearance of Melissa Packard, one of his earliest charity cases.

Her appearance stunned him, and the woman's kick stung him when her razor-sharp toenails dug deep into the skin of his left thigh. Her backhanded slap across his cheek cut his holler short. And when he raised his arm to block what looked like a two-fingered poke at his eyes, the woman grabbed the arm and swung him toward another.

The woman in the yellow gown had more than lady-like strength, possibly even more than human-like strength. Her swinging motion propelled Darryl at least fifteen feet across the floor. He would've stumbled on even farther if not stopped by a flat-footed kick to the center of his chest. Darryl fell on his back, hard.

The lady in lime who'd kicked him bent over Darryl and grabbed the top of his head with her right hand. She used just one arm to pull him back up to his feet. He didn't marvel at her strength; he marveled at her face, the face that had taken on the appearance of another past charity case.

"Jana?" Darryl stuttered the name.

"Uh-huh," the smiling woman said, "and nuh-uh," before punching him in the nose. Darryl felt the impact, starting at the point of contact and rippling outward toward the forehead, ears, and chin. If she'd let go, he would've fallen straight to his back again. But as he was still standing and staring at the grinning woman he both knew and didn't know, he couldn't do anything but breathe through his gaping mouth while a thick, sticky stream of blood flowed from his nostrils.

The woman stared back at him as she recited a verse of something that was either terrible poetry or horrible pop-music lyrics. As bad and pointless as it sounded to him, it had the effect of changing the shape and contours of its speaker's face. The words acted like a spell. A Dirty-Light Magick trick. When she stopped reciting, Darryl saw the woman appeared as yet another charity case.

"Irma—"

The woman punched Darryl in the nose again and, with the hand that had a firm grasp on his head, shoved him to stumble several feet across the floor, into the presence of the pale woman in black.

The porcelain-skinned woman appeared as she had before, her face wide-eyed and her mouth tight-lipped, unblinking and unexpressive. She grabbed Darryl by his shoulders and dug her broken-glass-sharp nails into his skin, looking him in his wincing eyes. Behind him, Veronica spoke.

"Vanessa there actually believes you to be much sexier than I ever did." Snideness coated each word. "Now, don't get me wrong, you are a very handsome man, with that vanilla-violet tan and all, but I just never felt the desire to go as far with you as she would. That level of passion just isn't in my blood."

As if reacting to Veronica's cue, Vanessa opened her mouth wider than she should've been able, thrust her face closer, and closed her eyes and mouth. Her eyelids finally touched each other, but her lips didn't. They were still apart, touching the skin of Darryl's lower neck as Vanessa's long, sharpened cuspids bit deep into his flesh. Darryl screamed louder than he'd screamed in years. The sight and sound of it all seemed to excite Vanessa. She opened her jaws and licked the neck wound, lapping the blood as it seeped out.

Darryl struggled, trying as best he could to ignore the pain, the pain in his head and the pain on his body. But Vanessa's grip was much too strong. He couldn't get free. Worse, he began to feel a cold, tingly sensation where her hands touched his skin, a sensation steadily spreading outward, getting colder as it moved toward his neck and down toward his elbows. Numbness. Soon he wouldn't be able turn his head or move his arms. Soon he wouldn't be able to fight back with anything but his legs, assuming he could remain conscious long enough to use them. He had to do something now.

Darryl reared back and kicked Vanessa's shin. He hollered when the impact of his unprotected foot against her skin made him feel as if he'd kicked an unyielding slab of ice. He may've broken his toes.

Veronica laughed. "Looks like he's trying to break up with you, Vanessa. Why don't you let him go? I'll be glad to welcome him back into my arms."

Vanessa ran her tongue across Darryl's upper lip and the area under his leaking nostrils. She pulled back her head and made sure Darryl saw as she mixed some of her saliva with the blood and mucous on her tongue, giving the thick substances a bit more fluidity.

His mouth was wide open. It was his only way to breathe. But when Vanessa kissed him, forcing the repellant concoction from her mouth into his, Darryl couldn't breathe or move. Only a small part of his consciousness realized the action was perversion of his very own honey-kiss, his method of making his saliva more like honey before kissing his charity cases for the final time. Most of his thoughts, however, were focused on how to get free as he gagged and continued to struggle. It wasn't until Veronica asked for him again that Vanessa spun him around and shoved him away.

As dizzied as he was, as battered as he was, Darryl's victimizers had made a mistake—they'd announced what they were going to do before they did it. He went on the offensive the moment he was released.

He could only see through bleary eyes, but indistinct shapes were enough for him. He swung his right fist at Veronica's head. Thanks to the disorientation, or the impaired vision, or the height difference, the punch only hit her in the neck, but it was enough. It hurt her. It did its job.

The blonde stumbled backward a few feet then sprang forward, her hands in front of her, her fingers bent and curled to resemble a hawk's talons.

It was far too dark and Darryl was much too weak to manipulate light as he would've wanted. In other circumstances, he'd have blinded her with an old-fashioned-camera-like flash, or he'd have shot a thin ray of infrared radiation at her forehead. Instead he had to rely on the basics.

He grabbed one of Veronica's wrists and ducked, dipping down to his knees, as he pulled the woman's long body onto his shoulders and dumped her on her back, onto the floor, using a fireman's-carry wrestling technique he'd learned from Robert.

He hopped back to his feet and rushed for the first woman he saw, the lady in the lime-green gown. He was stopped after three steps. The woman in tangerine blindsided him with a sharp-toe-nailed kick to the kidney.

Darryl fell down to a knee.

The lady in lemon helped him back up to his feet. She grabbed him by his bleeding neck, made fresh wounds with her fingernails, and shoved him back toward Veronica.

Veronica used her own wrestling technique to trap Darryl's arms behind him and lock her hands. It was an unbreakable hold. The blonde chuckled before leaning in to whisper into his ear.

"Watched you fight on the Mall," she said. "Just watched; didn't need to study. You're beyond pathetic."

Darryl struggled as best as he could manage. He might as well have been frozen.

"Fighting is futile," Veronica said. "It's all *Charma,* and it's all good."

Darryl cursed at her.

Her response was to shove him away as she shouted, "Ladies! Level two!"

The painted patterns on the floor began shifting from concentric circles to intersecting triangles.

Instead of standing and walking on the painted lines as they had been, the ladies in the fruit-colored apparel began to walk and stand only in the black spaces between the new geometric shapes.

Darryl continued to move wherever he was pushed; the ladies in orange, yellow, and green continued to shift and shape their faces into those of his past charity cases; and he continued to try to fight them. But he hadn't been lied to. It was futile.

No longer constrained to circles, the women fought in a more sophisticated manner, using graceful styles of fighting that were foreign to Darryl. Even when he tried to dodge their blows or run away, he couldn't escape. When he moved too far away from the colored lines, he felt as if he were suffocating on the shadows; he could only breathe when a foot or fist emerged from the black air, causing him to inhale with shock, and exhale on impact. As if to accentuate their new style and manner of combat, some of the ladies also broke out into song or recited familiar lyrics as they moved, avoiding the glowing lines, and making spot-on contact with some part of Darryl's weakened, bruised, and increasingly bloody body. In between his hollers and screams, Darryl heard sounds he hadn't heard in years, songs he had once associated with happy times or beautiful moments. But, as his torment went on and on, these sounds devolved into mere noises, purplish-white sounds, pale, irritating, drained of all meaning. He began to feel the noise was an appropriate accompaniment to the scene. As the ladies had hinted before they attacked, his life was being bleached of any purpose it ever had.

Chapter 13

Robert tried to double the legal speed limit on the way to Darryl's apartment. The Stang's V8 engine was up to it, but at this point in the evening, it wasn't easy to move so fast. Traffic was thicker than earlier in the day, thicker than usual. A lot of folks had come out with the sun after the midday rain shower.

When they finally arrived, Robert asked Ava to stay in the car while he took a quick look around. She didn't like it, but she didn't fuss.

Darryl's Miata was parked in its usual spot. Its hood was cold, and the space under the vehicle was drier than the space around it. Robert still took the time to peer through each window, looking for anything of interest. He found nothing and moved on, up the stairs to the fourth floor of the garden-apartment complex.

The key-tool he'd borrowed from Zel got him into the apartment.

Robert's first reaction on stepping into the one-bedroom was always the same. Darryl had "convinced" a talented interior designer to lavishly decorate it for free. The place was stylish and no doubt aesthetically pleasing to certain types of women and men, but to Robert, it all seemed a bit overdone. With all the plants, the randomly placed knickknacks, the framed photographs and other wall hangings, and the furniture chosen and arranged to match Darryl's "life compass," Robert felt like choking each time he crossed the apartment's threshold. But he had a job to do, and he proceeded to do a thorough survey for clues to Darryl's whereabouts.

After examining everything else, Robert turned his attention to the real potential treasure chest—Darryl's laptop. He turned it on, entered Darryl's password, and searched through his recent e-mails, his website history, recently saved documents, and anything else that might've been helpful.

On Saturday, his partner had apparently done a lot of searches on swastikas, the Star of David and, to a lesser extent, something called "Charma." The strange word seemed distantly familiar to Robert, but all he knew—based the web pages Darryl had found—was that it referred to some kind of esoteric spiritual philosophy. There were no real details. And there'd been no other searches within the past twenty-four hours.

Robert left the apartment with no more useful information than when he'd entered, but there were other leads to follow. One of them was leaning against his car with her arms crossed.

"Well?"

"No luck," he said.

"What're you thinking?" Ava asked. "You know he's not just missing. I can tell, you think something else is up."

Robert looked straight at her eyes for the first time since she'd put on her new glasses. However crisp and clear the world now appeared to Ava, to him, her eyes were now obscured by the glass, which offered him a pale-but-detailed reflection of himself. Too close to a mirror, he found it difficult to look at the lenses. It made him queasy, but he maintained it, staring at this ghostly apparition of himself as he leveled with her.

"I found out how you lost your memory."

"What?" She unfolded her arms and started toward him.

"At least I think I did," he said. "At the house where we found you, you were beat up by two women. They were angels. That's how you got your bruises, and it's probably how you lost your memory."

"How do you know this? How *long* have you known this?"

"I just found out this morning." He purposely ignored her first question.

"Who told you? Adam? What else did he find out?" Her questions came out rapid-fire. Robert answered her in a slower manner, hoping to calm her a bit.

"There is nothing else," he said. "I haven't told anyone at the Institution about this yet."

"Why the heck not?"

"Because I haven't had time."

"Use those stupid watches on your stupid wrists!"

"That's something that has to be told in person, face-to-face." Not necessarily, but Robert had set his own priorities. "Right now, we've got to find Darryl before the same thing happens to him."

"Robert, you better take me back to that house—*now*." Ava opened the car's passenger door and slammed it behind her.

"Why?" He said it even though he already knew the answer; asking the question was just a natural reaction. He knew taking Ava back to the scene of her vicious beating—the crime scene where she was robbed of a portion of her mind—might perhaps trigger a recollection, a memory of where her attackers had come from, or a thought about the place the two women might currently call home.

When Robert got behind the wheel, Ava only said, "I want to look things over for myself." That's all she said, but he knew what she meant.

As they raced down Arlington's streets, Robert told her Adam had contacted him while he was in the apartment to tell him the entire IAI had been alerted Darryl was missing. All anyone knew at the moment was Darryl had gone to brunch on Sunday morning. All Watcher agents not too deep into other research had been ordered to enter the field and follow up on any hunches they might have.

"None of them will even get close."

"That's some faith you have in your brethren," Ava said.

"That's not a commentary on them," Robert said. "It's an honest fear of what I think we're dealing with."

Ava didn't ask for a clarification. She seemed to become lost in her own thoughts and stayed there until Robert turned the corner that put the house into view. They got out of the car together. He followed behind her as she took her first tentative steps across the street and onto the sidewalk. The streets weren't as empty as they'd been the first time Robert was here. He saw a few dog-walkers and two strolling couples, all minding their own business; that was it. Police tape was still around the property. Neither Robert nor Ava paid it any heed as they stepped onto the lawn, but Ava stopped after two steps. Her face went blank. Robert saw her expression and thought it best to give her some breathing room.

"I'm going to check out the inside." He might as well have been talking to himself.

Robert opened the front door and walked in, searching for clues like he did at Darryl's, by manipulating light and his eyesight in every manner he could think of. With his eye and mind, he counted all objects and measured every distance between one and the rest of them, hoping for a hint of anything askew, anything out of place. He looked for anything the police might've missed, or any sign left behind by someone who might've come back after the authorities left. He wasn't completely sure what he'd do with anything he found; he wasn't exactly the world's greatest detective. But, depending on what he spotted, Robert figured maybe his mathematical instincts or the intuitional processes in his subconscious might push him on to the next step.

When he left the house, he saw Ava hadn't moved a muscle. He didn't want to risk breaking whatever trance she might be in, so he circled around to the backyard to give her a few more minutes of privacy. But he shouldn't have bothered.

"Nothing," she said when Robert stepped back into the front yard.

"What?"

"I don't remember a thing about this place," Ava said. "Or about what happened to me here."

"Oh." He shared her disappointment even though he knew her failure to recall anything was a much greater loss for her, a much more significant blow to her sense of self, her sense of wholeness.

"What about you?" she asked. "What'd you find?"

"Nothing useful."

Ava blew a puff of air through her nostrils. "So we've come full circle. All for nothing."

"No." Robert looked at his left wristwatch. "We're not done. It's time for us to go speak with a friend of mine."

∞　　　∞　　　∞

"Dawn club?" Ava said.

Robert rolled down the driver's side window and glanced both ways before making a left turn. "Yes," he said. "Dawnclub."

"They don't have those where I'm from."

Robert didn't much feel like engaging in small talk. But in his mind, in his mood, he felt as if too many periods of silence would have the same effect as tiny pellets bouncing up against his ear-drums—damn irritating.

"It's a metropolitan thing," he said. "Primarily on the East Coast. They're all lounges and clubs that open up around four in the morning and stay open till about eleven, noon, or sometimes one in the afternoon. They're a quieter answer to nightclubs. No alcohol, little noise. Most promote local performers—musicians, singers, poets. Mostly amateurs, but they're all practitioners in the quiet arts. No rockers, angry rappers, or screamers. Just something to help the sun get smoothly into the sky."

"They sound nice."

Robert pulled the car into the lot, trying his best to avoid running over any busted bottles.

"Some are nicer than others," he said.

"Quite a few hours till four A.M.," Ava said as they got out of the car. "Aren't they closed?"

"The woman we want to see is here. She'll let us in."

Ava stood still, surveying her surroundings. Robert just glanced at her and kept moving; there was nothing he needed to see on the outside. He knocked on the club's front door in a rhythmic manner, alerting the few people inside to his presence and his identity. He had to follow the same pattern twice more before the door finally cracked open. Half a face appeared in the opening.

"Hey, Rob. What's up?"

"Hey, Julio. Sonya's around, right?"

"Yeah." Julio pulled the door all the way open. "At the bar."

"Thanks. Didn't see my boy here this morn, did you?"

"Darryl? Nah. He's rarely here unless you are."

Ava followed Robert to the bar, where two women were sitting and talking. Seeing Robert, one of them smiled and waved.

"Rob!"

He nodded in return. The other woman said nothing. She just tightened her lips and widened her eyes. Robert narrowed his as he met her stare, searching for any recollection that he might know this person. He then turned to Sonya.

"Got a minute?"

"Sure," Sonya said. "I'll meet you for a smoke out back, VaShawna."

The other woman stood up, looked at Robert with no sense of pleasantness, and headed toward a side door.

Sonya grinned. "Nice to see you up past bedtime for once."

Robert waited until VaShawna had vanished before responding. He nodded in the direction of the slammed door. "Who's that?"

"New employee," Sonya said. "Bartender. Get used to her."

Robert made a noise in his throat—part grunt, part hum—then said, "Sonya, this is Ava. The girl Darryl and I found on Friday."

"Oh!" Sonya rushed to embrace Ava before she could back away. "We're so glad you were found!"

Ava looked embarrassed. "Did I—did I know you?"

"No," Sonya said, "but every found person is a recovery for us all."

Ava looked at Robert; he only looked at his left-wristwatch and asked Sonya, "Can I get some water, please? Lukewarm."

"Oh, sure." Sonya went behind the bar and retrieved a plastic bottle.

"Thanks." Robert untwisted the cap and sipped a little, just enough to wet his tongue and throat. He then took a pill bottle from his jeans pocket, untwisted it, and shook out the last two multicolored capsules. His regular dosage was four; he'd have to remember to refill at The Burrow as soon as he returned. He swallowed the two pills together, gulping them down as Ava eyed him curiously. He ignored her and asked Sonya, "You haven't seen or heard from Darryl, have you?"

"Not since Saturday. Why?"

"One day we find one, another day we lose one."

"Seriously?"

Robert nodded.

"Well, he can take care of himself, Rob. You know that."

"I know he can't take care of himself in the situation I think he's in," Robert said. "On Saturday, you saw that blonde he was speaking to, right?"

"Yeah," Sonya said. "She asked me about him before she went over."

"What'd you tell her?"

"Just his name, and that he wasn't married."

"She give you a name?" Robert asked.

"You mean hers?"

Robert nodded.

"It's Veronica Blake."

"You know her?" Robert asked.

"Of course," Sonya said. "She's a talent scout. And the manager of Phantasie's rEVEnge."

"You've got to be kidding me," he said.

"Why would I?"

"Any idea where I can find her?" Robert asked.

"She mostly goes where the band goes," Sonya said. "Find them, and she's probably nearby."

"Well, they were here two days ago..." Robert looked at the stage. "I don't suppose anyone here has a schedule of their performances?"

"I can do a quick search on the web," Sonya said. "Benjy's got a laptop in back. Hold on."

After she left, Ava asked, "You really trust her?"

"What do you mean?" Robert asked.

"I mean you believe she's not going to send you running after red herrings? How do you know she's not friends with this Blake woman? How do you know she's telling you everything, or that she's not back there making phone calls?"

"Because I trust her absolutely," Robert said. "One hundred percent. I wouldn't have come to her if I didn't."

"Well, I guess that makes one person on the planet who can fit into your little circle."

"It's an exclusive club," Robert replied. "Maybe one day you'll have the currency to pay your way inside."

"I can think of better ways to waste my money," Ava said with a snort.

The amusing comeback almost put a smile on his lips, but Robert was quick to prevent it by taking another drink of water.

Ava waited for him to finish the bottle before asking, "What were those pills?"

"Huh?"

"Those pills you took a few minutes ago."

"A placebo," he said with a joyless grin. "Something to help keep the visions of sugarplums dancing in my head. Without it, I'd trip on my feet and fall right on my ass."

The poor joke most likely went over her head, but one thing he'd said touched a nerve.

"Language." Ava shook her head. "All the cursing is really annoying."

"Then bless me, Arkangel. Maybe that'll help me keep balance."

Ava started to respond, but Sonya rushed back into the room, waving a piece of paper. "Their schedule for the whole month!"

Robert grabbed the sheet and quickly scanned it.

"Sorry it took so long," Sonya said. "The printer kept jamming. I hope it's useful."

"It is. Let's go," he said to Ava.

The pair rushed toward the door.

"Thanks again," Robert said over his shoulder. "Call me if you have any other ideas."

"I will, but you really need a *burner*," Sonya said, referring to the prepaid disposable cell phones popular with criminals. "Landlines are no good for you, or anyone else these days."

The moment the door closed behind them, Robert saw VaShawna leaning against a wall, glaring at him as she took a drag on her cigarette. Without being too obvious, Robert kept her in his range of vision as he and Ava made their way to his car.

"You should go back and give it to her," Ava said.

"What to whom?" He kept his eye on the potential enemy, paying only partial attention to Ava.

"Sonya. You should give her your watch number."

"Funny, Arkangel. You're hilarious." He saw VaShawna take a long last drag, throw her cigarette to the ground, and walk back inside the club.

"I was trying to make a serious point," Ava said as Robert, seeming to forget himself, opened the car's passenger-side door for her. "Who doesn't have a cell phone? How is anyone supposed to get in touch with you in an emergency, or a moment of desperation? Anyone who doesn't have one of those heart-to-mind readers is out of luck."

Her comment surprised him, but Robert kept his face blank and his mouth closed. He started the car and waited until he'd driven it out of the lot before he asked, "And just what makes you think you know how the watches work?"

"Just a lucky guess."

Doubtful. Robert himself had little idea how they worked; he just knew they did. The devices had been a joint invention by Zel and Vince. All Watchers had taken a training session on how to use them. Not once during the session were the exact mechanics explained to them; intuition had been emphasized over hard science. No words or sounds were used to create messages, just thought and touch. Psychic Morse code. Robert had always figured the method of message transmission had to do with some kind of connection between electromagnetism and the human nervous system. Even though the watches wrapped around pulse sites, he never once considered the heartbeat—not until now, anyway.

"I don't give a damn how smart cell phones are today," he said, "there are plenty of folks out there who are smarter, and up to no good. Whatever you write or say, someone could easily intercept the message, maybe an important one. Transmitting directly from mind to mind is the only truly secure way to communicate. The watches are the best instruments we have for that."

Ava said nothing for the next several minutes. During that time, Robert dwelled on VaShawna. He'd never seen her before, and yet he had a sense of familiarity when he saw her today, much like he'd had when he saw the word "Charma." It was possible—even probable—the woman was a previous charity case of Darryl's, someone who hadn't been left to stroll on the straight path to *peace* but instead had been dumped on the muddy, rocky, winding road to *nowhere*. Such a one couldn't help but feel wronged, angry, peeved toward others, particularly men, and especially Darryl and his associates. The woman must've seen Darryl and Robert together in the club—or together in another club—at some point. She must've known they were close.

The only things Robert knew for sure were that he was losing time, he was probably losing his partner, and he was definitely losing his patience.

"Maybe I should sign on formally," Ava said. "As an IAI agent, I mean. I could use that generous allowance Mister Smith mentioned. I wouldn't mind buying a cell, or even a burner. And I don't know if you noticed, but I've been wearing the same clothes for a couple of days now."

"I noticed," Robert said. "Where'd you snatch them?"

Ava at first seemed confused by the question. It couldn't have been because Robert had blurted it out without thinking; he suspected instead she hadn't meant to draw attention to her clothes. Or she thought he'd been too stupid all this time to notice the obvious.

"I didn't *snatch* them. I…well…I borrowed them. From the hospital. From some girl's suitcase before I left."

"Bullshit." Another blurt. "And what the hell do you need a cell for, anyway? Who do you need to call?"

"Anyone and everyone," she said. "My friends in The ID have a great calling plan. I want to get in the network."

Robert blew a puff of air through his nose, and then he shut up. Clearly that'd been her intent.

"Where are we going, anyway?"

"The Phantasie played at this lounge in Alexandria on Sunday," Robert said. "It's near the Eisenhower Metro stop."

"We're going to get on a train?" Ava asked.

"No time. We're driving. They close at midnight, and I don't know the secret knock."

"Then why bother telling me about the train stop?"

"Because once we get there," Robert said, "we're going to do some searching. If we get separated, or if anything crazy happens, that'll be the point of reference."

When they arrived in the area, Robert parked his car in the lot across the street from the movie theater, next to the Metro station.

"This is our spot," he said as they got out of the car. "You can remember this, right?"

Ava sneered at him then followed as he walked across the street.

"The club is several blocks that way." Robert pointed his thumb toward his right. "I don't know how he got there—by car or foot or piggyback—but from this point on, keep your eyes open for any sign of him passing by, or falling down."

Both took a quick moment to survey their surroundings before walking on. The sidewalks and parking lots were mostly empty. The few people they saw seemed to be making their way toward the movie theater for a late night showing. The theater's sign was one of the most prominent sources of light in the area, but it wasn't bright enough to illuminate the streets and sidewalks. The area was almost pitch dark. Robert and Ava walked slower than they would have during the daytime, four blocks down Eisenhower Avenue, neither seeing anything of even mild interest. When they reached the corner of the street, where the row of buildings ended and a grassy lot lay across the street in front of them, Robert pointed to their left.

"The lounge is two blocks down this street," he said.

Ava glanced in that direction then looked back at the darkened lot of lavender wildflowers and green-and-brown weeds. She took a longer look at the tall trees across the street on the other side, and then the taller buildings nearby.

"You go ahead," she said. "I want to get to some higher ground and scan the area. See what I can see."

It was a good idea, and even though Robert preferred they stay together, he wasn't in the mood to argue.

"All right," he said. "When I come out, holler if I don't see you."

A brief discussion with some of the lounge's waitstaff didn't give Robert much more information than he already had. Yes, The Phantasie had performed on Sunday. Yes, a guy fitting Darryl's description had been in the audience. Yes, a striking blonde woman had been with him. No, they had no idea where the two went once they'd left the establishment. And "No," Robert said in response to their question, "I don't need to know what they ordered."

He left the lounge and took a little time to peer through the fence at the project that would one day be John Carlyle Square. Seeing no bodies and nothing else of interest, he continued on toward Holland Lane. He crossed the street in front of the park and saw Ava, about two blocks down on his right-hand side, waving at him. He took his time getting there, making sure no step was neglected, no potential clues passed over. It wasn't until he reached Ava that he saw the first sign of something out of place.

She pointed triumphantly down at the small object lying on the sidewalk.

"It's all I found," she said. "But it tells us something."

It was a lighter, lying several blocks away from the lounge whose name was imprinted on it.

"Yeah," Robert said, "it tells us that people have no respect for the environment. They litter. I could've told you that as soon as you woke up."

"But look at it," Ava said. "It hasn't been here all that long."

"So?"

"Well, look at it," she said. "I saw the fingerprints. Look at them and see if they're Darryl's."

"How the heck am I supposed to know what his fingerprints look like?"

"You're his partner, aren't you?"

Robert sighed. "Darryl doesn't smoke. You find anything else?"

"No," she said. "I even took a quick look over the park. And the cemetery. You find anything?"

"Yeah," he said, "the last place Darryl was probably seen alive. The lounge. Once they left, Miss Blake must've whispered the magic words to make him disappear."

Ava crossed her arms and began to pace as Robert focused on the lighter, kneeling down to get an even closer look. The same word flashed across his mind as the first time he'd glanced at the object: *Charma*. There was something about the lighter, or something about this spot. But it was a mystery that would have to be put on the back burner.

"You could be on to something," he said. "It's possible someone dropped this on purpose. But it's telling us nothing, except we're at a dead end."

"So, you're giving up?" Ava asked.

"On this method, yeah." Robert picked up the lighter. "But I have another idea."

Chapter 14

The ladies helped Darryl through the darkness, up each uneven step of the spiraling staircase.

No lights. No windows. There was nothing to help him see clearly in the cramped area. It took energy to use his parasite-given abilities, and the gauntlet of taunting and whipping he'd just endured had sapped almost every bit of it. He couldn't even stand without assistance, let alone walk by himself. Even with assistance, Darryl tripped on every third or fourth stair. He knew Victoria and Verdad—the two women who'd draped his arms over their shoulders—were doing their best to ensure he didn't fall on his face. What he didn't know was *why*, especially after everything they'd just put him through.

A black wall was at the top of the staircase. Vonda, the woman in lime-green who was leading them, knocked on it in three different places before rubbing her hand against it at waist level. Something clicked. A long sliver of light appeared, then widened. The wall became a door.

The four entered a bright room; Vonda closed the door behind them. On its other side, the door appeared to be just one of the hexagonal room's many ten-foot-tall mirrors, all of them seemingly positioned to break up the white walls' monotony.

The shock and abundance of the light shining from the room's many bulbs caused Darryl's eyelids to close, twitch, and scrunch together. But he didn't have the strength to keep them pressed together for long. So he succumbed, again. He couldn't withdraw. He'd no choice but to watch whatever new torment awaited him. As he let his fluttering eyelids pull farther and farther apart, his trembling lips mimicked them as they parted and let a shaky voice accompany his vision.

"Where—?"

"You know something funny?" Vonda said. "The Beautiful One used to have a stuttering problem too. Quite awful. In fact, you're in much the same situation she was in a year ago—battered, bruised, confused by all manners of tricks. Looks like you two were made for each other."

"What? What's—?" Darryl stammered while Victoria and Verdad, his two living crutches, moved him across the room and ignored his malformed questions. He stopped trying to speak when his eyes finally adjusted to the bright environment, bringing into knife-sharpened focus the room's centerpiece: a glass coffin.

It stood upright, hovering a foot above the floor, suspended from the ceiling by four thin wires connected to each of its top four corners. Darryl could tell the coffin was comprised of several different types of glasses and mirrors, but it was mostly transparent—enough for him to see the nude body of the girl inside.

Her body was shapely, and short. She wasn't much taller than five feet. And not a single inch of her body was touching any part of the glass or mirrors. As the device itself was suspended in the room, the girl's body was suspended within it.

Rays from the twenty or so light bulbs that ran in a circle around the room bounced off the walls' many mirrors until they hit and filtered through the coffin's glass. When the rays of light hit the girl's skin, Darryl knew the parasites within her skin cells would use the radiation in their recipes of blood and other ingredients; they'd feed on it, process it, regurgitate it, and feed on it again, or work with it, or play with it. However the parasites used the radiation, Darryl knew the indirect results of all this was to cause the parasites' host to levitate in the air—or, in this case, within the coffin.

It was beyond the spectrum visible to most humans, but even in his condition, Darryl could see the grand web of light threading through the girl's skin, keeping her afloat within the coffin.

He gazed through the glass, staring at the girl from behind. That stout body. That wild, curly red hair reaching and stopping just a few inches below her bare shoulders. The patches of mud-brown freckles and varicolored rashes, scars, remnants of acne, and other types of bumps and bruises blemishing her pale skin. With only these pieces to form the puzzle, Darryl knew the lost girl had been found. The body in the coffin was Marie-Lydia McGillis, the Virus-infected girl who only a year ago tried to take out an entire high school in rural Virginia and almost succeeded. What had the five other women in the room done to her? What were they planning to do to him?

Three of the women—Vonda, Victoria, and Verdad—had participated in the beating he'd received in the dark room. He'd heard them named by the now-absent Veronica and Vanessa. The other two women—one in red, the other in blue—were new to him. All five were nearly seven feet tall. Darryl knew enough to know he was being used in some sort of elaborate ritual that was probably sacrificial. He just didn't know why. It all seemed so senseless.

"You see," Vonda said as she walked toward the room's fireplace, "it all went wrong for your zero-hero Vastion when his baby died—"

"Where's Veronica?" Darryl asked. "She led me to this…this execution. She should have the guts to face me."

"I've got your answer right here."

Darryl turned to look at the woman in the crimson gown as she picked something off of the fireplace's mantle and held it up by her face. It was a book.

"A full, complete copy of *Death's Heart*," the woman said.

"Let me go," Darryl said to no one in particular.

"Yes, do," Vonda said. "Victoria, Verdad—please give the dirty boy a bath."

The women in tangerine and lemon led him toward a claw-foot bathtub standing less than twenty feet in front of the glass coffin. The tub was filled with a gleaming ivory-colored liquid, a substance concealing golden-brown globules that sometimes rose to the surface and bobbed before sinking back out of sight.

Victoria and Verdad kicked Darryl's legs out from under him, hitting just the right spots to make them go numb, and forced him to lie backward in the tub, submerging his body in the creamy substance. The two were careful to position him so that his head stayed clear while the rest of his body remained immersed. It seemed they didn't want him to drown, at least.

Darryl couldn't put up a struggle, but he refused to give in. He opened his mouth to shout in protest, to shout insults, to shout threats—but nothing came out. He remained silent when he saw the golden globules beginning to elongate and wriggle, struggling and swimming like snakes in the milky substance surrounding him. Whatever the globs were made of, it was a substance that didn't dissolve in the creamy liquid. Darryl soon regarded the caramel gels less as snakes and more like eels as he became aware that something in the milky substance was actually soothing his body, giving a skin-tingling comfort to his many sores and wounds, calming his aching muscles…But his sense of dread remained. He wouldn't be soothed or calmed while he was facing the front of the suspended coffin, the front of Marie-Lydia McGillis.

Even though the texture of the skin and the condition of the body didn't look any different from the front, from his new perspective Darryl was able to do two things: confirm the girl really was whom he thought, and see the expression on her face. There was just a hint of it, at the corners of her mouth, but it was unmistakable to Darryl. It was the expression of someone sleeping sweetly, pleasantly. He wondered about it as the vapors from his bath wafted toward his nose to be inhaled, to be absorbed into his system.

"As I had been saying," Vonda said, "it all went wrong for Vastion's plan, his mission, when his baby blew itself out before its own birthday. His love child died—born stillborn—all because Vast settled for an *unfair* woman, a capricious tramp, an imperfect match. But all of that, all of *this,* it's really just a fiction."

The woman in red tossed the book into the fireplace.

Darryl should have shouted or screamed at the sight—his bible was *burning*—but the bath's vapors had already begun to affect him. While the liquid was doing something to his body, its odor was doing something to his mind…synesthesia. He began to taste the liquid through his wounds. He could taste the cinnamon-spiced honeymilk, with its hints of peppermint. It was delicious… intoxicating. Layers of his consciousness were being peeled back as he savored the flavors of the layered concoction, and Darryl didn't mind it at all.

He watched silently as Verdad, Victoria, and the woman in periwinkle-blue walked to stand against the white spaces of the room's walls. He then rolled his head and looked at the woman in red, the one Vonda called "Vesuvius." She was using the iron poker to jab at something in the fireplace. When she'd finished,

Vonda thrust a shovel into the same spot. She pulled the shovel out of the fire and looked at the mound of smoldering black-white ashes with a satisfied smile. Darryl stared as Vonda gracefully approached him, not spilling a single ash, looking at him with a grin the entire time, until she was close enough to dump the shovel's heap into the tub.

"The allegory is no more," Vonda said. "In Reality, we'll do things differently."

In another state of mind, Darryl's reaction might've been different; as it was, he just barely felt the hot ashes reacting with the tub's liquid as they were subsumed, altering the liquid's properties so the golden-brown eels were finally able to dissolve and fully mix with the rest of the concoction. The bath soon had the appearance of liquid sunlight, but Darryl had no reaction to the sight of it. The property of the liquid that had entered his nostrils like incense had been successful in putting him into an altered state of consciousness. The long-legged ladies no longer worried or scared him. What they were doing seemed one part elegant and one part absurd. Darryl stared with removed fascination as Vesuvius and Vonda walked to stand at another point in the room.

"We don't want you to follow the path of an anonymous poet's sad creation," Vonda said. "We think you're destined for greater things. You're going to start all over, play a variation on a bad poet's theme, revise the book by living it, in accordance with how The Beautiful One instructs you to."

Darryl had just enough of a stake in the reality before him to determine that the five women were standing equidistant from one another, defying the room's hexagonal design by standing against three walls and in two corners. If lines were drawn from each to the four others, the resulting design would resemble a pentagram within a pentagon. The suspended coffin was at the exact middle of the ladies' design.

"Get set," Vesuvius said.

The electric lights shut off, and the ceiling began to recede, sliding away to be hidden by the room's upper corners, revealing in its place a grand skylight. The large window not only allowed the overhead moon's light into the room, it also seemed to amplify it. The usually wan moon glow was more like bright baby-blue sunlight that spilled into the room and was amplified even further by the walls' many mirrors.

"It's time, ladies," Vesuvius said.

"Five," the lady in periwinkle said.

"Four," Vonda said.

"Three," Verdad said.

"Two," Victoria said.

Vesuvius said, "One," a cracked second before all five ladies released a harmonic wail that pierced the air, changing the atmosphere of the room.

It seemed with each breath Darryl took, twice as much air left his body as he brought in. The sound of his heartbeats increased in his ears; he heard them skip, jump, stop, and thump, playing music at war with the continuing song of the women. And his eyes…

Darryl lost complete sight of everything except the glass coffin. He stared as the eyelids on the redheaded girl twitched twice before jerking apart, as if pulled by fishhooks. And the coffin itself…

As cracks, hairline fractures, and wider fissures appeared in the glass, the coffin's shape transformed from rectangular to oval. The coffin appeared as a painted, glass egg a moment before the glass shattered. Its shards carpeted the floor under the girl, who was now unencumbered and hovering in mid-air.

Darryl couldn't blink. His eyes and hers had linked. His peripheral vision was being extinguished. Those green eyes were dominating him. Comely, expressive, endearing, it seemed impossible to look at anything else, even when she winked her left eye and the iris of the right flashed a bright fire-truck-red before the left eye reopened with a brighter puff of scarlet light. Both eyes were then a slightly different shade of green than they'd been before. They faded to yet another shade after she winked again. And they changed soon again, as if she were trying to find just the right color for whatever task she had in her newly awakened mind.

Darryl had little in his conscious mind. He gazed without words at the color-shifting eyes. He had nothing to say even as his peripheral vision returned enough for him to notice the pinpricks of white light flaring up and out from every pore of the girl's skin. He saw but didn't comment when the particles of dust in her immediate presence began to sparkle and move about her as if alive and dependent on her. Darryl saw and didn't question the bat's wings of light as they extended out, flaring, from her bare shoulders, displaying colors beyond the most exotic parrot's. Darryl thought nothing of the disappearance of her body's many blemishes, scars, bumps, and bruises. He was almost oblivious to the fact that the surface of her skin was tightening, smoothing itself out. He was just conscious enough to notice the skin's refinished tone looked like vanilla-bean ice cream, with cinnamon-brown freckles.

But the overall metamorphosis meant nothing to him. Darryl was only focused on those eyes, whose irises had finally settled on a bright-green jade.

He didn't care to see her smile. He didn't care to see her take the unsure-but-secure steps on the air as she approached the tub, as she approached *him.* He was like a drunk drowning in those eyes, one of them still winking, both of them still flashing several varieties of red, and both of them returning to the same glimmering shade of jade. He'd no desire to save himself. By the time the redheaded girl had perched herself, crouching, at the foot of the tub, Darryl was ready to do anything for her, this beautiful one. All she had to do was ask.

The girl gracefully positioned herself so that her hands and feet remained on the tub's rim, her unclothed body remained untouched by the sticky yellowish-brown glop, and her face and eyes hovered just a few inches away from Darryl's.

He was speechless. She wasn't.

"Hello, honey," she said with a slight rasp. "Are you ready to come into me, so we may beautify the world?"

Darryl said nothing. She didn't need to say anything more.

With those big, beautiful, green eyes, the girl winked one last time at him, bit her tongue, and exhaled. His vision began to get cloudy.

Darryl didn't know anything about beautifying worlds, but on some level of his subconscious, he knew he'd never again see the only world he'd known intimately.

Chapter 15

Darryl was lifted down into XynKroma. Plunged into the hole of his own mind, he fell into the pit of Ultimate Reality, a plane of existence ruled by dangerous metaphors, a dimension where killer poetry held sway. A modern-day Dante on the ultimate psychological trip to Inner Space, surfing the Scalp of the Creator—he should be so lucky to live to rhyme about the experience.

He initially felt and knew nothing about his situation, perhaps for the best. Between a boundless sky of honey and equally limitless sea of syrup, a grape-colored glob of jelly hovered, convulsed, and undulated, gradually becoming self-aware it was the essence of Darryl Ridley…There wasn't much he wanted to feel or know about the situation prior to that.

So close to the Source of Creation, the only way Darryl or any human could exist in the extra-dimensional realm was by a figurative representation of the essence of his consciousness—his "soul." He was all too familiar with the realm polluted with the detritus of every sentient being's imagination, but it was rare for Darryl to visit involuntarily. And the fact his soul was represented by a glob of jelly did not portend a happy journey.

Those afflicted with the ability to manipulate light usually had an advantage in taking control and maneuvering through the dirty-light realm's nonsensical, ever-shifting, ethereal terrain. At the moment, Darryl was having trouble maneuvering his senses within his own unshaped and uncontrollable soul. Despite the lack of blood or bones or organs, and in spite of his transformation and transfer to this lawless, old realm, the senses were still present. But with the exception of his sense of hearing, they were all garbled within him, and Darryl couldn't manage to untangle them or position them so they might be of some use.

His attempts to make sense of himself had the unintended consequence of stretching his soul in multiple directions. The jelly glob sprouted gooey limbs that reached and stretched (and twisted, when becoming too close to one another) as they went on and on, the tips extending farther and farther beyond their source. This process continued as the honey sky and syrupy sea underwent their own changes—in tone, in currents, and in contents.

The sky more and more resembled the roof of an icy cave; rows and rows of icicles resembling stalactites jutted downward. If Darryl's seeing-sense had been in order, he would've looked and—if sensibly possible—expressed horror at the images of these long, thin, and pointed ice-lances, each of them impaling a partially transparent human body. Ghosts were stuck through their centers, hanging upside down, and—whether living spirits or truly dead—positioned so they were forced to face and perhaps see the sea as it became suffused with the color of indigo while rushing upward, toward the sky.

By the time the sea had engulfed everything, Darryl's soul was stretched in ninety-nine different directions.

He needed assistance. He desired help. He wished to be saved.

Granted.

Something with multiple appendages snatched at the ends and captured the wayward limbs of Darryl's confused soul. This same something brought everything together, molding Darryl's shape into a ball, before destroying the perfect sphere to fashion it into a shape to which Darryl was much more accustomed: a humanoid body.

He felt much more comfortable. All his senses were now in place, except one. He noticed it right off. He'd been left blind.

"Like the creator who cares nothing for its own creation."

Darryl heard a voice. He also felt it as an immediate then quickly subsiding sensation of warmth surrounding him in the water.

Whatever the symbolic material composition of his soul, he was now imbued with pure fear. He didn't want to see what had spoken to him, what had read his thoughts. He very well knew there was no limit to the type of phantasmagoric beings that lived in the realm. There were no constraints of any kind to Xyn, neither in its expanse nor in its variety of contents. The wisest of its visitors knew to succumb, submit, and operate within whatever was imposed, until the moment a sure advantage could be discovered. Darryl considered himself nothing if not wise.

"What's happening?" he asked in a near-whisper.

"You will see for yourself," was the water-warming response. "Then you will see much further."

This time the warm-water sensation did not fade when the voice went silent. It grew warmer, hotter, until Darryl's soul felt as if it were enveloped in steam. He felt the hot-then-warm water droplets settling onto his soul's skin. Once settled, the droplets dropped further in temperature, altered their shapes, changed their composition, and became harder, became like crystals, became sharper and more pointed as they burrowed under the surface of his soul.

He was all too sensitive now. Darryl felt every single gelid particle within his soul moving, each of them making its way upward toward his soul's neck, into his soul's head, where they began to amass in the area that, on Reality's surface, would've been occupied by gray matter. The crystalline structure resulting from the inner-soul migration raised its temperature and, while inflicting tremendous pain, melted away the sticky, viscous substance surrounding it. Darryl was left with nothing but a diamond-like brain, sitting alone atop his soul's shoulders, a gem that allowed him to see in every direction, at every angle, simultaneously.

Unfortunately.

He was now able to take in the entire scope of the monstrous leviathan that had been addressing him. The deep indigo hue of the watery environment didn't matter. Darryl's vision was of such a quality that he could pierce through it, clearly taking in the giant's entire form.

In spite of his enhanced vision, though, it was difficult for Darryl to determine the amount of distance that actually existed between the giant and him. He hoped it was much farther than it seemed. From his fresh perspective, it appeared his soul was one-third the size of the leviathan's head, which resembled a giant squid's. The tentacles coming out of the being's neck were most likely what had gathered Darryl's wayward soul, rolled it into a ball, and fashioned it into a human form. It wasn't surprising the creature chose a human form for Darryl. Below its tentacles, it too had the body of human. It was neither male nor female, but a hermaphrodite.

Clothing was uncommon among the visitors and permanent inhabitants of XynKroma. Although parts were revealed that Darryl would've preferred hidden, the creature did have some covering on its arms and legs: scales, which were congruous with the claws it had as hands and feet, and with the dragon wings protruding from its back.

While Darryl's primary attention was diverted toward the primary inhabitant of the surrounding sea, he did notice it was also populated by much smaller and more nebulous beings whose bodies seemed almost gelatinous. Some of them swam about like jellyfish, while others swam about in the manner of eels. All possessed a certain electrical quality. There was a bright flash of pale-green light when two or more almost touched. When two or more passed through one another, branching veins of dark green lightning traveled through their immaterial bodies, tangling with the gossamer innards. They were far more fascinating than frightening.

Darryl's gemlike brain did more than allow him to see all around. The multifaceted organ also gave him knowledge of the immediate past. He could see the entire progress of his soul's most recent journey through Xyn, from its emergence between honey skies and syrupy seas down to the present. He knew the beings swimming around him were the ghosts who'd formerly been impaled on the sky-roof's icicles; they were now free, half-living, and adapted to a new environment. As for Darryl's own immediate environment, a pocket of air had been created around his soul. He was no longer in the water, but suspended within a transparent bubble surrounded by water.

"What are you?" he asked his current master.

"I am MadaMadaM," it said. "The sentinel at the beginning of your path to redemption."

"Redemption?"

There was no response.

"How?" Darryl asked.

"First, by not asking me any more questions," MadaMadaM said. "Second, by answering one of mine. One and only one. If you do not guess it, your fate will be worse than anything you can comprehend."

Of course, Darryl thought. So no need to bother using words to describe what might happen.

"How many faces can a man wear," MadaMadaM asked, "before he wears himself out?"

Darryl recognized the question. How couldn't he after what he'd so recently endured at the hands—and feet, and teeth—of five vivid women in a dark room? The question was a quote from the very last poem in the first volume of *The Blackbook of Autumn Numbers*. After violently confronting his falsely loved female acquaintances (one-day lays) in a dream, and then confronting his true love in a heated, damning argument in reality, the young-but-repentant womanizing protagonist of the story put the question to himself and followed it with: "Inquiries such as these find their answers in my tracks." But MadaMadaM didn't want that line as a response. It wasn't an answer, only a pointed line, an arrow leading to the answer.

Darryl in his younger days had been much like the main character in the book, pursuing whichever female caught his fancy until he caught her. Shortly after he was done with her, he would run away—fast enough to duck and hide so she'd lose sight, or far enough for her to be dissuaded to pursue. But it had all caught up with him. All of it—in the form of one virus, a virus that made his skin ultrasensitive to light, that gave him epileptic seizures, that gave him constant bouts of queasiness, that had affected his nervous system, that enabled billions of parasitic microbes to live in his skin and blood, and that made him unable to survive without the parasites and unable to exist happily and healthily with them. There was no telling which girl or woman had given him the virus. Darryl didn't remember most of their names. He remembered numbers. The numbers in his own little black book. He had kept score. And in the end he'd lost. After all the scores of women and girls, he'd ended up with nothing. Zero. Love.

"Seventy-eight," he said in a whisper.

That was it. The number he'd wantonly bedded before he knew he had the White Fire Virus. The number he'd happily and carelessly seduced before he became sick and scared. The number he'd played with before he began to wonder, ponder, obsess over how he'd gotten it, who may have given it to him, how long he'd had it, and to whom he may have given it. He had wondered in circles, and ended up with zero. Nothing. Love.

Darryl said it again, louder. "Seventy-eight."

The number of recognizable faces three of the five women in the dark room had worn as they extracted blood and exacted indirect revenge on behalf of the unknown seventy-eight. These dark avengers probably hadn't known the names or faces of his seventy-eight either, but they somehow had known about his charity cases, and they'd selected seventy-eight faces from them. And Darryl, for each of those unknown seventy-eight, when he had been with them in reality, he'd blindly put on a different face, an indifferent act, whatever it took so he could get all he desired from them. Now he was so, so tired.

"Seventy-eight!" Darryl said one last time. "That's how many faces!"

The beak on the leviathan's face couldn't show any expression, but MadaMadaM seemed satisfied with Darryl's response.

"The answer is different for each individual," it said. "The key to answering correctly is to answer honestly. And the only way to answer honestly is to exercise all available faculties to remember past moral crimes. Remembrance leads to absolution. Absolution leads to Salvation."

MadaMadaM stopped speaking, but Darryl continued to sense vibrations of sound emanating from the leviathan. It was the equivalent of humming, but it wasn't meaningless sound. It was a communication. While Darryl remained motionless, trying to determine what it meant, he saw jets of pale-blue ink shooting out from the neck of the giant. He watched and soon understood. The leviathan was communicating with ink and noise, communicating in order to scribble out and redraw the environment. Although they were still in XynKroma, still in that ambiguous dimension of damaged archetypes, the symbols were changing.

Darryl's spherical range of vision began to extend farther and farther, providing even more detail as the indigo sea receded from view. When the process was complete, the entire ground was over-laid with white cirrus and gray stratus clouds. In patches where there were no clouds, there was a blue soil, dotted with little black stones. Standing securely on a cloud, Darryl looked down at a nearby blue patch and followed his attention to some of its ebony pebbles. He found that the stones operated like peepholes, giving him as he concentrated a view of the orange and red forests, all situated amid turquoise-tinted blades of grass, miles below the ground of clouds and blue soil.

Darryl shifted his focus. The air surrounding him was replete with tri-colored rings, floating about like incomplete bubbles blown by a playful child, all of them bouncing away from one another when two or more came close enough to almost touch. The moody sky not-too-far above him churned, appearing one moment like a thick, reddish mud and the next like a more fluid, creamy substance that appeared to be milk. Even though there was no sun or other source of light, much of the atmosphere was as bright as that of an afternoon on a clear spring's day. But the leviathan overshadowed the ground on which Darryl's soul stood.

Although he now saw it in a different environment, Darryl still had the same level of fearsome awe when looking at the giant riddle-maker. It was positioned on all fours, standing on dirty-white cushions of clouds. Darryl stared and studied its silvery green scales, its orange-brownish claws, it blue-grayish squid's head, and its tentacles, each featuring a variety of colors that tangled together while maintaining the integrity of their distinct hues.

"As you have answered your question correctly," MadaMadaM said, "I shall give you the gift of a helpmeet in your quest."

Darryl wanted to ask "What quest?" and "What's a helpmeet?" But he remembered the leviathan's earlier admonition and kept silent, hoping it would explain all he needed to know.

"The quest to earn redemption for your soul," MadaMadaM said. "At a particular location in Xyn, well guarded by the minions of another, the soul of a young one, a beautiful one, is being kept prisoner. She is a prisoner of twisted love. The soul was imprisoned by a very sick lover who now walks freely on the surface of Reality. You shall be well on your way to Salvation if you free her."

"If I can't?" Darryl found the courage to ask.

A chain appeared out of nowhere. One end of it was buried underground; the other trifurcated and ended in manacles shackled around Darryl's neck and wrists. Darryl couldn't speak. Even though his soul had no mouth and no larynx, somehow the manacle at his neck took away his voice.

"What should happen to a man unable to save his own soul?" MadaMadaM said.

The patch of blue soil in front of Darryl shook, experiencing a very localized quake. Among the clods of speckled blue clay thrust upward and outward leapt a creature with the shape and face of a wolf, the size and skin of a tiger, and the spanning wings of a mutated eagle. A chimera. Darryl saw the other end of the chain that bound him was attached to a collar on the beast's neck.

MadaMadaM said nothing more. There was no advice, no warnings, no riddles, not even a nonsensical explanation of what was happening. There was only a silent signal that prompted the eagle-winged creature to spring into the air, dragging the shackled soul of Darryl behind it like a slightly weighted kite string as it flew higher and higher, faster and faster, toward the sky of mud and milk.

After penetrating the sky's barrier, Darryl saw sights he never could've conjured words to describe even if he'd been able to speak as they travelled through mixed terrains, bizarre environments, and impossible habitats. As his soul was dragged through it all, he experienced a sensation similar to the one his body of flesh had felt when pushed into the tub of spiced honeymilk.

The chimera eventually stopped, bringing them to rest in an area of XynKroma consisting of dark green trees and brown, red, and silver leaves. Most of the trees were rooted and stretching upward for miles, but others had fallen to lie on a foot-high bed of foliage. The chain and shackles that had bound and connected Darryl and the chimera were now gone; they'd dissolved at some point during the journey. Darryl briefly considered maybe the reason they stopped was because the chain was gone. He then considered another one.

The chimera was resting on its haunches, gazing at Darryl's soul. Darryl didn't like the look in its eyes, nor the manner in which its mouth hung open, but rather than engaging it in a staring contest, he focused his attention on the appearance of his soul. It was revolting. Humanoid shape notwithstanding, his soul's composition resembled something a disturbed child might concoct if left unsupervised for too long: a milky blood-mud-honey pie. He then understood the look in the chimera's eyes. He was only thankful that, after the beast opened its jaws wider and pounced, he didn't experience the sensation of being devoured. Darryl didn't feel his sloppy self being chewed, swallowed, and consumed. The sight and thought of it were confounding enough; to actually feel the pain and torture of it would've been too intense for him to withstand.

While his soul slipped into darkness, Darryl sensed he remained in one piece. The chimera's teeth weren't rending him into parts; its teeth, tongue, and jaws only helped reshape him, making him easier to swallow. As his substance mixed with the acids and other substances in the creature's stomach, through the immediate sounds of swishing, churning, and rumbling, Darryl heard a more distant sound of gagging, heaving. He realized exactly what it was when he felt a sudden shift in the processes inside the beast.

The chimera was vomiting. After being swallowed and partially digested, Darryl was being regurgitated. Since no part of him had ever been separated from the whole, Darryl's soul came up and out all in one piece, out and down all over the body of the beast as it stood on its hind legs, its face pointed upward toward the blank, wintry sky.

Darryl's soul covered every single inch of the beast, leaving not even the smallest part or patch of skin or fur exposed. Freshly introduced to the atmosphere, the regurgitated soul hardened, and the shape of the body underneath it transmogrified, assuming a human's shape, a human male's shape, with broad spanning wings jutting out from its back.

Darryl stood erect. He folded and respread his wings before picking up a fan of silvery leaves in order to examine himself in their reflection. His head had a wolf's shape, with tiger-striped eyes. His skin had a violet tone. He was nude, but he wasn't cold. The surface of his form was firm but soft, similar to the skin of his body on Reality's surface. And his vision, much like that on Reality's surface, was limited; he could no longer see in every direction at once. All in all, he felt comfortable. It was a change, but was it an improvement?

"That is irrelevant."

Darryl heard a voice speaking simultaneously with the appearance of a transparent bubble in front of his face. The bubble contained black letters clearly spelling out the words as he heard them. It gave him the impression of a bubble one might see in a comic strip, but it wasn't a cloudy thought bubble or a clean speech bubble; it was something in-between the two, and something beyond.

"You are now outfitted for battle."

The bubble popped after Darryl heard and read the word "battle." He looked all around for the source of the voice and its accompanying visual effects. He discovered it only after he'd turned a full circle and stopped to look directly above him.

Another chimera. This one also had wings, but these were colored like the most exotic parrot's, shaped like the most horrific bat's, and flapping in a manner contrary to a hummingbird's, something approaching the slowest motion—but it was apparently enough to keep the two-foot-long, silvery crimson fish's body afloat. In Darryl's current condition, neither the chimera's hawk-talons nor its piranha-teeth were enough to scare him. The incongruent creature provoked only one reaction.

"What next?" Darryl asked.

"Now that you have been acquainted with your helpmeet, Sprat—"

"Who?"

Darryl's interruption of the creature's words didn't cause the bubble containing them to pop. The black letters inside the bubble only disintegrated into a nectarine-shaded mist as the bubble's skin took on a tint of coral-green. The letters and bubble went respectively back to black and clear when the creature resumed speaking.

"Sprat. The one who consumed you so you could assume its necessary qualities."

The other chimera, Darryl thought.

"The other pole-pet," the creature said. "Only the specially chosen are gifted with the assistance of a pole-pet in XynKroma. I am VanJill, the pole-pet of The Beautiful One, whose soul you must free if Creation has a hope of being saved.

"Come."

Chapter 16

"Come on," Ava said, "are you going to tell me your great idea or not?"

"I told you twice in the car," Robert said as they stepped out of the elevator. "I need to make a call."

"Sure, and that's all you said. Your friend Sonya was right about you needing a burner."

Maybe. Up until recently, Robert felt he'd no reason to own a cell phone. His watches worked just fine for instant communication to Darryl and to Adam—the Institution's heart and lifeline—and his apartment's landline was used mostly for ordering pizzas and cursing at telemarketers. Normally he would've made the call from home, but it was impossible when his new self-proclaimed partner refused to leave his side.

"No burner is more secure, or *private,* than what we have here," he said.

"Aren't you at least going to tell me who you're going to talk to?" Ava asked.

Robert felt a sensation on his right wrist. He put two fingertips to the face of his watch.

"Right now," he said, "we're going to talk to Adam."

The two rushed through The Burrow's halls toward the chairman's office. Adam wasn't waiting for them in reception room. To Robert's surprise, he and Ava were allowed to enter Adam's main office. This wouldn't be good.

"Sit down, Mister Goldner, Miss Darden."

Both did as instructed. Neither said a word.

"What I am about to show you is extremely disturbing. But it is necessary for you both to see this. It was posted on the Internet sometime within the past hour, and probably recorded only a short time before that."

When Robert and Ava had entered the room, all of the monitor screens in Adam's office were scrambled, as was normal. But after warning them, Adam picked up a remote control with one hand and typed something on his desk's keyboard with the other. In a few seconds, one of the larger screens gradually gave a clear picture.

Darryl was in a dark room. A dark room with splashes and flashes of colors. A dark room with a group of five women. Robert sat in a cushioned chair, removed from it all, watching the colors, watching the women, watching them all gracefully and mercilessly thrash, beat, humiliate, and torture his partner.

He'd known something like this was coming. He'd hoped he was wrong. Robert hated being right about things going wrong. But here he was, staring at a violent action flick, a movie clip featuring an adventure in meaninglessness. Brutality for the sake of brutality.

Ava gasped, mumbled, and made other vocal noises as she watched, but Robert mostly tuned her out. After getting over the initial shock of seeing Darryl in such a predicament, he took in the entire presentation of the film. There was sound and there were voices, but none of them were produced by the people on the screen. What they were watching had been recorded and the soundtrack added later. Music and dialogue that was both spoken and sung; it was like a snippet from a movie musical. Robert recognized some of the words. They were from *The Blackbook of Autumn Numbers*. He was watching a scene snatched from the book and dramatized for others' enjoyment. He was also watching two sickeningly familiar faces. Among all the shifting faces on the screen, theirs were the most recognizable. Another MC³ Production, just as he feared. He hated being so right about things going so wrong. Robert itched even more to make his delayed phone call.

"Mister Smith," he said, "those women, in the white and black, they're the same two who attacked Ava. They're the two who beat her up before we found her."

"Mister Smith," Ava asked, "who are they? Do you know?"

Robert could hear it in her voice. She was struggling to suppress her anger. Maybe it was anger at the fact she'd been taken out by the pair, or maybe it was anger that Robert hadn't even bothered to describe the women to her earlier. He hadn't given her descriptions because he hadn't felt it was necessary, and he knew it'd lead to questions about how he knew. But he wasn't ready to discuss those videos with her just yet. First things first.

Adam paused the film on a shot where both women could be seen on the screen at the same time.

"The blonde one is Veronica Blake. The dark-haired woman goes by the name Vanessa Blight. Both names are most likely pseudonyms. What is certain is that, together, they once comprised the pair of Infinite-Definite terrorists classified as 'Initials V.V.' They left these initials written at the scenes of their assaults, usually using the blood of their victims to write them. We stopped hearing reports of their activities about a year ago. Some figured they had been captured or killed, but apparently they were somehow recruited and initiated into a new and far more danger-ous sect of angels."

"More dangerous than what?" Robert asked.

"Than anything with which you are probably familiar, Mister Goldner. They are Sprytes, very unique angels who can somehow hide their status from the eyes and senses of other angels. Sprytes seem to be very skilled in the practices of a highly advanced form of Light Magick. For instance, they do not need to use the eyes to gain access to the soul of a victim. Skin-on-blood contact works just as well. In addition, they can read minds like one reads a Braille book, simply by placing their fingers on or near the pulse of their subject. They are very few in number, and all of them, to my knowledge, are female. Together, those two have been making a name for themselves as 'Blink & Blank.'"

"I suppose Blink is one-eyed blondie." Ava spoke slowly as her fingers slowly curled, straightened, and curled—making fists and relaxing them—over and over again.

"Yes," Adam said.

"Why haven't I heard of these two before?" Robert asked. "Or anything about these Sprytes?" Or anything about rare types of Virus-carriers like Ava?

"I only divulge information to Watcher agents on a need-to-know basis," Adam said, "when they need to know it."

Robert fought hard to keep his facial expression respectful, as blank as Adam's mask, though he was becoming more and more bothered by Adam's manner.

"Anyway, Mister Goldner, what I know is very little. My file on them is minimal. Perhaps they are adept at other arts of which I am unaware."

"That's all we need to know right now, huh?" Ava said, almost under her breath. Robert was starting to find her manners a bit refreshing.

"That is all I can tell you, Miss Darden."

"We also know another thing," Robert said. "They have Darryl. Right?" He wanted to know how the film ended but didn't want to ask outright. And he didn't want to have to watch it. He knew how the scene from *The Blackbook* ended, but how faithful were the filmmakers in adapting it?

"As far as we know," Adam said, "yes. He is most likely still alive. We do not know where, and can only guess at why."

"I don't want to know why," Robert said. "I want him back."

"I have contacted the proper authorities on this matter," Adam said.

"Fine. They can back us up."

"Mister Goldner, you should know the Heartland Security Agency is becoming increasingly concerned some of our agents are overstepping their bounds. It may be wiser to allow them and other law enforcement agencies a period of doing without us, just to see how well it works for them."

"Finding Darryl is well within my bounds, sir." He found adopting the same tone with the chairman as Ava even more refreshing than hearing her do it.

It was impossible to know by sight alone if Adam was taking offense, annoyed, or on the verge of rebuking him, but out of respect, Robert put a damper on his manner. He didn't waver on anything else.

"Mister Smith, you know he's not just an associate or acquaintance to me. Darryl's…He's more than just my partner. In Sterling, in those woods years ago, he *saved* me. And if after I get him, the HSA wants to play alone in what they probably think is just a game, well, that's their business. And yours, too, I suppose. But I'm going out there to bring him home."

"I cannot stop you," Adam said.

"But you won't be able to help me," Robert said, "you or anyone else at the Institution."

Adam nodded. Robert wished he could see behind the mask, read a facial expression, take a shot at determining what Adam was really thinking.

"I understand," Robert said.

"Good luck."

Robert knew that was the cue for him to get out of Adam's office. He'd almost forgotten about Ava. He didn't notice she was right behind him until he was more than halfway down the hall.

"What do we do now?" she asked.

"I'm going to make my call," he said. "May I have a little privacy please?"

Ava looked ready to snipe back at him, but her expression quickly changed, as if a better idea had popped into her mind.

"Okay." She used an index finger to push her glasses higher on nose. "I'm going to see if Mister Bernard's around."

Robert watched her walk down the hall. The moment she turned a corner and was out of sight, he rushed into one of the little rooms with the most secure phones. He dialed. After ten rings, a sleepy voice finally answered.

"Rob?"

"Yeah, Kurtis, it's me."

"What's up? It's the middle of the night."

"I know," Robert said. "Sorry. It's an emergency. My laptop's still broken, and I need someone I can trust to do some super-quick sleuthing for me. Only people who'd be willing to do it for me here are out or asleep."

"Yeah, it's the middle of the night." Repeating himself, Kurtis sounded less groggy and much more irritated.

"Yeah, I've heard. I—" Robert hesitated, rethinking his strategy. "You know, never mind. I just remembered that Anika could probably do it twice as fast anyway. I'll give her a call."

"Hold it," Kurtis said. "I'm turning on my laptop now."

Robert smiled. He knew just how to push his old friend's buttons; just imply his girlfriend was much more talented. In all honesty, he knew both Kurtis and Anika were equally adept, but Anika would've been harder to reach. She kept her cell in her purse, stuffed in a drawer. Kurtis slept with his phone next to his pillow.

"Remember our meeting yesterday?" Robert asked. "That outfit, MC³ Productions?"

"Yeah, okay?"

"Do they have any kind of roots in the metro area? Like a production studio, or a local distributor, or anything?"

"You know we tried to find out about them the other day," Kurtis said, "and didn't have much luck. It's not like they're registered with the SEC. With the type of stuff they're putting out there, they're not exactly operating like a public company."

"I know," Robert said, "but you guys said they wanted their name out there. Can't you pull up something they posted and backtrack it or something?"

Kurtis didn't respond, but Robert could hear him tapping away on his keyboard and whispering to himself. After five minutes of listening to this, Robert was about to ask another question. Then Kurtis shouted.

"What's the matter?" Robert asked.

"My laptop just died!"

"What? How?"

"I don't know *how*—the screen just went red, then black! I'm pushing the reset button, and not a damn thing's happening!"

"Kurtis—"

"Damn it!"

"Kurtis, please," Robert said, "what's the last thing you saw on the screen?"

"Before the red fucking screen of death? Just some code. Symbols…"

"Nothing intelligible?"

"Yeah," Kurtis said. "Reston."

"Reston, Virginia?" Robert asked.

"Maybe. Or maybe it was just a man's name."

"Thanks, Kurtis. Listen, can you run over to Anika's and ask her to see what she can find?"

Kurtis responded with a long string of curses. Robert hung up and rushed out of the room. Ava was waiting for him.

"Get all that you needed?" she asked.

"No," he said as he hurried past her. "But I'm about to get one thing I need."

"I'm right behind you."

"Ava," he said over his shoulder, "I don't need your help. Why don't you go take a nap and refresh yourself so you can be ready to go shopping in the morning?"

"Ha ha, jerk."

Robert didn't mean it the way it sounded. She'd said she needed clothes, and he wanted her to stay out of this. But she could take his comment however she wanted, as long as she backed off.

"I want to help," Ava said, "and I'm going to. I have a stake in this too, you know. Those two bimbo-tarts beat me up pretty badly too, remember?"

Robert stopped and looked at her. He did remember. She'd been in the same situation as Darryl, and she'd come out of it okay. They could've killed her, but didn't. And she'd recovered physically, if not psychologically. There was hope for Darryl. But time was still their chief enemy.

"You want to help?" Robert asked.

"Yes," she said.

"Tell me then, is Zel in his office?"

"Yes."

"He's awake?" Robert asked.

It was normal for the chairman to be awake at this hour, but unusual for the toymaker. Robert had planned on entering the workshop on his own, and leaving a note behind when he left.

"Yeah," Ava said, "but—"

"Thanks."

Robert ran down the hall with Ava close behind. He'd simply have to ask for what he wanted and refuse to accept a negative response.

Zel almost looked as if he'd been expecting them. "Welcome back, Miss Darden. Robert, always a pleasure."

"It would please me," Robert said, "if I could borrow Darryl's corresq."

"Oh?" Zel said. "But it's not finished yet."

"It doesn't need to be," Robert said. "Whatever modifications you're making can wait. I can use it fine just the way it is."

"And I'd like to borrow the bow," Ava said with a raised voice.

Zel and Robert both looked at her.

"Please," she said. "I don't want to go out in the field unarmed this time. I'd rather just have to use my eyes for searching and watching."

Zel looked at Robert, who only shrugged.

The toymaker pulled the bow down from its wall rack and said, "I presume you two are going out to try to find Darryl. Guess it's appropriate you're going armed with toys made for him."

"It'll be more appropriate to hand them back to him," Robert said while scanning the workshop table for other devices he might like to borrow, "after we bring him back alive."

"Yes," Zel said, "and when you bring him back, Vince may have his project finished."

Robert looked from the handheld laser he'd picked up to Zel. "What project?"

"The morning he left here, Darryl asked Vince to work on some kind of map for him."

"What kind?" Robert asked.

Zel glanced at Ava. "I don't know. All I do know is that Vince has been working on it feverishly since the alert about Darryl went out."

"I've got to go see him," Robert said. "Is he up?"

Zel nodded as Ava said, "I'll come with you."

"I still need to tell you how the bow works, Miss Darden."

"I'll come back for you, Ava," Robert said over his shoulder while hustling through the door. "Promise."

Vince was on his way out of his office and, after almost bumping into him, was startled to see Robert.

"Sorry to bother you, sir, but…Darryl's missing."

"I've heard," Vince said. "I was just on my way to discuss the matter with Adam."

"I heard you were working on some kind of map for him," Robert said. "Can I see it, please?"

"Well, it's not exactly finished," Vince said as Robert followed him into his office.

"How did it start?" Robert asked.

Vince explained the project, giving Robert the overview Darryl had given him.

"So far," Vince said, "it's not much."

"It's enough for me," Robert said as he ran his eye over the map. "Can I borrow this?"

"I have a copy."

"Thank you, sir. And I realize Darryl came to you with this in confidence—"

"Yes, Robert," Vince said with a weary smile, "and you borrowing it will also remain in my confidence."

Robert put the map in his jacket's inner pocket, thanked Vince again, and left the office. Ava was waiting for him outside the door.

She was holding the crystalline bow. To Robert it looked natural in her hands, as if she'd been using it for years.

"Ready?" she asked.

"Even more than before," he said. "Come on, let's go for a ride."

Chapter 17

Darryl flew as fast as his wings would carry him in Xyn, at nearly the speed of light. VanJill maintained a steady lead ahead of him—incredibly far, but still within range of Darryl's far-reaching sight.

They flew through a burning blue, a purifying azure. That's how, in a flickering moment of reflection, Darryl described it. Nothing but blue in every direction—he had to follow VanJill just to ensure he was actually going anywhere. Darryl had intuited the purifying aspect of the flight. There was no wind in this section of Xyn, but he felt breezes stirring and blowing within his soul, through passageways that would've been occupied, on Reality's surface, by his body's bones. He was sure this feeling, this process—whatever it was—was toward his overall betterment.

The pole-pet had said nothing to him beyond, "Come." After that instruction, VanJill had spread its parti-colored wings and taken flight. Darryl had instinctually done the same. Harboring his own pole-pet seemed to give him certain advantages in the realm. Nothing, however, had given Darryl the advantage of being prepared for the sights he saw when—out of the blue—they entered a blinding blizzard.

Darryl lost sight of VanJill, but he tried to keep moving in the same direction he had been. It was difficult. The blizzard was a furious whirl of segues and incongruities: a storm of circuit boards that weren't stiff boards, but rather white handkerchiefs imprinted with circuitous designs sparkling and crackling with blue sparks and green noises. The intricate cloths flew and waved like flags before turning into dead, gray leaves that displayed throbbing veins of sunshine-yellow and bloody-blue liquids. He saw what looked like leaves blowing in the currents of the angriest gusts until they all color-switched into swatches representing every hue imaginable and imprinted with an unending array of incomprehensible symbols.

The whole frenzied experience was like traveling through curtains and veils that can warp space and time and sense.

VanJill and Darryl emerged from this grotesque storm into the storm's eye. They stopped and hovered, staring at a sight that could only be hidden at the center of such a bizarre blizzard.

The decapitated giant was standing on a frozen lake at least the size of Lake Superior. Maybe. Darryl always had trouble judging the true size of objects in XynKroma. He had no trouble judging gender, but this nude giant, whose jade-hued body was modeled generically after a human's, showed no sexual organs, nothing to distinguish it as tending toward a male or a female. Its head didn't help Darryl reach a conclusion. Gone, but not forgotten, it had been skinned down to a crystalline skull, a prism on which nothing could be seen but broken light. The skull was being held at the end of an arm stretching rightward, dangling by two short tangles of red-and-golden hair. The hair had been braided in such a way as to resemble chains. Three misshapen spheres were in the headless giant's left hand, at the end of the other outstretched arm.

They hovered above the upturned palm and seemed like giant grapes, already well on their way toward devolving into giant raisins, or evolving into giant, wrinkly brains. The spheres' skins were translucent, and colorful gemstones could be seen at the core of each—an emerald was in one, a red ruby in another, and amethyst in the third.

"Her prison hangs in its right hand," VanJill said as a bubble spelled its words.

"Her?" Darryl asked when the bubble popped. "The giant's?"

"The Beautiful One. Her soul is inside, waiting to be rescued by one worthy."

"Me, huh?"

"If you so believe."

"And I'm guessing," Darryl said, "no, I'm *believing* that prison there is full of all sorts of traps waiting to trip me up once I'm inside."

"No," VanJill said. "If you make it into the skull, you will find and deliver freedom."

If? Darryl looked over the scene again, this time focusing on all the free-floating rectangles. Each projected a ghost-like image of one of many different varieties of flowers. There were seventy-eight rectangles, he just knew without counting. Each was silvery white on the image-projecting side and ash-blackish on the other. They surrounded the giant from the waist up, the silvery sides facing outward. Darryl imagined the giant had once been wearing armor that had come undone; its pieces fragmented and were gradually floating away from the body, much like Earth's moon was slowly floating away from its source. But the flowers comprising the holographic garden only puzzled him.

"This environment has changed immensely since The Beautiful One's soul was imprisoned," VanJill said. "She changed it, using the sheer strength of her will, trying to get free. This is the result."

Darryl looked down below the giant's waist, all the way down to the lake. Trees surrounded it on every side.

"She is still imprisoned," VanJill said, "and she is still being guarded, but at least she managed to kill all of the mares and other equine monsters her jailor conjured. Your chances are greater than ever. But, in the end, your success depends on you."

Darryl knew the danger was in the rectangles, the two dimensional cards, each of which was twice his soul's size. But he had no strategy. He only knew what he needed to do. Darryl flexed and flapped his wings, and he flew straight toward the hanging skull.

Darryl didn't see them emerging. They were so swift—moving, shifting, and striking faster than thought, coming at him at once from all sides, stinging his shoulders and wings, rendering him helpless. Darryl knew his attackers had jumped out of the cards, but he hardly saw them. Next thing he knew, his face and eyes were pointed toward his new uninviting destination: a section of the tightly packed cluster of trees surrounding the frozen lake.

It seemed to take him an hour or more to fall; gravity was fickle in Xyn, when it played a role at all. While he fell, and the breezes within the hollows of his soul turned themselves into several tiny hurricanes, Darryl thought about everything that had happened over the last few days, and about everything that had brought him to this scenario. Memories could be worse than any blade or bullet.

His soul crashed through the trees, breaking branches, bringing down a bewildering variety of leaves and fruit, until he hit the ground. Hard. But he was neither broken nor buried. Not yet. He was certainly in pain, but it was nothing like the level of pain he'd experienced on the way down, or even in the dark room on Reality's surface.

Darryl stirred. When he felt ready and able, rather than stand, he stretched his wings and floated, rising to hover just above the treetops. He stayed there for a while, gazing up toward where he'd been stung.

As well as his vision usually worked on Reality's surface, in XynKroma that vision might be enhanced or diminished depending on where he was and in what condition. At the moment, his eyes were operating like the most powerful telescopes.

VanJill was nowhere in sight. Darryl only saw the giant, the floating rectangles, and the seventy-eight beings that had come out of them. Comprised of a wide variety of green lights and black shadows, the beings were shaped like human women, nude except for the serpent-like organisms writhing, vining, and twisting about their bodies. Out of the card-garden of ghostly flowers, emerged seventy-eight evil Eves.

Seventy-eight women had caused him to begin this journey, and now seventy-eight stood in his way…Seventy-eight things that looked like women, but actually weren't. They were just symbols, killer metaphors. It was a taunt. It was supposed to be a deterrent. After what he'd been through in the dark room, after successfully answering the leviathan's riddle, this was supposed to scare and stop him; his drudged-up memories were supposed to freeze him.

It wasn't going to happen.

He knew what he had to do to make his way through.

Dare All, he thought, and Spare None.

He flexed his wings and flew, fast as lightning, straight as an arrow, as he ceded temporary control over his reflexes, over every possible voluntary and involuntary movement of his soul, to his pole-pet Sprat, the one that was of this realm and well-adapted to it.

Although an adroit manipulator of light on Reality's surface, Darryl couldn't figure how he might defeat beings comprised entirely of it at this level; so Sprat made the jump, not settling on a sure-fire way to control the beings, but on a definite way to annihilate them. As he flew, the feathers of Darryl's wings converted into razor-sharp shards of crystal. Each shard was to act as a prism, capturing light, breaking it apart, and holding it until extinguished.

When the seventy-eight phantasmal warriors converged on him, Darryl threw punches and kicks to get them where he wanted them while his wings performed multiple tasks: keeping his soul afloat, maneuvering his soul out of harm's way, and slashing through his attackers' bodies.

It was a massacre without the mess of blood or the echoes of screams. The warriors fought with skill, with vigor and, it seemed, with a purpose higher than simply keeping Darryl away from the skull-prison. But Darryl was relentless. He engaged them all as if he were just a shade away from berserk.

When it was all over, he didn't even pause to survey the results. He just flexed his wings and darted for one of the eyeholes in the skull, ready to take on whatever opponents might be waiting inside.

But there were none. There was nothing inside the cavernous skull except a lump of something floating in the exact center of all the otherwise empty space. Darryl approached it with caution.

He determined as he got closer that the hovering lump was nothing other than frozen light, sculpted to resemble the body of Marie-Lydia McGillis. Dark green, leafy weeds covered it in parts near the torso and strangled it in sections of the neck, arms, and legs; otherwise the opaque ice-light sculpture had the hue of an even-toned frost. Darryl stared at the head of the frosty figure, perplexed as to why it didn't move. It gave him a blank, unblinking stare in return.

With the elimination of the seventy-eight guards and the apparent passing of most of the danger, Sprat had returned control over most of Darryl's faculties back to him. Darryl was now faced with a mystery, and end-of-the-quest questions. Hadn't he succeeded? What's wrong with her?

He stood motionless, clueless about what he should be doing next as VanJill flew into the room. Darryl didn't in any way acknowledge the arrival of the pole-pet; he didn't flinch from the frozen girl's gaze. But VanJill spoke, offering a solution-in-verse encapsulated within algae-tinted transparent bubbles that floated and bounced in front, behind, and all around, in close proximity at all times to the gelid statue:

> "No more wondrous talk of clear-blue skies;
> no more crossing rivulets of honey
> and saliva. Approach closer, caress
> the shoulders of The Beautiful One's soul,
> finally breaking the spell with quaking thunder,
> with blind tenderness, pass a kiss
> of lightning, let her eight senses
> regain their reign, and fear nothing as you hear
> the Divine and Peerless address you."

After some hesitation, Darryl did as VanJill had instructed, moving forward to place his hands on the light-statue's shoulders and his soul's wolfish lips on hers. *No honey business this time,* he thought he heard some voice say as he continued to kiss, continued to caress, and sensed the amorous actions were having their intended effects.

Darryl soon felt the rapid change in the surface texture of the mannequin. He had to force himself to break the connection and push himself away. While the cavernous room trembled and began to shake away from monotony, Darryl watched as the frosty statue shivered, shuddered, and shook itself free of the constraint of its frozen form.

The frosted-glass appearance melted away to a surface that gave the impression of a pellucid gel as the dark forest-green weeds unstuck themselves and sunk beneath the surface. Darryl's keen sight saw some of the weeds lodge themselves between the second and third layer of what could be considered her "skin." Other weeds sunk deeper inside the translucent form as the statue itself slowly sank toward the floor. Darryl sank as well, keeping his head level with hers, watching her transformation.

Within the female's figure, Darryl began to see thimble-sized versions of all sorts of bizarre and otherworldly creatures: amalgams, made up of mixed parts picked from the salt-water and fresh-water creatures on Reality's surface. He could only presume they were, in a sense, her soul's organs (he briefly wondered what his soul might look like inside). The water creatures floated and swam freely inside her as the dark green, leafy weeds closer to the surface of the figure sprouted flowers that pushed outward to clothe the now-free, aware, and no-longer-naked soul.

She and Darryl now hovered a few feet from the cavern's floor. The once-frozen girl continued to stare unblinking at him, but the lips on her face finally moved.

"Why so frightened?" she asked. "Not used to seeing your actions having a stimulating effect?"

Rhetoricals. Her questions didn't need answers, but his did.

"You're the soul of Marie-Lydia McGillis?" Both a question to her and a statement of faint disbelief. Darryl needed reassurance he wasn't being fooled, that he hadn't somehow freed the wrong soul.

"No," she said. "I am not. That girl is dead. Didn't you see the coffin on Reality's surface?"

Darryl couldn't forget it. But the girl inside hadn't been dead. She'd appeared to be hibernating, until the glass shattered.

"A victim of lies, deceit, beatings, and all of false love's other treats," she said, "that girl has perished and passed through to the other side, beyond love, no longer resting in peace, but understanding it all. She's taken a more proper name for herself, for one who's taken on the burden of ensuring A Beautiful Creation."

VanJill produced a bubble, supplementing her words:

"The Beautiful One—
the Divine and Peerless, whose
saintly name is ****"

Hearing and reading that perverted haiku, Darryl almost felt like he was the victim of a bad joke. Marie-Lydia McGillis—the proclaimed Beautiful One—had apparently taken on a new proper name, a secret name he couldn't hear or read, not to mention several flamboyant titles. He wondered whether he was supposed to in some way intuit the blanked-out name, or if the defrosted girl's soul and her pet were just toying with him. Whatever torment the girl had been through, it had certainly affected her mind.

"For the ease of your mind," the girl said, "and the comfort of your soul, you may call me 'Marie-Lydia' for now."

Easy comfort—definitely a joke. Darryl's lycanthropic face couldn't show expressions, but something—a shift in his stance or the quick-flash of his soul's hue to another color—must've been enough of a signal to the one standing in front of him.

"Have you come so far," Marie-Lydia said, "only to express displeasure and doubt?"

Not a rhetorical. Darryl wanted to respond, but couldn't find the words.

VanJill blew another bubble into the ensuing silence and spoke its poetry:

"Liberty's secret: loving the work,
hating the outcome.
That's why the accursed process goes on
and on…"

"Yes, it is hard work, isn't it?" Marie-Lydia asked Darryl. "Liberating souls. Mine. Yours. So much easier to erase minds, isn't it?"

"What?" Darryl said.

"Before the Killer Vees found you, lost one," she said, "just how were you intending to spend the rest of your pointless life?"

"What?" His tone of anger doubled with the repeated word. If this was just another trial, Darryl would be damned if he'd go through it without at least attempting to defend himself. He was more than ready to do so.

"My life had meaning," Darryl said. "I *gave* it meaning. I'd dedicated myself to giving peace, giving security to the insecure. Yes, when I was younger, and before I got sick, I slept around, but not with just anyone. Others aimed high, I aimed low—for the plains, the forgotten, the rejected and neglected, and the ridiculed. Homely and plain and plump girls that most boys wouldn't even give the time to. I *loved* them—and, yes, I found out the hard way the error of my methods. But at least I tried to do something I thought was good. I looked for inner beauty and tried to bring it out for those who possessed it and were blind to see it. And I—"

"Yes, yes," Marie-Lydia said, covering a feigned yawn, "I know all those boring old stories. As unconvincing now as they were then." She cast a look upward toward her pole-pet. VanJill was perched upside-down on the shaky skull-chamber's ceiling. The creature had begun to produce a multitude of wordless bubbles.

Darryl tried to continue his self-defense. "You don't—"

"And I know the newer stories, too," Marie-Lydia said. "Sad boy meets sad woman or man, fries with glad passion, then dyes her or his bad brain. And on to the next one." She giggled. "Such a small, limited thinker you are. It's almost a wonder you managed to summon the thoughtful power to overcome and free me."

Darryl stifled his ruder response as Marie-Lydia turned her back on him. She began to touch and play with the objects, de-signs, and colors released by VanJill's bubbles. Darryl kept silent and looked on. He'd begun to detect subtle shifts in the room's atmosphere.

"I know you did all that you've done ultimately for your own redemption." Marie-Lydia spoke without looking at him. "You've finally come to the right place."

Darryl approached her, drawing her eyes back to him. "Repentance, redemption, whatever. But there's nothing selfish about it, as you seem to be implying. I've been trying to erase my past mistakes."

"By erasing others' minds," Marie-Lydia said.

"I was *changing* minds," Darryl said, "preventing tragedies, before they could happen."

"Daring all to accept what you call 'peace,' and reject what you call 'love'?"

"Yes."

"No," Marie-Lydia said. "You did nothing but contribute to the problem. Your alleged works of charity have only harmed the cause of Harmony."

"Bull—"

"Honey," Marie-Lydia said, "I've done more good here as a frozen lump than you have as a walking, talking body."

She turned her back to him again and took to the air, grabbing the contents released by VanJill's bubbles and transforming them before letting them fly free to decorate some area of the trembling chamber as it slowly transitioned into something else.

Darryl wondered just what was happening. Surely he didn't come here only to be insulted and berated. He considered the brutal obstacle course he'd recently been through: Vanessa and Veronica and their dark-room friends (presumably the "Killer Vees"), his entrance into XynKroma, the leviathan's riddle, and the seventy-eight prison guards, whose splendorous remains were still entrapped inside his wings' prisms. It was so much. Maybe too much. Darryl half-figured it was all for a greater good, but he couldn't fathom just what that good might really be. He began to consider whether it had all been a vicious trick to get him to free the girl's soul; after succeeding, he was free to be burned, buried, and forgotten.

While reflecting on his situation, Darryl picked up tones of sound in the air around him, and the faintest hints of melodies. He heard beginnings of melodies only, nothing complete. VanJill and Marie-Lydia continued to float and fly around the room, conjuring, playing, and decorating. Their actions were in some way making the music.

Darryl's eyes met Marie-Lydia's. She smiled and began to descend.

"Please don't think me ungrateful for what you've accomplished," she said. "You saved my soul from the prison of one even more misguided than you. I intend to return the favor."

"How?" Darryl asked. "By having your pole-pet eat me up and shit me out?"

Marie-Lydia laughed. "No, vulgarian. By releasing you from the head-cage of bad ideas."

VanJill blew a word-bubble and said:

> "If one loves nothing that one will want nothing—
> and live happily in peace…
> if that one is happy being fleeced
> and counting on oneself
> while perpetually falling asleep."

"Time to wake up," Marie-Lydia said, snapping her fingers as her pole-pet's bubble burst. VanJill went back to its decorative duties as its master stepped closer to Darryl.

"You see, I know you, Darryl Ridley. I know your entire history. A soul trapped in Xyn can't help but learn all manners of things—histories, futures, possibilities, *arts*—whether she wants to or not. And you, so near but still off of the right path, following an incomplete scripture that led you to wander around in zero, with holey goals, accomplishing nothing remarkable, only pitiful.

No gardens, just pits. You were never properly inverted; you never settled down with the right partner. But you had a reputation. There was something unique about you. You were a mystery that had to be solved. So I learned about you, saw your potential, and I was sure after you were properly seasoned, you could liberate me. And I might even be able to do a little something for you…

"So, tell me, Darryl Ridley, where would you like to go from here?"

Darryl felt he was in no position to make suggestions, and probably couldn't even if he'd wanted to. He felt funny, as if his soul were being jabbed from the inside by dozens of needles. Was Sprat trying to communicate something to him?

"No answer?" Marie-Lydia cocked her head. "Well, then, let me make a modest proposal: you and I, we become united, as One. We become as One and work together, using all of our *talents* to recover the self-aborted child of Vastion, the child who was created and lost in the service of false love. Remember what Vastion *was* and think of what his child might *be,* with the proper parents and upbringing: an artist, a supreme Artist, who may bring the reign of Harmony to Reality."

Her words were a torrent of metaphors.

"What are you talking about?" Darryl asked. "How?"

"Xyn is the source of all true magick," Marie-Lydia said. "A realm constituted of the fundamental levels of Reality, a realm of *absolute* thought and *ultimate* light…For light's most skillful manipulators and Reality's deepest thinkers, the metaphor-made-literal is more than possible here. Mind over matter, and all that. You and I, with the right amount of concentration, through our thoughts and our actions, we can create miracles.

"If you accept my proposal, we'll go forth from here, both of us fundamentally reformed, back to the surface of Reality, and—as One—we'll rewrite that vile book *Death's Heart* by living the revision. Our artistic contribution to the elect of humankind. At the same time, when here in Xyn, our souls shall work to remake and reconceive the babe—Kaprice's and Vastion's lost fetus—the would-be babe whose new birth and successful development will be the beginning and process of cleaning up the Flood."

The Flood. The insane and ultimate goal of The Infinite Definite to return all of Creation to a state of primordial chaos, or something worse. "You make it sound like it can't be prevented."

"I do," she said. "Because it can't. I've been trapped in Xyn long enough to see and learn of both possibilities and inevitabilities."

Darryl didn't buy it. Nothing was preordained.

"The Creator is dying, honey," Marie-Lydia said. "It came into being and lives only to bring Creation to completion. But the Errorists—those who are too far astray from any right or true path—they can't let a dying God die. They want a premature death. They are impelled to mess up the process of Creation, sending it as far astray as they. Using their Dirty-Light-Magickal talents, they are intent on cracking open God's Skull, setting off the ultimate bomb. They can't be stopped, but their anarchic game plan can be changed, by me, and you…

"You…" Marie-Lydia began to pace, circling him. "So intent on…*changing* the minds of women"—she paused for a quick chuckle—"and some men. All for no good purpose other than to make your sorry self feel better about your sorry self. With me as your now-and-future partner-in-art, we'll *change* the mind of the doomed Creator before it's too late. We'll shape the imagination of the senile old Fool whose creative process has allowed so much of nature to suffer under its false rule. And humanity—the most highly evolved creatures, who share an unbreakable psychological link to this silly deity and thus bear much of the responsibility for the state of the world today—unless we act, it may meet its end too. Humanity and its false philosophies of *love* and *peace,* and the results of the twisted thinking based on those two fundamentals: the sexism, the racism, the terrorism, the ecological rapes, the pollution, the wars…Think about those. Think about their reasons, both the stated and the real reasons behind them. The perpetrators and participants always claim to be acting out of love, not hate. They all claim to want peace, not what they actually produce. *Think* about it."

Darryl did think. Something about the subject of the Creator really got under her skin. He'd heard Robert often refer to the Ground of XynKroma as the Scalp of God, and here Marie-Lydia was making references to God's Skull. To say Robert was a skeptic and a nonbeliever was putting it mildly, but something about Marie-Lydia's harsh words…something about them seemed simultaneously dissimilar and familiar to casual discussions he'd had with his Watcher partner. And it wasn't just her words. Something about *her* made Darryl think of Robert for the first time since his ordeal began. Whatever it was, Darryl didn't think about it for long; Marie-Lydia had stopped ranting and started talking about him again.

"If you and I are successful in our arts—our beautiful actions—when the Flood occurs, it will have a far different effect than the Errorists intend. And in this new as-yet-indescribable environment, the lost-found babe, born in Xyn, shall be the one with the power, opportunity, and ability to shape it into a new Reality—finally, a universal Paradise, populated by transfigured creatures…under our rightful guardianship, of course."

Darryl almost felt like chuckling. It wasn't Marie-Lydia's words that inspired giddiness, but the stranger changes occurring in the atmosphere and decor around him. He heard increasingly complex melodies and various *musics* flowing through the skull-chamber. Something was happening within him as well.

He wasn't able to determine for sure just what it was, but it caused random spots about his figure to flare inward from his soul's surface, several at a time. He felt as if he were being pricked with fiery pins, more than a dozen at any one time, never in the same spot.

While watching and listening to Marie-Lydia, Darryl also noticed VanJill flapping, fluttering, and erratically flying around the room, as if the creature were riding on the currents of one complex melody before suddenly deciding to stop and hop on the currents of a simpler one, then back again. He thought about the pole-pet's poetry, and Marie-Lydia's proposal. Taken all together, it wasn't necessarily complete lunacy.

"In the Flood's Afterbath, my liberator," Marie-Lydia said, "we three shall ensure a perfect Creation. The End. The end of History, Art, and God. An unending realm of unending Beauty, physical and emotional; a realm were *no* child will ever again have any reason to live in fear…All we have to do is recover the fictional unborn. Save the Child, for the sake of Reality."

The surface of Darryl's soul frizzed. That was one awesome goal.

"You and I," Marie-Lydia said, "will first begin our own artistic project—revising *Death's Heart*—by confronting the wayward Errorists on Reality's surface, wherever we may find them."

VanJill blew bubbles, several of them at once, each containing only one or two words, as the pole-pet said, "But rather than giving the Errorists a false sense of love or peace, you will correct them, set them on the bright path leading to Xyn, where their souls shall be put to work at the tasks of cultivating our partition of the Ground and building a temple-palace for your Miracle."

Darryl noticed but wondered little about the metaphors; he was more taken by the fact that, considering the way VanJill usually communicated, the entire sentence was actually coherent to him. Neither the seen words nor the heard words were in any way lined up or presented in order. And they weren't presented as poetry. But Darryl had received it all as one plain—if quite lengthy—statement, just like he'd understood the pole-pet before it entered its master's presence.

Darryl soon realized what the transformative process had begun to do for him. Within this atmosphere, within what had been a cold, empty, skull-chamber, he was being enabled to better understand philosophic-poetry, with increasingly little effort. It was his pole-pet's doing—Sprat, his helpmeet—aided in some way by the enveloping sounds of tunes, melodies, and various types of music. Like Marie-Lydia's pole-pet, as a denizen of Xyn-Kroma, Sprat was conversant with all manners of philosophy and poetry, all the *arts* of thought and communication. Sprat's being inside of Darryl's transformed soul explained (or at least made intuitive sense to Darryl) how he was coming to an easier understanding of the meaning underlying VanJill's hard, gemlike words. Darryl was being *inverted,* coming around to their way of thinking. It wasn't a bad experience.

"True love is believed to transcend space and time," Marie-Lydia said. "The temple-palace and its cultivated section of Xyn's Ground will exist outside of those constructs as well. The temple-palace will be based on an architectural design I've learned during my time here. Those Errorists' souls delivered by you and me will be allowed to reform themselves by laboring to build the temple-palace and tend to the vineyard, a plot of the Ground where we shall make our magick wine to change the dull Creator's mind."

This almost made good sense to Darryl, but—

"What about the bodies left behind on Reality's surface?" he asked. "When delivering souls to Xyn, their and our bodies will be left on the surface in a deep-deep sleep. We'll eventually wake up to go about our 'artistic' business—but what about them? What are we supposed to do with the bodies?"

She smiled in a fashion Darryl had never seen before. "We'll have allies on the surface who'll know how to deal with those.

Your concern and mine are the souls." She then took to the air to assist VanJill with its current task.

Darryl stayed on the ground, but he followed her around the room, considering the entire proposal. A lost-found child, a great Artist, a *Miracle,* crying into reality—all levels of Reality—perfection. *A Beautiful Creation.* One finally fit for humankind, a species that has suffered gravely and incessantly since its inception…But there were pieces that didn't quite fit for him. Marie-Lydia had left something out of her proposal that he felt should've been obvious, but he just couldn't get his mind to settle on it.

While thinking about it all, he also looked around and considered the fact they were now standing inside an elaborately decorated room. What had once been the skull's eye sockets were now stained-glass windows. The entire scene was plainly set for some sort of ceremony. It almost seemed as if his acceptance of Marie-Lydia's proposal was a foregone conclusion.

"What if I understand I want no part of this engagement?" he asked. "What if I decide that, now that you're free from your prison, I should be allowed to go free and live my life as I please?"

"You may," was Marie-Lydia's surprising answer. "The choice is yours. And you don't have to make it now. Let your actions speak for you when you return to Reality's surface. Faith preceded by words but not backed by actions is *holey.* Empty.

"You'll take your final test after you leave Xyn. To pass, you'll send to me the soul of the Errorist who was most responsible for my imprisonment here for so long. Your success will be considered an acceptance of my proposal; your failure, a rejection. If you reject what I've offered, then you'll be free to follow your own pleasure, free to go in peace."

He wasn't trapped after all. But Darryl knew he couldn't go back to living and behaving as he had. There had to be other options.

"If I choose your way," he asked, "to pass this test, just how would I send someone's soul to this exact spot?"

VanJill interrupted its actions to respond, using one word per bubble. "Your jeweled brain was transplanted to the area of your heart as you were modified by Sprat. A faithful caretaker of The Beautiful One's body on Reality's surface has placed a replica of this jewel on your body. You may direct souls back to the correct section of the Ground with the jewel assisting your will and wishes."

"And just so you know that I won't feel bitter or wronged if you don't accept the offer I've given in return for your actions on my behalf," Marie-Lydia said, "my pole-pet and I will give you and yours a gift just to show our gratitude. Consider it an engagement gift you may keep even if you decide to break it off with me."

"What kind of gift?"

"It was simply described as 'Perfect Memory Recollection' when it was given to me," Marie-Lydia said. "It's an extrasensory ability. A truly valuable one. Your pet will best know how to put it to use."

Of course. Sprat would now be with him always. Just under the soul's skin when in Xyn, and deep in the subconscious while on Reality's surface.

"Now then," Marie-Lydia said, "you've heard my proposal. Go and give me your answer."

Darryl looked behind him toward the stained-glass windows, the now-plugged portals through which he'd entered. He wondered exactly how he should make his exit.

"And remember," Marie-Lydia said, "you *will* remember, if you want redemption, if you want to be saved, absolved, you need to know exactly what you're being saved from, what's being washed away. You won't be saved by interpreting someone else's attempts at art. You'll only be saved by creating your own."

Darryl felt the jewel at the center of his soul's chest beginning to throb, and quickly accelerating. His soul felt increasing pressure, from within and without, as if he were expanding and being crushed at the same time. He wanted to cry out in pain, but he no longer had a voice. The only sound he made was when his wings fell off his back and shattered on the floor; the crystal-feathers were reduced to colored dust. It was amid an expanding cloud of multicolored dust that Darryl's soul began to disintegrate. Its pieces and particles began to get carried away on the fierce breezes that had been contained within him. He was ushered out of the room, out through the tiny cracks in the stained glasses, the imperfectly plugged eye sockets. But Darryl saw much before his consciousness evaporated.

The giant had replaced its skull back onto its shoulders; the lifting and reattachment must've caused the skull-chamber's earlier trembling. The seventy-eight rectangles were now nowhere in sight. There was no more need for armor or guards, but the giant's body was most likely protected in some way by the grapevines entwined about its entire body. The soon-to-be-brains-or-raisins had turned into imperfect spheres, multicolored egg-shaped objects, each imprinted with the design of a globe—Earths with amethyst seas, emerald continents, and swirling wisps of ruby-red clouds. Bunches and bunches of the egg-shaped alternate-earth objects rested in both of the giant's hands, so many it seemed inevitable a few would spill and fall to crack open, or maybe to float in the fresh unfrozen water on which the giant's feet now stood.

The last thing Darryl saw before losing the sight and thought of it all was the face of the giant's newly replaced head as it acquired patches and pieces of something like skin. Each puzzling piece was a different pigmentation, none of them a hue found in familiar nature. Darryl was gone before he could solve that puzzle, but he was all set on the solution to another.

Chapter 18

Robert and Ava had been driving around for a little more than an hour. There were several more to go until dawn. Aside from the Mustang's headlights and the occasional unbroken streetlights and the unreliable moonlight, there wasn't much to help brighten their way. But Robert wasn't really relying on light for their search. He'd put his trust into Ava's intuition, particularly her sense of recollection.

He'd taken a good look at Vince's map, and without showing or even mentioning it to her, he'd been driving Ava to the places where Darryl had spotted the "Save the Children" graffiti in Reston, Virginia, and its surrounding areas. He'd hoped the places would provoke Ava's sense of familiarity. The forth spot did just that.

"I know this place."

"Here?" Robert asked.

They were driving through Herndon, Virginia, a few miles from the city limits of Reston.

"Yes," Ava replied in a voice that just rose above a whisper. "That group of trees. On the other side is a house. A pretty big house. Probably something in there worth looking for."

Robert drove for another half mile then pulled the car over to the side of the road. He shut off the engine. "We'll go on foot from here."

He popped the trunk so Ava could retrieve the crystalline bow. He removed the corresq from his jacket's inner breast pocket, tossed the jacket into the trunk, and secured the vehicle. He then motioned for Ava to move closer.

"We don't have watches to communicate with," he whispered, "so we'll go over the plan now, just so we're on the same page." Ava nodded. "This is a wealthy area. People guard their properties ferociously. So from here, we travel through the treetops, camouflaged. We don't want to trip anything lying out on the ground for trespassers. Once we get to the house, if it is the one we're looking for, we stay together. No splitting up."

"Seems like we could do a more effective search by splitting up," Ava whispered. "Unless you don't trust me to—"

"Damn it, I trust you!" Robert almost forgot to keep his voice down. "Like I said, we have no way to communicate with each other, no easy way of finding each other quickly if we need to. You said it's a big house, right? So we stay close." Robert attached the corresq to his belt buckle. "Let's go."

It was more difficult than it would've been in broad daylight, but they both managed to get to and move through the higher tree branches while making only a small amount of noise. If anyone had been listening, they would've been more likely to mistake the two as frisky owls or insomniac squirrels than as two people on a serious mission. Even with their toys in tow, neither Ava nor Robert managed to rustle the tree leaves any more than a small mammal would have. Robert was keenly alert to how they were moving and the results of those movements; he was impressed with Ava's skill. It was clear she'd had more than her fair share of practice at doing this—when, where, and exactly why he'd have to learn later.

Within minutes, the two were in view of the three-story house. The front door was on the second story, and the porch in front of it was larger than most backyard balconies Robert had seen—but it had no patio furniture, no flowerpots, and no decorations of any kind. A four-car garage was on the left side of the house, on the other side of the stone stairway leading up to the front door. The property's driveway, currently empty, was long and wide enough for more than half a dozen cars. All of it was impressive, but the first thing Robert noticed were the large windows. The black rectangles and squares were all tinted with something that prevented Robert's eyesight from penetrating through. When he tried, he only saw a tiny reflection of the trees.

"Damn it," he said. "If they have any special optical equipment in there, they'll see us coming the second we leave these branches. If they haven't already."

"It doesn't look like there're any lights on," Ava said.

"Yeah, the better for them to see us."

"I meant maybe no one's home. Or they're asleep. They can't be expecting us."

"Always expect that you're expected," Robert said. "You may be embarrassed later, but you'll survive long enough to enjoy it."

"That's a delightful little philosophy."

"Yeah, well, any delightful big ideas on how we can get in there? Front door is clearly out of the question."

Ava stared at the house for a moment. "There's a hidden entrance on the right side of the house. It's the main entrance for the first floor. Very inconspicuous. Even if we were facing the right side of the house right now, dead on, you'd have a hard time seeing it."

"Me?" Robert said. "I doubt that."

"I don't."

"Well, then, lead the way, Arkangel."

The two made as little commotion as possible as they maneuvered through the trees to get a view of the right side of the house. Ava was correct. There was no walkway leading to it, and the door wasn't visible to anyone looking at the house straight on. It was located on the side of a portion of the house that jutted outward from the rest of the structure, evidently an add-on. Robert wondered for what purpose. He then wondered why the light-posts in the yard and the light fixtures on the house were all shut off. The lack of light enveloped the entire property in darkness, a darkness enhanced by the surrounding trees and accentuated by the fact the fading moonlight didn't touch the house or the grounds.

"Any alarms?" he asked.

"Probably," Ava said. "But every door and window probably has one. This is the entry point they'll least likely expect us to use. It's our best bet."

"Good thinking; you're probably right."

"Quite a compliment."

"Here's another one," Robert said. "You're taking point. I'll be right behind you."

"Wow. You actually trust me to go first?"

"As long as you trust me to have your back."

Ava didn't respond.

"Turn invisible," Robert said. "Your bow too. When we leave the tree, don't touch the ground. We'll levitate a few inches above the grass blades and skate over."

Ava nodded and did as instructed.

As they cautiously approached the door, Robert had a fleeting thought. What if there were motion detectors on the property? Maybe the lights were set to turn on only if triggered.

His fear dissipated when they made it without even a flicker from the lights. He again, briefly, wondered why all the lights had been shut off. He then concentrated on the door. A thorough x-ray showed the only thing of significance on the other side was a stairway leading to the second floor, the primary floor.

"Got a key?" he said, half joking.

"I can get us in," Ava said.

She did something to the door's handle while her body shielded Robert's view of the process. He could've spent some energy and concentration to manipulate his vision in order to see exactly what she was doing, but he didn't. He needed to conserve. For all he knew, she really did have a key. Maybe Zel had given her a tool. Right now, it didn't matter. Getting in was most important. He trusted her to get them in.

Something clicked, and Ava cracked open the door. No alarm. She opened it wider and stepped aside to allow Robert to go first. He shook his head then pointed at her and the stairway. They'd be better off with her maintaining the point position on the assumption she'd know the inside of the house as well as she knew the outside.

Ava started up the stairs, her feet not touching anything but cushions of air. Robert gently shut the door behind them and followed in the same manner.

The stairs ended at another door, this one already ajar. Regardless, Robert adjusted his vision to x-ray and see if the other side was clear before they moved on. They entered the kitchen. Excepting the dirty wine glasses near the sink, the room was spotless. Ava motioned for Robert to move closer and whispered into his ear.

"There's another set of stairs on the other side of the house. They go downstairs, to the garage and bedrooms. One of us can go that way, the other can go upstairs."

Robert didn't want to repeat his feelings on the idea of them splitting up. He was beginning to think maybe it was a good idea.

After all, Ava's other recent ideas had been good ones. She'd gotten them this far.

"Let's say we do split up from here," he said. "Anything else about this place you want to tell me? Any surprises I should know about?"

"Surprises?"

"Booby traps."

"How should I know?" she asked.

"Same way you knew about the stairs," he said. "And the side door."

"Robert, believe me, I'm just going by sight and angelic intuition. A sight of something will push a thought into my head. I don't know what's coming next. I'll be just as surprised as you."

"Yeah." Robert took a look around him—peering, measuring, and searching. "Okay. Take me to the stairs that go to the upper level. I'll go up, you go down."

Ava looked at him and parted her lips as if she wanted to say something else. But it was only momentary. She closed her mouth, tightened her grip on her bow, and walked into the dining room. Robert followed, searching and measuring each new view with his eye. They both stopped after they left the dining room and entered the foyer. Ava pointed at the stairs. Robert focused on something else.

The mirrors. All of the various mirrors hanging in the corners and running all along the walls of the spacious two-story foyer. There were so many, Robert knew their purpose went beyond simple decoration. How far beyond, he couldn't figure. He didn't waste much of a thought on it. The sight of the potentially dangerous reflective glass made him think of a bigger potential danger.

He'd missed his last scheduled dosage.

He was supposed to take his Virus medication every two to three hours. It'd been a few more than that since his last dosage. His last *half* dosage. So caught up in worrying about Darryl, he'd forgotten to get a refill from Sam. He now realized he could be attacked at any moment from within as well as from without.

Ava had left him to his silent speculations and gone into the living room. After a few breathless moments, Robert inhaled, deeply, and started up the winding staircase. When he was two steps from the top, every light within range came on at once.

Robert cursed when the onslaught of radiance made him recoil and almost made him fall down the stairs. As he checked his balance and his eye adjusted to the bright atmosphere, he called to Ava. She didn't respond. He instead heard another female's voice shouting "Welcome back!" from the living room.

He ran down the staircase, almost tripping more than once, but not stopping until he reached the living room's entranceway.

In a split-second's survey, he saw Veronica Blake dressed in a white cropped T-shirt and denim cutoff shorts; he saw every window in the room had somehow converted into a mirror; and he saw Ava lying on her back on the floor, surrounded by a rectangular coffee table at her head, couches on either side of her, and Veronica at her feet. It seemed the Spryte had gotten the drop on the Arkangel.

Robert saw what he needed to do: run, leap onto the back of the nearest couch, jump off, and kick Veronica wherever he could land his sneaker. He moved.

On just his third step, Vanessa Blight slid out of nowhere. Robert didn't notice until after her foot kicked him in the ear.

He didn't go all the way down, but he stumbled; his knees buckled. Robert recovered in an eye's blink and reeled around to size up his enemy, to figure the best spot to hit her and do it without wasting a breath. Contrary to her partner, Vanessa wore a dress showing very little skin. Only her face, arms, and feet were bare. And even at this close range, in the bright light, Vanessa's eyes were in deep, deep shadow.

Robert squinted and concentrated to fire an infrared pellet at one of those pale arms, but he couldn't focus on the target. Vanessa had already moved, dashing for the stairs. Not expecting a retreat, Robert hesitated, then he hustled after her when he realized she wasn't running away. She was running to hide something.

The first thing Vanessa hid was herself. She slid back into invisibility as she placed her foot on the first stair. Robert kept moving, but with much more caution. He couldn't see her, couldn't pick up even a hint of her, but the Spryte could pop back into sight at any moment and shove him down the stairs. She wouldn't get him that easily.

Ava would have to deal with Veronica alone. Robert hoped she was up to it.

Chapter 19

Darryl was lying on top of a bed. He knew that much. It was his first thought, even though so far he'd seen nothing but a white ceiling and the dull-yellow bare bulb hanging from its center. His second thought was a self-directed question: Why did his left hand hurt so much?

He tried to raise his arm. It wouldn't move. Stiff, like a board. Like his back. He wasn't tied down or restrained in any way, but he couldn't move. Some dark spot in his psyche half encouraged him to laugh at the situation. After all, one should wake up from a nap well rested, invigorated, ready to hop up and hurry about one's business. Darryl wondered just how long he'd been asleep, how long he'd been unconscious, how long he'd been under…

XynKroma. That's where he'd been. And he was well aware that excursions in the realm, while seeming to last for several hours or even days, actually took place in the duration of a finger-snap according to the manner of time-flow on Reality's surface, or at least according to the manner of time-flow on the planet Earth. An exit from the realm always put the traveler into a long, deep sleep. Darryl knew a deep sleep for him after leaving the realm averaged about seven hours. Always a risk. He was supposed to take his medication about every three hours. Something in the back of his mind, though, told him not to worry about it this time. All the drugs to which he'd been exposed recently had probably been formulated to take the place of his usual pills; he would've been no good to his abductors dead. And however long he'd been lying dead-to-the-world in this brick-hard bed, now that he was awake, Darryl knew there was work to do, affairs he needed to finish.

He tried moving his left arm again. His entire body was sore. He remembered the how and why of it, but—never mind—Darryl knew he had to get up.

He bent both of his arms enough to get them into a position where they could help him sit up. While grunting, wincing, and taking long, halting breaths through clenched teeth, Darryl imagined and moved as if his bones had been transmuted into eggshells and his skin had been remade from their boiled yolks. His bones felt as if they would crack at any moment, and his skin as if it would do nothing to prevent the broken pieces from jutting through, causing even more pain. But with a sustained effort, and without breaking anything (plenty had already been broken by others), Darryl managed to get to his feet.

A quick self-examination showed the Killer Vees had left him completely naked. His boxer shorts had gone the way of his other clothes, and his watches. His attention turned to his throbbing left hand. It took only a second to locate the source of the discomfort. His middle and ring fingers had a tight new metallic decoration. The Vees had given him a replacement for the watches. Darryl smirked at the sight of it, shook his head, and looked away to survey his surroundings.

He'd been placed in a small and tidy room that had only four blank, white walls, one full-sized bed, a bedside nightstand, and, on top of it, a lamp. The lamp was unplugged, its bulb missing. He spent a few moments looking harder, looking closer, but there was nothing of interest in the cramped quarters. He began to move toward the door, cursing and fearing for his brittle joints with each step.

After what seemed like five full minutes, Darryl made his way out of the room and into a dark hall. He made a few failing attempts before successfully managing to adjust his vision, enabling him to see as if the hall's lights were on and the fixtures had been set with 100-watt bulbs. He took two tentative steps forward, then a more confident one. He stopped on the fourth.

He'd come to another door, closed. Darryl looked at it and concentrated. Nothing. He concentrated harder, then felt a trickle under his right nostril. His nose was bleeding…No matter. He'd had success with seeing through the door. It was another bedroom, of the exact same size and layout of the one he'd just left. And it was still occupied.

Darryl thought about turning the knob. He thought about entering, showing his face, making a new introduction to the person inside. He looked at her, and he thought about revenge.

And that was the whole point, wasn't it? Revenge, or something like it. He'd been living the fantasy of it, deluding himself he'd been doing good when he'd been doing nothing but contributing to the fallen state of the present world. He'd been no better than an Infinite-Definite terrorist. An *Errorist*. Taking person-by-person revenge to earn a personal (false) redemption. That was the revelation. That was the lesson of his journey through Heaven&Hell.

The idea caused a few lights to brighten his path to true Salvation. His mind was recovering…Darryl had conceded he'd been going about his life the wrong way, but he hadn't gone so far off he couldn't find his way back.

He heard a sound and turned to his right. Another sound. The noise was coming from another part of the house. His ears had recovered. Darryl closed his eyes and listened, trying to decipher the sounds, dissect them and reconnect the pieces.

Voices. Two of them. Both hysterical. One joyous, the other not so much. Darryl opened his eyes and took a step back from the bedroom door, looking through it one last time. Revenge. He'd have it soon enough. The *right* way.

He followed the sounds to a door that hid a stairway. The stairway led in only one direction. Up. Darryl took the steps slowly, more out of trepidation than in subservience to the pain still wracking his body. He stopped before the door at the top of the stairs. He knew what he'd heard, but he wanted to get a clear picture of what he might be jumping into. Once again, he took a good look at the wood—causing a leak in his other nostril—until he saw through to the other side.

At first, Darryl couldn't understand what he was seeing. Swirling varicolored lights mimicking liquids and winds engulfed the room. It appeared to him as if a typhoon of light was battling a tornado of random shades and hues. But with a bit more concentration—and no small increase in the intensity of the throbbing at his temples—Darryl saw through the confusion. His eyes cut through the room's colorful chaos and located two people. Two women. Two strong angels. And one of them…At the sight of her, the intense desire for revenge washed over him, saturating him.

Darryl flung the door open and waded into the room's magick show.

The torrents of colorful radiation would normally have been a torture, unbearable to Darryl only a short while ago. It was now emboldening. Here was the invigoration one should have felt after a good night's rest. Here was refreshment. Here his strength rapidly returned. Darryl didn't feel his brittle joints, his aching muscles, the throbbing in his temples, or the soreness on his hand. He was sensitive only to the experience of his skin, which felt as if it were being massaged, delicately, by billions of pin-sized therapists. There was no stinging. There was no burning. There was only comfort as he walked in his element, his body enshrouded and draped in unnamable blurs. Darryl walked unnoticed though the colorful commotion.

Stopping to stand behind an oblivious Veronica Blake, he looked over her shoulder at Ava Darden, lying flat on her back, wide-eyed, resting on fear, ensconced in stark panic, grasping the prismatic bow to her chest. Darryl looked into those wide bloodshot eyes of hers and somehow managed to snatch away and view glimpses of what she was seeing, the living phantasms of liquid light overwhelming her, suffocating her, burying her, playing on the concealed terror she'd held and carried for more than fifteen years: the dread of immense bodies of water, the disdainful awe of rushing water, the horror of an unwanted child being drowned—again. A grotesque baptism. He saw all of Ava's memories of the day she almost died, both her imaginings of a belated attempt at infanticide and the facts of a parental suicide gone wrong.

Darryl's mind and senses could only take so much. He'd seen all he needed to. There was only one act left to perform. Finish off the kidnapper, the tormentor, the jailor, the wayward artist, the true *Errorist*. Send her to where she belongs.

Darryl placed his hand on Veronica's shoulder, squeezed, and spun the startled woman around to face him. The Spryte opened her mouth—to shout in realization, to scream in retaliation, to curse in anger, to laugh in nervous amusement—which or whatever, it didn't matter. He took the opportunity to pull her close, holding her with all his gathered strength as he kissed her.

Both of their eyes remained open as intangible wings of rust and bleeding scarlet thrust up from Darryl's shoulder blades, flared out, and flapped against the living room's colorful currents, beating against them like an eagle's wings on the currents of the sky. His wings of light, however, had a purpose different than flight. He'd no intention of lifting himself and his enthralled above and beyond. He didn't want to lift and carry her away. He wanted to push and usher her down deep toward another level of Reality.

He held her tight. He handled her exactly like he'd been wanting to for some time now. Radiation coiled around and strangled the blonde's bare skin as—by his mouth, through his lips, thanks to his tongue and gums and bloody saliva—Darryl wordlessly told Veronica exactly what he'd been thinking about. The radiation sank into her skin and entangled her blood vessels, scribbled through them, enraging her blood, causing each molecule to shake, shudder, and vibrate more and more rapidly as Darryl caused the torrential currents of light in the room to calm themselves, settle down, and smooth into a uniform blue.

In a flash, the blue engulfed every man, woman, and stone in the room.

Chapter 20

It took four times longer than it should have, but Robert's caution paid off. He reached the top of the stairs without getting blind-sided. He was just as careful walking down the upstairs hallway, x-raying each door and searching the rooms behind them. He saw nothing of interest and detected nothing of potential danger until he came to the room of white walls and mirrors.

Robert took a steady breath before entering, leaving the door open behind him as he began to conduct his usual mathematical survey.

Like all the other rooms, the lights in this one were on. Unlike the other rooms, this one had twenty-two bulbs lining the corners where the ceiling met the walls, and no visible light switch. Excessive lighting and mirrors. Never a good combination. The parasites infesting him would go berserk if given the opportunity, and they'd devour him in the process.

Damn his forgetfulness. And damn his decision to leave his windbreaker in the car, thinking he wouldn't need the extra covering in the predawn hours. Most of all, damn his self-pity—there was no time for it. Robert tried to focus on the task at hand. He was getting a little help.

His senses were sharpening, through no voluntary effort of his own. His body's invaders were becoming more attuned to their host's environment. Robert swallowed hard and tried to ignore the inevitable, tried to use the good of a worsening situation. He tried to use his enhanced senses to pick up any sign of his enemy.

The room had a fireplace, but no fire. He could smell there'd been one recently, but there were no ashes. The large clawfoot tub was even more curious; it was empty and clean like the fireplace. Robert wondered about it as he moved closer. He stopped one step before one of his sneakers would've landed on the carpet of broken glass.

"The hell happened here?" he said.

"Prelude to a honeymoon," a scratchy voice behind him responded.

Robert spun around and saw her, but he wasn't quick enough to move out of the way as Vanessa swiped at him. Her nails caught his T-shirt, piercing the fabric and ripping a large hole in the front. As he tried to pull away, Vanessa's left hand swung across his face. The fingernails drew streaks of blood on his right cheek.

She remained expressionless, but the sight of the ruddy lines on Robert's face seemed to excite the porcelain-skinned woman. He saw her body experience a moment of frisson before she swiped with her right hand at his other cheek.

Robert ducked out of the way and threw his body forward, ramming his left shoulder against Vanessa's right knee.

The Spryte crumpled to the floor with a shriek and slid herself back into invisibility.

On his hands and knees, Robert looked around him and listened. He saw she'd shut the door before she'd attacked him, but now he couldn't pick up even a hint of her presence in the room.

He felt alone, but he knew he wasn't. No—never alone. His blood was now exposed to the bright environment. The parasites in his blood cells began to drink in the sea of light surrounding him. Robert felt and heard the reaction on his rough, drying cheek—it frizzled and burned.

He clenched his fists, tried to put it all out of his mind, tried to think how to prevent half of his face from burning off. Then he heard the chalky voice speaking to him.

"I'm going to peel off all your skin and knit it into a blanket thick enough to smother all your friends."

Robert took a deep breath and held it as he tried to figure out where the voice was coming from. He held it as long as he could. Failing, he exhaled, and responded.

"You're under the weird impression you're going to leave this house in one piece."

"Me?" Vanessa said. "I assume nothing…except everything."

The twenty-two bulbs in the room began to flicker, each one at its own pace. When they settled, each gave off a very different type of light.

Something else had entered the room. Something Robert couldn't smell, or see, or hear—his enhanced senses weren't in fact perfect. He only knew it was *something*. Something dangerous.

Robert squinted, running his vision through every range accessible to him as he spun around, trying to find where the raven-haired Spryte was hiding. He didn't see her; he didn't hear her; but out of the silvery blue, out of the reflective glass, he saw *them* stepping out, stepping forward, grinning, winking, taunting: Anika, Kurtis, Sam, Zel, three people who lived in his apartment building, and several others. Friends, colleagues, neighbors, ac-quaintances, trusted confidants…

No.

He didn't trust any of it.

They were all illusions.

Robert grabbed the corresq on his belt, unhooked it and flung it. The silver circle sailed and hit the corner of the room he'd aimed for, at just the angle he'd wanted. The corresq ricocheted off in another direction, at another angle, crashed into a mirror, and ricocheted off into another direction, toward another mirror. The sounds of shattering glass dominated the room while Robert waited, waited for his toy to finish the job he'd assigned it and come whizzing back, close enough to him so he could reach out and grab it without getting cut or stung.

He'd figured it perfectly. After first stepping into the room, out of habit and caution, Robert had counted all of its major objects, measured all distances, and taken account of all angles. His mathematical mind and his geometrical instincts had guided him; they'd guided his arm and wrist so he knew exactly how hard to throw and what point to hit so the metallic circle would break and demolish all mirrors after one toss. It was another sort of instinct that allowed him to snatch the device in mid-air without hurting his hand.

The conjured illusions faded away as the mirrors that helped produce them fell apart.

"What else you got, Blight?"

Robert reared back and prepared to fling the corresq at the next target, but a shrilling Vanessa jumped out of nothing and knocked the toy from his hand with a well-placed chop as she ripped off his tattered T-shirt with her other hand.

Before he knew what had happened, Vanessa had tossed the rag to the floor, kicked the corresq across the room, and scratched at Robert's bare stomach—drawing more blood—before blanking out of sight again.

Robert flinched and grunted, but through it all, he'd kept his footing. He also kept his eye open, searching for his elusive enemy as he inched his way toward the corresq.

Something shifted in his abdominal area, around his stomach, squeezing it. Worse than any cramp he could recall. He couldn't run, but he could still walk. He made the best of it, ever aware of his surroundings.

Vanessa wasn't anywhere to be found—until she again slid from behind an unseen veil, scratched, drew blood, and slipped back to a place Robert couldn't see or sense.

If nothing else, the attack settled the contents of his midsection. Robert no longer had a cramp. There was only a burning sensation there now, like he'd downed a jarful of sliced jalapenos.

He scrambled for the corresq; the raven-haired Spryte followed her now-familiar pattern twice more before he could get his hand on it. A lack of perfect balance forced him to toss it more than once, but he managed to extinguish all of the light bulbs in the room before Vanessa could strike once more. He and whoever or whatever else was in the room with him were now in complete darkness.

Even though his body ached all over, the parasites now seemed somewhat soothed. Still, Robert had only an inkling of how the darkness might give him an advantage. Despite all of his training and abilities, he couldn't think of any sure-fire way to defeat the Spryte.

The lack of light was certainly no hindrance to Vanessa. If anything, it seemed to make her more self-assured of her eventual victory. There was no longer complete silence. Robert now thought he could hear her breathing. He even pictured her smiling. Could be the result of his enhanced senses, or maybe the parasites were beginning to play tricks on him. Whichever, the faint sounds might as well have been silence; he still had no clue where in the room Vanessa might be. She could be close. She could be by the door. She could strike him again at any moment.

"Wise move, Rob." Vanessa's voice came from nowhere, and everywhere. Gone was Robert's fleeting idea of locating her position by hearing her speak. "I do my best work in the dark."

"I figured as much," he said after taking a moment to listen for a heartbeat. "You certainly look like that type."

"The use of sight doesn't appear to be one of your strong suits. Not at the restaurant. And certainly not now."

No use arguing. She'd made a good point. She'd also given Robert's inkling more definition. He reattached the corresq to his belt and reached inside his jeans pocket. He'd almost forgotten about what he'd picked up outside of another restaurant. Thank fortune he hadn't been stupid enough to put it in his jacket pocket.

Robert closed his eye and listened, not for a heartbeat, not for breathing, but for something else entirely. While shifting his body, slowly turning around in one spot, he also shifted control of his reflexes, his instincts, and waited. Let the parasites have their last hurrah.

"Aren't you going to ask me where your loving partner is?" the chalky voice said.

Robert didn't respond.

"Or what I'm going to do with Anika, after I'm finished with you?…Sorry—I'm sure you prefer to hear about Kurtis."

Robert kept silent.

"Or maybe I'll just escort you to Xyn…and arrange a play-date for you and your lost little brother—*Charles*."

A hand contorted into a talon swept down and scratched the back of Robert's head, behind the right ear. The hand's nails drew blood and severed the strap of his eye patch. Robert's right eyelids parted as he caught Vanessa's wrist and, with his free hand, struck the lighter, placing it in front of his face. The blackball in his right eye socket cracked, releasing a sliver of radiation that combined with the flame to produce a broader ray.

There was no time for Vanessa to duck or dodge. No time to disappear or even shut her now-shadowless eyes. In the spark of the moment, the Spryte could do nothing but look dead on at the ray as it illuminated her face, passing its skin from a clean, pale sheen to a cleaner lucidity, raising the vitreous fluid within her eyes to just a few points short of boiling while—in a brief mind-to-mind link—Robert saw her brain hiccup, erasing each layer of her conscious mind.

Creature of the fire.

Vanessa collapsed to the floor. Her body landed at Robert's feet.

He knelt down and grabbed her in order to ensure she wouldn't slide away again and, almost as an afterthought, to ensure she was still alive. Her skin was cold and clammy, but she was still breathing, if just barely.

Whether stable or on the brink of death, there was no question in Robert's mind she'd stay put for a while. He grabbed his eye patch and tied it back on as he raced out of the room.

He made a quick detour into the bathroom. After wiping away all the wet and dried blood, he tried his best to cover his exposed skin. He tied one bath towel across his chest, under his armpits, and he draped another across his shoulders. Short on materials and time, it was the best he could do. He had to hurry and help Ava finish off her opponent, if he wasn't too late.

When he got to the living room, it appeared he already was.

Ava was lying on the floor, unconscious.

Veronica Blake was lying next to her, in the arms of Darryl. Neither one appeared alive.

Chapter 21

Robert checked the blonde one first.

Veronica was still alive—barely. Much like her partner-in-crime upstairs. He took a deep breath before checking on his own partner.

Alive.

Darryl was naked, bruised, scarred, and bloodied—far uglier than he'd ever want to see himself—but he was still breathing. Still tethered to the land of the living, holding on to fraying ropes.

Robert put his trembling fingers on the face of his right-wristwatch. Adam got the message and responded—tersely, it seemed—he'd be sending someone to clean up the mess.

Robert sat on the couch and stared at the three bodies on the floor. He tried to ignore his now erratic breathing, tried to ignore the truck-on-gravel sounds as he also tried to reconstruct what could've happened. Best he could figure it, Darryl had probably freed himself and, while making his way out of the house, had come across Ava and Veronica, fighting. Or maybe he'd come on the scene shortly after Veronica had gotten the best of Ava. But then what? The crystalline bow on which Ava had been so keen probably hadn't been of any help. It lay by her side, colorful as a pattern seen through a kaleidoscope.

Robert focused on Darryl. Minus a lot more clothes, his body looked very similar to the way he remembered Ava looking when they'd first found her. He also noticed something else. A diamond-encrusted band was on Darryl's left hand, encircling his middle and ring fingers. Robert looked closer. It was a golden ouroboros, twisted into a figure eight—a diamondback snake eating its own tail.

No clothes, no watches, but an expensive ring—two rings attached to one another, and to Darryl. Robert wondered about it. He then looked at Ava and wondered about her diamond pendant, the pendant she didn't have when they first found her but which she'd been wearing when she broke in to his apartment. Ava and Darryl—Robert tried to draw connections…

But it was hopeless. He was losing himself, was soon to be lost to the world.

He saw the dots, the tiny little blisters running up and down his arms. They were swelling—mushrooms—starting out cream-white and turning pink, then darker pink as they grew. He saw the wavy lines on his palms, electric blue, clustered, out of which radiated a skin rash, black, the color of mold. And something was crawling on his chest.

Robert grinned, then chuckled, then launched into an all-out hysterical laugh.

He could smell it—the odor that was putting poetry in his mind. Not some nineteenth-century English poet; this time, some nineteenth-century French poet, named…He couldn't remember. Memory was fickle in one's death throes. He could remember the poem itself. Hell, he was living it…

Odors. Potent perfumes that could penetrate glass. Or bone. Rotten marrow. A rotting brain…leaking the acrid aroma of time.

A thousand thousand sleeping thoughts awakened to intoxicate the evaporating soul…drunken, and dunked into the miasmic pit of infinity.

This isn't how Davin went. His first. His first time. And Leigh… This is how her father, the surgeon, feared she'd end up if she kept up with a black, diseased bastard like Robert Omari Goldner. The thought of it, that's what could compel a prominent doctor to—in a fit of rage—aim a shotgun at his daughter's high-school classmate. The woods outside Sterling were an escape—then Xyn—then Darryl…Or did he have the order confused? Maybe he had it all confused. His memories were absconding, leaving him in bits and pieces.

Robert heard a noise. It wasn't his lungs. It was kind of like a droning sound. Low, barely detectable, but he heard it. It was coming from another level of the house. Downstairs, through the open door to the right of him. It wasn't like anything he'd ever heard, at least not while on Reality's surface.

He summoned what strength and energy he could, focused it toward one goal, and heaved himself off the couch. He stumbled toward the door, the corresq in his hand. His legs weren't very sure of themselves, but he made damn sure his fingers were. He wasn't about to take any chances. He'd a feeling that whatever he was going to find down those stairs, he wasn't going to be happy about it.

With an equal mix of clumsiness and carefulness, Robert made his way down, looking every which way with every type of vision the rebellious parasites would allow him.

He saw five doors when he entered the hall. Four of them were shut. The droning was coming from behind one of the four. Robert performed a quick-and-smart search of the other rooms first, looking for people or anything else of interest. There was nothing. Just that droning sound behind door number five.

He got into a safe position and, after three failing attempts, x-rayed it.

He couldn't believe what he saw.

It was her. Behind this unlocked, wooden door. Awake. Alert. Waiting. She'd probably even seen him before he saw her. This could be bad. And he was nowhere near full strength.

Robert turned the doorknob.

Marie-Lydia McGillis was sitting cross-legged on a bed, naked, her left hand resting on her stomach, her right clutching a stained bedsheet that covered her knees and feet. She was sitting in an imperfect circle of blood. It had come from somewhere between her legs. She wasn't bleeding anymore, but she'd bled long enough for it to soak through the bedsheet underneath her and the mattress pad underneath it. And she hadn't just sat still. There were bloody footprints leading from the bed to where she'd used bloody fingers to write "alVa" on one wall and "saVes" on another.

The rest of her body looked as if it had been through plenty of abuse as well. Acne, scars, blemishes, scratches, bruises. Some of it was normal for a fifteen-year-old girl. Some of it was normal for a Virus-carrier not on the proper medication. The rest were signs of someone who'd had a rough time in life, age and sickness notwithstanding. Robert's body was slowly transitioning into a funhouse mirror version of hers.

Whatever else had happened to the girl, whenever it had happened, she seemed oblivious to it all. She only stared at Robert, her lips shaped into a Mona-Lisa smile.

Robert stared back. Head tilted and slack-jawed, apparently. He felt a foam-like substance bubbling, oozing out of the left corner of his mouth. He didn't know what to say, or do. The entire scene was shocking enough to leave him at a complete loss. Marie-Lydia broke the silence.

"Congratulations, Robert Goldner. Looks like another successful hunt."

Robert tightened his grip on the corresq. "How do you know who I am?" His words came out like a last gasp.

"You're a friend of the family."

She'd hardly finished the last word before Robert's legs gave out. His knees were jelly. He fell to the floor, his skin tightening all over, hardening, cracking. A vomit the color and consistency of oatmeal shot out from his mouth like a Jack-in-the-box's surprise. It had the scent—*he* had the pungent scent—of raw sewage.

It was his time. But he refused to take his eye off of the angelic face of the recovered treasure. Another lost child found. Sad parents soon to be so happy…

Marie-Lydia stared back at him, her picture-perfect smile unwavering. She winked her right eye as her left flashed an odd hue of red. The right flashed a stranger red color when she opened it. Then both eyes quickly settled to a piercing jade-green.

Then…

It was gone. All of it. The queasiness. The burning. The smells. The rubbery bones. The bumps, rashes, and glowing lines on his crusty skin. The dementia.

Robert now felt strong—as strong as an *angel* could be anyway—and he knew Marie-Lydia was the direct cause. But he wasn't about to thank her.

He got into a defensive position. Marie-Lydia cocked her head.

"Don't worry," she said as she lowered her eyes toward his corresq. "You have nothing to fear from me. I'm not going to hurt you."

Robert took a full passage-clearing breath, elated that his lungs and throat were clear, noiseless.

"I'm not worried about you," he said. "I know who you are. I know what you've done. And I know where your mind has been. I've already contacted the authorities. They'll be here any minute to help you. They'll clean you up and, when you're ready, take you back home."

"Home?" Marie-Lydia laughed. It was an uncanny laugh, filling the entire room, echoing off the walls. Robert thought he also heard wind chimes as he listened to it. When she stopped, he just heard the droning again. The initial shock of the scene and his subsequent collapse had blocked it out of his ears, but it had never really gone away. The droning had actually become more prominent since he'd entered the room.

"I'm not going anywhere near those people you think are my parents," Marie-Lydia said.

"No. Not anytime soon, that's for sure," Robert said. "You'll need to be rehabilitated first."

"Oh? Like you were?"

Robert knew better than to say it. He learned within the first year of living in the DC-area that one should never entertain the questions or comments of a crazy person. Smile, nod, give them spare change if you must, but don't ever engage them in any type of conversation. He knew better, but he reflexively asked, "What are you talking about?"

"The Institution to which you pledge allegiance," Marie-Lydia said, "and the hack-job they did on you. Instead of avoiding mirrors, you should start taking a good look at yourself, Mister Goldner. A watchdog being robbed of his soul, and too dumb to know it. Wasting all of your time trying to find children who were never truly wanted in this world the first place. It's a fool's game, and you're one of its best players. A true, clueless champion. Working tirelessly to find the children…Haven't you ever once thought to ask, 'Where are the parents?'"

Robert heard sounds coming from the main level of the house. Local Herndon cops or HSA Peacemaker agents had arrived.

"Time to go," he said. "Please, come peacefully."

"Of course," she said. "As peaceful as a little lamb."

She smiled her Mona-Lisa smile and rubbed her stomach. Only then did Robert realize that's where the sound was coming from. Something was happening inside of her, in that area. He didn't dare x-ray her to see just what.

Someone called his name out in the hall. He slowly backed out of the room, keeping the girl in view the whole time. He wasn't going to let her disappear on him.

"I'm Robert Goldner," he said when he saw the Peacemakers. "I found a lost girl, in here."

Marie-Lydia shook her head at him.

"Flood's coming," she said. "Who's going to be lost then?"

∞   ∞   ∞

Robert was brusquely escorted from the house.

He wasn't arrested, or even accused of breaking the law, but he received stern warnings from the two ranking HSA agents on site as Peacemakers made a sweep of the entire house and the injured were carried out on stretchers to the waiting ambulances.

The most senior agent hustled Robert into the backseat of his car just as the news cameras arrived. The car's windows were tinted, but Robert blurred his facial features anyway. He wanted to start making it a habit.

The agent drove Robert to The Burrow, where Sam gave him a thorough examination and surprisingly concluded he had only minor injuries. He told her about Marie-Lydia. He wasn't cured of the Virus—far from it—but she'd brought him back from the brink of death, if only for one day more. Sam had no explanations or theories. Vince was the guy he needed to talk to. But first, Adam wanted to see him.

The lighting in the reception area of Adam's office seemed dimmer than usual. This had the ironic effect of making Robert even more uncomfortable than he would've been, not that receiving a good talking-to from the chairman was anything he could ever take in complete stride. Adam didn't waste a lot of time going into details. When he told Robert he'd placed the Watchers program in serious jeopardy, he understood what he meant. It wasn't just the trespassing, the home invasion, and the near-fatal assaults of its not-yet-proven-guilty occupants, it was the fact they committed all these acts without any official sanction. His and Ava's actions were no different from those of reckless vigilantes, or common burglars.

Robert tried to put up a defense, saying not only had they found Darryl, but they'd also recovered a missing child. And no one was killed. Adam didn't say a word to this. He couldn't. Robert understood that while the chairman in no way condoned what Robert and Ava had done, he was pleased with the results. But to say so would give license to Robert and other Watchers to act reckless in the future. Rules could be bent, but not broken. It'd be a slippery slope to getting the Institution shut down and the whole lot of them thrown into prison.

Adam concluded their brief meeting by saying he and the IAI's government liaisons had worked out a deal with the HSA. Robert wouldn't face formal charges, but he'd be suspended for two weeks from all IAI activities. During that time he'd essentially be under house arrest, confined to his apartment and closely monitored by the HSA. Adam had also swung it so that his accomplice, Ava Darden, wouldn't be charged. He'd told the authorities she was a Watcher agent-in-training and had asked that her punishment be the same as Robert's. She had no apartment or any other home to go to, so once she recovered from her injuries, she'd be confined in one of The Burrow's apartments and monitored by Adam himself.

If there was ever any doubt, it was now certain that the chairman held some definite sway in certain circles. Even a cop couldn't do what Robert and Ava had done and get away with a little off-the-books suspension. Robert couldn't tell if Adam was serious about Ava being an agent-in-training, but he'd never known the man to joke, or to lie. Well, there was nowhere else for her to go, and no better place for her to be; she certainly couldn't do any harm locked up in The Burrow under Adam's watchful eye, so Robert didn't sweat it. He'd figure out Adam's real plan for her—and her real plan for Reality—once he was free, if he should live so long.

Robert met Peter Levy in the hall outside Adam's office. Peter was a founding member of the IAI and its chief government liaison. A veteran lobbyist and old hand at understanding how things really got done in Washington, Peter had undoubtedly been instrumental in helping Adam work out this deal with the HSA. He was now taking it on himself to escort Robert from The Burrow to the parking garage, where HSA agents would be waiting to drive him home, secure his apartment, and fit him with monitor bracelets, anklets, and a collar.

Robert had never spoken with Peter much. There'd never really been an opportunity or reason. Peter's realm was politics; Robert, his respect and admiration for President Jenifer Sagan notwithstanding, had never cared much for the subject. Today, however, he thanked Peter for his efforts and, during the elevator ride up, grilled him for information Adam hadn't bothered to give out.

"Well, you don't have to worry about Darryl," Peter said. "They took him to a very secure, private hospital in Reston. Sam and I spoke to one of his doctors while you were in with Adam. It turns out his injuries aren't that severe. He should recover in a couple of days."

"Good," Robert said. "I guess he's also going to need take a little time off from the Institution."

"The vacation may be longer than you think."

"What do you mean?"

"We had a briefing meeting with the HSA this morning," Peter said. "They want to see Darryl for a final round of interviews."

"For the Peacemakers?"

"So they said. But I've heard through the grapevine that the Agency is creating a special operations force, pending authorization from the President. My gut tells me Darryl will find a new home there."

Well. It looked like Darryl might have a shot at his dream after all. Robert wasn't sure he truly deserved it, but what the hell. It was time to give the guy a break.

"I can't wait to congratulate him."

Peter chuckled. "Well, you won't be making any calls for a while."

"Yeah," Robert said, "don't remind me."

"You'll be fine. We had to pull a lot of strings, but there was no way we could convince anyone to let you off with just a warning."

"I understand," Robert said. "And thanks again for what you were able to do. But for the record, what Ava and I did was nowhere near the heinous level of what those other two have done. Veronica and Vanessa, or whatever the hell their real names are."

"We know all about it," Peter said. "Adam is sharing the footage he found with the HSA. Guaranteed those two are never going to see the light of day again."

They stepped off The Burrow's elevator and waited for the one to the parking garage to arrive.

"And what about Marie-Lydia McGillis?" Robert was worried about her most of all. She was in a dangerous state. Her mind was clearly warped. They couldn't just give her a bath, a new dress, and send her home.

"That's a trickier subject," Peter said. "The HSA has a lot of questions about her disappearance, her alleged abductors, and a whole host of other things. And she's certainly in no condition to give straight answers right now. But that'll change, with the proper care and treatment. Regardless, from what I've been told, she's going to be kept in a special facility until they're sure she's fit to reenter society. Her parents will be notified she's been found, but they won't be allowed to visit her just yet."

That was probably for the best. Robert considered if he were in her situation. If he'd committed the acts she had, had subsequently been forced into XynKroma, and then had gone through whatever-the-hell for more than a year, would he want his parents to come see him? Could he face them? He laughed a short, bitter laugh as the elevator door opened. Yeah, he could face them. That wasn't the right question. What else did he want to do before the Virus or a bullet or whatever else made him breathe his last? His mom was dead, but he'd almost kill to be able to see his dad again—if he was alive.

"Don't worry," Peter said. "Brighter days are ahead for Marie-Lydia. There are some experimental drugs that came on the market in June that may help her better cope with the Virus and help her readjust to the world relatively quickly. Whatever the case, she's going to be a lot happier than she possibly could've been over the past year. There's no reason to have anything but a positive outlook. Remember, things could always be worse, for any of us."

True enough. Robert had kissed death, he'd kissed the heart of it, and he'd come back to himself. But it was only now, now that he and Darryl were no longer officially together, that he felt it was time, it was safe, to let him go. Let Darryl spread his wings, whether metaphorical or real, and let him find his true happiness while Robert moved on to find the something else that may hurry up and kill him, or make him stronger.

Love…fuck it. Maybe it really was just a dangerous myth, the product of a multitude of diseased brains, a sick hive-mind producing a mass delusion—at least in this world.

Don't worry, be happy.

The elevator door opened on the fifth level of the parking garage. Robert followed Peter toward a black SUV parked at the far end, straight ahead, against the low wall. Two men in suits were standing near the vehicle. One of them was looking out over the wall's ledge, probably at all the morning rush-hour traffic on the street below. Peter greeted the men when they were within non-shouting distance and shook hands when closer.

"Before you take Mister Goldner here," he said, "I wanted to ask you…"

The three men began to discuss something that had nothing to do with Robert, so he moved closer to the ledge, looking out and all around as he took deep breaths. Polluted as it was, he wanted his fill of outdoor air before being shut away. He spent a minute taking in all he could before he felt a scratching at the back of his neck, inside the skin. The sensation simultaneously ran down his spine and crawled all over his scalp. He shuddered, then instinctively looked up into the sky. He had to squint and concentrate to telescope his vision, making its range travel much farther than usual, but it didn't take him long to spot them. A whole flock of them.

They were arranged in a hexagonal formation, flying in a zig-zag fashion. Not in the manner of birds, or even in the manner of bats, but in the manner of creatures made up from the constituent parts of other creatures, some of whom were adapted to the sea, some of whom were adapted to the sky, and some of whom were adapted to an entirely different environment altogether.

Chimeras. Denizens of Xyn. There'd been a dimensional breach.

The creatures had left their old habitat and entered a new realm, Reality's surface. It appeared they were becoming adapted to their new environment in fits and starts.

Robert watched as the flock flew into a cloud and disappeared. He shuddered again and backed away from the ledge.

"What's the matter?" Peter asked. "You okay?"

"Yeah," Robert said as he got into the backseat of the SUV. "I just saw a dark cloud in the sky. I think it's about to rain."

Postscript

"Why so disturbed?" the girl asked. "Isn't this the beginning of the Happily-Ever-After you wanted? The one you agreed to?"

Darryl's soul stood next to hers on the giant's left shoulder. He was gazing down at the two other souls tilling the Ground of Xyn near the giant's feet, far below. The giant had walked away from its lake to stand in a stranger terrain of gloppy, inhospitable soil. Darryl had been wondering what kind of seeds would work here, and just where they'd come from. Yes, he knew they were only to be metaphorical seeds, but it and similar questions nagged him. Unlike his companion, the angel formerly known as Marie-Lydia McGillis, he hadn't spent enough time in XynKroma so that the answers to all questions, riddles, and arts were clear to him, or easily discovered. But now he and she were a couple. Inseparable. *One.* He trusted her to give him everything he needed. She'd certainly trusted him well enough to reveal her secret name when his soul had returned to hers after their first meeting. "St. Alva," she'd said, "because I am nothing if not a martyr." But so much still remained a mystery.

"I'll tell you my opinion on the beginning," Darryl said, "once we've reached the end."

He focused again on the souls below them. Veronica Blake and Vanessa Blight. VanJill and its assembled crew of pole-pets were overseeing the two souls and their work. No need for Darryl or St. Alva to go anywhere near them. They could keep their distance. But they couldn't rely on just two souls to complete the work that had to be done. They needed more. A whole town's worth. Maybe a whole city's, or a country's. The mother and father of the latest and greatest Miracle had to do their parts to ensure a perfect End.

"Any idea what happened to their bodies?" Darryl asked.

"Yes," St. Alva said. "I have an idea. And so should you. Heartland Security agents took them and shut them away."

"I only just started there," Darryl said. "I'm lucky I know where the bathroom is. Info on captured terrorists isn't something they'd give to someone like me."

"Do you think they gave it to me?" St. Alva asked. "Here in XynKroma, knowledge of the entire world is open to us, potentially. Learn to manipulate the bits and pieces to find out what you want."

Inside and outside of XynKroma, his so-called Perfect Memory Recollection ability wasn't working as well as he'd imagined it should. Instead of an accessible ability, so far it seemed to be operating more like a trick—a trick elbow or a trick knee—acting up only when it wanted to, giving him only imperfect pictures of others' pasts and secrets. Maybe it would work better in time.

"You'll have to teach me your arts," Darryl said.

"Of course, honey."

"And maybe tell me just where in the world you're hiding your body on Reality's surface," he said. "Since we've become so close, it would be nice to be able to see you face-to-face. Under better circumstances than last time."

Only a few days had passed since Darryl's first meeting with Marie-Lydia McGillis. During that time, Darryl had been hospitalized, released, interviewed by the HSA, and hired on the spot as one of their agents. During the same time, the girl had been examined at a hospital, taken to a high security center that specialized in caring for dangerous Virus-carriers, and held for two days before disappearing. This was their fourth meeting in Xyn.

"You can't see me now," St. Alva said. "It's too dangerous. Rest assured I'm being kept safe. The fewer people who know where, the better."

"Having trust issues?" Darryl asked. "After all I've been through for you? For *Us*—honey?"

"You know the answer to that. Our relationship is stronger here, at the fundamental realm. Our bodies will be transformed anyway in the Afterbath. The surface doesn't matter. Paying too much attention to skin is one of the primary faults of humanity, leading to so many other ills."

She had him there. It was a good point. But Darryl wasn't dissuaded. During his first visit back to XynKroma after accepting her "modest proposal," she'd insisted all the activity needed to make their child a body-and-soul reality could be performed in Xyn. Darryl still insisted on seeing her in the flesh. He wanted to get a good look to make sure it was healthy enough, fit enough to gestate their child. The child would be like no other, but its body would still be carried in the body of its mother, if not necessarily for nine months.

"I need to stay hidden until our child is born," St. Alva said. "I need to maintain that wall of security. If my body is returned too soon to Mister and Missus McGillis, they'd force an abortion."

"What?" Darryl expressed disbelief even though he knew exactly where she was coming from. A fifteen-year-old daughter returned to her parents after missing from the face of the earth for a year and a half? A fifteen-year-old pregnant daughter? Even the most religious parents would question the tenets of their faith and wrestle with the very concept of morality in such a situation.

"Evil adults," St. Alva said. "Thankfully we're no longer related. I'd love to tell them to their big wicked faces their little girl Marie-Lydia is dead."

They both fell silent. Below, the pole-pets were allowing Vanessa and Veronica to take a break. The two humanoid-shaped souls stood knee-deep in the oatmeal-like soil while VanJill lectured them on their necessary duties and the final Reality to come. The two may've heard the pole-pet's words, but neither was reading the text in its bubbles. Both were glaring, staring all the way up at Darryl and St. Alva.

Darryl had delivered Veronica's soul directly to the giant's feet. The diamond ring had worked as promised. Someone unknown to him had sent Vanessa's soul to Xyn and, as a result, it had landed far from where St. Alva and Darryl needed it to be. St. Alva had found the soul wandering in a maze and captured it, brought it to the giant.

Both Vanessa and Veronica could've met far worse fates in Xyn. Neither seemed to appreciate that fact. But there was nothing to fear from either of them. Superior angels on Reality's surface, they were now inferior souls at its base. Veronica's and Vanessa's souls couldn't fly. They couldn't change their souls' shapes or compositions. They could only manipulate the polluted light of Xyn within a tiny radius of their soul's figures, and only for the few purposes allowed.

Darryl could still feel their hatred. VanJill's words had been ineffective. If they'd been listening to the pole-pet, if they'd taken a moment to try to understand, they would've been thankful for the opportunity Darryl and St. Alva had given them.

"It was a struggle," St. Alva said. "Such a struggle. The tug of war between me and those two..."

The first time Darryl returned to Xyn after accepting her proposal, bringing Veronica Blake's soul with him, St. Alva had praised his wise decision, then she'd told him the whole story of her soul's imprisonment. She'd told him how, shortly after Ava Darden, her would-be mentor, had brought her to Xyn against her will, the dirty-pool-dipping souls of Veronica and Vanessa had found her. Veronica had suggested and Vanessa had agreed to take her soul and make it their plaything. The two attacked the hundreds of teacher-guardians in whose care Ava had left her and captured eighty or so with the intent of converting them into prison guards. They then took her soul to another section of Xyn and stirred up the storm that would prevent anyone from locating her. They began molesting their new plaything immediately, siphoning what energy they could from the soul to make themselves stronger, smarter, more powerful. The two became more and more ambitious.

St. Alva's true mentor, the one who'd originally inverted her and had shown St. Alva her full potential, had kept her body safe on Reality's surface while trying to find a way to free her soul and reunite her mind and body. The Killer Vees were the acolytes of this mentor and, by default, loyal to St. Alva; Veronica and Vanessa were loyal only to themselves. After some time, St. Alva had managed to establish periodic physic links with her mentor. Together, bit by bit, piece by piece, they'd devised a plan that would allow them to not only gain temporary mastery over the minds and bodies of Veronica and Vanessa but to also steer a liberator to St. Alva's soul. Through a vast network of contacts, they'd learned of the name and reputation of Darryl Ridley. He had the near-perfect psychological makeup for the task. All they had to do was lure him and cleanse him before outfitting him in *white* to be St. Alva's shining knight.

Darryl had wondered about the coincidence of the women's names, all them starting with the letter "v."

"It's no coincidence," St. Alva had told him. "It's HyperVersism, otherwise known as 'Word Magick.'" Her mentor had come up with a verbal concoction, a *charm* whereby, to match Veronica and Vanessa, the ladies would adopt pseudonyms beginning with the same letter to better effect the primary charm they were using on the pair. It would tighten the circle, help ensure the two wouldn't deviate from the grand plan.

Veronica and Vanessa had been useful artists. St. Alva had manipulated them into performing all sorts of neutral, good, and great deeds—steering the course of a band of artists, capturing the interest of Darryl Ridley, and keeping Ava from recovering St. Alva's body before Darryl could recover her soul. Now the former Infinite-Definite terrorists served in another useful role.

A full understanding of magick of any kind was beyond Darryl, at least at this point. Whatever the women had done, it had worked. But Darryl wondered more and more about this mentor, more and more about this mystery woman. If Stavan "Ava" Darden wasn't her true mentor, why had the girl formally known as Marie-Lydia McGillis adopted—or been given—a name so similar to hers? More so-called Word Magick? And if Darryl and St. Alva were to be the parents of this child, this great Artist of The End, what role would the true mentor play? Critic? Editor? Questions, questions—a vast number of them...

St. Alva grabbed the hand of Darryl's soul and tugged.

"Come," she said. "Before we return to the surface this time, I want to show you what VanJill and I have done with the chamber since your last visit. I need your opinion on a few things."

"My opinion?" Darryl asked. "What do you expect me to have to say about it?"

"Plenty, I hope. We are One now, honey. And the chamber has to be perfect if it's where our child will guide the unfolding of A Beautiful Creation."

They lifted their souls from the giant's shoulder and floated gently into its left ear. As they traveled through the canal toward the chamber, Darryl considered the giant's ear, its head, its face, and the fact it already had its own vineyard wrapped around its body, threading in and out, stitched to its skin. What did it mean that the souls they brought to Xyn were to grow a vineyard from nothing while the giant was already outfitted in one? In XynK-roma, symbols weren't merely harmless symbols; they had stark translations to hard facts. This giant heard. This giant saw. And if its face wasn't blurred to him, Darryl would know exactly for whom to search on Reality's surface, exactly whom to confront, exactly whom to accuse of being the near-future abductor of his and St. Alva's child.

About the Series

Eve of Light is a Dark Metaphysical Fantasy series chronicling the surreal events leading up to the Apocalypse—the Death of God. The setting is a contemporary, alternate Earth on the verge of a cataclysm that will warp space, time, and minds. The main narrative of those plotting and battling to save humanity is told in the *Eve of Light* series of novels. The short stories and novellas are simply flashes on the fringe—episodes told from the perspective of everyday men and women living in a world turned weird.

The Core Novels
BloodLight: The Apocalypse of Robert Goldner
Broken Angels *(Eve of Light • Book I)*
Divinities, Entangled *(Eve of Light • Book II)*

Stories on the Fringe
FoolKillers
The Lark
Heaven's Gun
Knotty & Ice
Rogue Beauty
Deviant-Hunter's Sabbath

About the Author

Harambee K. Grey-Sun writes under the broad umbrella of speculative fiction. He integrates elements of fantasy, horror, noir, black humor, and science fiction into his work and spins dark, surreal, mysterious, grotesque, at times challenging, and often blasphemous tales. Many of his stories can be categorized into one or more of the following subgenres: speculative thriller, urban fantasy, metaphysical fantasy, superhero, occult/supernatural, slipstream, and–*of course*–weird fiction. His Dark Metaphysical Fantasy series *Eve of Light* examines the dark nature of God and what it really means to be human. Find out more at the **Hyper-Verse Blog**: www.harambeegreysun.com

And SIGN UP for the **HyperVerse Blog Newsletter** to be among the first to learn about new releases, discounts, freebies, and other special deals: http://eepurl.com/_tzUv